To: Steve,

I'm memory of you lovely wife Gillian and all that you two, working together, did for the Attaché Corps and America!

Chuck Scanlon

December 1999

Attachés II

RETRIBUTION

A Novel by

Chuck Scanlon

Foreword by
LTG Patrick M. Hughes
USA (Ret)

IM Press, Inc.
Fairfax Station, VA
1999

Please direct all correspondence and book orders to:
IM Press, Inc.
P. O. Box 377
Fairfax Station, VA 22039-0377
or
IM Press, Inc.
P. O. Box 372884
Satellite Beach, FL 32937

Library of Congress Catalog Card Number 99-97132
ISBN 0-9660137-1-9

Published by IM Press, Inc. and
Gateway Press, Inc.
1001 N. Calvert Street
Baltimore, MD 21202

Printed in the United States of America

DEDICATION

To the memory of
Army Sergeant Kenneth R. Hobson, II
who died while serving the United States in the Defense Attaché
Office in Nairobi, Kenya, on August the seventh, 1998,
as a result of a terrorist bombing
of the U.S. Embassy.

FOREWORD

Suddenly, everything has gone wrong. A conventional bomb has recently destroyed a key U.S. embassy. A nuclear terrorist attack against the U.S. is underway; a biological agent has been deployed; and, a cyber attack has begun.

What next? The end of the world as we know it?

The real question is… could this really happen? Could three terrorist events involving weapons of mass destruction happen in the United States, simultaneously?

Having served as the Director of the Defense Intelligence Agency for the past three and a half years, and having contemplated these ideas in real life, I was asked by the Author to comment on the plausibility, the level of realism, the sheer possibility, of three potentially catastrophic attacks occurring at the same time, as described in this novel. The answer, unfortunately, is… yes. Yes, it is possible. It could happen. Let's pray that it won't, but it could.

The premise General Scanlon has used, multiple acts of terror where weapons of mass destruction are used by utterly ruthless madmen, is implicitly possible. The shortage of people and resources in our intelligence and police structures, the involvement of organized crime in the transfer of threatening weapons and technologies, the vulnerability of modern systems to cyber attack, the importance of random events, and the clever use of description—all are well covered in this keen story. At the same time, for many reasons, it all seems somewhat unrealistic (or is that wishful thinking?). Is the plot a bit too thick with challenges? Are there too many problems, happening concurrently, for the heroic agents of the government to deal with? Is the reader forced to zig and zag through the intense plot of *Retribution*, without regard to the many barriers and impediments that would surely be placed directly in the path of the perpetrators of these horrible acts by a confident and capable government? Do we give the terrorists too much credit?

The reader will have to decide. From my standpoint, Chuck Scanlon has adequately described what could happen in the real world, in a work of fiction, well crafted, and filled with accurate detail and professional insight. He has been in the game, and has the knowledge and experience required to imagine and portray the possibilities in a highly readable and believable way.

Perhaps the main reason to doubt the multiple acts of terror occurring at once is the complexity of the tasks involved to bring such events about, and if any hint of such events should reach the authorities, the expected immediate and strong response from the leaders of the very government the terrorists seek to destroy. The public expects, indeed assumes, that if a single attack, a conventional attack against an embassy as an example, happened, the resulting security offensive and the attendant defensive blitz, would swing into place and subsequent attempts would be forestalled or intercepted. Thus multiple strikes, concurrently, following so closely on the heels of the initial conventional attack, are thought by some to be unlikely. But Chuck Scanlon has woven a believable pattern of possibility over real events, which we cannot deny.

Meanwhile, the terrorists who may be out there plotting just such a set of attacks, are predictably detached from anything that will interfere with their single-minded purpose. There are no rules. They plot and act in spite of the expectations of the public and the actions of the governments who are the target, and in spite of the ever-watchful intelligence system and the established counter-terrorism organizations who work in the shadows to deny the terrorists their ability to act with impunity. This is why, in this book and in real life, we are surprised when an act of terror occurs, even though we knew it could. The asynchronous and asymmetric nature of terrorism is at the heart of this conundrum. The irony of this is not lost on the reader, who will recognize this ebb and flow of real terrorism against the backdrop of accurate intelligence and inspired action by those who are entrusted with our safety in the face of such threats. How can we always intercept the terrorist when there are so many possibilities for the terrorist to act? The answer, in real life and in this book, is hard work, dedication and devotion to duty, and sheer good luck.

In fact, those who expect their government to act in a way that will give the terrorists pause are not completely confident in the bureaucracy and its ability to correctly anticipate and judge the impending threat, and then to act to prevent it from happening. This is Scanlon's not-so-subtle point, and he's right. After all, many crimes, perpetrated by diverse and dispersed criminals, happen every day, day after day. Terrorism, perhaps the ultimate "crime," has happened to us, infrequently to be sure, but often enough, and with heartbreaking effect and with tremendous consequences. The odds are… it will happen again, despite our best efforts to see that it does not.

The fictional account in this book has all the elements of a true story. One can only hope that it never happens, but the concerned reader would do very well to read and think about this book as if it could happen, and then support relevant public information, the national intelligence system, the preventive organizations and the training and equipment they require, and everything else needed to ensure that America is not victimized by terrorists who have the means to attack us in such dangerous ways.

Patrick M. Hughes
Lieutenant General, US Army, Retired

Washington, DC

ACKNOWLEDGMENTS

I am once again grateful for the generosity of many friends, professionals, and family without whose assistance and advice this book would not have been possible. I want to thank Keith Alexander, Charles Battaglia, Barbara Morrison, Steve Norton, and Dick Powers who helped me with my early research and brainstorming; Barbara Duckworth and Bob Harding for their perspectives on the national security community and Jim Ritchey and Marc Powe for their Middle East expertise.

My thanks also to Tom Dahlstrom for his technical counsel and to my classmate and fraternity brother, Dick Ragland, for aviation advice and lifelong support.

Appreciation must also go to my comrades-in-arms, Cal Korf and Mike Mastrangelo, for their manuscript reviews and recommendations. My gratitude to Pat McCord and the Pentagon Book Store and Arnold and Linda Dupuy of Nova Publications for sharing with me their knowledge of the fascinating world of books.

To Ann Hughes of Gateway Press, and my naval connection, Mike Messman, for their superb editorial direction. A special thank you is due to my longtime friend and fellow soldier, Stan Hyman, for his untiring support, advice, critiques, and guidance and for believing in this effort from the beginning.

My love and thanks also to my family for their understanding and backing during the long periods of writing, and especially to my daughters, Teri, who served as my literary point-of-contact in Washington for all things and Kellie, who was the mainstay for IM Press in Virginia, and my publisher, Keith Paradyme. And of course, thanks, as always, to my smiling typesetter, RoseMarie Dorer of The Write Word, for her ruined evenings and weekends and unfailing support and loyalty. And to all those people in Satellite Beach, Florida, who, by word or deed, contributed to the writing of this book.

AUTHOR'S NOTE

The Defense Attaché Service, like this story, is fictional. It is however, fashioned after the real-world men and women who are part of an organization of military attachés existing within the U.S. Defense Department.

My intention was to create a work of fiction dealing with terrorism grounded in reality and possibility. The main characters in the story are the results of my imagination. Where real and recognizable characters play supporting roles, their words and actions are the results of my creativity. Any similarity to real world events is purely coincidental.

The terrifying events I describe are, to my mind, more than just potential threats to Americans. These kinds of unimaginable terrorist attacks could happen, and very well may happen unless the U.S. resolve to combat terrorism is strengthened and our preparedness is dramatically improved.

CHAPTER 1

WASHINGTON, DC/BAGHDAD—1999

It was a cold and rainy January day in the nation's capital. President William Jefferson Clinton, in a speech before the National Academy of Sciences, warned the nation that terrorists, recognizing that they cannot defeat the United States with military force, are seeking "new tools of destruction."

The President said, "We must be ready for attacks against computer networks and the use of chemical and germ warfare. This is not a cause for a panic," he said. "It is a cause for serious, deliberate, disciplined, long-term concern." He spoke of deepening concern and anxiety in the White House and recalled the shock the world felt four years ago from a nerve gas attack in the Tokyo subway. He then cited the rash of anthrax hoaxes in the Los Angeles area.

Later, when the Washington Press Corps asked the White House about the terrorist threat, Richard Clarke, the President's national coordinator for anti-terrorism, reluctantly admitted, "We do not know of any imminent attack being planned in the United States using chemical or biological weapons, or using cyber attack techniques. But we do want to raise consciousness that such attacks are growing increasingly likely."

The President's concerns about the growing terrorist threat to the United States were said to be shared by the U.S. national security agencies, FBI, CIA, NSA, DIA, and others. And it was dutifully, if not dramatically, reported to the American public by the print and television media. However, any real clear and present danger was widely discounted in follow-up comments. To an American public that had been deluged by the steady stream of politically pleasing

1

announcements pouring almost daily out of the White House, this latest clarion was viewed by most as just one more attempt by an embattled President to divert attention away from the painfully embarrassing impeachment proceedings against him taking place in the U.S. Senate. This naiveté on the part of the Americans, regarding threats to the United States during times of economic wellbeing in spite of the past New York City World Trade Center, and Oklahoma Federal Building bombings was unfortunate, certainly not shared by America's adversaries around the world. That could prove to be incredibly costly!

While Americans in Washington during that last week in January were chilled by the rainy cold weather outside and the sordid revelations unfolding inside the well of the Senate about their Commander-in-Chief, the mild climate in Iraq belied the inner-most feelings of its volatile leader, Saddam Hussein. He was seething! He did not know whether he was more angered by the dog of a President of the United States' war mongering suggestion that Iraq and its unworthy neighbor, Iran, posed the biggest threat to the "Great Satan" or the characterization by some so-called U.S. experts that the terrorist threat to America could be likened to "an insect or mosquito threat."

The flood of articles on the terrorist threat that continued in the world's media for several days caused Saddam's rage and hatred of the United States to rise to unprecedented levels. His anger was so fierce and obvious to his closest aides and family that they feared not only what it might portend for Iraq but for their own safety should they somehow, however unintentional, offend the mad one.

Saddam's angst continued through the first week in February then, suddenly, the calmness that his aides recognized when Saddam had decided on a course of action or a response appeared. He then summoned one of his most trusted and feared generals, Ali Hassan al-Majid.

Ali Hassan was in the North at the time but returned immediately to Baghdad when he was informed that Saddam wanted to see him. He neither shaved nor changed his clothes after the long journey but, went directly to Saddam's Republican Guard's Security Headquarters, where he was blindfolded, searched, and relieved of his sidearm, and placed in a blacked-out Mercedes and driven to Saddam's closely held and extensively guarded location for the day. Once inside, Saddam's "hiding place" for that day as it was known by his most senior aides but never mentioned to Saddam's face, Ali Hassan's blindfold was removed. He did not recognize the surroundings but could immediately tell by the closeness of the rooms he was led through that it was probably going to be a one-on-one meeting with Saddam, without an entourage and the tea serving formalities that Saddam sometimes preferred. As he entered the small, windowless room, he was surprised to find Saddam already there and seated in one of only two easy chairs that Iraq's dignitaries prefer for personal meetings. Ali Hassan snapped to attention and gave Saddam a smart salute in the old British colonial fashion. He did not apologize for his appearance or the dirt on his field uniform knowing that Saddam would take that as a mark of respect and urgency on the old soldier's part in responding to his leader and superior.

Saddam did not get up and embrace his long-time colleague, some would say henchman, and ally in countless atrocities against enemies and their own people. He did smile broadly and point for Ali Hassan to sit down in the other chair.

When Saddam was satisfied that the steel encased door by which Ali Hassan had entered was securely closed, he began immediately. "I have something in mind for our former friends, the Americans."

When in the best of moods, Saddam delighted in referring sarcastically to Americans as "former friends." He

3

did so because of the stupidity he thought the Americans had displayed during the Iran-Iraq war in providing the Iraqis information and technology against the U.S.'s former ally, Iran. He knew the Americans would never understand the Iraqi thinking and culture.

As Saddam was saying, "I have something in mind for our former friends, the Americans," Ali Hassan, although completely ruthless himself, mentally shuddered. He remembered the disaster of the Kuwait War and Desert Storm the last time Saddam had something in mind for the Americans, not to mention the current problems being experienced by Iraq in Saddam's "no fly" zones plan. Ali Hassan knew that even the slightest reservation over Saddam's ideas could, and had for many, resulted in sudden death and therefore, he displayed a deadpan but, interested expression as his leader and benefactor told him what he had in mind.

"I want you to travel to Afghanistan and contact Mullah Mohammed Omar, the Taliban leader and ask him to arrange safe passage for you to Osama bin Laden's place of hiding. Omar will not be comfortable with this request and will try to offer up many excuses why it cannot be done. But you must remind him that he is beholden to me and Iraq and I will that it be done. He will comply. He will, of course, insist on the utmost security in order that bin Laden's whereabouts not be discovered by the western infidels. He is being handsomely rewarded for his hospitality to bin Laden and he will not want to endanger his arrangement. You must cooperate with Omar's security people but, when you see bin Laden insist that no other person, even his own people or Omar, be present. Then I want you to inform bin Laden that I desire to see him on a matter of gravest importance to the true Arab World. Our meeting must take place in Iraq and only his most trusted aides will be permitted to accompany him. He may also bring along his own security and that of the Taliban if he desires. Bin Laden will also resist this meeting, pleading any number of excuses, but you, Ali Hassan, will insist and pass to him a sealed personal note that I will give to you.

He too will, reluctantly, agree. He is dependent upon our help and particularly our intelligence support without which he would have had no success against our enemies."

Ali Hassan was surprised at Saddam's task having heard Saddam speak disparagingly of bin Laden, a number of times referring to him as the "little Saudi entrepreneur." But he also knew that no one in Iraq knew everything that Saddam was involved with, or who, for whatever reason, was in his debt. Saddam had gone on to say that if asked by bin Laden who would attend the meeting between Saddam and himself, Ali Hassan would reply that only two others would be present, Saddam's son, Uday Hussein and Ali Hassan. Another involuntary shudder by Ali Hassan. Saddam would prefer Baghdad for his meeting but would be willing to compromise if bin Laden would feel more secure at a location closer to Afghanistan. But Saddam would, of course, pick the place. Ali Hassan thought to himself that this meeting surely must be important to Saddam because Saddam was not known for his willingness to compromise on anything. Saddam then quickly turned the conversation, a monologue really, to a few pleasantries about the General's family, passed the sealed note for bin Laden to him and dismissed Ali Hassan.

The mission given to Ali Hassan by Saddam Hussein was not an easy one. First, he had to establish a secure communication with Watil Ahmed Miettatil, Mullah Mohammed Omar's Chief of Staff, to inform Omar that Saddam wished to dispatch a high level dignitary to him immediately to discuss a matter of the utmost importance. Ali Hassan would not name himself as the emissary. This, because of concern for his own security in traveling outside Iraq. Traveling for him was always a high risk based on his own, brutal and deserved reputation. He, too, was both feared and hated and would be a high value target for many enemies. Second, the journey to Khandahar in Afghanistan was not the easiest place in the world to get to, particularly with Iran in between the two countries. He would have to travel under a cover identity, a disguise, and take some of his own security detail with him.

Three weeks had passed since the day that Saddam Hussein had given Ali Hassan the mission of arranging a meeting between Saddam and Osama bin Laden. All the obstacles to the meeting that Saddam had predicted took place and some others but, Saddam's will and Ali Hassan's forceful ways of carrying Saddam's message had finally prevailed. Bin Laden had agreed to come to Iraq to meet Saddam but he would not agree to meeting in Baghdad. He was concerned that even Saddam Hussein could not guarantee his security there. Too many foreign devils there and who knew when Baghdad might be subject to American or British air attack. Saddam did not hesitate in selecting an alternate site for the meeting and chose Basra, a well-known city near the Arabian Gulf. The one-day meeting was scheduled in three parts. Saddam would meet alone with bin Laden in the morning, shortly after their arrival in Basra to discuss privately Saddam's idea. After the noon meal, assuming agreement between the two principals, Saddam, Ali Hassan and Saddam's son, Uday Hussein, would be joined by bin Laden and his two chosen aides for more detailed discussions. Then, following the afternoon prayers, the six men would again meet to share a meal and conclude the day's discussions. All would depart Basra that night.

Saddam had selected a secluded and well-secured safe house in a quiet neighborhood in the outskirts of Basra. The house was on a knoll overlooking a battlefield used in the Iraq-Iran War. The large house was one of many owned by the Tikriti Clan in Iraq. The neighborhood housed members of the ruling elite Sunni Muslims. The advance party of Saddam's Security Guards had arrived two days prior to the meeting time and Ali Hassan and his own security people came in the day before to insure that all preparations had been made for Saddam's arrival the next day by helicopter from a nearby Iraqi Army installation.

The Colonel in charge of Saddam's advance security party and Ali Hassan's Security Chief assured him that all necessary measures to insure iron-clad security had been taken. And at midnight, Ali Hassan himself, had made a final walk-through to personally inspect the guards posted at all entrances and exits to the house. The final place he stopped on his inspection was in a facility in the basement of the house where the meeting would actually take place. It was an area that was totally self-contained. It had been constructed to be free of any electronic eaves dropping and reinforced with enough steel in the walls to also serve as a bomb shelter. Once the room had been inspected and electronically swept by Saddam's technical specialists, it was guarded 24 hours a day to ensure continuous security. The room contained only a small conference table and six chairs. No writing tablets or pencils were on the table. Saddam wanted no notes taken. Ali Hassan thought to himself, "When your leader is a madman, who knows what mad ideas will come next or where they will lead?" And with that, he went up to his bedroom to get a few hours sleep.

As planned, Osama bin Laden was the first to arrive. He and his security party drove up to the gated entrance to the house in three black, bulletproof Mercedes sedans. Once bona fides were established by the outer perimeter guards, the cars and their occupants were allowed inside the wall but still far enough away from the main entrance to the house to minimize any car bomb threat. Bin Laden and two other men and several of their security people were then escorted to the house's main entrance where they were searched, passed through the electronic security detector and met by Ali Hassan. Ali Hassan, a stocky, short, swarthy complected man in his late fifties, was dressed in a gray business suit rather than a uniform for security purposes. He recognized bin

Laden right away and some of his security guards from his earlier meeting with him in Afghanistan. He was again struck by the simplicity of bin Laden's dress that was almost Bedouin-like. He wore a shalwar qamese, or the white pajama type trousers, sandals and a long flowing and loose coat and a plain, colorless, head wrapping. Bin Laden was a tall, thin man, well above six feet but his dress made him seem even taller and with a certain majestic air. Not at all the way you would picture one of the world's richest and most feared terrorist, thought Ali Hassan.

Bin Laden was accompanied by two men that Ali Hassan had not seen or met before. Both men, Ali Hassan estimated, were in their mid-forties, dressed similarly to bin Laden, and like him, were bearded. One man following closely behind bin Laden looked like a Saudi but the other, slightly younger looking man, had a certain western look about him and Ali Hassan guessed he could pass for a Brit or American.

Ali Hassan escorted bin Laden and his aides to a room where they could freshen up and then directly to the basement room where bin Laden and Saddam would meet. Saddam was scheduled to arrive in fifteen minutes and would be accompanied by his son, Uday. Uday would then join Ali Hassan and bin Laden's two aides in a nearby waiting room until summoned by Saddam.

Saddam Hussein and his son, Uday, arrived on schedule; both dressed in business suits. Saddam seemed in the best of humor, smiling broadly and obviously pleased that Ali Hassan had been able to arrange the meeting with bin Laden. He went directly to the basement meeting room and after the standard Arab greetings and exchange of kisses, the door was closed and the others moved to the nearby waiting room.

Uday Hussein was Saddam's eldest son and while certainly not as smart as his father, he was equally brutal and had been taught by the master, since birth, the virtues of torture and execution of one's opposition and enemies. Next to Saddam, he was the most hated, closely guarded man in Iraq against the fear of assassination. He was thought by many to be a ruthless psychopath and he had demonstrated on many occasions, to his father's satisfaction, an eager willingness to murder any one who opposed Saddam. Ali Hassan had once read an intercepted CIA report characterizing Uday as a "loose cannon." An apt description, he believed.

While Saddam and bin Laden were meeting privately, the four other men sat quietly in the nearby waiting room. Uday was aloof, not talking with the others, and occasionally pacing back and forth. "A Doberman-pinscher disposition," thought Ali Hassan. He, on the other hand, tried to engage bin Laden's aides in conversation. They volunteered their names. The older man called himself Wadih Mohammed and the younger, Abdul Khalid. Ali Hassan doubted that these were their real names. In the dangerous business of terrorism, real names are rarely used. They, too, like bin Laden, were very conservative, almost stoic, in their mannerisms, and behavior. Both could have passed for clerics. They were the kind of men that typified the term "Jihad," referring to those involved in a "holy war." Ali Hassan didn't have any time for that kind of thinking but he had to admit that the fundamentalist groups such as the Hizballah and Hamas could produce people willing to do anything for what they fanatically believed to be their holy cause.

The morning passed without the four waiting men being summoned by Saddam. Just at noon, the door to Saddam's meeting area was opened and Saddam, followed by bin Laden, headed to the nearby dining room for the noon meal. Ali Hassan, Uday, and the others followed and took seats around a table set for six with Saddam at the head, bin Laden on his right, and his son Uday, at his left. Uday Hussein was introduced to bin Laden and bin Laden, in turn, presented his two assistants to Saddam Hussein. During the midday meal of dates, cheeses, tea, and soft drinks, Saddam smiled a lot. In fact, he was rather expansive in describing to bin Laden how pleased he was over the dilemma he had given the Americans by his tactics in the "no fly" zones. It was only a short matter of time before the American Congress and the public would grow tired of the daily American air strikes in Iraq and demand that the U.S. military stop the death and destruction they were carrying out against Iraq. "The Americans don't have the focus and stamina for anything that lasts more than a few weeks," he boasted. Ali Hassan read Saddam's smiles and good humor as a sign that whatever it was that he wanted bin Laden to do, Saddam had been successful in gaining bin Laden's agreement. Saddam could demonstrate an instant insider's malevolence toward anyone whenever he was unable to impose his will. There was a black, cruel side of Saddam that could strike fear in the hearts of even the most ruthless and resourceful of men, including Ali Hassan.

At the end of the meal, Saddam announced that following a short break to relieve and refresh themselves, all present would join him in the secure meeting room. Personal aides then escorted each man to a nearby private toilet. As Ali Hassan leaned over the lavish tile wash basin of his facility, he threw cold water in his face repeatedly in order to be able to be as alert as possible when receiving whatever it was that Saddam Hussein was about to give them. Again, one of those involuntary shudders. "I must really be getting old," he thought.

When tea had been poured for each individual around the small conference table and the tea pots refilled and the door closed, Saddam began, "As you all know, that cur of a President, Clinton announced in January to the world that the Great Satan feared nuclear, chemical, biological and cyber attacks by terrorist forces. Particularly those who he said knew that they could not defeat the American military. We also know that whenever the Americans talk about terrorism, no matter who is to blame, they always think of Iraq, and the great Osama bin Laden. Never, of course, as freedom fighters, but only as dreaded terrorists. We also know that this scare tactic announcement was just one more lying ploy to disguise his whoring with the bitches of Washington. When I heard this, I was deeply offended, as I am sure all of my Arab brothers were, too. I laid awake at night thinking, is there no end to the pain and shame that this infidel and his followers cause us to bear." As Ali Hassan listened to Saddam, he privately expressed admiration for Saddam's ability to deliver a message—any message. The longer he talked he seemed to feed on his own emotion and each word, phrase and sentence was stronger than the last. Saddam was only talking to five others but he might as well have been talking to a thousand, he was that animated. And Ali Hassan had no idea where Saddam was going but he had a premonition that something far more risky than ever before was about to emerge from Saddam's mouth.

"I agonized and agonized over this insult to all Arabs and prayed and said to Allah, must we, all our lives, continue to suffer at the hands of this foreign devil? Will there never be any peace of mind for us? Will there never be any retribution?" Then, with his voice rising higher, "It came to me. Why not let the sum of all the Great Satan's fears become reality? Why not make those things happen that he seeks to frighten his own people about? Why not make the false threat that he claims may possibly happen… take place? Why not make his own words, his worst self-fulfilling prophecy? And make that our long sought after retribution?"

Saddam had so worked himself up over this emotional delivery he suddenly realized that he could be thought of as out-of-control and he quickly returned to a more normal tone of voice.

"My idea is simply this. If the United States fears most a nuclear attack, let's make that happen. If they also fear a chemical or biological attack, then let's make that happen. And if they also fear a cyber attack, then let's make that happen. And let's make all of these things happen at the same time, then that will truly be our retribution. A long awaited and fitting retribution for the Great Satan."

11

Saddam then paused to gauge the impact on the faces in the room. Bin Laden was stoic. His aides looked somewhat surprised but, definitely curious. No reaction on the part of Uday. But then, thought Ali Hassan, "he was as mad as Saddam." And Ali Hassan, through a lot of practice, had become successful at maintaining a poker face at Saddam meetings. But he was worried that he might have paled at Saddam's mention of a nuclear attack.

Saddam seemed satisfied that he had everyone's attention, so he continued. "Now you are thinking how can this be? How could we carry out nuclear, biological, chemical or cyber attacks against the United States? Clinton is right about one thing. We do not have the military forces or delivery means to carry out those attacks across the great distances and waters. But the master terrorist Osama bin Laden," Saddam said, nodding toward bin Laden, "has set the examples for us all that a few determined men, using the element of surprise can inflict grave damage on even the most powerful of enemies. And it is in using the successful techniques perfected by bin Laden that I believe, working together, we can be successful against our most hated enemy the "Great Satan.""

Saddam then went on to explain that he believed that bin Laden's successes against Americans around the world and within America were due to the combination of his vast financial resources, small organization, compartmented operations and the ability to recruit a cross section of true believers across the Arab world that were willing to carry out the will of Allah, even if that meant martyrdom.

"What I have proposed to bin Laden is that Iraq will now take on the responsibility of obtaining the necessary weapons, and the chemical, biological, and cyber agents, now that I am free from the United Nations' inspections. Iraq will also provide him with increased financial, logistics, operations, and even more intelligence support than we have provided in the past. All of these will be your responsibility to coordinate Ali Hassan." And then pausing, Saddam said to bin Laden, "I want you to know that I have the greatest confidence in Ali Hassan. He has for years, been my foremost expert in chemical warfare which he used against our enemies in Kurdistan when he was our Governor there, and against the Americans in the Gulf War. They still don't know what hit them, but I credit Ali Hassan with more than 70,000 casualties that continue to the present day."

"Osama bin Laden has agreed to recruit and train three teams to be used for the attacks on the United States. Ali Hassan, you will coordinate any support that bin Laden requires in this endeavor."

Turning to Ali Hassan, bin Laden pointed toward Wadih Mohammed saying, "Wadih will carry out this operation for me, and he will be your point of contact." Ali Hassan acknowledged this and then turned back to Saddam who continued, "At the same time the strike teams are being recruited and trained, my son Uday will coordinate the preparation of a list of targets for nuclear, chemical, biological and cyber strikes in the United States. The list will contain at least fifty targets of each type and will include an estimate of the strategic, military, economic, and psychological impact on the Americans, as well as an estimate of the degree of difficulty of striking the target based on location, access, and security. The targets will then be ranked in order of value and difficulty.

When the strike teams are trained and ready, I and Osama bin Laden, will choose three primary, and three alternate targets, to be struck. The only other persons to know the targets selected will be the three team leaders. And then, only just prior to strike time."

Bin Laden pointed to his other aide and said, "Abdul Khalid will assist you in the selection of targets. He lived in the United States for many years and will have first hand knowledge of many of the targets. Please call on him for any help you need, General Uday."

Uday acknowledged bin Laden's offer with a slight nod and turned again to listen to his father, something he developed a lot of practice in doing. Ali Hassan made a mental note to make sure Khalid was involved in the targeting process with Uday. It made Ali Hassan nervous to think that Uday was going to be involved in something so important as this latest scheme of Saddam's. Ali Hassan did not trust Uday, but then, who in Iraq trusted anyone.

The rest of the afternoon was spent in discussing how long it would take for the recruiting and training of the strike teams and the types of weapons to be used. Ali Hassan, a man with much blood on his own hands over the years that Saddam and the Takriti clan had ruled Iraq, was struck by the matter-of-fact, almost clinical way that bin Laden and his two aides discussed the various options in which large numbers of men, women and children, buildings, monuments, and military installations could be inflicted with the maximum pain, damage, and destruction. Ali Hassan knew that Saddam was driven by the madness of power and would continue to do anything to survive. But these other younger fundamentalists supposedly derived their strength from prayer and their undying faith in Allah. Did Allah, Ali Hassan wondered, really want the kind of retribution they were now planning to inflict? Somehow he didn't think so, but he wasn't sure what to do about it. Maybe he would actually pray later at the afternoon prayers they would all observe.

CHAPTER 2

BART LOWE—1999

During that same week in January that the President of the United States started beating the drums about a terrorist threat to the country, on an overcast Friday afternoon, a black Lincoln official car from Capitol Hill pulled up at the River Entrance to the Pentagon and deposited Senator Robert Jones, a ranking member of the Senate Select Committee on Intelligence, or SSCI. Jones had an appointment with the Secretary of Defense, William Cohen. Cohen, himself a former Senator, and Jones had been colleagues and friends in Washington for many years.

Senator Jones was met by one of Secretary Cohen's military aides and escorted through the Pentagon security guards to Cohen's E-Ring office overlooking the Potomac River. After being seated on one of the Secretary's plush leather chairs and served a cup of English tea, his favorite, Senator Jones said, "Thanks for seeing me, Bill, on such short notice."

"Bob, you know I'd never be too busy to see the distinguished Senior Senator from Florida," Cohen replied, using the formal and still very familiar language of the U.S. Senate.

"I know you're very busy, Bill, with the many challenges of Defense and I suspect even more busy than you were in looking out for the great State of Maine."

"You can say that again, Bob, and I might add, I never realized when I was on the other side of the river, just how many demands you and your other distinguished colleagues generate for the guys on this side of the river."

"Amen. The shoe is on the other foot, huh, Bill?"

"I just wanted you to know that I am earning all of that taxpayer money that you have thrown our way."

"Never a doubt, Bill. Never a doubt! Which brings me back to why I am here today. Unlike the media and the American public, we in the Senate, and particularly, in the SSCI, are even more concerned than the President over the possibility of a terrorist threat to the United States. And you know as of late, we have done all we can do to strengthen the posture of the military counter-terrorist forces and the counter-terrorist capabilities of the FBI, CIA, and NSA. But I am concerned over the continuity of operations in the Defense Attaché Service."

"Oh, how so?" asked Cohen, the start of a frown appearing on his forehead.

"To begin with, we all saw the announcement this week that General Don Odom is moving to the National Security Council to be the Deputy National Security Advisor. And if I am not mistaken, Don has only been head of the DAS for less than a year."

"Yes, Bob, I am well aware of that move. Madeline Albright called to complain about that the day the announcement was made. And I can tell you what I told her. Odom is the President's choice and he will not take no for an answer. We will just have to suck it up somehow." Cohen's face was beginning to redden.

"Bill, I am not here to try and get into your business. I hope you know me better than that. What I want to do is to offer a suggestion. My staff head is Teri McCannon; you remember Teri, don't you, Bill?"

"Yes, of course. She's been with you a number of years, right?"

"Yes, indeed. Well, she pulled together some information for me and if it's correct, it says the DAS Director's job has turned over four times in the last five years. And not because of any fault of the military officers. They have all been outstanding people. It's just that someone thinks they are needed somewhere else more."

"Yes, yes, I know all of that. When we move a General Officer in the military, it causes 16 other moves," Cohen said, a touch of impatience beginning in his voice.

"Teri also says that the military services are not always anxious to nominate their best people for the DAS job and often, the candidates nominated are not ideally qualified, not a former attaché, etc."

"Yes, yes, my people tell me we often have to intervene and identify the best qualified officer we want and direct that he or she be assigned. But that's nothing new for the military, Bob. Too many requirements, not enough of the right set of people and the frequent crisis that we are dealing with... like Kosovo." Cohen inched forward in his chair and said, "Which reminds me... my next meeting this afternoon is in the tank with the Chiefs to discuss that quagmire. What is your suggestion, Bob?"

"Bill, you know after the leadership problem we had at the FBI someone came up with the bright idea of recalling Louis Freech and giving him a ten year tenure so that continuity would have a real chance for success. Why not recall Bart Lowe for the Defense Attaché Service job? You remember Bart, don't you, Bill? In my opinion, he was our best Director of the DAS and the State Department people loved working with him."

"Yes, I remember Bart," the Secretary said, now shifting back again into his chair. "He was from Florida as I remember, right, Bob?"

"As a matter of fact, I think you are right, Bill," the Senator acknowledged, smiling. "But his credentials were exceptional."

"I believe I would agree with that, but in what capacity? As a civilian, or a military officer. Wouldn't he be too old for that now?"

"My thought was that you would recall him as a military officer. Say at the rank of Lieutenant General, but make it one of those commissions like General Hershey had for years at the Selective Service. And I think you could gain

Congress' support for whatever tenure you wanted the job to have—5 years, 10 years, whatever. Your call."

"And what about Lowe's availability? Would he want to do it? Have you checked that?" Cohen asked.

"No. I have not. I do see him from time-to-time in Florida. He works for one of my best constituents, Dick Groveland."

"Oh, yeah. Groveland Enterprises. Smart guy. Has a finger in many pots. If Lowe is working for him, my guess is that he is making more than you and I combined. Would he be willing to give that up?"

"I honestly don't know the answer to that question and it would have been inappropriate for me to even raise the subject with him before contacting you, Bill. I do know he is a staunch patriot and like you, would probably respond to the call of duty." Senator Jones replied referring to Cohen's willingness to serve as Secretary of Defense rather than return to a lucrative law practice in Bangor, Maine.

"Well, Bob," Cohen answered as he rose from his chair, signaling the meeting was at an end, "It is a good suggestion and I'll give it some thought and put our people on it to see if it would be feasible."

The two friends shook hands and Senator Jones departed with a politician's smile on his face.

Major General Barton Scott Lowe retired from the U.S. Army and as of head of the Defense Attachés Service, or DAS, in August 1991. At that time, he had been in charge of the DAS for five years and served 31 years in the Army. His last two years as Chief of the DAS were busy times for Bart and his Attachés, filled with problems stemming from the war in southwest Asia, Kuwait, Iraq, the civil war in the former Yugoslavia, and the never ending unrest in the third world countries such as the Sudan, Somalia, and even closer to home, Haiti.

At his retirement parade at Fort Meyer in Virginia, Lowe was decorated by the Vice Chief of Staff of the Army, receiving the Defense and Army Distinguished Service Medals and the Intelligence Distinguished Service Medal from the National Intelligence Community. He was commended by the Secretary of Defense for his earlier work on HEAT SEEKER and his support to the other national security agencies. He even received personal notes from the President and the Secretary of State. His most prized memento of his time in service, however, was a bound leather book of farewell messages that was sent to him from the more than one hundred Defense Attaché Offices, or DAOs, around the world. The Attachés were lavish in their praise for the many ways in which General Lowe had carried their water in Washington and for his tireless dedication to those serving in the field. To a person they said that he had carried out his responsibilities better than any other who had held the job. Bart was not sure of that, but he was deeply touched by their thoughts and knew that his five years with the DAS had been the most fascinating and exciting times of his life. He knew it was time to go, but was saddened that that phase of his life was coming to an end.

During the summer of 1991, Bart finally accepted the long-standing offer from his developer friend in Florida, Dick Groveland. "Rags" Groveland, Bart's classmate and fraternity brother from college days at the University of Florida, lived in Miami, but had been expanding his land development business in central Florida and wanted Bart to take over that effort. Bart's mother, a widow for many years, had passed away in their home in Miami in 1989 and he had no compelling reason to return there.

Immediately after his retirement, Bart, with the help of Master Sergeant Sam Mills, his long time enlisted aide, packed up the furniture and his belongings from the quarters at Fort Meyer and went to Barbados in the Caribbean for a two week vacation with his longtime female friend, Assistant Secretary of State, B.J. Ross. Ambassador Ross had served as head of the State Department's Intelligence and Research Bureau for most of the time that Bart had been Director of the DAS. They had worked well together and the cooperation and coordination between State and Defense's worldwide diplomatic and attaché operations had never been better. They were each other's frequent escort at the various government and foreign affairs in Washington and considered by many in State and Defense to be a romantic item. In truth, Bart and B.J. were romantically involved with each other, but never to the point of seriously considering marriage. They both were people who were so deeply engrossed in and committed to their work that it never occurred to either of them to take on the additional responsibility and commitment to each other of marriage. Their relationship was one of mutual convenience and support. And it had worked well for both of them. When Bart made the decision to retire from active service, the thought went through his mind that now might be the time to reconsider his feelings on marriage. However, he knew that B.J. was a couple of years younger than he and wanted to serve at least ten more years at State. In fact, she was scheduled to return to the field again in the fall of 1991 and was looking forward to the major responsibilities of being a U.S. Ambassador abroad after her extended time at the "Foggy Bottom" in Washington.

They had a great time together in Barbados; it was both a romantic and bittersweet time. B.J. had learned that she was being posted to Albania and had much to do in the way of language training and other orientations. She was anxious to get started. Bart, on the other hand, was just finishing his life's chosen work and going off to a future for which he wasn't really sure he was qualified. He wondered if old soldiers did just fade away. Also, for the first time, he wasn't sure how much he would miss the companionship of B.J. and when he would see her again. The past five years had been great for Bart Lowe and the future was a question mark.

However, Bart Lowe, consistent with his track record, was not only a survivor, but an eternal optimist. From the first day he reported to his new boss, "Rags" Groveland in Miami, Bart simply got off of one fast track and immediately got on another. Bart flew from the Washington-Dulles Airport to Miami International and took a taxi directly to the Groveland Enterprises Building on Brickell Avenue, just south of downtown Miami. When he was shown into Rag's expansive office overlooking the emerald hues of Biscayne Bay, Bart's first words were, "And I thought the Secretary of Defense had a great office."

"Not bad for a country boy. Huh, Bart?"

Rags Groveland was relatively short, about 5'5", with broad shoulders and large, muscular arms from his early years in the construction business. When younger, he'd had short, reddish brown hair but, it didn't stay long and he had been shaving his head for as long as Bart could remember. Bart and Rags met in college and became lifelong friends. They had gone into the Army at the same time but Rags had served only three years and then returned to Miami to marry his high school and college sweetheart and make his fortune.

And make his fortune, he did. He was now one of the richest men in Florida, and perhaps, the nation. Everything he touched from housing development, to malls, to theme parks, you name it—they turned to gold. *Time Magazine* had said he was a man with a Midas touch. And for all Bart could tell, it was true.

"How're Mary and your beautiful girls?" Bart asked.

"Mary hasn't talked about anything else except you since we got back from your retirement ceremony and party. You know you have always been her hero. And the girls never have figured out why you haven't married one of them. Mary says it is because you are a true straight arrow. I know it's because you have more women than you can handle in Washington. Right, Bart?"

"Yeah, I wish." Bart replied. Rags had always been the kind of person that made everyone feel at ease, had a great sense of humor, and was liked equally by men and women.

21

Rags invited Bart to sit down in one of the flowered, rattan easy chairs and asked his administrative assistant to bring them both tall glasses of iced tea.

"Bart, the first thing I want you to do is to get rid of that suit and tie." Rags told him. This is a casual world we live in and I want you to relax and have some fun. The way I'm dressed in just an open collar, short sleeved shirt and trousers. That's the way we do business here in south Florida.

"Oh, I can handle that," Bart said and nodded.

"As I told you earlier," Rags continued, "I have been successful beyond my wildest dreams in Miami, Hollywood, Fort Lauderdale, West Palm Beach, and Key West. And there are enough projects already on the books to last a lifetime. As a result, I have not been able to pay enough attention to central Florida, nor find the right person to head up our expansion efforts there. And besides, I always wanted to save that for you, my old friend."

"I'm delighted that you did, Rags, and I know that it is going to be great working with you after all these years. I can only say that you must have taken leave of your senses to offer me the six-figure salary you did. I'm not sure that I'm really worth that kind of money. Was there someone you wanted me to put a contract out on?" joked Bart.

"Not to worry, buddy. I know what you are worth and I guarantee you will earn every penny of it and have some fun while you are doing it.

"What I have in mind is that you start with us here in Miami. Get to know the organization and all our people, our long-range plans, who our contacts are, and with whom we are doing business; I think that'll take you three or four months. Then, when you say you are ready, you can head up to Orlando. I already have a small advance party in Orlando. They are in temporary spaces but are getting the lay of the land and will be prepared to give you some recommendations when you get up there. In the meantime, while you're here in Miami, if you haven't already made any arrangements, I hope that you will stay with Mary and me at our place on Key

Biscayne. It's really only about twenty minutes from here and since all the girls have grown up and moved away, it's only Mary and me rambling around in that big old place."

Bart had accepted Rag's invitation to stay with him and Mary and thoroughly enjoyed being with his old fraternity buddy again. Rags insisted that Bart leave work each day at the same time he did, and as a result, Bart was no longer burning the midnight oil in his new profession.

Bart quickly picked up the essentials of what Groveland Enterprises was all about and by the end of November, he deemed himself ready to head north to Orlando. Once in Orlando, Bart had quickly found out that the small Orlando town he had known as a college student was long gone. The Orlando, Florida town that Disney had put on the map was more akin to a sprawling Los Angeles and the shortest distance between any two points was under construction. Groveland's people were located in an area close to the busy airport and most of them were staying at the nearby Guest Quarters. Bart did likewise until such time as they had finalized their lease for offices in a new building, also near the airport, and then he took a furnished apartment near work.

For the next year, Bart had been on a steep learning curve picking up the usual ins and outs of the development business. Surprisingly, to him, there was still an abundance of undeveloped or underdeveloped land and areas in central and northern Florida and more than enough people and investors with deep pockets looking for a promising project.

Rags Groveland had done a great job of surrounding himself with honest, competent people and the organization had an excellent reputation in both the building and banking communities in Florida. Bart's job as Vice President for Central Florida Operations was old hat to him. In his military career, he had spent countless hours in taking on new requirements, identifying a solution, pulling together the right people, resources, and funding, and riding herd on the project to fruition, and then moving to the next project.

During his first three years in Orlando, Bart had traveled a good deal throughout the state and to other business centers in the southeast United States. In his frequent trips to the main office in Miami, Bart renewed many friendships he had had with high school and college classmates. He dated, when in Miami, the widow of a high school football teammate.

By the end of 1994, Bart felt comfortable in his new job. He was successful in building a solid foundation in central Florida for the Groveland Long Range Development Plan. Bart believed in The Plan. It certainly would be good for Florida and its residents. He liked his work and having Rags for a boss couldn't have been better. He even felt as though he was earning that six-figure salary. But Bart was not an altogether happy camper. He didn't like living in Orlando—too hot and congested. He also missed B.J. Ross. She had corresponded regularly about the first six months but that dropped off to infrequently.

One day, on a road trip returning from Vero Beach to Orlando, Bart had chosen to take the more scenic and slower route back along the coast on Highway A1A. That route runs through Patrick Air Force Base and Bart had decided to stop and visit the Base Exchange and the nearby small beach community of Satellite Beach. Bart had been there a few times over the years during visits to space events either at Patrick or nearby Cape Canaveral. But he had completely forgotten how pleasant Satellite Beach was and how it was relatively undiscovered by the hoards of tourists and snowbirds that flocked to Florida each year. He had made a note to check it out.

And check it out he did. By the summer of 1995, Bart had purchased, at a surprisingly reasonable price, an ocean front, eighth floor, northeast corner, penthouse at the Buccaneer Condominiums in Satellite Beach. He retained his small apartment near the Groveland offices in Orlando and spent Monday through Thursday there. On Friday afternoons, he headed for the beach and spent Friday, Saturday, and

Sunday nights there and commuted the 53 miles to Orlando on Monday mornings.

The next three years were good ones for Bart Lowe. He greatly enjoyed being on the ocean. He joined the Officer's Club at Patrick Air Force Base and the local Yacht Club. He bought a speed boat and logged in many pleasant hours on the Banana River and racquetball courts at the Patrick Air Force Base Gym. He enjoyed the camaraderie of the active duty and retired military families living in Satellite Beach. His social life even improved. He hit it off well with the attractive woman and successful realtor that helped him locate his condo and they became frequent companions at many of the areas' cultural and entertainment events. He even discovered that Eckler's, one of the country's best known vintage Corvette facilities was a mere twenty miles from Satellite Beach. There he found many a sympathetic ear about the virtues and needs of his old '75 Stingray. No, he had not yet been able to deal with the thought of parting with it. But he had added a green '95 Jaguar XKE to his garage and used that for his Florida travels.

Still, for a man who to most appearances had everything—money, a good job, a fantastic place to live, more social contacts and invitations than he could accept, the carefree life of a bachelor, usually with an attractive woman on his arm, and the well groomed look of a healthy man who had successfully completed one career, and was deeply enmeshed in another—Bart Lowe was not completely happy. Something was missing in his life and he was not sure what it was. More and more he found himself lying awake at night wondering, "What the hell is missing?" He guessed that the most obvious missing piece was not fully sharing his life with another person, a wife and companion, and children. Yet Bart, deep down in his inner self, was not sure he was fully capable of that. He had recalled a number of times in his life an incident that had taken place during his senior year in college. He had gone steady for three years with a girl who had been his high school sweetheart. Although they were not engaged, most of their friends, and really themselves, thought they would marry after college. They were very close and Bart had never had any other romantic interest. But the girl was very keen on going back to Miami and making a life there among their families. When Bart told her that he wanted to go into the military and see the world, she was heartbroken and accused Bart of only being interested in himself. She had said that she doubted that Bart Lowe would ever be truly able to love someone else. They broke off their relationship and went their separate ways but the accusation his sweetheart had made had had a profound effect on the young Bart Lowe. It had stayed with him all of his adult life and had probably kept Bart from establishing too close a romantic relationship with anyone. His self-doubt was somewhat reinforced during his military career when a close friend whom Bart considered a very professional and successful military officer confided to Bart that he considered himself to be only half-a-man. While his friend had worked very hard and succeeded in his professional life, he had done so, he believed, at the expense of his family and concluded that he had let them down. Bart had worried at the same time that he, if married too, might be that same kind of person.

While all of this was going through Bart Lowe's mind in Florida and 1999 had begun with many new opportunities for Groveland Enterprises, something most unusual occurred. He received a call from William Cohen, the Secretary of Defense, who asked Bart if he would be willing to return as head of the Defense Attaché Service.

What a shock! Secretary Cohen, whom Bart had known years ago when Cohen was a U.S. Senator on the SSCI, explained to Bart that he was acting on a recommendation from the Congress, specifically, Senator Robert Jones. Jones and Bart had worked closely during Bart's time with the DAS and he had been one of Bart's and the Defense Attaché Service's biggest supporters. Bart had always considered Jones a true statesman and had the greatest respect for him but, "My God," Bart thought, "Is this really happening?"

Cohen went on to explain that in the seven plus years since Bart had left the DAS, there had been no less than five successors. "They were all good people," Cohen said, "but other requirements had taken priority and they had been moved along. In fact," Cohen said, "the incumbent DAS Chief had been selected by the President to be the Deputy National Security Advisor and the President was not about to take 'no' for an answer."

The Secretary of State had complained to Cohen because of the importance of military attachés serving as members of the U.S. Embassy teams. "The coordination," she said, "between State and the Defense Attaché Service is vital to U.S. Foreign Policy and the frequent turnover of DAS Directors is impacting on both Agencies' continuity."

"It was the continuity thing that gave Bob Jones the idea of recalling you. As you are probably aware, because of some earlier problems at the FBI, the Congress had urged that Louis Freech be recalled to be the Director of the Bureau and be given a 10-year tenure for the sake of long-term continuity. That precedent by the Justice Department led Senator Jones to think that Defense could probably make a similar case for you. My people think it is a good idea and I agree. So what do you say Bart Lowe? Are you interested?" Cohen had asked.

CHAPTER 3

CHERRY BLOSSOM TIME

Bart Lowe had received the telephone call from Secretary Cohen in mid-February. He could hardly believe his ears! Adrenaline had rushed throughout his body the whole time he was on the phone. While his life after the Army was both interesting and financially rewarding, it never came close to the feelings of excitement and accomplishment he had known in the Attaché Service. Cohen's offer seemed almost too good to be true. But, Cohen assured him that the offer was really on the table and the job was Bart's for the taking.

"Mr. Secretary, I can't think of anything that I would rather do at this time in my life."

Bart had asked for 30 days to extract himself from Groveland Enterprises before reporting to Washington. Cohen had agreed and thought that would be sufficient time to allow the President to nominate Bart Lowe as a permanent Lieutenant General and get Senate confirmation. Cohen planned to ask for a five-year tenure for the DAS job with an option of offering a second assignment if all parties agreed.

When Bart had asked his old friend Dick Groveland if he would be willing to let Bart return to the DAS, Groveland had answered, "You've done everything I asked and more. I'd hoped that you would consider taking over the whole operation here, someday soon, but I always knew that if the call of duty ever came again, you would be the first to go. You will always be a good soldier, Bart."

True to Secretary Cohen's estimate, by mid-March, the Senate, coaxed by Senator Bob Jones, approved the President's nomination of Bart Lowe as Director of the Defense Attaché Service with the rank of permanent

Lieutenant General. Bart was sworn in for the second time in his life as DAS Director in a ceremony in the Secretary of Defense's office on the nineteenth of March. To his delight B.J. Ross, recently assigned as the U.S. Ambassador to the Ukraine, was in Washington and attended the ceremony along with the Grovelands and a number of Bart's friends from Florida, and certain key officials from the National Security community and the Congress.

Washington in March and April is normally one of the best times of the year. The long winter is over. Springtime is in the air. Spring Break school children and their families are visiting in droves and everyone is anticipating the cherry blossoms and a fresh new year. This year, however, there was a political tension hanging over Washington like a damp, heavy fog. You couldn't see it, but you could feel it. It was present in the national media, in the Congress, at the White House and in the frequent meetings taking place throughout the U.S. Government, not only during the day, but often throughout the night. It all had to do with the crisis in Kosovo.

Kosovo was an unknown name to most Americans prior to 1999 but it was fast becoming a household word. It had started in the summer of 1998 when the "ethnic cleansing" by Serbs of the ethnic Albanians in Kosovo province of Serbia of the former Yugoslavia became known to the world press. And when diplomatic efforts by the U.S. and its NATO allies failed to persuade President Slobodan Milosevic to halt the brutal killing of Kosovars by the Serb military and police forces. NATO decided to intervene. NATO's plan was to bomb Milosevic and the Serbs into submission and President Clinton and some of his advisors, although not all the military ones, thought the bombing had a good chance of success. However, as it turned out in the short term, the bombing appeared to have triggered events which led to the departure of ever increasing numbers of Kosovars into Albania and Macedonia, creating hundreds of thousands of refugees. As the numbers of refugees increased, the media, as it is always want to do, began its second guessing of the President's plan to bomb Yugoslavia, and the political second guessers in Washington had a field day on the battered U.S. President's decision not to use ground troops to stop the Serbs. Against this backdrop, Bart Lowe resumed his duties as Director of the Defense Attaché Service.

Bart was impressed with the DAS' progress during his absence. A new building had been constructed in Northern Virginia to serve as DAS Headquarters and it was located only minutes from the Pentagon. The multi-story building was a considerable improvement over the old building in Rosslyn! The DAS staff now enjoyed modern offices and work areas, and their proximity to the Pentagon and downtown Washington gave them an advantage over their colleagues at NSA and CIA who faced a considerable commute to and from the many impromptu meetings that took place with maddening regularity in the halls of the U.S. Government.

While many of the outstanding military and civilian professionals that Bart had been privileged to serve with before had departed the DAS or retired from military or government service, such as George Martin, Chuck Gregorios, and Pete Kalitka, Bart was pleased to learn that Barbara Barnsworth had, as he always thought she would, continued to demonstrate exceptional talent and had advanced to being the civilian Deputy Director of the DAS. Also, he learned that Colonel Jim Poreman who had played such a key role in Iraq before the war as Defense Attaché, had retired from the Army and accepted the Senior Executive Service position responsible for Middle East DAS operations. And in one other important development, Bart was informed that Navy Captain Mike Stanik, a former Attaché and DAS Eastern Europe Division Chief had been selected by the Navy for Rear Admiral and would be coming on board in mid-May as Bart's Director of Operations. And last, but not by any means least, Bart was pleasantly surprised to find out that his former secretary, Joan Weber, was still serving as the administrative assistant to the DAS Director.

Although he was chomping at the bit to get to work, Bart did not want to spoil anyone's weekend and he decided to leave steerage of the DAS in Barbara Barnsworth's capable hands until the following Monday. Barbara had been the acting Director for over a month due to the departure of General Don Odom to the National Security Council.

B.J. Ross had kept her apartment at the River House across from the Pentagon and had invited Bart to stay there until he got settled again. She would be returning to Kiev in the Ukraine on Monday, but they had the weekend together and had dinner Saturday night at one of their old haunts, The Chart House, on the Potomac River in Old Town Alexandria. B.J. had served in three ambassadorial posts since they had served in Washington together and her current position in Kiev was said to be a prep for moving the following year to Moscow as the U.S. Ambassador there. Bart was really pleased to be with B.J. again although the time was short. He had only seen her a half a dozen times during the last seven years and their lives had taken different paths. They did, however, make love on their last night together but he could tell the old romantic spark was no longer there and it saddened them both. But once again, they were two people with very important roles to play for their country and they were more than ready to get on with it.

"I have your coffee ready, General," announced Joan Weber when Bart Lowe arrived at his 14th floor office on Monday morning.

"Sounds familiar, Joan," Bart replied with a not unpleasant feeling of déjà vu. The years had obviously been good to Joan Weber and none of the DAS front office tension that comes with a steady diet of crisis management had affected her cheery, upbeat manner.

"We are so happy to have you back, General Lowe. You were always my favorite," said Ms. Weber, following Bart into his corner office. Whether or not that was actually true, Joan Weber made it seem so and Bart was, in truth, absolutely delighted to be back.

"You have thirty minutes to look over your new office and tell me any changes you would like to have made before Ms. Barnsworth comes in to give you your first round of briefings. We have set aside two hours for that and then the admin people will be in to give you the security procedures and get things going for all the new clearances you will need. Then, this afternoon you will have a tour of our facilities and get to see all of our people. I think, General, you will be surprised how many people that you knew when you were here, left, went all over the world, but are back here again."

"I'm looking forward to that, Joan, and let me say how pleased I am that you are one of those people. I feel like I am home again."

When Barbara Barnsworth came into Bart's office from her adjoining one, he was immediately struck by her professional appearance and manner. He had seen her only briefly at his swearing-in ceremony and had not had the opportunity to speak with her at any length. Still a blonde, her figure and stylish dress would be enough to turn male and female heads in almost any walk of life. But in addition to that, she exuded executive confidence. The same kind that Bart had seen in the boardrooms of power in the civilian world that he had just left behind. She was dressed in a black business suit, matching pumps and carried a small black leather portfolio under her arm. She asked Bart to join her at the briefing table across from his large executive desk. When he was seated, she slipped into the first chair to his left and began:

"General Lowe, again welcome back to the DAS. I am sure that you know that your many friends here and at the other agencies in town are happy and feel very fortunate to have someone of your experience and outstanding reputation return to serve with us again."

"Thank you, Barbara, and again, congratulations to you on your continued success in this business. The career civilians like yourself and many dedicated others provide the continuity and experience that keeps the military attachés out front. And let's do away with the title between you and me. The name is Bart. I know I'll need a lot of help from you and others in order to get back up to speed and carry my weight around here."

"Very well, Gen-- ah, Bart. I'll be happy to help you in any way I can. Now let me tell you what the DAS is all about in 1999. We have a lot of ground to cover in the next two hours."

Bart wondered as she began if he detected a slight coolness in Barbara Barnsworth's words. Then it came to him. She had probably thought that she was ready to be the first civilian Director of the DAS and then somebody came up with the not so bright idea of recalling an old fart like Bart. It was way too soon, of course, but Bart wondered if he might have to watch his six with Ms. Barnsworth.

During the next hour and forty-five minutes, Barbara Barnsworth went on to give Bart a superb, *one over the world* briefing of current, DAS operations, trouble spots and Defense, JCS, and Joint Military Commands' priority requirements for the DAS. Bart could not remember having received a finer, more articulate briefing.

"So General Lowe... I mean, Bart," the first sign of a smile now appearing on her face, "in summary, the most important missions now facing the DAS and our Attachés are one, supporting the NATO and U.S. efforts in the war zone in Kosovo, two, monitoring and reporting on the worldwide terrorist threat to the U.S., three, keeping tabs on our longtime adversary, Saddam Hussein... He was a pain-in-the-ass when you were here for Desert Storm and he is still a pain-in-the-ass. And four and five six and seven include the Chinese, our technology that they are stealing everywhere, the threat of war in North Korea and the Russians, because of their failing economy, and the large number of weapons of mass destruction still there and not always properly safeguarded."

"No small plateful, Barbara. And how is our talent in the field? Are our attachés up to the job?"

"In spite of the cutbacks and the constant downsizing, we are holding our own. We are going to have to close down Belgrade. Unfortunately, as the Kosovo thing continues to heat up, it is not possible to keep the embassy open. However, our teams in Albania and Macedonia are doing a first rate job and the allies who are still in Yugoslavia and Serbia and will remain there will take up the slack for us. Iraq and Iran are tougher problems with no embassies in Baghdad and Tehran. But between us and the Military Assistance Groups that belong to CENTCOM, we have good observation from the periphery countries. Also, the J2s in both CENTCOM and EUCOM are great to work with and strongly reinforce and support our attachés. In the Far East, we have two outstanding Defense Attachés. Both DATTs are Army Foreign Area Officers and serving second tours in China and Korea. In fact, the DATT in China is Brigadier General Ron Lee. He was the Army Attaché in Hong Kong when you were here."

"That's right. I remember Ron. He was a first class linguist.

"In Russia, we are about to lose another Army FAO. We have had back-to-back Army Brigadiers there, both FAOs. Now it is the Air Force and Navy's turn. In fact, Navy is overdue. They keep nominating people who are good officers but, don't have the Russian language or the aptitude to learn it in time. I'll make a note to come back at you when we have a solution to that problem."

"I had heard, Barbara, that both the Air Force and Navy have begun FAO programs. Is that true?" Bart asked.

"Yes, sir. And they say they are both serious about having quality programs. But it is too soon for us to benefit and we will have to rely on sending prospective attachés for all services to language training for some time."

"And the terrorist thing. How are we doing with that?"

"That is, of course, the toughest one. Most of the threat groups are still from the Middle East but the bin Laden attacks against our embassies in Africa got all of the attention in Washington. Our inability to move around easily in those Middle Eastern countries makes gathering of terrorist related information difficult but Tim Poreman, your Middle East Division Chief and one of the your best attachés when you were here, has done a remarkable job in obtaining important reporting from our attachés in that part of the world. Quite frankly, everyone, and particularly the FBI, is very concerned about terrorism, but we all agree it's a very tough nut to crack. It's a requirement you will want to devote your attention to as soon as possible. In fact, I recommend that one of the first places you visit in town is the Counterterrorism Center at CIA Headquarters. Although it's located at Langley, it is really an interagency operation and they are doing a good job for us all."

Bart added the Counterterrorism Center to his list of growing notes. "What else do you recommend I do right away, Barbara?"

"Well, I think you need to quickly get around town and meet the national security agencies' heads so that you can call upon them when we need support. They are a relatively young group and I think you will find them easy to work with."

Bart hoped that his 59 years didn't put him too far outside of Barbara's relatively young definition.

"After that, I would suggest that you visit first the EUCOM Headquarters in Germany. They are responsible for the U.S. portion of the NATO actions against Serbia, then NATO Headquarters in Mons and our attachés in the Balkans. When you return from Europe, I recommend you go directly to Florida and see the CENTCOM folks and get their take on Iraq and Iran. I figure if you are anywhere as fast as you used to be, and have at least half the stamina, you can get all that in by the end of April." The smile on her face was now broadening.

Bart doubted that there was little that Barbara Barnsworth forgot.

"And the Headquarters during that time? Will it be okay for me to be away so soon?"

"Not a problem. I'll look after things here," answered Barbara. And Bart had no doubt she would.

After his official calls with the Secretary of Defense, the Chairman of the JCS and the Chiefs of the Military Services, Bart Lowe used the rest of March to get settled and reacquaint himself with the national security agencies' key personnel. John Kitchen, Bart's friend at the FBI from HEAT SEEKER days (the sensational espionage case that Bart Lowe worked with the FBI and CIA), was now the Deputy Director of the Bureau. At CIA, Bart remembered the Director from when he was a General Counsel for the SSCI and the Deputy Director of Operations was a man Bart had known as the Chief of Station in China. The head of the National Security Agency was an Air Force Lieutenant General that Bart had not previously known but assured Bart of his cooperation. And the DIA Director was an Army three-star that had once served as one of Bart's Brigade Commanders, Pat Eways. Also, Bart recognized the woman heading up the Counterterrorism Center, René Softly, as the wife of an Army General Officer that Bart had served with in an earlier assignment. Mrs. Softly, an attractive black woman in her mid-forties, was a remarkable intelligence careerist who had served with Army Intelligence, OSD, the Congress, and the Defense Investigative Service. After he had received the Counterterrorism Center briefings, the main ones from Mrs. Softly herself, Bart was certain that his attachés needed to work closely with the CT Center and that there was much to be learned from the smart set of men and women working there.

Bart remained at B.J. Ross' condo at River House for two weeks while he looked into the possibility of government housing. Unfortunately, Fort Myer would not have any housing opening up until late August. However, Bolling Air Force Base in Anacostia offered Bart one of their General Officer Houses and he quickly accepted their offer.

The Army did agree to provide Bart Lowe, as a three-star general, an enlisted aide to staff and manage his quarters at Bolling, and after interviewing three candidates, he selected a smart and enthusiastic, Sergeant First Class, William Childs.

Childs was nowhere as experienced as Lowe's former aide, Master Sergeant Sam Mills, now retired in Florida, but Bart liked his cut and thought he would work out just fine. With SFC Childs' help, Bart moved into Quarters #7 at Bolling Air Force Base using government-owned furniture as he planned to keep his personal things in the condominium at Satellite Beach, Florida.

Bart Lowe had been out of uniform more than seven years and most of his work had been in casual clothes in Florida, and so he really had to scramble to come up with the right uniforms and clothes for his new responsibilities. Bart had remained in good physical condition over the years but he knew he no longer looked as young as he once had and he wanted to be sure that he would not in any way embarrass the uniform. Secretary Cohen had suggested that since he had fundamentally changed the way in which future heads of the DAS were selected, Bart Lowe should now consider the position of DAS Director as a mix of civilian and military responsibilities. Bart thought that was a good idea and decided to wear a mix of civilian clothes and the Army uniform. As a result, Bart gave a tailor that he had used in the past in Arlington, Virginia, a landfall amount of business in the form of new suits and uniforms. Bart's dark brown hair was also somewhat thicker and slightly longer than when he had been on active duty with more than a little graying at the temples. Joan Weber said, "A number of the women working at the DAS Headquarters have commented that they thought the Director looked a lot like Harrison Ford." And Joan agreed.

By the first of April, General Lowe had selected an Air Force Colonel Ted Wenke to be his Executive Officer. Col. Wenke had served as an Air Attaché in Morocco and as the DATT in Portugal. He was a senior Colonel and Bart had decided that this time around he didn't need a traveling XO as George Martin had been but rather someone experienced and steady to look after his office in his absence. Ted was a family man who would enjoy the time at home with his spouse after so many years on the road for the Air Force and the DAS.

Bart was, once again, ready to let the adventure begin.

CHAPTER 4

BAGHDAD

The cool daytime temperatures of March had all disappeared from Iraq and April brought with it the high 80's that would soon climb to the 90's and 100's as the brutally hot, dry, and dusty summer approached.

Ali Hassan sat in his new, and as yet unairconditioned office that had been arranged for him by Saddam Hussein. A drop of sweat rolled down his nose and onto the paper on the desk where he was making notes on the progress of the *Retribution* project Saddam had given him. Ali swore and then quickly wiped the drop of moisture away from his notes. Unlike most Arabs, Ali perspired profusely and he wasn't looking forward to the long, hot summer in Baghdad. He would much rather be in his headquarters in the north where the higher elevations always brought a cool breeze. But he didn't have any choice. Saddam wanted him close by.

"Allah! Saddam has already summoned me six times since we returned to Baghdad, and tomorrow's session will be seven," he muttered to himself.

On their return Saddam Hussein had given Ali Hassan a chit written in Saddam's own hand that virtually gave Ali authority over anyone in the Iraqi government for any support that Ali required for *Retribution*. While Saddam had insisted that the details of *Retribution* be limited to those who took part in the Basra meeting, Ali had carte blanche for coordinating the very sensitive project. Ali had been with Saddam for many years and he had known his leader often to change his mind about some plan or objective he had ""dreamed" up. But that was not going to happen in *this* case. Not since the early days of the Iran-Iraq war when Saddam was convinced Iraq could defeat Iran had Ali seen Saddam so keyed-up about anything.

His eyes almost glowed when he discussed any details with Ali. Saddam was not, however, in any way careless about the security of the compartmenting of *Retribution* and questioned Ali at great length at each of their meetings on who knew what about anything relating to *Retribution*. One of Ali's greatest concerns was that he alone would know more about *Retribution* than anyone else save Saddam. That, on the one hand, would make him indispensable to Saddam until the project had been executed. But, on the other hand, if and when the project was accomplished, "Allah, forbid," he thought, then Ali would be the only one who could lay the blame at Saddam's feet. Ali's usefulness at that time would be at grave risk. "What a choice," Ali thought to himself. "If I refuse to help Saddam, my family and I would be shot and if I help him and he is successful, he probably can't afford the risk of letting me live." A knot in Ali Hassan's stomach had begun to show up with regularity and he wasn't looking forward to his evening meals anymore.

Saddam Hussein surely did have great confidence in the loyalty of Ali Hassan. He had provided him a special encrypted cell phone that was a direct line to Saddam's Security Chief. When Ali needed to see Saddam, as he did for today's update, he merely punched in the Security Chief's number and a car was dispatched for Ali, usually within 15 minutes. Once the security precautions had been taken and Ali was blindfolded, he was then rushed to Saddam's location. Ali noted that Saddam must have been close to his location today because he was seated across from Saddam in less than forty minutes—a new record.

"So, Ali Hassan," Saddam said, gesturing at Ali with his right hand and smiling broadly. "What have you to report today?"

"Sir, there is progress," began Ali, being careful not to use any descriptors such as good or much as he knew Saddam alone would decide how much was enough. "I have taken control of the building in the commercial quarter, a safe distance away from the Government Offices, but still close enough for convenient access. The building is secure, the guards and electronic security measures are in place, and we have established our presence as conducting a special scientific research project directed personally by yourself."

"Good."

"The cover will extend to any and all requests that will be made to the Iraqi Intelligence, Armaments, Communication, and Logistics Ministries. I have directed each Ministry head to establish a dedicated and compartmented cell of people who will be available 24 hours a day, seven days a week, to support the project. This cell in each Ministry now has its own Chief's authority to act on any request that I or my assistants make."

"Any resistance?"

"None. The written authority you gave me made it absolutely clear that all were to comply. And none would dare to challenge your directions," Ali reported.

"Good," Saddam said, obviously pleased that his iron hand rule continued unchallenged.

"I have taken full leave of my responsibilities and turned over all my duties to my second in command," Ali continued.

"Can he be trusted?"

"Without question," was the only acceptable answer that Ali could give to Saddam but his number 2 was a loyal Sunni Muslim without much imagination and Ali hoped he wouldn't do something for which Ali would be blamed.

Saddam nodded.

"At our new building, I have assembled six assistants. Four from my most trusted people from my headquarters in Kurdistan and two from the chemical section of the Logistics agency that I worked with previously. In addition, I have established a dedicated communications center with secure communications between bin Laden and his two assistants and your son, Uday. Who, by the way, has had the Iraqi Intelligence working on a target list since the day we returned from Basra."

"Yes, I know," Saddam acknowledged. "Uday is often impetuous and I don't want our intentions compromised through his efforts to please me. I am going to tell him that I want him to coordinate everything he does with you so that you can ensure the overall security of the project."

"Uday is not going to like that," Ali was quick to react, thinking, "All I need is to have to look after that 'loose cannon'!"

"I am aware of that," Saddam just as quickly responded, his eyes flashing and the pleasant look on his face disappearing. "Son or no son, I don't want this project screwed up. Am I clear?"

"Yes, sir," Ali acquiesced realizing that he had touched a sensitive nerve and could not further debate the subject. He would have to think of a way to deal with that idiot, Uday.

"And I can report that the six assistants I have pulled together will work in three compartmented teams of two each. Two will work on obtaining a man-portable nuclear weapon, two will work on a cyber or computer attack, and two will work on formulating the best chemical or biological attack. I will closely supervise and guide their efforts which have already begun."

"And how difficult will this be to accomplish?" Saddam asked.

"As you know, sir, our efforts to locate and avoid the UN inspections significantly retarded our nuclear weapons program and we neither have the critical components or the time to build a weapon from scratch. We do, however, have the necessary expertise to know what we need and what kinds of weapons will be suitable for the kinds of targets we select. Our best chance of success will be to buy an existing weapon from someone else in the world, the Russians or Chinese, for example, or even better, to buy the components of a weapon and assemble it at the time it is to be used."

"And the cost?"

"The cost to buy an existing weapon will be very high, even for us and bin Laden sharing the cost. The most cost effective way will probably be the component approach. The limitation there is making sure we have the expertise to assemble the various components."

"Is it really that difficult?" Saddam naively asked.

"Not under controlled laboratory conditions but under field conditions, it could be very difficult."

"Well, whatever it takes, Ali Hassan. I want it accomplished! It is the will of Allah." Saddam almost shouted and banged his hand on the table.

Ali Hassan thought, "The mad one is really reaching on this one. The will of Allah. I don't think so." But he responded in kind with a loud, "Yes, sir!"

As Saddam Hussein regained his composure, Ali Hassan continued his report.

"I can also report to you that Osama bin Laden and his assistants have lost no time in taking advantage of your generous offer of increased support. Their requests for intelligence on the Americans have increased almost two-fold. And not just in America, but around the world. Requests for weapons, explosive materials, and trainers to assist in training their trainers have greatly increased. It appears to me that these requests are to support all of bin Laden's operations, not just *Retribution*.

"Yes, I know, those requests have been reported to me through the General Staff and I have agreed to support them. It is to our advantage to support bin Laden in all of his efforts. However, I am more concerned that we see some indication of what he needs to support *Retribution*. Have you noted anything?"

"Yes, sir. In truth, both Wadih Mohammed and Abdul Khalid have contacted me through our secure communications. Wadih Mohammed reports that a list of forty individuals having some expertise in the skills required for strike teams against nuclear, chemical, biological, and cyber targets have been compiled. The individuals will be further screened and 25 selected and brought in for some preliminary training prior to final selection for *Retribution.* Khalid tells me that the final phase of training cannot be conducted until more specificity on the type of target is produced and the timing for the target strike. After that, sixty days will be required for final phase training."

"Is that much training time necessary?" Saddam asked.

"In going against the best counterterrorist, counterintelligence, and security systems in the world, I would say that even that is optimistic," replied Ali.

Again Saddam nodded.

"Abdul Khalid has provided a preliminary target list to Uday from the bin Laden holdings. He has promised a refined list with some specific recommendations by the first of June. Uday has passed the list along to our Intelligence Service Cell for integration into the targeting work they are doing for him."

"Did Uday tell them the purpose?" Saddam asked, his eyes narrowing.

"No, sir," Ali responded, "Uday gave me the list for passing to the cell and I told them that it was for future military training exercises."

"Good."

"Both Wadih Mohammed and Abdul Khalid have pressed for a time that the attacks will take place. They say that the time factor is important to planning the training and target selection."

"I'll determine the time. But you need to know that I have a definite time in mind and it is not too far away. I want all things to be ready before the pilgrimage to Mecca."

"Sir," Ali protested, "I'm not sure that it is feasible to obtain a nuclear weapon or design a chemical or biological attack in that time."

"Do it," Saddam said, striking the table for the second time, anger flaming through his body.

Ali could think of no other reply at that time except to say, "Yes, sir."

Saddam Hussein then sat back in his chair once again and said, "I am pleased with your progress, Ali Hassan. I, also, have been doing my part. I decided to reduce our visibility with the Americans. I have issued orders that the provocation flights into the no fly zone shall be scaled back. After all, they have enough to worry them with the debacle going on in Serbia. And we can save our forces for another occasion. Also, I have communicated with my old friend in Tripoli, Muamar Qadafi and suggested that this time might be a good time to release those terrorists that he has been protecting, to the West. This concession to the West could result in even less attention paid to us while NATO and the U.S. dogs are bogged down in the mud of Serbia." And with that, Saddam stood, and without another word, left the room.

Ali Hassan was covered with sweat. Even though the car returning him to his new building was air conditioned, he could feel the perspiration running down his face under the security blindfold and beneath his uniform shirt. Saddam not only wanted the impossible; he wanted it right away.

Unbeknownst to Ali Hassan and Saddam Hussein, Osama bin Laden had made arrangements with the Taliban in Afghanistan to provide him with a new hiding place on his return from the Basra meeting in Iraq. Bin Laden's concern was twofold: prior to the Ali Hassan visit, a number of bin Laden's terrorist operations had been compromised and he did not completely trust Saddam Hussein or his representatives with the knowledge of his whereabouts. He was not sure if his own organization had somehow been penetrated or if the western satellites were monitoring his communications, or even if one of the Taliban security people had given them up. Nevertheless, it was time to move along from southern Afghanistan. The new location was more secure than the old and the Taliban agreed to leak information to the West that bin Laden had departed Afghanistan.

Before leaving Basra, Ali Hassan had provided bin Laden's assistant, Wadih Mohammed, a set of one-time encryption pads for communication between Baghdad and bin Laden's location. The preliminaries were accomplished and the new and dedicated secure channels of communication were initiated. At that time, bin Laden, a man of few words, but absolutely serious in his determination, summoned his two deputies, and explained his own intentions regarding *Retribution*.

"All communications between Saddam Hussein and his representatives will be personally cleared for release by me. No agreements will be reached without my personal approval. The scope of the *Retribution* operation is far greater than anything we could undertake alone. While my resources are significant, they do not equal with what Iraq can bring to bear. For those reasons, I am willing to support Saddam Hussein's schemes. In truth, however, I am not convinced that Saddam is a true believer and his motives are far different than ours. I have pledged my support and will do all in my power to strike a blow against the United States if all that Saddam Hussein has promised is fulfilled. I am sure of one thing, however; if we are successful in this ambitious endeavor, Saddam will want to take all the credit, even at his own peril. But if something goes wrong, he will want to find a scapegoat. We must not allow that to happen to our holy cause."

CHAPTER 5

BELGRADE—STUTTGART—TAMPA

Two days after Bart Lowe received his initial briefings from his deputy, Barbara Barnsworth, in Washington, Army Colonel Karl Vukovitch, the Defense Attaché or DATT to Serbia and Montenegro, closed and locked the front door to the two-story brown house that had been his official residence in Belgrade for the past two years. It was a quiet house that he left because his wife, Meriam, had departed for their home in Augusta, Georgia a week ago as part of the planned evacuation and upcoming closing of the U.S. Embassy. Gone also was the Serbian family that had served as the houses' staff for more than a decade. Not by their own choosing, but at the direction of the Serbian government.

As Colonel Vukovitch passed through the iron gate in the center of the security wall that surrounded the house, the Serbian sentry saluted him and nodded good morning. The once friendly guards had taken on a more official demeanor with the deteriorating relations between the U.S. and Slobodan Milosevic's government. Vukovitch suspected that the security guards provided by the Serbs were now there to keep an eye on him more than watching out for his safety.

"Well, you have got to take the good with the bad," thought Vukovitch, an Army Foreign Area Officer (FAO) and veteran of three Attaché tours.

It was a few minutes after 7:00 a.m. as he began the six-block walk to the U.S. Embassy through one of the better neighborhoods in Belgrade. He was a stocky man dressed in a brown business suit and blue raincoat and cap. His features were dark and Serbian-like and his linguistic ability was flawless. His parents had emigrated to the U.S. from Serbia and he spoke three languages found in the Balkans. It was his second tour in Belgrade and he was very effective with the Serbs.

It was a windy and gray morning and he could feel the dampness from the always present cloud cover in March. There were not many people on the residential streets early in the morning and it gave him a chance to review in his mind what had been accomplished in the last fifteen days since hopes for the peace process had failed and the Embassy had received word from Washington to prepare for evacuation and closure. The Ambassador had called him and the Deputy Chief of Mission, or DCM, in and said, "Well, Vuke, it's no surprise but now, it's official. The EVAC order came in just a few moments ago from the Department. We have a green light for moving out the dependents and non-critical personnel. I want you to take the lead for all evacuation actions, coordinating with the Embassy Security Officer and the Chief of Station. We will inform the Serbs of the evacuation of dependents as a precaution and not mention closure until the last possible moment although they will suspect it. Do all that you can to gain the Serb military's cooperation and support, or at least acquiescence, as I will with the Foreign Office. Then prepare a list in priority for the departure of the U.S. dependants, then Embassy staff. I'll be surprised if you, the COS, the DCM, and I are not the last four on the list," the Ambassador said and wanly smiled. No U.S. Ambassador liked to give an evacuation order. "At the same time, and I know you know this, we need to maintain our reporting capability on what goes on here on the ground until the last possible moment. Clear?"

The guidelines had been clear and Colonel Vukovitch and the other Embassy key personnel moved out smartly. The hardest part of what had been done in the days and weeks since the order had been given was the movement of the dependents and the families. When a situation deteriorates in a foreign country, emotions run high and the fear of the unknown creates tension. The unspoken but present thought in everyone's minds was, "Will they let us out or will we be interred like the Embassy staff in Iran?"

The Serbs did cooperate and, albeit reluctantly, followed the international rules governing diplomatic immunity, and all the families and non-critical personnel had been safely evacuated. "Thank God for the Black Passport," Colonel Vukovitch had said many times. "The rapid scaling down of an Embassy of more than 250 people to less than 25 is no small undertaking," Vukovitch thought to himself, "but my seven people have been magnificent and the Embassy has made a Herculean team effort. Since the last of the non-critical staff departed yesterday, more emphasis can be given to the destruction of Embassy classified information and files, and the disposition of the secure communications gear."

As Colonel Vukovitch entered the ground floor entrance to the six-story U.S. Embassy, he passed through both reinforced Serb security forces and the U.S. Marine guards who had doubled their numbers on guard shift, added rifles, shotguns, and armored vests, to their side arm armament and had changed to their combat utility uniforms. The Serbs maintained that the increase in their security forces outside the U.S. Embassy was for the purpose of providing better security for the Embassy given the rise in anti-American feeling now taking place in Belgrade. But the Embassy had to guard against the possibility of a Serb government staged riot and any rushing of the embassy entrance. Accordingly, the entrance had been semi-barricaded and the Marine sentries had rehearsed and were prepared to seal off the embassy entrance on split second notice.

"Anything new, Gunny?" the Colonel asked the Marine Gunnery Sergeant in charge of the Marine Guards.

"No, sir. We are all secure here and standing by. It does, however, look as though the Serbs further increased their security forces out front last night."

"Yes, I noticed that they have added more men and vehicles. Has your sentry on the embassy roof post noticed any troop movement in the surrounding neighborhood?"

"Not as yet, sir."

"Well, okay. Let the Embassy Security Officer and me know the moment any substantial changes are noted. And by the way, Gunny," Vukovitch said, noticing the sergeant's red eyes, "you look as though you could use a couple of hours of sleep. I know you have been putting in the long hours around the clock but if all hell breaks loose, we are going to need your leadership. Better get some sleep while you can."

"Aye, aye, sir."

Colonel Vukovitch then took the elevator to the fifth floor of the embassy, punched the cipher code lock, and entered the Defense Attaché Office (DAO) spaces. As he passed the offices along the hall leading to his own office in the rear of the building, he noticed that all his seven people were already at their desks.

"Don't you guys ever sleep," he yelled as he passed attempting a little humor but not getting any humorous replies—not even a smile.

Thirty minutes later, after he had reviewed the overnight cable traffic from Washington, and a note from the Ambassador, he sat in the DAO conference room with his assembled attachés and operations support staff. He was looking at a sea of tired, red eyes. Particularly from the attachés who had been working the streets and their contacts in the Serbian military. They had worked tirelessly in getting their reports on Kosovo and the Serbs out to the hungry Washington consumers throughout the U.S. military and government and devoting every other available minute to the imminent Embassy shutdown.

He asked for and received their updates. He learned that DAS headquarters had directed that all DAO classified files either be shredded or burned in the Embassy basement furnace. And that a decision had been received that no attempt to transport any of the highly sensitive technical and secure communications equipment in Diplomatic pouches would be made for the fear that the Serbs would be watching for such an opportunity and would seize the diplomatically protected pouches in spite of the usually accepted immunity. That equipment would be destroyed in place. And if for any reason, the self-destruct mechanisms that were an integral part of the equipment did not work, then fire axes would be used to destroy them.

After he had heard from everyone, he shared with them that the Ambassador had informed him that they were now on 24-hour alert for Embassy shutdown. He explained that meant when the order was given, they had, as he put it, "a maximum of 24-hours to get out of Dodge. So make sure before anyone goes anywhere today that you have re-reviewed the Embassy shutdown plan, that we have overlooked nothing, and that we can be ready to go on a minute's notice. Bag and baggage, as we used to say in the Old Army! And by the way, I think you all know that when we leave here, we will all be going to the European Command Headquarters in Stuttgart, Germany, for an in-depth debriefing and if we are lucky, a little R&R with our families. But we have our work cut out for us, so let's get with it!"

A week later, Bart Lowe was sitting to the right of General Wesley Clark at a table in the briefing room known as the "big bedroom" at the headquarters of the U.S. European Command (EUCOM) in Stuttgart, Germany. Clark, the Supreme Allied Commander of all NATO Forces in Europe was also dual-hatted as the EUCOM Commander or Commander of all U.S. military forces in the theater. He spent most of his time at the NATO Headquarters in Mons, Belgium, but fortunately for Bart Lowe, he was located in Stuttgart at the time of Bart's visit.

The current intelligence and operations briefing was given at 0800, six days a week, for either General Clark, if he was in Stuttgart, or his deputy in his absence. On those days, when Clark was in Mons, the briefing was sent to Clark via the secure J2 closed-circuit television. The briefing covered the intelligence, operations, and logistics of the now ongoing NATO actions against Serbia. In this morning's briefings, extensive coverage of the NATO bombing campaign was presented. The bombing of Serbia had begun on 26 March and was receiving as much coverage in the world's press as it was by Clark's battle damage assessment specialists, according to the local Public Affairs Officer.

When the last briefing was completed, General Clark dismissed his staff, poured himself another cup of coffee, and turned to Bart Lowe, "Well, Bart, how does it feel to be back in the saddle again?"

"In all candor, Wes, it is probably too soon to know. I do know that the night's sleep I lost coming from Washington to Germany isn't as easy to recover as it used to be, judging from the number of times I've yawned this morning," Bart said and laughed. "I better have another cup of this good coffee," he concluded, reaching for the urn in front of him.

Bart Lowe had sat on the General Officers Selection Board that had selected Colonel Wes Clark to be a Brigadier General years ago and recalled how impressed the entire board of General Officers had been with Clark's performance and potential. It gave Bart a sense of pride to see how far Clark had gone in serving his country.

"Then let me say, Bart, I noted with pleasure, as did many others, your return to the Defense team. A steady hand such as yours is always welcome and needed as we take on the challenges of today's volatile world."

"Thanks, Wes. I hope that I can contribute."

"Believe me, you will. And that leads me to my pitch on how you can help us here in the European Theater. Our bosses at the White House are hoping we can win this thing with Serbia with just the use of air power. Their political counterparts in the other NATO nations share that hope. You, as an old infantryman, know the limitations of air power. The Chairman and I are on record with the President on this score and we will just have to see how it plays out. All my experience tells me it is going to get worse before it gets better and however it turns out, I smell long-term role and obligations for the United States and its military. Remember we went into Bosnia for just a year, five years ago."

Bart Lowe sagely nodded, thinking to himself, "How monumental are the tasks the United States passes to its military and how fraught with grave risks those tasks are when we commit America's youth in harm's way."

"Having said that, let me now say that the role the U.S. Military Attachés play in this theater has never been more important. I know you must have heard this before, but I didn't realize, until I came to this four-star billet just how much we depend on this set of men and women for their information and assessments. For example, I have personally read each report that Colonel Vukovitch has written about Kosovo and Serbia in the last six months. And the DAO reports about military and government facilities will be the foundations for the targeting of the NATO bombing effort. And for the duration, what your people in Albania, Montenegro, and Macedonia are able to glean with the inevitable refugee flow coming in every direction out of Kosovo will be vitally important to our total war effort. And one other important role that your attachés must play is to be at the vanguard of the U.S. and NATO efforts to persuade the other neighboring countries, their government and their military of the right of our cause and our need for them to help in bringing Milosevic to the peace table. And the attachés that these other countries will continue to have resident in Belgrade and Serbia will be of immense help."

As Bart Lowe sat listening to General Clark, he was somewhat amazed to hear the Commander-in-Chief (CINC) of the European Theater telling him almost verbatim the points that Bart's staff in Washington had suggested he use to tell the CINC how the Defense Attachés could be of help in his war effort. "God damn!" Bart thought, "maybe the DAS has really come a long way in the education of senior military officers as to the value of the Attachés since my retirement.

And maybe, just maybe, my job will be a little easier. But then," he concluded, "Wes Clark was always a fast study."

While in Stuttgart, Bart met with Colonel Vukovitch and the other military attachés from the now closed DAO Belgrade. He commended them all and decorated them on the recommendation of the U.S. Ambassador for their lead action in the Embassy closing. He, unfortunately, had to give them the bad news that they would not be rejoining their families in the United States right away. Because of the importance of the NATO combat bombings against Serbia and the attachés' obvious expertise regarding the Serbs, General Lowe had made the decision to keep them in theater for the time being and split them among the DAOs in the three countries most affected by the Kosovo situation. Vukovitch would be going to Montenegro and taking the Operations Coordinator with him to handle the build-up of what had, until now, been a small DAO. Three of the other Attachés were being sent to Albania and two to Macedonia to assist with the dramatically increased workload at those two DAOs. The news was received with mixed enthusiasm by the attachés, but they were all pros and followed their marching orders with the hope that they would get a well-deserved break as soon as there was a lull in the NATO action.

Prior to returning to the United States and visiting Central Command Headquarters in Florida, Bart visited the DAOs in Albania, Macedonia, and Montenegro. He came away confident that he had the nucleus of a good team in each country although they would need more people soon to stay abreast of the new, and ever increasing, work brought on by the NATO action. The refugee flow was almost beyond comprehension and Bart realized with grim certainty and deep sadness that what was taking place in Kosovo at the hands of the Serbs contained elements like the Holocaust!

General Lowe was able to get a non-stop flight from Stuttgart to Tampa, Florida. As he settled into his business-class seat, he recalled how important the use of frequent traveler miles had been to him and his attachés in getting some rest on the long international flights. George Martin had worked miracles with the airlines in getting seats that would allow for both work and rest. Fortunately, now the frequent traveler miles were not as important for him because the government had changed its policy since he retired and LTGs were permitted to use business-class travel tickets.

Bart had spent his last night in Europe at the Distinguished Visitors Quarters at Patch Barracks at EUCOM and had a good night's rest. EUCOM had provided him with military aircraft for his visits to the Balkan Countries and he had been able to wear his new camouflage Battle Dress Uniforms. They were, of course, more comfortable than the more formal dress uniforms, but the thought occurred to him that he must be the oldest American man in uniform. Even so, he had lost eight pounds since he returned to the DAS and he felt and looked fit. Last night he had had dinner with the EUCOM J2, a new U.S. Air Force Major General whom Bart immediately liked. Flying along now over the Atlantic Ocean, he remembered something profound the J2, Len Fisher had said, "I am concerned that the United States is biting off a commitment in the Balkans that may tie up a sizeable part of the U.S. military's fighting capability for a long time. That is understandable because we believe it is the right thing to do, but if something else happens in another part of the world, another crisis, we may be unable to successfully take that on. Given the post Cold War force reductions and the other cutbacks placed on the U.S. military over the last few years, the military's capacity to take on two major contingencies in the world at the same time is long past. And I wonder how many Americans really know that!" The thought was chilling, but Bart suspected that Fisher was right.

Bart's host at the sprawling Central Command (CENTCOM) Headquarters at Macdill Air Force Base in

Florida was the J2, Army Brigadier General Keith Great. General Great had met Lowe at the Tampa International Airport, planning to drive him to his accommodations at Macdill where he could freshen up prior to beginning the Florida afternoon agenda that had been arranged for his visit. Bart remembered Keith Great as a Battalion Commander of one of the Army Military Intelligence units in Augsburg, Germany, during the earlier years that Bart was at the DAS. And during his recent visits to the Pentagon, both the JCS, J2 and the Army's Deputy Chief of Staff for Intelligence had spoken highly of Great.

As they drove in the official sedan along Bayshore Drive heading south toward Macdill, Bart recalled fondly his many previous visits to CENTCOM Headquarters both in Tampa and then later at the forward base in Saudi Arabia during Desert Storm. He recalled some of his fiery exchanges with "Stormin' Norman" Schwartzkopf. General Schwartzkopf didn't always get his way, but he always had his say and sometimes, at the top of his voice.

"General Zinni regrets that he will miss your visit and asked me to pass along his regards and best wishes. As you know, he is in the forward area visiting a number of those 19 countries in Southwest Asia and the Middle East that CENTCOM is responsible for monitoring. However, the CINC is very attuned to the important support that the Military Attachés provide CENTCOM. He gave me a number of specific items to be passed to you and I'll cover those with you this afternoon during the briefings we have scheduled," said Great, passing to Bart a folder containing the afternoon's agenda.

After Bart had scanned the CENTCOM program he said, "It looks fine, Keith. As you know, one of our most important missions is supporting the 'war fighter.' And although I have been away for some time, that is a mission that will never change for Military Attachés. I'm interested in knowing how well CENTCOM thinks we are doing that and if there is something more you think we should be doing to assist you in your mission."

"I think, sir, that you will find that our briefings this afternoon will answer those questions. Now, can we get you something to eat after you have changed, and before we begin this afternoon? Or, perhaps a sandwich or salad during the briefings?"

"Good Lord, no. They fed us three times on that flight. What I would really like is a jog or possibly a game of racquetball this afternoon after we finish. Is that a possibility?" Bart asked.

"General, I thought you would never ask. I'd be delighted for you to give me a racquetball lesson."

That afternoon as Bart sat through the political-military, operations and intelligence briefings, he was once again fascinated with the developments in a region of the world that represented the last place that the United States had gone to in an all out war. "Hundreds of thousands of Americans under arms and engaged in mortal combat," he remembered. "Is the same thing about to happen in the Balkans? Certainly Washington is preoccupied with the possibility," he thought. "And what about the potential for further trouble in that part of the world and will this command be up to handling it if it comes along while we are engaged in Europe?" These thoughts were racing through General Lowe's mind as the formal briefing ended and the room cleared, leaving just Lowe and Great behind.

"Do you have any other questions, sir?"

"Thank you, Keith, that was an excellent overview. I hope you will pass my thanks along to all those fine briefing officers who participated. I appreciate your candor in highlighting where our Attachés are doing well for CENTCOM and where you believe our efforts can be improved. I can't promise you anything yet. I simply don't know our people in the field well enough yet, but I will look into it and see what we can do."

"Fair enough," replied Great.

"Now as to questions. Tell me, what are the CINC's concerns?"

"General Zinni's first concern is that a major contingency may arise in our area of operations while the United States is heavily committed in Europe. He is concerned that if that happens, there will not be sufficient trained and ready forces to respond. For example, there are only so many Apache helicopters, so many fighter aircraft, so many multiple rocket launchers, etc."

"And is he worried about any particular place or contingency?"

"Iran and Iraq are our flash points of most concern. Relations with Iran seem to be improving slightly, but Iran remains unpredictable and their armed forces are formidable."

"And Iraq?" Bart asked.

"Iraq is problematic. We don't see Saddam Hussein going away anytime soon. And now that the U.N. inspections are no longer possible, there is no telling what he will dream up next. We really need your help with Iraq. The boss is concerned that with the problems in Europe, the national intelligence agencies support we are so dependent upon at DIA, NSA, and CIA will be reduced because of the priority to Europe and our ability to watch Iraq closely will be further weakened."

"Hasn't Saddam's activity in the No Fly Zone all but dried up?" Bart questioned.

"Yes, but not because of the damage we inflicted on him. It wasn't that much. And we think that he is probably up to something else, but we don't know what."

"I hear you. Tell the CINC I share his concern and I'll do what I can."

"Also of concern to us is the growing threat of weapons of mass destruction in the hands of terrorists. Take bin Laden for example. He has been developing for years his own intelligence and strike capabilities. They give him respect and access to many of the countries in our AO. He is like a state without borders and can influence others to support him, shield him, and even provide him arms. If he can persuade any of the states in the region to sell him weapons of mass destruction or assist him in obtaining them, we would be looking at a difficult situation and one that could not only threaten CENTCOM's AO but also the continental United States."

Bart nodded his head and said, "It's a tough target for the DAS, Keith, and we are looking for ways to cover it better."

CHAPTER 6

AFGHANISTAN

Osama bin Laden sat cross-legged on a cushion in a rear room of his new house. Sunshine and a warming, but still cool, April mountain breeze came through the open window. His hideaway was now located in the northwest quadrant of Afghanistan near the town of Herat and just south of the mountains of northern Afghanistan. Bin Laden was pleased with the new location. It afforded excellent security in a sparsely populated, difficult terrain area and was not far from border exits to Iran and Russia where he had contacts and a support apparatus in the event he had to depart Afghanistan quickly. The Taliban had also provided him with an excellent training facility near a small village known as Yazdan along an isolated stretch of the Iranian border south of Herat. He had moved Abdul Khalid there to be in charge of all the training the bin Laden organization required, but he had already decided that Khalid would be the logical one to be responsible for selecting the strike teams and supervising their specialized training for action against the United States and, if necessary, to lead and coordinate their efforts in America. Bin Laden knew that Khalid would represent one more person than Saddam had suggested, but bin Laden had been impressed with the work Khalid had done already on the targeting project and he knew America better than anyone in bin Laden's movement. When the time came, he was certain he could convince Saddam. As these thoughts went through his mind, an assistant knocked on the door and quietly said, "Abdul Khalid is here."

"Good. Send him in."

Khalid entered the large room and, after showing respect to bin Laden with, "Assalam Alaykum" (an Arabic greeting meaning, 'Peace be upon you'), was motioned to another cushion near him.

After he was seated, bin Laden asked, "How goes the training and the new location?"

"Training at our several locations elsewhere for our already planned actions over the next year is proceeding on schedule. The Iraqis have responded to all our requests for assistance, funding, and materials, and even send specialized trainers to assist our people. There are no security problems to report from those locations. There was one personnel problem—an Indian that had been recruited in Calcutta. He was quite capable and passed all of his training requirements but we discovered that he had been in touch with some relations in India in violation of his contract. He was not a believer, but only in it for the money. Unfortunately, we had to eliminate him."

"Any chance of compromise or trouble?"

"None. He died from an accidental electric shock. His family will be quite pleased with the settlement."

"Very well."

"The new location is quite suitable. It was originally a large sheep and goat farm. The original perimeter fencing is still in place and has been reinforced by the Afghanis. Modern security devices and electronic surveillance equipment have been installed and one of the old barns has been converted into a sleeping and eating area. The cover for the facility is an Afghani Microwave Station and a regular government security force is in place. The inside of the main house has been modernized and I will take up residence there today. The rest of the cadre that I have selected will arrive this week, and next week we will complete the outdoor training areas. Initially, this location will be used only for our *Retribution* project."

"You may say that word but you will never put it in writing," bin Laden directed.

"Of course. I understand that." replied Khalid.

"And those to be trained?"

"I have now further refined the list of candidates from 25 to 21. They will be here in two weeks for thirty days of intensive training. All these candidates have been trained by our people and demonstrated some success in various operations. They have all shown exceptional skill and dedication to our cause."

"And what will you do with them for a month?"

"It will be refresher training in all the skills Allah's successful and resourceful soldiers need. I will add a number of intensive physical training items and self-confidence tests to determine which ones are the best of the best. And from that number, we will have our individuals for the three strike teams."

"Confidence building. Isn't that what the Americans do?" bin Laden asked.

"Yes. The U.S. Army taught me well and now I will use what I learned for our cause and the glorification of Allah."

Ben Laden smiled. "Now tell me, Khalid, how do you envision actually training for the strikes in America?" he asked.

"Most important is knowing the targets to be struck and the time of the strikes," Khalid replied.

"And, if, in the interest of security of the operation, it will not be possible to let you know the target selection until the last possible minute, then how will you proceed?"

Khalid took a minute to reflect. He had anticipated being asked this question. He also knew it was a test. He had thought about his answer and had given careful thought to his response.

"At the end of the 30 days of rigorous training, I will return them all to their home locations. They will be told they have all satisfactorily completed the training, if that is the case, and that they will be summoned when and if a need arises. That way, the security of the nine strike team members will best be protected and even they will not know it until they are notified. I will require sixty days for training but would not want to begin that phase of the training until the candidates have had at least two weeks at their home locations. When they are summoned for the second phase of training, they will be told to be prepared to spend at least six months on the task we will assign them."

"And what will you do in this two month period?" asked bin Laden, sounding somewhat skeptical.

"If, as you have suggested, I still do not know the targets to be struck or the time table, I will select a range of representative targets of each type from the list of fifty that we have provided to Saddam Hussein. I will ensure that the selected targets for training purposes range from relatively easy, to relatively difficult. The group of nine individuals will be broken down into three groups of three each. Each group will train for twenty days on one type of target, for example, a nuclear device target or a cyber target or a biological target. Then, at the end of the twenty days, the group will be rotated to training on the next target."

"And to what advantage is this rotating? Would not it be easier to train all the groups together in one-third the time?" bin Laden pressed, appearing more skeptical.

"If time was of the essence, yes. But given the time, this compartmenting of the training will assist in maintaining security and allow me and my trainers to select the very best individuals for each target."

"And at the end of the sixty days, if the targets become known, will you just send them off to attack them?" a slight tone of scorn now evident in bin Laden's voice.

"No. At least thirty days additional training will be required when each team's target is identified and the type of weapons are known. This final phase of the training must include the development of the operational concept for attacking each target, the security plan, and rehearsals to detect any flaws. This will be the most important phase of the training. If all goes well here, we can expect the strikes to be successful." Khalid reported this with a strong sense of confidence that was evident and reassuring to bin Laden.

"And the necessary time for putting the strike teams in place?"

"I would ask for thirty days for the implementation of the operational plans. If absolutely necessary, it could perhaps be done in less time."

"And what else will you require?"

"When the weapons and targets are determined, I may need additional materials and training devices. I believe we can count on the Iraqis for that assistance. And when the targets and weapons are finally known, the teams may require assistance and support from those true believers we already have in America."

This last answer caused bin Laden to slightly raise one eyebrow. The facial movement was not lost on Khalid. The exact number and locations of the members of the bin Laden organization was tightly compartmented and up until now, had not been shared with Khalid. Bin Laden's only reply to this comment was, "When the time comes, speak with Wadih Mohammed regarding your requirements."

Khalid received the minor rebuke with steady eyes and hands and, as a result, grew in stature with bin Laden.

"Finally, Abdul Khalid, what assurance will we have when we send these strike teams on missions of such importance that we can count on their allegiance, and if compromised, their loyalty?"

Khalid found this question the easiest of all to answer. "Inshallah," (with Allah's help), "all members of the strike teams will be true believers and have volunteered and fully expect their martyrdom on this, the most holy of missions."

"And does that include Abdul Khalid?"

"Without question." But to himself, he thought, "It will never come down to that for me."

"Very well. I am satisfied. However, you need to know that for security's sake, Saddam Hussein will not wish to select the targets until the last possible minute. And I agree. You need to proceed accordingly. Allah be praised."

Abdul Khalid, a fictitious name, was born Talal Muhammed-al-Jabr to Palestinian parents in Amman, Jordan in 1954. His parents, who had relatives in the United States, moved there when he was two years old. His parents, his sister and he, all later became naturalized U.S. citizens. His family first lived in Connecticut but when Khalid was five, they moved to New York City. When Khalid started to school, his full name was shortened to Talal al-Jabr for ease of understanding and acceptance by the school system and his schoolmates. He was raised as a devout Muslim and although he was living in America, learned the ways and beliefs of Islam, which he accepted early on as his faith. He did well in school and gymnastics, graduating with honors and receiving an academic scholarship to the City College of New York where he majored in Middle Eastern studies, hoping someday to teach, he told administrators. However, after graduation in 1975, he joined the U.S. Army, and because of his Arabic language skill learned at home and his expertise on the Mid-East, he became a Green Beret.

The young al-Jabr was an outstanding soldier, excelling in all skills required by America's finest soldiers. His fitness and leadership were indefatigable and he was promoted rapidly up through the ranks to Sergeant First Class. He spent a total of 15 years in the Army, most of which was spent at Fort Bragg, North Carolina, although he served a tour in Bad Toltz, Germany, and went on numerous deployments to the Middle East. Much of his time at Fort Bragg was spent as an instructor for other Green Berets in the use of explosives, surviving in a hostile environment, and teaching about Islam and the Middle East. He was disappointed to find that most of the soldiers he taught were not interested in learning about the Arab world and Islam. Many were prejudiced against Arabs after Desert Storm and often referred to soldiers in Arab armies as "Ragheads." His disappointed turned to resentment.

In 1990, when SFC al-Jabr told his superiors he was resigning from the Army to take a career-enhancing job as a security officer with a large corporation in New York City, they were shocked. Although somewhat of a loner, he was an outstanding soldier whose potential for continued advancement in the U.S. Army was certain. His fellow NCOs friends thought he had taken leave of his senses. But what none of them knew was that a Muslim whom al-Jabr had met at a small Arab cultural center in Fayetteville, North Carolina, had recruited him to train militant Islamic extremists in Brooklyn, New York. What al-Jabr did not know at the time of his recruitment was that the financial and operational direction for the militant activity in New York was coming from a Saudi named Osama bin Laden.

When he returned to New York, al-Jabr was indeed provided a cover position as a security officer, but one that allowed him the maximum latitude in recruiting and training potential terrorists for planned bombings against landmarks in the New York-New Jersey area. So effective was al-Jabr's training and knowledge, that he was brought into the Brooklyn Islamic extremists most ambitious operation—the planned bombing of the New York World Trade Center. He helped develop the operational concept and he personally selected the type and quantities of explosives to be used in the bombing. When the day for the strike came, he was confident that it would be successful. Then, when the news came and it was clear that the bomb damage was only a fraction of what had been intended, he was concerned that he had overlooked some flaw in the operational planning and had failed Allah's bidding. Later, he learned that circumstances beyond the terrorists' control had prevented the terrorist operations from gaining access to the building, resulting in only a partially successful strike.

As the follow-on investigation by the FBI intensified, it became evident that al-Jabr could be linked to the bombing and a decision was made to relocate al-Jabr from New York to a safe location outside of the United States. At that time, al-Jabr became Abdul Khalid. He learned that bin Laden was the head of the Islamic Jihad organization that he had become a part of, accepted all of that as Allah's will, and made a commitment to carry out bin Laden's bidding in the name of Allah. Since then, his devotion to bin Laden had not wavered.

In Afghanistan, as Abdul Khalid drove his Toyota land cruiser carefully along the winding, narrow dirt road that ran south from Herat to the Microwave Station that was now his headquarters near the small village of Yazdan, he reflected on the morning discussion with bin Laden and on the years since he had left his old life in the United States. He had no regrets. The only thing that really mattered to him was his family but they knew that he had gone off to serve Allah. He had not communicated with them since the Trade Center bombing. He had never married. And it was not because he didn't care for women; he would occasionally take one, but that was just for the physical pleasure of it, much like a good meal or a good workout. Allah had blessed him. He never wanted for anything and Allah had always provided him what he needed. His needs were simple. When he wasn't studying in school, when he wasn't on duty in the Army, and when he wasn't carrying out the needs of the Jihad, he read the Qur'an (or, to the Americans, the Koran) and reflected on his destiny. He had never known what that was, but he believed he had a special destiny in doing Allah's work. And he believed with all his fiber that when the time came, Allah would reveal to Khalid that purpose for which he had been placed on the earth.

He recalled, as the vehicle bumped along and he steered to avoid the potholes, a tingling feeling throughout his body when he accompanied bin Laden to Iraq and heard Saddam Hussein speak of a strike greater than Khalid ever imagined. He had felt that same tingling again today as he was telling bin Laden of his concept for training for such a great strike. Could it be that his true destiny, his reason for being, Allah's role for him was at last being revealed? As a true believer, he had always known that he must be patient and carry out Allah's will in all that he did. But then, he had always believed that there was something special for him to accomplish. And perhaps Allah was beginning to reveal that special task to his humble servant! "Allah, be praised," he thought with more than a little fervor, as he approached the steel gate. The Afghan guard recognized him and pushed the electronic switch that would open the gate and permit him to drive inside.

CHAPTER 7

BACK IN THE SADDLE AGAIN

General Lowe's Executive Officer, Colonel Ted Wenke, had made arrangements for Bart to return to Washington from Macdill Air Force Base by military air. The C-20 aircraft picked him up Saturday night and flew him directly to Andrews Air Force Base in Maryland. From there it was only a short ride to his quarters at Bolling. Prior to leaving Florida, Bart had received updates from both Barbara Barnsworth and Ted on the secure phone. He told Ted that it wasn't necessary for anyone to meet him—just the car and driver. He also let it be known that he planned to go into the DAS Operations Center on Sunday morning but insisted that he didn't want anyone else to come in. Barbara Barnsworth had offered to meet with him on Sunday morning but she was not surprised when Lowe declined. She remembered well his preference for coming into the DAS Operations Center on the weekends so that he could hear first-hand how the people manning the long and tedious watch shift in the center were getting along in their very important, but often overlooked roles. He also liked to get their thoughts or take on a particular event or crisis somewhere in the world such as Kosovo.

Bart arrived at Andrews at 2100 hours and by 2130 was chatting with his aide, SFC Childs, over a cold turkey sandwich in the dining room of his quarters at Bolling.

On Monday morning after the regularly scheduled 8:00 a.m. DAS around the world update for the DAS leadership and Division Chiefs, Bart returned to his office and accepted a fresh cup of coffee from his secretary, Joan. Flashing her famous, and always welcomed, Monday morning smile, she said to Lowe, "General, when I came in this morning and emptied your Out Box, I couldn't believe my eyes. All that pile of stuff that was in the In Box on Friday night had somehow magically moved to the Out Box. I thought 'Good Lord! What time did the poor man come in?' And then Colonel Wenke told me you were in the Operations Center yesterday and that's when you did all that work."

Bart laughed and replied, "It certainly seemed like déjà vu sitting there in the Operations Center yesterday, facing those huge stacks of paper. Is it possible that the flow is even greater than when I was here before?"

"I don't know about that, but let me assure you, Boss, there is plenty more where that came from!" The smile now disappearing, Joan asked, "Have you looked at today's schedule? If so, you will see the first hour is with Ms. Barnsworth. She directed us to schedule that today and for the future, on the first day you return from any absence from the Headquarters. I trust you approve?"

Detecting a slight tone of turf concern, Bart replied lightly, "Oh sure, it's always a good idea for the Boss to meet with his deputy first after a trip to make sure he won't be blindsided by something that took place in his absence. And by the way, please tell Ms. Barnsworth that I'll come over to her office this morning for our meeting."

"Very well, sir. I'll inform her," Joan answered with one eyebrow slightly raised.

Bart could not help but laugh to himself thinking, "Some things never change—either in, or out, of government."

Bart Lowe was now seated across the table from Barbara Barnsworth in her somewhat smaller, but quite tastefully decorated office. Her sky blue business suit and light blue blouse seemed almost to be color coordinated with the color of her office. The office looked professional but had many touches of Barbara Barnsworth's personality. It was neat, orderly, and accentuated with color in the form of pictures, plants, flowers, and softly lit lamps. The government furniture had been rearranged to suggest inviting comfort rather than the stilted, often bare, straightforward look of most government offices. There was simply nothing to suggest disarray. Bart was impressed. Even her conference table was round and seemed less formal. But in spite of the inviting atmosphere, everything about Barbara Barnsworth said, "No nonsense" and Bart wondered if he would ever get to know the unofficial Barbara.

"Barbara, before you begin, let me say the daily update cable you provided during my trip was very helpful in keeping me abreast of what was going on here. Frankly, I hadn't been here long enough to even think about it before I left on the trip to Europe and the first one came as a pleasant surprise. I thank you."

"Not at all," Barbara said. "I remembered it was a technique you used when George Martin was your XO and Ted Wenke and I talked about it and decided it would be a good idea. Ted deserves the lion's share of the credit. I just gave him the essential headlines and he handled the admin to put it together. A piece of cake really. I am glad you found it useful."

"Piece of cake, my fanny," Bart thought to himself. "A great deal of work went into those cables and someone burned the midnight oil. I'll have to ask Ted about them."

"At any rate, they were very helpful. Now what do we do need to talk about today?"

Obviously pleased that Bart had come to her office, Barbara smiled and said, "I have three major items that I want to cover and then I would like to hear your impressions from the trip and what that entails for the DAS."

Bart was somewhat surprised by this request from Ms. Barnsworth thinking to himself, "Does she think that I have information beyond that that I shared with the assembled leadership at this morning's update? Does she think that there are hidden agendas that I plan not to share with the staff? I'm not sure where she's going with this but, by damn, I'll find out soon!"

"Okay," he said aloud, "you first."

"One, the letter I prepared for the Chairman of the JCS directing the Chiefs of the Military Services to get cracking on our requests for additional language qualified people to staff our DAOs in the Balkans was signed last week and the results were immediate. The numbers we asked for were accepted and orders have been cut and the additional people should all be in place within fourteen days."

Surprised that this was the first time he was hearing about the subject, Bart asked, "Was this something initiated before I came on board?"

"No. Our people were having such a struggle dealing with the Services personnel people and the need was so great, I just decided last week that some kind of drastic action was needed. I had this idea. I talked it over with the JCS, J2, Admiral Dylan, and he agreed to get me five minutes of calendar time with the Chairman. I briefed him myself and he signed off and the results speak for themselves."

"Isn't there still a system for coordinating papers through the JCS? And did you coordinate this action with the Services Personnel Chiefs?" Bart asked, his ire becoming more pointed.

"No. I did not. In my judgment, the situation taking place in the Balkans is extraordinary and our need to support it called for extraordinary action." The first bit of red color now appearing on Barbara Barnsworth's cheeks in response to Bart's rapid-fire questions.

"And not a word of this in the daily updates? Didn't you think I might be interested in the things you were asking *my* boss to do? What if the Chairman had called me and asked, 'What do you think, Bart? Is this really necessary?'"

"I did not think that was very likely. Particularly since I was standing right there and could answer any questions." Barbara replied, becoming more defensive.

"And what would your answer have been if the Chairman had asked, 'How does *your* Boss feel about this?'"

"I would probably have said, 'General Lowe is visiting Europe and the Balkans and he is still in the orientation phase getting his feet on the ground. In the interim, he has delegated the day-to-day running of the DAS to me."

With that, Bart Lowe stood up, leaned across the table so that his face was closer to Ms. Barnsworth, and through clenched teeth said, "The orientation phase for the new Director of the DAS is now complete. Is that clear, Ms. Barnsworth?"

"Well, uh, uh, yes, General Lowe, that is clear," an equally surprised, and somewhat rattled, Deputy Director of the DAS replied.

"Good. Then excuse me for a moment," Bart announced and strode out of the office down the hall into his own office and into its private bathroom. Using a technique that he had derived from his earliest days as a leader whenever he felt his anger toward a subordinate was about to get out of control, Bart called a halt to the discussion or whatever and took a short break to collect his thoughts and make sure what he was about to do was the correct and fair thing to do. He now threw some cold water in his face, thoroughly washed his hands, cleaning them to the point he was sure he could be accepted into any hospital operating room and then looked into the mirror. The traces of anger had all but disappeared and the man in the mirror once again looked like the calm and reasonable man Bart Lowe believed himself to be. He was ready to sit down with his deputy again. And he promptly returned to her office.

As he entered Barbara's office, he found that she had left the table and returned to her desk. When she saw him, she stood and appeared somewhat tentative—not sure of what to expect.

"Let's resume, shall we?" Bart said and took his place at the table. Barbara did likewise but, before she could begin again, Bart carefully and slowly told her, "Barbara, my old boss in the Army, General Gordon Reiley, used to tell his subordinates, 'Work your lane.' That was good guidance and meant that if everyone did their job, and did not try to do the other fellow's job, everything would work out okay. I believe in that philosophy. Do you understand my meaning?"

"Yes, sir. I believe I do." And like the pro she was, Barbara recovered her bearings and pressed on with her briefing.

"The second subject I want to cover is that the Navy has just informed us that the promised Naval Officer, Admiral Mike Stanik, who was scheduled to be your Military Deputy, in May will now *not* be coming."

"And why is that?" Bart asked.

"According to the Navy, overriding operational requirements. You will recall that Mike is a surface-warfare officer and the build-up of ships to deal with the problems in the Balkans is putting a new squeeze on Navy manpower."

"Can we, should we, fight it?"

"I recommend, no. Given the shortage of Flag Officers in the military today, I think you will lose that one. After all, Ba--, uh, General, isn't that why you are here now?"

"The name is Bart, Barbara. Nothing's changed. I have to agree with you. Let's get through this Kosovo crisis and then we'll look at the Military Deputy option again," Bart replied, obviously disappointed.

He felt strongly that a uniformed leader at DAS Headquarters was critically important to the military attachés in the field. There was, and always would be, a cultural difference between the uniformed military and the civilians who worked as part of the military and government. And he wasn't sure how he would be perceived now by his attachés. True military, or civilian, or a little of both?

"The third item I have, is to suggest a meeting between you and Senator Karson."

"Senator Karson? Is that Kit Karson, the Medal of Honor winner?" asked Bart.

"The same."

"What's the connection?"

"As you probably know, he is a member of the oversight committee, the SSCI. Next to your old friend,

Senator Jones, he has been our strongest supporter. We do have budget issues and he can help us. He is a proponent for covert action where there is no alternative and while the CIA is willing to carry it out, the Clinton Administration has been strongly opposed to any form of covert action. Senator Karson is looking for any way to strengthen his hand or any fresh ideas."

"But where does the DAS come in? That's not our cup of tea. And Karson doesn't know me from Adam!"

"Do you remember a woman named Maureen Gately who worked in the DIA Director's front office when you were here before?"

"Vaguely."

"Well, she moved to the Hill shortly after you left. She has had several jobs as a staffer there and is now Senator Karson's Chief of Staff. She and I are friends."

"A connection emerges."

"No," said Barbara, slightly irritated, "When she learned that you were returning, she mentioned you to the Senator. He thinks that you and he, because of your mutual military service backgrounds, will have a lot in common and will work well together. Maureen and I agree."

"Barbara, all of that sounds good but, I am not convinced. I will be on a steep, relearning curve for quite awhile just getting the hang of the job at hand and I don't want to get bogged down in someone else's concerns. If you feel strongly, give me a paper that I can look at, outlining the covert action problem and the specifics of the budget items you believe Senator Karson can help us resolve. And then I'll consider it."

"Very well. I'll have a paper prepared and on your desk by tomorrow morning."

"Is that it?" Bart asked.

"Yes. Unless you have anything else for me," his Deputy inquired.

"Barbara, there is nothing really beyond the debrief I gave to all our people downstairs except to say that our mission is clear. We must do all that is humanly possible to support the NATO and U.S. war effort in the Balkans while continuing to support our other customers around the world and in Washington even though some are working altogether different scenarios. I must admit that this 'other contingency' scenario that I heard about in Europe and Florida also has me concerned as well as our role in terrorist related activities. I want to study both these areas further in order to know the best way for us to take them on. If none of this sounds clear to you, it's because it is not yet clear in my mind. But here's how I want to begin. I want you to arrange for me, by the end of April, a mini-conference on the probability and location of other contingencies taking place in the world during the Balkan crisis. Also throw in terrorism reporting. No more than three days in duration. Informal, but structured enough that we can get through the most likely areas, i.e. Middle East, North Korea, China, Russia, Arabs and the terrorist organizations. Invite the analysts from DIA, CIA, NSA, the Military Services, and the State Department and bring in our DATTs from those areas so that I can personally talk to them."

"We might get some resistance to taking some of the Attachés away from their posts."

"Let's insist pleading that it will be only for a short time. And let's keep it low key enough so that it doesn't alarm any of the elephants in town or, God forbid, leak to the media. Let's emphasize that we are looking for analysts' level views for my edification as a new boy on the block, not agency positions."

"Yes, sir. I'll see to it right away."

CHAPTER 8

THE THREAT

On a beautiful spring morning, the last day of April, with the temperatures in the low 70's, Bart Lowe's official sedan passed by Arlington National Cemetery and crossed the Potomac River over the Memorial Bridge, heading for downtown Washington and FBI Headquarters. Now driving along Constitution Avenue, the White House, the Washington Monument, and the Jefferson and Lincoln Memorials all came into view. Bart never tired of these symbols of American history and greatness. Seeing them always sent a tremor of patriotism and inspiration surging through his body. This morning was no exception, in spite of the weight of responsibility he was already feeling after being back on the DAS job for just six weeks. "Well, no one had promised me it was going to be easy. I just forgot," he thought, "how many problems, in so many places around the world, could arise in a single day or week." And he could no longer say to himself, "That's why I am getting paid the big bucks!" In his earlier career, he had never realized the disparity between military and government pay, and that found in the civilian sector. But fortunately for Bart, that was not a real problem. He had only himself to worry about and in his years working in Florida, he had put away all that he needed.

He was looking forward to his lunch with FBI Deputy Director, John Kitchen. Kitchen met him at the Hoover building entrance, gave him a Security Badge and they went directly up the elevator to the top floor and the FBI Executive Dining Room. It was an early lunch, 11:30, and there were only a few people in the large, glassed room, overlooking the Nation's Capitol. Kitchen led him to a small, semi-private table in the far corner with a view of the Potomac boat docks.

"Beautiful day, isn't it, Bart?" John said as they were taking their seats.

"Yes, indeed, John. These are the kind of days that makes being in Washington seem all right! You can almost forget all your problems on a day like this."

"Not quite, Bart. Not quite," replied John, "but I hear you and then I remember you are the guy, when the going gets tough in Washington, who can head off to Hong Kong or Brazil or wherever, right, Bart?"

"I guess I plead no contest, John," answered Bart, holding up his hands in mock surrender.

"Seriously, Bart, it is good to have you back in town. I especially enjoy the resumption of our racquetball. Before you came back, there was nothing but a sea of young guys who just lived to humiliate the 'Old Deputy Director.' And now I can hold my own with an 'Old Soldier' like you, Bart."

"Thanks, John, you ringer!"

Both men laughed and accepted a menu from the white-coated waiter. After ordering, John informed Lowe, "Bart, all the people who work here are cleared for classified information and the dining room is secure. We can discuss anything you like."

After the meal of bean soup, salad and iced tea that both men ordered had been eaten, Bart explained to John his and others shared concern that a second contingency or crisis could arise somewhere else in the world while the U.S. military was heavily engaged in the Balkans. Bart needed to posture the DAS to be alert to that possibility and to provide early warning to their supported commanders and customers if such a contingency materialized.

"How do you see the threat, John?"

"Tough question, Bart," John replied, sliding down in his chair, signaling to the waiter for coffee and getting ready, Bart suspected, for delivery of a thoughtful answer.

"Remember, Bart, that the greatest number of FBI resources, dollars and time is spent chasing crime in the United States and fully 80% of my day is spent in that endeavor. As to my old responsibilities, and real love, Foreign Counterintelligence, as you know, we participate with CIA and DIA and the other big boys in the National Intelligence Estimate process and generally come to the same conclusions as they do."

"I'm aware of that, John, and I've just read all the current NIE. I am more interested in your gut feeling."

"Well, Bart, sometimes gut feelings can be way off the mark, but if that's what you want, here goes. The Chinese are stealing us blind. They have the greatest number of people both overt and under cover in the United States involved in espionage—both military and industrial. They are good, and they're successful."

"And what about your counterintelligence efforts?"

"Our guys are good, too, but we are simply outnumbered. The various trade agreements between China and the U.S. and the private sector deals that this permits give the Chinese a field day. Frankly, the best we can do is slow them down. When we bust one, they will send four more to replace that one. Also, I am sure you know that because of so many political scandals involving the Clinton Administration, so many of his people being indicted, so many Special Counsels, the Justice Department is under immense pressure to make sure that everyone's rights are looked after and not violated. As a result, it makes it tougher for our investigators to get a green light on the true bad guys. The biggest case in point is the investigation concerning several of the scientists at Los Alamos. When our guys and the managers at Los Alamos wanted to look into their computers, the Justice Department would not allow it on the basis that the search would produce tainted evidence. Tainted evidence or not, had we done so, we would have at least stopped the flow of information then. And now the secrets are in the hands of the Chinese and we will spend years on the damage assessment."

"And where is all this going, John?"

"I don't see much changing until we have an administration and a Congress that is willing to take the political heat from the Chinese. And the current ones aren't going to do it so we will continue to look for scapegoats. Now having said that, Bart, I don't see the Chinese causing a shooting contingency anywhere in the world. They are getting too much just for the asking. But you guys would know more about that than I would."

"Okay," Bart acknowledged. "And the other traditionally bad guys? The Russians, the North Koreans, the Arabs, others?"

"They have become manageable for us. The Russians are still active, and in many ways are still the smartest. They have good taskings, they know where to look for what they are interested in, and they are still getting into our secrets. That is, the ones we don't give them. And I must admit that the exchanges we have had with them have been helpful in clearing up many of our old espionage cases. I don't see them causing trouble for us anywhere except maybe in the Balkans because of their alliances, but they too, have too much to gain just for the asking from us. I don't see that happening from their government; maybe from one of their radicals, but let me talk to that later. Regarding the Arabs, the North Korean, and all the others that are in the U.S. to get something from us, I don't see any sizeable threat. A great and continuing nuisance factor, but that's all."

"And now the terrorists?"

"And now the terrorists. I have saved the best or, should I say, the worst, for last. The nations that sponsor or condone terrorism—the Libyans, the Syrians, the Iranians, the Iraqis, the Sudanese, the Islamic Fundamentalist groups, the Hamas, the Hizballah, the Islamic Jihad, Abu Nidal, and our latest tormentor, bin Laden—these are the guys that scare me the most. In fact, they make my blood run cold. I say that because in spite of our best efforts, I'm not sure we really understand them fully yet. The cultural differences between our societies are enormous and yet, they probably know us better than we know ourselves. These guys are clearly the biggest challenge for the Bureau today. And Bart, they just may be my and your greatest threat."

"Why do you say that, John?"

"Why do I say that? Let's start with the New York Trade Center bombing. It was bad enough but if a few minor things had gone the terrorists' way, then it could have been the country's biggest disaster. And as we investigated it, and by the way, the investigation is still going on, we find these things are not planned and carried out by a small group of radicals, but rather, they have large organizations, even countries, behind them to include unlimited financing and logistical support. And their Arab bases in the United States are everywhere and growing. New York, Chicago, Los Angeles, Washington, Dallas, you name it. Virtually every big city in the United States has a large Arab presence."

"John, do you see this terrorist threat primarily internal or external to the U.S.?"

"Both. And I see it coming in what I call a high-low mix."

"How's that?"

"First, low, where this guy, bin Laden, continues to hit us externally in places like Saudi Arabia at the Air Force billets, like the embassies in Africa, and against soft targets that have only the minimum of security. Then high, when these guys lay their hands on a weapon of mass destruction and get into the United States."

"Do you think that is going to happen, John?"

"Absolutely. I think its only a matter of time. Until the set of bad guys like Qadafi and Saddam Hussein pass from the scene and until we can convince nations like the Sudan, Syria, or Afghanistan to give up terrorists like bin Laden, until then, we will be vulnerable, and as much as I hate to say it, I believe it's inevitable that both the citizens and the government of the United States will be a victim of some fanatic's revenge. It's amazing what these people will do in the name of God."

"John, that's a sobering thought. I can only hope you are wrong."

"Right on, Bart. My sentiments exactly."

"And finally, John, how are your guys doing against bin Laden, and is there anything more my guys and I can do to help?"

"You probably know this from your own security people, but working with the other U.S. intelligence agencies and some of our allies, we have prevented seven bomb attacks by bin Laden sponsored people since the east Africa embassy attacks. All were targeted against U.S. embassies and of course, your Defense Attaché Offices were all in on the countermeasures. The targeted embassies, if memory serves me, were in Albania, Azerbaijan, Ivory Coast, Tajikistan, Uganda, Uruguay, and one other. The U.S. Embassy in Uruguay was the first one we have seen in South America. A large number of people were arrested in each of these countries, but so far, have not provided enough information to locate and target bin Laden, or his key people. We know, of course, that there are at least six Middle Eastern countries that have provided him a base of operations. We are offering a five million dollar reward, hoping some brave soul will come forward with the information of where we could grab him. We believe it is only a matter of time before he strikes again," Kitchen grimly concluded.

"John, just what I needed. Thanks. You and your guys keep up the good work. We need you."

"Anytime, Bart. Anytime."

As Bart rose from the table to leave, he paused briefly by the window looking at the serene, green horizon across the river and said, "John, I wonder what it is that we Americans do that make some people hate us so?"

It was now 6:30 p.m. on the Friday that Bart had lunch with John Kitchen and the last day of the three-day mini-conference that Barbara Barnsworth had organized at Bart's request on other "contingencies." Bart had spent the entire afternoon with the interagency group that had participated and was pleased at the range and depth of estimates he had heard that afternoon, and at the conclusion, he sincerely thanked all those who attended. Near the end of the conference, on a spur of the moment, Bart had asked Joan Weber if she could quickly pull together some wine and cheese so that he could host an impromptu after-conference drink for a few of the conference participants. Never one to back down from a challenge, Joan organized a remarkable spread inside of an hour. The people he had asked to stay behind were now assembling in his office and admiring the spectacular view of the northern Virginia and Washington skyline. Those that he had asked to attend were Brigadier General Ron Lee, the Defense Attaché to Beijing, China; Dr. Winifred Samuels, the senior Russian analyst for the Defense Intelligence Agency (DIA); Mr. Tom Mellon, the current head of the Defense Human Intelligence Service; Mr. Tony Roper, the National Intelligence Officer for Terrorism for DIA; Mr. Jim Poreman, the DAS' Division Chief for the Middle East; and Lowe's deputy, Barbara Barnsworth.

At first, the select group of military and government civilian achievers in each of their different areas of expertise, remained standing, circulating and moving among themselves, trading barbs, banters and repartee as they relaxed. Because it had been a long day, they soon settled into the various chairs around the room and became receptive to the additional questions that General Lowe obviously wanted to ask them.

By way of preface, Bart shared with the group the essence of his conversation with John Kitchen and then went around the room with a specific question or two for each person.

"Ron, do you agree with all we heard this week, vis-à-vis, the Chinese?"

"Yes, General Lowe," the tall, crew-cutted, uniformed officer answered, "I do. These accusations of Chinese espionage, which are no doubt true, are making it more difficult for me and our attachés to have access to the Chinese military and government officials that are essential for us to obtain the kinds of information we need. But the increased trade with the U.S. and the rest of the world has made the general population more open to contact and that helps us in our jobs. The NATO bombing of Serbia and the Chinese embassy has certainly increased tension in Beijing, but I don't see the Chinese moving to any kind of confrontation involving force in the near future. Now where they are going in the long-term, the bidding is still open on that."

"Okay, Ron. Now, Dr. Samuels, what do you see as the single area of greatest concern for us with respect to Russia?" Bart asked the bespectacled, brilliant, but petulant and well-known Russian-basher.

Dr. Samuels, as was her style, did not answer immediately but then said, "Bart, as you know, Russia is still imploding. All parts of her society, including the military, are in disarray. Our greatest fear should be for the control and accountability, or I should say the lack of control, of their weapons of mass destruction. While we have tried to assist them, they have not been entirely forthcoming and we know that more than a few weapons are either missing or under the control of radical elements in Russia. If these weapons should fall into the hands of some of the world's crazies, there will literally be hell to pay."

"Not a pleasant thought, Dr. Samuels."

"Jim. What about the Middle East? Are CENTCOM's concerns well founded?" Lowe asked the slim, brown-skinned Arabist.

"No question, sir. Hatreds in that part of the world do not die easily. Iran and Iraq are tinder boxes that may blow up at any moment. Our problem is that without embassies in either Baghdad or Tehran, we are at a great disadvantage in keeping our eyes on either of these two. Technical intelligence, of course, helps us but so much about our capabilities has been compromised in the media that everyone now knows how to hide from or evade our technical intelligence. And the loss of the inspections in Iraq was a severe blow. It's clear that both Iran and Iraq will continue their own programs for developing weapons of mass destruction. They've seen the western world's paralysis in dealing with Israel, India and Pakistan, and so they also want their own ace-in-the-hole. No one wants to get left behind by a hostile neighbor."

"Thanks, Jim. And now, Tony, any news—good or bad—about the terrorist threat?"

Before answering, Tony Roper stretched his feet out and placed his hands behind his head. It was hard to tell which was more rumpled—his coat or his trousers. However, there was nothing rumpled about the bald and bearded analyst's judgments. He had been working the terrorist problem for years and had served at the State Department and CIA prior to beginning his long tenure at DIA. Bart had met Tony when he first came to the DAS in 1985 and had great respect for his views as did the entire Washington community.

"Not really, Bart, although the FBI and NSA and especially, CIA, have geared up to much better coverage of the terrorist target. And the DAS has become an important reporter on terrorism. But I am very concerned. The terrorists are watching other terrorists' results against us closely, and they see how effective some terrorist activities have been. The Oklahoma federal building, even though it was home grown, had a tremendous psychological impact on the nation. And that kind of stuff is not lost on the bin Ladens of the world. Even as we sit here discussing this, I am confident that somewhere out there, more than one group are plotting an attack against us."

As Tony Roper said these words, Bart noted a smile or two among the group, probably because Tony had the reputation of sometimes over-dramatizing his points. "If I were going to predict something, I would say that I fear that the year 2000 will be the 'Year of the Terrorists' no matter what happens in Kosovo."

The smiles quickly disappeared and Tony's words had a sobering effect on the group.

"Any specifics that you can share with us, Tony?" Barnsworth asked.

"No, Barbara. It's just that bin Laden has been thwarted several times over the last year by the FBI and others, and he thinks he is better than that. It's only a matter of time until he has a successful hit against us, unless we get him first."

"And where do you see that happening, Tony?" Bart asked.

"Who knows. We are probably more vulnerable at some of our overseas posts, but I am guessing that he wants us to think that is the only place he can hit us and for him, hitting us on our own turf would be his greatest achievement."

"Thanks, Tony," Bart said, feeling the concern of the others in the room as they heard Tony's pessimistic but realistic view of the future. "Now, Tom, can you bring us up to date on how our human intelligence efforts and sources are fairing?"

Tom Mellon, a stocky, gray-haired man, was a retired Army military intelligence officer. He had spent his military career in clandestine operations. He was fluent in German, Russian, and Serbo-Croatian. He had spent many years in running agents and had worked closely with CIA on numerous occasions. He had been an ideal candidate to be the first head of the Defense HUMINT Service. The idea for the HUMINT Service had been borne during Bart Lowe's first watch but the actual implementation did not take place until years later. Bart's job at the DAS still had the over sight responsibilities for the HUMINT Service, but they were now separate operations at separate locations.

"General Lowe, as you know, a few months ago, our priorities turned to Kosovo and we are focusing our support on the U.S. and NATO effort. Our debriefers of the refugees coming out of Kosovo will play a major role if the war continues. The amount of useful information coming from human sources on what is happening in Kosovo has already tripled and our capability for coverage will continue to increase. Our human source capabilities around the world designed to provide us early warning of any imminent hostilities against U.S. forces or interests is well established and recently strengthened by our improving liaison and rapport with CIA. As to the terrorism target, that for us, like for CIA, is our toughest target. We have had only limited success on the fringes of terrorist groups and we are constantly trying to improve our techniques and capabilities. The bottom line is, we aren't anywhere near comfortable with what we have so far to monitor the terrorists."

When the meeting broke up a few moments later, Bart stayed behind to reflect on all that he had heard that day and learned over the last week. He was clearly now more knowledgeable about the state of the world and possible contingencies for the U.S. beyond Kosovo. He felt better prepared to take on his responsibilities now and had some definite ideas on how to strengthen the DAS' capabilities for anticipating, recognizing, and providing early warning of contingencies in areas other than Europe. Everywhere, in fact, except terrorism. It was still an area of uncertainty for Bart.

As he rose and walked over to the window to take one more look at the imposing skyline before heading home, he suddenly realized he was bone-tired. A new feeling for Bart Lowe. And the first element of self-doubt surfaced in his mind.

"Was it really a good idea for me to return to the DAS? Am I over the hill? Well," he guessed, "only time will tell."

CHAPTER 9

KIEV

On a rainy and still cold day in May, a man dressed in a bowler hat and raincoat and carrying an umbrella came out of the main entrance of the Alexander Hotel in downtown Kiev. He quickly ignored the line of waiting and anxious taxi cabs and walked north on the wide boulevard. He opened his umbrella against the moderately falling rain and set out at a brisk pace. After two long blocks, he turned to the left on Georgi Street and continued on for another block and a half. Seeing the sign he was looking for—the Bakal Restaurant, he entered the front door, checked his umbrella, hat, and raincoat, and spotted a hand raised in one of the booths running along the back wall. He headed toward the booth and its occupant, a swarthy, dark-eyed man in a heavy gray suit, extended his hand and said in good English, "I am Igor Solov and you must be James Bryce-Kent."

"Yes, of course I am, Mr. Solov. So good of you to see me."

After he was seated menus were presented by a waiter and Bryce-Kent, a fair-skinned, ruddy-cheeked, slightly balding man, suggested that Solov order for them both since he was a stranger to Kiev.

"I recommend we begin with some caviar and a glass of cold vodka," Solov said, knowing the English reputation for enjoying a drink. "Then we can try some stroganoff. It is excellent here."

"Splendid," replied Bryce-Kent.

After the caviar had been eaten, the vodka drunk, and the stroganoff ordered, Bryce-Kent began. "Well then, as I indicated to your law firm in my communication, I have a client who is interested in obtaining a certain, shall we say, industrial demolition. I have some specifications here," he said, reaching into his coat pocket and pulling out a single, folded piece of paper, which he passed to Solov. After looking over the specifications, Solov replied, "I am in touch with a client who has access to these kind of devices, but because of the sensitivities of such things, the price would, of course, be very, very dear, and I must tell you that my client has had other offers in the past but none so far have been able to meet the price."

"Very well, I understand. Let me say that I believe that a reasonable price is not a problem for my client, provided the item is workable and the terms of the sale and delivery can be met. I also have a list of those terms," he said, reaching into his other coat pocket and passing another single sheet of paper to Solov.

When Solov unfolded the paper, he read:

TERMS

- Item to be inspected by our representatives prior to purchase to verify specifications. After a satisfactory inspection, one-third of purchase price to be electronically transferred at that time to your numbered account.
- Item to be delivered to country of mutual agreement and upon arrival re-inspected by our representative to insure operability. Remainder of purchase price transferred as before when we accept the item.

"I am not so sure that my client will agree to the third country scenario. That will be very difficult," Solov commented, his eyes narrowing.

"I can assure you, Old Boy, that one is non-negotiable."

The two attorneys finished their lunch in good spirits vowing to do all that they could to work out a mutually acceptable arrangement between their clients, recognizing that their fees alone for closing such a deal would be worth a king's ransom. Solov promised an answer to Bryce-Kent at his London office within thirty days.

Three weeks later at the U.S. Embassy, at number 10, Yuria Kotsubynskoho Street in Kiev, Ambassador B.J. Ross was working at her desk in her third floor offices overlooking the tree lined street below. Her secretary entered and announced that the Chief of Station and the Defense Attaché were in the outer offices and wished to see her. Ross, slightly irritated, as she was struggling with a cable to State on the recent firing of Russian Prime Minister Primakov, asked, "Are they on the calendar?" She already knew the answer but asked for effect. Ambassador Ross was a stickler for schedule.

"No, ma'am, but they said it was important."

"Alright, but ask them to stand by for a few moments. I need to get this out. I'll buzz when I'm ready." She picked up her pen and went back to work.

Ten minutes later she came on the intercom and said, "Marsha, this cable is ready to go to the Com Center. Please take it down for me and then send in Arlen and Joe."

After Arlen Garrand, the COS, and Colonel Joe Farrar, the DATT, entered, Ambassador Ross rose from her desk, walked over to the table that held an urn of hot coffee and said, "Coffee?" When both men declined, she then said, "To what do I owe this unscheduled pleasure?"

"Ambassador Ross," Mr. Garrand, a well dressed man in his early forties, began, "do you recall a briefing that you received at my headquarters at Langley, before you arrived here, on the subject of unaccounted for nuclear weapons in the former Soviet Union?"

"Yes. Yes, I do."

"Then you know that any information on that subject is one of the highest priority reporting requirements for both myself and the DATT."

"Yes, of course. Do you have such information?"

"Maybe, yes. Maybe, no," replied Garrand. "But, first let us give you some background information."

The Ambassador nodded for the two men to continue.

Colonel Joe Farrar was an Air Force command pilot with many hours in the cockpits of B-1 and B-52 bombers. Joe was a math major who had also always done well with languages and had studied Russian in high school and college. When he completed the one-year Russian language refresher course at the Defense Language Institute prior to attaché duty, no one was surprised when he scored well on his Russian Language Proficiency Test. He and Arlen Garrand, also a Russian linguist, worked well together, and newly appointed Ambassador Ross knew immediately after her arrival that she had good country team members in those two.

"Soon after the Soviet Union began to disintegrate, was when the nuclear accountability problems started for the Russians," Colonel Farrar began. "The essence of the problem was that the records in Moscow at the General Staff level reflected false figures to be used for the SALT Talks so that negotiations with the U.S. would allow the Soviets to hedge on numbers of weapons to be destroyed. When the old Soviets were thrown out and a new set of people came along, they discovered that no one knew exactly how many nuclear weapons they actually had, where they all were located, and exactly who was controlling them. These new folks sought the assistance of the U.S. in establishing a viable control and accounting system. We provided the help and now feel confident that the devices that we found are now being accounted for and the control measures are sufficient. However, our continuing concern is for those weapons that existed, at least numerically, and have not been accounted for.

"Unfortunately, the number may be significant. Our current supposition is that there are actually unaccounted for nuclear weapons in Russia and that, unfortunately, they are in the hands of two groups of people. First, a few former senior military leaders who knew where the weapons were located. Some of these people have become disenchanted with a 'free'

Russia and may try to overthrow the present or future elected governments. The second element that especially concerns us are the now very powerful criminal elements throughout the country who command large sums of money, and influence, and have worldwide contacts. We know that many former military members have gone into the group for the money. We believe that some of the missing weapons are in the hands of these criminal groups. And we believe these groups include former military personnel with the know-how to maintain, transport, arm and use the weapons."

"Joe, I do recall most of this. Where is this going?" Ambassador Ross, not known for her patience, asked.

"There is one element that is especially worrisome. When we were assisting them with their accountability methods, we learned that they had created a number of 'suitcase bombs'."

"Really. You mean you can get a nuclear weapon in a suitcase? That is scary."

"These suitcase-type devices were created by the Soviets for the purpose of terrorist-type attacks. The nuclear yield is somewhere between one-tenth to one-kiloton.

"They made the bombs from the fuel that they used to operate their nuclear submarines. This kind of fuel is fresh and does not radiate intensely. It is actually a highly enriched uranium. It needs no special protective gear and can be easily linked up with a detonating device. The suitcase bombs can be transported as packages. They only weigh tens of kilos apiece so individuals can easily carry them or disguise them in other containers. We believe the Soviets made one hundred and three of these devices but can only account for fifty-five. That means up to forty-eight are unaccounted for. They have been the subject of an intense search by the Russians themselves and all of the U.S. intelligence agencies. We and the Russians believe that the missing suitcase bombs, if there are forty-eight of them, are still in Russia or their former states. We believe at least five of them are located in the Ukraine."

"Joe, Arlen, this is not only a scary story but also a fascinating one, but, what's the connection to us now?" an impatient Ambassador demanded.

"Joe has a contact in the Russian Military Nuclear Control Office located in Kiev," the COS continued. "Joe believes, and I agree, that his contact wants to find those missing suitcase bombs as much as we do. He is privy to the information that the Russian and Ukraine intelligence and police agencies intel about for the bombs. He has shared with Joe what may be a significant development."

"My contact," Joe explained, "says that the Russians have been watching the largest criminal group in Kiev for some time suspecting that they may know where some of the suitcase bombs are located. Perhaps they may even control them. My contact agrees with this premise because he knows that one of the key people in the criminal group is a former USSR Strategic Rocket Corps major."

"And the significant development is?" Ambassador Ross asked.

"It seems the Ukrainians and the Russians have a Kiev attorney-at-law under regular surveillance because of his work for the criminal group. Earlier this month, the attorney met with a British lawyer in a local restaurant. The Ukrainian police queried the British Special Branch and Special Branch reported to them that the English attorney's law firm represents several Arab countries.

Then just yesterday, my contact learned that the Kiev attorney had a second visitor from London, an Arab official from a London-based Iraqi oil company."

"Well, what's the big deal? Aren't there oil interests in the Ukraine?" the Ambassador wanted to know. "And there certainly have been many Arabs visiting Kiev," she added.

"The kicker is, Ambassador Ross," Joe Farrar answered, "the second day, the oil rep was here, he was picked up at his hotel by the former Soviet Strategic Rocket Corps major and they left Kiev by auto and did not return until late that night."

Ambassador Ross then turned to the COS, "Arlen, can you verify this with your contacts in the Ukrainian and Russian Intelligence Services?"

"No, we can't do that. First of all, their official position is that there are no missing suitcase bombs and there is no continuing investigation. Secondly, if I go to them with this, it would likely compromise Joe's contact."

"If there is something to this and the Ukrainians and Russians learn more, will they share it with Joe's contact?" asked Ambassador Ross.

"Maybe, yes. Maybe, no. We'll just have to wait and see," the COS replied.

"Arlen, Joe, what is the worst case scenario you can imagine?"

The two men looked at each other and Garrand spoke first.

"Simple. That the unaccounted for devices are for sale and we are witnessing the start of a buy by an Arab government or Arab terrorist."

"Joe?"

"I agree. I have been working with my contact for more than a year and I trust him. He is convinced that the former Soviet major knows where at least some of the suitcase devices are located and he would be involved in any sale or transfer."

"Well, gentlemen, you certainly have my attention. Now what's to be done with this information?" the Ambassador asked.

"The important thing is that Joe and I write this thing up and get it into our two reporting systems, CIA and Defense. The problem is that this will be an unconfirmed piece of information and intelligence that, without the other pieces, may mean nothing. But the analysts at CIA and DIA will have it and it could fit with other reports."

"The operations people at the DAS and at Arlen's headquarters will likely pass it on to our people in London and Moscow for further follow-up," Colonel Farrar added.

"Okay. It's a wrap. Make sure the distribution of your reports includes a copy to Intelligence and Research at State. When they are written, give me copies and I will pen a note to our nuclear proliferation guy. And Joe, make sure your new boss, Bart Lowe, reads a copy of your report."

Colonel Farrar and the COS took their leave. Joe Farrar said to no one in particular, "I wonder what she meant by that?"

CHAPTER 10

BEIJING, CHINA—BALLSTON, VIRGINIA

If Bart Lowe thought that April had ended on a good note, May dispelled that and went quickly to hell in a hand basket. The NATO bombing of the Chinese Embassy in Belgrade immediately caused reactions against U.S. embassies around the world, the greatest being in Beijing.

It was 6:00 o'clock Sunday morning in Beijing and Brigadier General Ron Lee, the Defense Attaché to China was just getting up from the makeshift cot and sleeping bag in his office in the U.S. Embassy. His office, fortunately, was in one of the inner corridors of the embassy and not subject to the pelting of rocks that the windows in the front of the embassy had been subjected to from demonstrating Chinese students the last forty-eight hours. Navy Yeoman First Class Wally Shields, one of the DAO's non-commissioned officers, entered Lee's office with a steaming hot cup of tea.

"Good morning, sir. Here's your tea and a summary from the night watch team on events since you turned in last night."

"Thanks, Wally. No breeches of the embassy, I assume?"

"Oh, no, sir. We were aware of your instructions to wake you if anything new happened here or at the housing complexes."

"Good," replied Lee, moving over to his desk which was in great disarray, not having received much attention since the announcement of the Chinese Embassy bombing was made on Friday. He reached for the tea that Shields had placed there and then scanned the night's one-page report.

"We are ready for your call to Lieutenant General Lowe whenever you're ready, sir."

"Okay, let's do it."

The Stu-3 secure telephone call was placed in a matter of minutes to the DAS Operations Center in Ballston, Virginia where Bart Lowe was standing by for the morning update from the DATT. Because of the thirteen hours difference in time between Beijing and Washington, it was actually 7:00 p.m. Saturday night in Ballston.

"Good evening, General Lowe. How are things in Washington?"

"Much better, I suspect, than in Beijing, Ron, and a good morning to you."

"Not much new to report this morning beyond that which I gave you twelve hours ago after that single Molotov Cocktail thrown late yesterday afternoon—the volume of rocks, and other debris tapered off. The fire didn't reach the inside of the embassy. Just some scorched outer walls, but I think every window on the front of the embassy that faces Xiu Shui Bei Jie Avenue is broken. Our people are staying away from the windows and so far, only a few minor injuries have been sustained from the flying objects coming over the embassy wall and gates."

"Have any problems arisen in the housing quarters?"

"No. As you may know, our people and the other people from the embassy are all in three large building complexes in the diplomatic housing subdivision. As soon as we got the word about the Belgrade bombing, we anticipated trouble, and sent some of our personnel to the housing area so that they could be there to help the families. So far, no incidents. Our inside contacts at the Foreign Ministry gave us an unofficial heads-up to expect trouble when they learned of the bombing and also gave us an idea of what to expect from the government-staged demonstrations. Unfortunately, they tell us that tomorrow will probably be the worst with the number of demonstrators increasing and the potential for violence escalating. They do say however, that the police forces and the military will not let the situation get out of hand. I don't believe, nor does Ambassador Sasser that we face the threat of the embassy being stormed or overrun."

"How's the morale of our troops?"

"Pretty good, I'd say. As you know, the DAO folks are used to dealing with the unexpected and we have enough emergency gear here to hold out for at least a week. The toilet and washing facilities are limited and some of the Foreign Service people are having a hard time dealing with the emergency Meals-Ready-to-Eat cuisine."

"I'll bet. I haven't eaten one of those in years. Ron, do you see this thing possibly getting out of hand, along the lines of the Tehran embassy takeover?"

"I know, of course, that concern for those kinds of things have been foremost in the Ambassador's mind and in the minds of a number of people in the embassy and in D.C. Being cut-off from the families is very stressful on folks, but no, no, sir, I don't see the Chinese authorities losing control here. Control is the key word. My read of the Chinese authorities is that the orchestrated demonstrations that show their outrage will meet their objectives. Please don't misunderstand me. They are upset as we would be if the table was reversed. But, the moment they sense that they have gained the world's attention and sympathy, they will wind the whole thing down. They would not want to send the message, for any reason, that the government can not control the people."

"All right, Ron. Is there anything we can do for you here?"

"No, sir. Everyone's been great. The Country Desk Officers at the DAS and at State have been in touch with our people twenty-four hours a day and responded promptly to every request. We appreciate the help."

"Goodnight then," Bart said, forgetting for the moment the time differences. "Keep your heads down and hang tight!"

Following his conversation with Ron Lee, Lowe left the busy Operations Center, took the elevator to the ground floor of DAS Headquarters and then walked out to his official sedan which was waiting to take him into Washington to attend a reception at the Lebanese Embassy. The driver opted to avoid the heavy traffic going into the Nation's capitol across the 14th Street Bridge, and instead, headed north through Rosslyn across the Roosevelt Bridge and up Foxall Street through Georgetown. This area on the Potomac where northern Virginia and Washington come together was one of Bart Lowe's favorite settings, particularly at twilight when the skyline was beginning to fade and the lights of Georgetown were just beginning to emerge. There was a peacefulness there that belied the turmoil taking place as close as the inner city of Washington, D.C. and as far away as Kosovo and Beijing.

A reception at the Lebanese Embassy was one that Bart Lowe would normally have passed up but Jim Poreman had recommended that he attend so that he could meet the Lebanese Military Attaché, Colonel al-Khouri and a woman who was the Lebanese Intelligence Service representative to the U.S. Government, Maria as-Salah. Both of these people had been very helpful to the DAS and other U.S. agencies in their work on counterterrorism, according to Poreman.

The ride from Ballston to the Lebanese Embassy took just twenty minutes, but to Bart, who was deep in thought about the situation in China, it seemed even shorter and he was almost surprised when the sedan deposited him at the front entrance of the embassy.

"I'll pick you up in an hour, sir?" the driver asked to confirm his instructions.

"Okay, great." Bart replied, and climbed out of the car and went into the embassy.

The first face Bart recognized as he started toward the crowd in the main social room of the embassy was Jim Poreman.

"Good evening, General. Glad you could make it," Poreman said, extending his hand to welcome him and shake Bart's hand. Jim Poreman was dressed in black-tie, formal evening wear and on his left lapel, were two rows of miniature military decorations proudly indicating his previous military service. Bart was dressed similarly having made the decision to wear his military dress uniform only at U.S. sponsored events and ceremonies. He was comfortable in the tux.

"General, if you will allow me to escort you, I think I can get you through the receiving line and around the room in about thirty or forty minutes introducing you to those key players from the Middle East who are here tonight. After that, you may wish to freelance it because I see many of the key national agency officials are here."

"That suits me fine, Jim. Please lead on." After they had moved swiftly through the Ambassador's receiving line, Poreman quickly obtained a drink for Bart and then they were off to work the room. Bart Lowe was once again impressed with the confident manner in which the former Attaché moved them smoothly from group to group, conversing as easily in Arabic as in English, presenting his boss to a host of military and civilian dignitaries. Their movement was so easy and fluid that Bart was amazed to find that thirty-five minutes had passed and he felt as though he had probably already met upward of thirty people. And Jim had also managed to swap a new drink for the empty one in Bart's hand.

"I saved the people I mentioned to you at the headquarters for last. That is because they are working and, of necessity, have been moving around greeting the embassy's many guests. It is also because, as I told you earlier, they are two of our important contacts for the Middle East and I wanted you to get to know them beyond just the usual social amenities," Poreman whispered to Bart and then steered him toward a distinguished looking man in a Lebanese Army uniform and an attractive woman in a royal blue, high-necked evening gown. These two had just left a larger group of people and started toward the tables where huge amounts of colorful and tempting foods were being offered on silver serving trays.

"Mrs. Salah, Colonel al-Khouri," Poreman called, gaining their attention and causing them to pause and wait for the approaching gentlemen to join them.

The woman quickly extended her hand reaching for Jim Poreman, and said, "Jim, how good to see you. Thank you for joining us," and quickly turning her gaze toward Bart. "And this must be your new boss, General Lowe? Welcome, General Lowe. And may I present Colonel al-Khouri, our Military Attaché."

The next five minutes or so were spent with Bart Lowe listening to a series of friendly exchanges passed among the three individuals. Theirs was, by all appearances, a mutual admiration society. But Bart's respect for the professionalism of Jim Poreman led him to believe that interpersonal rapport was an important element for the DAS and the United States. As Bart listened to Mrs. Salah as she expounded on Jim Poreman's astuteness, he was struck by her extraordinary beauty. He guessed she was a woman in her late forties, taller than most women at about 5'10", medium brown eyes, and very long, dark brown hair, almost flawless olive-colored skin, a trim figure and a full bust line. Her very white teeth were surrounded with full red lips and the sparkle in her eyes and ready smile suggested that she had a good sense of humor.

When the two finally took their leave, pleading the need to look after their other guests, Mrs. Salah once again grasped Bart's hand, and with a more than polite squeeze said, "General, we must meet again soon. I know that we will have much to talk about." In spite of his normally reserved manner, the pure male in Bart Lowe wondered if the invitation was really meant for General Lowe, the Director of the DAS, or was it for Bart Lowe, the man. As she walked off, he faintly heard someone behind him calling his name, "Bart, Bart, are you with us tonight?"

Startled, Bart turned and saw it was his old friend from the FBI, John Kitchen. "I can see Bart, that you have been hypnotized by the radiant beauty of Maria Salah."

Recovering his bearings, Bart answered, "Sorry, John, you got that right. You know her?" a boyish grin covering his face.

"Indeed I do. Along with most of the players in counterterrorism in town. Mrs. Salah and her small group of people here in the Lebanese Embassy have been of considerable assistance to just about every national security agency during the past three years. You now know that CIA and the Lebanese Intelligence Service in Beirut have had an intelligence exchange program for years. Mrs. Salah is here to look after that. But because of her foresight, the exchange program has been expanded to cover just about every agency in town. I have a full-time Legal Attaché in our embassy in Lebanon to look after our interests on that end. And you guys have a piece of that action, don't you, Jim?"

"Yes, sir. As you say, our Attaché is looking after Defense interests in Beirut and Mrs. Salah has been most helpful to us," Poreman agreed.

Looking at both John Kitchen and Jim Poreman, Bart asked, "What does her husband do? Is he here with her?"

"Colonel Poreman here knows more about that than I do," John answered.

"Yes, sir. Mrs. Salah is a widow. Her husband was a Lebanese Army major who was killed by a Hamas car bomb in Beirut and she has never remarried. She has dedicated her life to her country and the Lebanese Intelligence Service. She is one of their very best and is quite senior. Their Ambassador here gives her wide latitude."

"Sounds like a fascinating person," Bart commented.

"She is that, Bart. She is that. And say, look, isn't that René Softly over there? Let's go over and talk to her and see what the CT Center folks are up to," John Kitchen joked, grabbing Bart by the arm and dragging him away while Jim Poreman saluted good night to his boss.

"After all," Bart thought, "what better hands to be in than those of the FBI."

Two weeks later, Barbara Barnsworth knocked on General Lowe's office door, stuck her head in and reported, "I just had a call from Maureen Gately. She and Senator Karson are on their way and they should be here in twenty minutes."

"Thanks, Barbara. I better check with Colonel Wenke and SFC Childs to see if they are all set for the lunch."

"No need to do that, Bart. I just left Sergeant Childs and he's all set. Corn chowder, sliced turkey sandwiches, and fresh melon balls for dessert. And plenty of iced tea and Colombian coffee. Joan rounded up some flowers and the place looks great. I must admit that your idea of fixing up that unused break room into a secure guest mini-dining room was a good one. And Ted's idea of putting some of the memorabilia from the Attaché Hall of Fame in there makes it look like a historic site. I don't know why we didn't think of it long ago."

"I didn't mind hosting guests at my quarters, and SFC Childs really likes to display his culinary talents, but it was a long haul to Bolling and this way, we can relax and still deal with classified or sensitive information.

"By the way, Barbara. I think it a real feather in your hat to have gotten Senator Karson to agree to come here for our meeting. As I remember from my earlier time in this town, it was always difficult members off the Hill and on our turf except for their overseas visits."

"I can't take much of the credit. Maureen Gately felt strongly about the meeting between you two and pushed for it taking place sooner rather than later."

The informal lunch went off without a hitch. Senator Karson had not previously visited the adjacent Attaché Hall of Fame and he'd requested that Bart give him a quick walk through before they ate. At lunch, the Senator demonstrated the charisma that his supporters said made him a natural candidate for president in the next election. And yet, Bart could also sense a feeling of humility and dignity that you would expect in a Medal of Honor winner. Bart's long time friend and supporter, Senator Bob Jones, had told him, "Kit Karson is no ordinary politician." Jones had recommended that Bart meet with him and agree to assist Karson in any way he could.

The lunch had run beyond the allotted time and finally Ms. Gately, the Senator's Chief of Staff interjected, "Senator, I know you are enjoying this, but we have a full afternoon of commitments and I need to tell you, if there are any serious issues to discuss, there are only a few minutes left."

"The good thing about Maureen is that she never beats around the bush. She would have made a hell-of-a-Sergeant Major. But as always, Bart, she's right, and so, here's my pitch. I'm concerned first about the declining strength and future of our military forces and secondly, the growing threat of a terrorist attack in the United States involving weapons of mass destruction, particularly chemical or biological agents.

"The administration has reduced the capabilities of our military forces to an irresponsible level, while steadily increasing their piecemeal commitment to conflicts like Bosnia and Kosovo—a formula for disaster in my opinion. As a member of the SSCI, I am charged with exercising oversight of America's intelligence agencies to make sure their operations are consistent with our laws and policies on human rights. Although we keep our eyes open for human rights issues, I am more concerned with insuring that those agencies are doing all within their charters to identify the real threats of violence against the United States. By-and-large, the intelligence community seems to be doing a good job at that. For example, CIA and DIA analysts were right on the mark when they said that NATO bombing without ground force action would result in defiance from Milosevic, increased Serb ethnic cleansing in Kosovo, and massive movement of Kosovar refugees into Albania and other Balkan countries. The administration chose to not accept those estimates thereby widening the problem, adding many uncertainties, and increasing the U.S.'s long-term commitment.

"Now! While we are stretched thin in Europe concentrating most of our energies there, what better time for the terrorist powers of the world to take a shot at us on our home ground? I am personally convinced that the center of mass of that threat is located in the Middle East in the form of Saddam Hussein and Iraq."

"I hear you, Senator and I am aware that the CENTCOM and its commander share that concern. But what is it that you want from me and our attachés?" Bart bluntly asked.

"Bart, I'm simply asking that all concerned do all they can during what I consider to be a vulnerable time to root out any indication of terrorist attack coming toward the U.S. As an example, I have asked the CIA to re-look at some of their covert action plans and thinking for Iraq. I believe the U.S. should not rest easy until that bastard is dead and gone."

"Do you have anything in particular in mind for the DAS, Senator?"

"Yes. I am looking for fresh information and ideas on how to deal in a pro-active way with this terrorist threat. I know you have a set of bright military people serving in the Middle East and here at your headquarters who have dedicated their lives to studying the culture and behavior of those Middle East countries and people. I am interested in their ideas to include brain storming on solutions. I am also interested in information on developments in that part of the world as they happen, rather than after they become a part of a finished intelligence estimate. The bottom line is that I would like to set-up an informal flow of pertinent information from the DAS that will be helpful to me in carrying out my responsibilities."

Before Bart Lowe could respond, the Senator stood up preparing to leave and said, "Please think it over and if something can be worked out, we can leave the details to the ladies," waving his hand at Barbara and Maureen. "And by the way, I am prepared to help you with your budget and resource needs." After handshakes and thanks all around, the Senator and his Chief of Staff were out the door and soon on their way back to Capitol Hill.

As Bart and Barbara were walking back to their offices, Bart, with a frown on his face, turned toward Barbara and asked, "Did you know the Senator was hoping to acquire his own military-political information service?"

"Not exactly, Bart. Not exactly!"

"God, I love this town." Lowe mused.

CHAPTER 11

BANGLADESH

The end of May in Dhaka, Bangladesh, brought with it the end of the rainy season and hope in the minds of its people for the end of the flooding that had been so disastrous this year. Certainly that was foremost in the thoughts of Lieutenant Colonel Frank Windom, the Defense and U.S. Army Attaché to Bangladesh. In the six months he and his wife Jan had been stationed at the embassy they had been severely limited in their travel because of the heavy flood waters and both were anxious to see more of the country. Both held Ph.D.s in Indian Subcontinent Studies, his degree from Georgetown, hers from Northwestern. Frank had met Jan in New Delhi, India, in 1984 during his Foreign Area Officer studies while she was researching material for her first book. A whirlwind courtship led to a quiet marriage, and their mutual academic interests and subsequent Army tours in southwest Asia were considered blessings by them both. When Frank volunteered to serve in Bangladesh, the Army and DAS assignments officers both breathed a heavy sigh of relief. The Dhaka DATT billet was one of the most difficult to fill.

Frank Windom was an immediate success with the Bangladesh military. He'd met many of the upper and mid-level officers in prior assignments, and his knowledge of the region and the language was exceptional. After mastering Hindi in India, the Bengali language came easy to Frank. Jan Windom had taken the DAS language training with Frank and they quickly became a popular couple among the diplomatic circles in Dhaka.

In keeping with Moslem custom, the work week was from Sunday through Thursday, with Friday and Saturdays as holidays, and the U.S. Embassy followed that schedule. On this Friday afternoon Frank and Jan Windom sat at a table in a computer-coffee house that was just down the road from the Madani Avenue diplomatic enclave where the Windoms lived in a fifth floor flat.

"Hon, I'm going to have some more coffee. How about you?" Frank asked.

"Uh, yeah, sure," Jan replied, engrossed in the small keyboard and screen on her side of the table. The coffee shop known as Compute-a-Cup was one of their favorite places. Both had been surprised at the technological advances that the business elements of Bangladesh society had made in the field of computers. Like their Indian neighbors to the west, the people of Bangladesh seemed to have a particular gift for understanding computer applications, particularly software.

"Where is Turan Dey today?" Frank asked the man who brought them new pots of steaming dark coffee.

"Mister Dey is in Calcutta today. He will be back on Sunday, Colonel Windom."

Turning back to Jan, Frank said, "Turan must have gone on another buying trip."

"Uh, huh," Jan replied, still fascinated by the computer program she was working.

Both Colonel Windom and his wife Jan, were longtime computer buffs. Before coming out to Bangladesh, it was not usual for the two of them to spend an entire evening in silence in their apartment in Bethesda, Maryland, surfing the Internet on their separate PCs—this, after a full day's study of Bengali. There was an Internet terminal in the U.S. Embassy but it was located in the Public Affairs Office space and shared by the whole embassy and it was not yet economically feasible to connect the Internet to the Diplomatic Quarters. The Windoms had their own Internet access from their apartment but they had other reasons for frequenting Compute-a-Cup.

The coffee house had an Internet terminal but it was wildly popular, particularly with young people, and so the

Windoms usually contented themselves with the wide variety of computer games when they visited. Frank Windom had only a passing interest in the games, but rather his primary focus was on Turan Dey. The Compute-a-Cup coffee shop, with its tables, terminals, and monitors, was just a showroom extension for Bangladesh's largest computer and computer software business with several outlets throughout the country. Its owner and founder, Turan Dey, was one of Dhaka's brightest business stars. He was a brilliant math student as a young man and was drawn early to the fascinating world of computer science. He earned a doctorate degree in that field at Oxford at the age of 24 and soon became a moving force in his country for computer literacy and technical applications for business and government. His computer business, the first of its kind in Bangladesh, became an overnight success and Turan Dey was sought after regularly as a consultant for other businesses, the government, and the Bangladesh military. Turan Dey had been to the United States on many occasions and considered it the center of the computing world. And he liked Americans.

From the first time Lieutenant Colonel Frank Windom came into the Compute-a-Cup and met the charismatic Turan Dey, they liked each other immediately. Dey was a frequent guest at the Bangladesh hosted functions and Windom became a regular at the coffee shop. As time passed, Dey saw in Windom a rare individual. A soldier-scholar-intellectual who knew more about the history and culture of Bangladesh than did most of its citizens and Windom saw in Dey a gold mine of knowledge of all that was going on in south Asia—its strengths, vulnerabilities, politics, and potential. Windom always benefited from Dey's wise council, whether it was for a simple computer game or the merits, or lack of, of the Bangladesh Army's latest reorganization.

The following Sunday afternoon when Lieutenant Colonel Windom returned to the DAO after a visit to Bangladesh Army Headquarters, he asked his Operations

Coordinator, Air Force Master Sergeant Glynn, "Anything up, Bud?"

"Yes, sir. The Deputy Chief of Mission has called a staff meeting for 1600 hours today and you are requested to attend. The scuttlebutt is that the latest Ambassador nominee has fallen out and that the DCM will probably be in charge for at least six more months."

"Unfortunately, that's not too unusual for some of the smaller and less desirable posts like Bangladesh, Bud," Windom commented.

"Yes, sir. Also there are about two dozen cables that came in over the weekend on your desk. I put what I considered the three most important on top of the pile. One is a message from the new DAS Director, General Lowe, concerning contingencies."

"Contingencies?" Windom asked.

"Yes, sir. About the possibility of something happening somewhere else in the world while we are involved in Serbia and Kosovo. It's a pretty good message and really makes you think about whether the U.S. military can handle more than one war."

"Okay. I'll look forward to reading it."

"The other two are the weekly Intel updates from the Pacific Command Headquarters in Hawaii and a DIA update on operations in Kosovo. Both are very interesting," Sgt. Glynn concluded.

"Oh, I almost forgot, sir. That guy who owns the computer coffee shop, Mr. Dey, called for you and asked that you call him back right away."

"Right. Bud, why don't you get some lunch and I'll hold the office down."

"Roger that, sir. I'm out of here!"

Lieutenant Colonel Windom read General Lowe's heads up to the worldwide DAS calling their attention to the vulnerability of the U.S. military while the country was so heavily engaged in Kosovo, and enjoining all military attachés to the absolute necessity of being vigilant and on the lookout for any indications of new crises or hostilities in order to provide the earliest possible warning to the responsible U.S. combatant commanders. Frank Windom understood what his boss was saying but could not conceive any scenario in which rain-soaked Bangladesh would play a major role. After finishing the rest of the cable traffic and making some notes for follow-up action, Frank Windom picked up the phone on his desk, pushed nine-nine for an outside line, and then the seven digits of the Compute-a-Cup wondering, "What exciting new development in computer technology does my friend, Turan Dey, have to share with me?"

The phone on the other end of the line rang several times and then was answered in English by a man's voice, "Compute-a-Cup. How may I help you?"

"Mr. Turan Dey, please."

"He's in the back of the shop. Who is calling, please?"

"Lieutenant Colonel Windom."

"Ah, yes, Colonel Windom," the voice said recognizing the name, "Right away."

After about four minutes, the voice of Turan Dey came on the line. "Is that you, Frank?"

"Yes, Turan. You called me earlier?"

"Yes, Frank, I did. Can you come round and see me?"

"I was planning to drop by on Tuesday. Will that work alright?"

There was a pause on Turan Dey's end of the line, then he said, "Actually, I found that new accessory you were looking for and thought you might want to check it out later today."

Since Windom hadn't expressed an interest in a new accessory, his ears immediately became more alert at Turan Dey's request." He couldn't imagine what it was but he had far too much respect for Turan Dey to turn him down.

"Good idea, Turan. Good idea. Will seven o'clock be satisfactory?"

"Indeed. And I'll have a cup of our finest coffee ready."

The DATT replaced the phone receiver and thought to himself, "I wonder what that's all about."

That night, Frank Windom had an early dinner in his quarters with his wife, Jan, and after the server had cleared the table and brought coffee, Frank told Jan about the call from Turan Dey.

"What in the world could it be? Probably something the United States has done to restrict the dissemination of computer technology information. I'll go along if you like," Jan volunteered.

"No. I think not. If it had been something like that, I am sure Turan would have invited you, too."

"Okay. Do you want me to drive you over since there's no parking in that area?"

"Once again, no thanks. It's only about a twenty minute walk and I can use the exercise." Looking at his watch, Frank said, "I'd better get going."

"Don't forget your umbrella. There is still the odd shower falling," Jan reminded Frank.

By the time Colonel Windom arrived at the Compute-a-Cup, he was grateful that Jan had reminded him to take his umbrella. The odd shower showed up with a vengeance. Even with the umbrella, he was soaked from the waist down, and a moped had added insult to injury just a block away when it hit a king-sized mud hole and sprayed mud over Windom from head to toe.

"Out for a bit of a walk, are we?" asked Turan Dey, when he spotted the attaché coming in the front door. "Get the Colonel a towel," he said to one of the passing waiters, "and bring it along with some of that Black Pearl coffee to my office," motioning for Frank to follow him.

Once they were in the spacious office located in the rear of the building, Dey, a large, heavy-set man, dressed in white silk trousers, a matching white shirt, and a waist coat of crimson and black, sat in one of two recliners and offered the

Attachés II—*Retribution*

other to his American guest. As he sat, he removed his slip-in sandals, leaned back, and folded his hands across his stomach. The waiter poured coffee for both men before departing.

"Frank, I went over to Calcutta last Wednesday to do some software buying and then on Friday and yesterday, I attended a regional conference on computer technology developments. I have found these very useful in the past and it also provides me an opportunity to see and meet with many of my colleagues. I had dinner last night with an old friend of mine from New Delhi. We'll call him Parkeet. He and I were at Oxford together. He has been a pioneer of sorts for India in spreading the knowledge and value of computers. He is well respected for his expertise throughout what you Americans call the 'third world.' He was concerned about something that happened in New Delhi and sought my advice. He related a story to me, the essence of which follows.

"Two weeks ago, Parkeet was contacted by an Arab gentleman who said he was from Abu Dhabi. He asked Parkeet if he could recommend some freelance computer experts that might be available for a scientific project the man was conducting. The man specified that the individual would need to be knowledgeable of large-scale computer operations to include work with viruses. When Parkeet suggested to the man that he could recommend any number of well-respected and highly competent firms in New Delhi, the man rejected that due to affordability and repeated that he was only interested in individuals. He further specified that he would prefer an individual of the Islamic faith. The next day, Parkeet provided the gentleman a list of six individuals in New Delhi that met his qualifications. One of the individuals on that list was a brilliant young man in his early thirties from Bangladesh living in New Delhi. The man, Abdel, was well known in the New Delhi and Dhaka computer communities. Interestingly," continued Dey, "Aziz is one of my former students. I remember him because he gave me concern regarding his research methods and use of computer manipulations for other than strictly ethical purposes; nevertheless, his competence and innovation were unquestioned. On the evening that Parkeet was scheduled to leave for Calcutta, Parkeet was surprised when Aziz stopped by Parkeet's residence to tell him that he had been selected for work on the scientific project and to thank Parkeet for recommending him. Parkeet was, at that moment, literally walking out the door of his home to go to the airport and only had the shortest of time to speak with Aziz. They spoke for barely two minutes. Later, on the flight to Calcutta, Parkeet remembered two comments that Aziz made that were inconsistent with what the gentleman from Abu Dhabi had told him. Aziz said that the fee offered was greater than anything he had ever received and that he was looking forward to seeing Baghdad, having never been there before."

"Hmm. That's interesting," Windom observed.

A short time later, walking home, Frank Windom pondered what Turan Dey had told him and what, if anything, he should do with it. Dey was a Christian and viewed Saddam Hussein as a dictator and international troublemaker. That view was not shared by the Islamics in government and the Hindus were neutral. Bangladesh did not see Islamic fundamentalism as a threat to the country. The bottom line was that Turan Dey was unsure of who in the government he should give the information to and decided it might be of more interest to the Americans who had taken on the responsibility of keeping an eye on Iraq.

When he returned to his quarters, Colonel Windom called the COS on the secure telephone line and relayed the story to him and asked for any suggestions. The COS recommended that Windom contact the DATT's counterpart in New Delhi to see if they could persuade the Indian authorities to contact the Aziz before he left and determine his purpose for traveling to Iraq if that were, in fact, the case. Frank agreed that was a good idea and immediately made a secure call to Colonel Russ Jonah, the DATT in India.

"Sorry to bother you at home Russ, but I have a funny one I want to run by you and see if you can help."

After Windom explained the situation, Colonel Jonah agreed to ask the COS at his embassy to request assistance from Indian authorities and told Frank he would get back to him as soon as he knew something.

The following afternoon, Colonel Jonah called to say, "The Indians were quite helpful. However, they determined that Aziz departed two days ago on a flight to Abu Dhabi. Whether or not he was going on to Baghdad, they couldn't say. They checked his home address in New Delhi and found out he gave up the apartment he was staying in and so he may be planning to be gone for awhile. They pointed out that since he is a citizen of Bangladesh, and traveling on a Bangladesh passport, he might return there. At any rate, they have promised to put him on a watch list and if he shows up back here, they will try to determine the purpose of his visit to Iraq."

"Is there really a chance they will watch for him, Russ?" Windom asked.

"Oh, yeah. They are sincere but candidly, they have so many people on their watch lists for their own priorities, I wouldn't count on it."

"Understand Russ, and many thanks for your fast response."

"Glad to help out. Out here."

Later that day, Colonel Windom wrote a priority Information Report under the subject, "Possible Iraqi Computer Activity," and transmitted it into the DAS message system. He doubted that it would get much attention by the community of national security analysts in Washington, but, "What the hell," he thought, "every little bit counts."

CHAPTER 12

YAZDAN—BAGHDAD

June brought warmer weather to the mountainous region of Afghanistan where Abdul Khalid now resided full time. On this Monday morning he was sitting at a writing table in his private rooms of the main house of the Afghan microwave station that served as a cover for bin Laden terrorist training activities. "The Goat Farm," as it was known to those individuals who trained there, was to Khalid an ideal training location—completely isolated so there were no distractions for either those to be trained or those doing the training. And bin Laden's generosity had allowed Khalid to acquire and put into place the best training aides and devices that money could buy for the few necessary classrooms, and for the practical exercises and the mock-up training areas. "Even the Army Special Forces, who normally received the best resource support in the U.S. Military would be impressed," he thought.

The two rooms and private shower he used were very austere. Just the essentials—a bed, a night table and light, an easy chair and a small portable storage cabinet for his clothes. In the second room he had a writing table, and lamp, where he now sat, where he could meet with trainees or instructors. The half dozen instructors he had chosen lived in the large barn-like building that also housed those to be trained, in even more austere accommodations. The Afghani security detail was housed in yet another building and their contact with Khalid and his people was limited with only the Officer-in-Charge reporting to Khalid.

Khalid's rooms looked as though they were ready for a military inspection. His training and many years in the U.S.

Army had given him a disciplined and structured way of life that he still preferred.

The twenty-one trainees that Khalid and his instructors had taken through thirty days of extremely demanding physical and mental training had all departed at the end of the previous week. One individual had lost a hand in a bombing exercise when a defective detonator went off prematurely. The loss of the limb limited the usefulness of the individual and he was taken out of training. The others all did very well and Khalid had no problem in selecting nine people for the *Retribution* project. Khalid was now preparing himself for the afternoon visit of bin Laden, and Wadih Mohammed. Wadih Mohammed had been with bin Laden from the beginning of the movement and was his most trusted assistant. Khalid knew that bin Laden had great faith and confidence in Wadih Mohammed's judgment, and Khalid, in going over his notes, was careful to not propose anything that Mohammed could not support. Now as he looked over the notes he would use, his hands almost trembled in anticipation of being a part of something so important. "Praise be to Allah," he said aloud.

That afternoon, when Osama bin Laden and Wadih Mohammed arrived, Khalid took them to one of the small classrooms and with the assistance of one individual that Khalid had designated as the Chief Instructor they briefed them on the training just concluded. It had consisted of a number of sabotage-like objectives to be accomplished by the trainees under the most arduous harassment, mental and physical barriers, sleep deprivation, and food and water rationing. Bin Laden listened without interruption until the briefing was completed and then asked Khalid, "Abdul Khalid, what do you believe you have accomplished by this very difficult, very physical, very demanding, even cruel, training?"

"It is my belief we will not know how well an individual will perform a mission of grave importance under the most stressful conditions unless in training we have taken

117

that person to the limits of human endurance and evaluated his performances under those circumstances."

"And did you do that with these twenty-one people?"

"Yes."

"And do you believe that these people can now serve Allah better?"

The last question worried Khalid but he answered, "Absolutely!"

Bin Laden then turned to Wadih Mohammed who nodded slightly, indicating his agreement.

"Then proceed," bin Laden said.

At that point, Khalid excused his assistant and when the Chief Instructor had exited the room and closed the door, Khalid opened his small black leather portfolio and passed a list of nine names and pictures of each individual to bin Laden. Bin Laden looked at the names and pictures and then passed them to Wadih Mohammed.

"If you approve, these are the nine individuals I have selected for *Retribution*."

"And how did you arrive at these nine?" bin Laden asked.

"In truth, Osama bin Laden, any of the twenty-one would be satisfactory. They are all true believers and have served your cause for at least five years. However, we devised a grading system for the trainees unbeknownst to them and these nine had the highest achievement scores. I believe they will give us our best chance for success," Khalid responded. Again bin Laden turned to Wadih Mohammed who again nodded. "These three individuals," Khalid said, indicating the names and pictures of the next highest scorers, "will serve as back-ups if anything should happen to the first nine."

Seeing the affirmation, Khalid continued, "I now propose for training purposes that we designate these nine targets in the United States as the most likely targets for strike," again removing a single handwritten sheet of paper from his portfolio and passing it to bin Laden.

"How did you decide on these nine?" Wadih Mohammed now asking the question.

"It is, as the Americans say, 'a straw man.' I started from the Iraqi list of fifty targets that we received from Ali Hassan. I compared that with your and my own input to their list, and using the two criteria of most valuable and most easy to strike, I arrived at these nine proposed targets. Subject to Wadih Mohammed's and your approval."

A frown was already appearing on Mohammed's face as he suspected that Khalid was getting into his area of responsibility. Turning to bin Laden, he said, "I will need some time to review this before agreeing that these would be the most likely targets. Then too, Saddam has his role to play and who knows what targets he will consider most important," this last addressed to bin Laden.

Bin Laden responded, "On the other hand, Wadih, Saddam and Ali Hassan are pressing us to be prepared to strike as soon as possible. Khalid says we cannot train realistically without knowing what the targets will be. Let's press Ali Hassan to get Saddam to agree to at least ten likely targets. Tell him we can't begin the second phase of our training until we have an agreed list of ten targets—four nuclear, three chemical or biological, and three cyber. Agreed?"

Both men agreed.

It was Friday afternoon on a hot, dry day in Baghdad in mid-June. Ali Hassan was sitting in his now plushly furnished and comfortable office. The temperature was a cold seventy degrees. He had spared no expense in converting the small office building into a first class facility, as indicated by the ornate goldleaf sign at the entrance of the building which read "Scientific Studies and Applications, Ltd." State-of-the-art security systems and a guard force had quickly been installed and operated vigilantly around the clock, but this had been accomplished discretely to mask the sensitive activities taking place inside the building. Ali knew that the office equipment, technology, and communication suites within the building were the best the Western world could design. Great care had been given to disguise the exterior antennae array on the roof so that high altitude reconnaissance could not determine the building was an Iraqi government facility.

Ali Hassan found that it was necessary to increase the number of people in the building to twelve, not counting the security people, who had no access to the inner offices and compartments. The additional people were primarily full time support and administrative types allowing Ali and his six assembled smart people to concentrate on *Retribution.* This number was greatly increased if you counted the number of people in the cells or compartments that Ali established in various government ministries to provide instant information to him and his people's requests. But then they only saw a small piece of the larger undertaking at any time and in Ali's judgment, did not pose any serious security threat to the project. Ali himself had added a female captain from his former headquarters in Kirbuk to act as his aide and admin assistant. She was very efficient but did not have access to any of the papers or notes that Ali or his people generated. All documents were kept in a small safe next to his desk. The sound proofing of each room allowed for secure discussions anywhere in the building.

The sign outside of his office said simply "Director" in Arabic and English which was normal for Baghdad. Ali liked the sound of it and required his staff to address him as Director rather than General in the interest of security. Ali no longer wore his uniform—only business suits. Captain Bassari had just served him hot tea and a sweet meat. She rotated her daily dress from the traditional Iraqi gown and scarf for women and the Western, far more revealing, style. Today she had on a gray two-piece suit and high heels that was quite complimentary to her light complexion, dark short hair, and healthy looking figure. Ali smiled at her as she sat the cup, saucer, and plate in front of him, noting her feminine attractiveness with pleasure.

"Director, please do not forget your two o'clock appointment today," she said and returned his smile.

"Of course not!" he scowled, thinking to himself, "It'd be unlikely that I would forget my weekly update with the Mad One," as an unintentional tremor passed through his body.

When he finished his tea, he rang for Captain Bassari to summon his assistant who was working the cyber weapon problem. When the bespectacled, slight, balding lieutenant colonel entered, Ali Hassan motioned him to a chair and asked, "Tell me once again the status of our cyber weapon development."

With the slightest of sighs because he had been over the subject in great detail just yesterday with Ali Hassan, the studious looking man began, "As you are aware, sir, over the years we have been moderately successful in developing three cyber programs designed to disrupt large scale military or commercial type computers. The shortcomings of our programs are that we have no standoff capability and thus, must have direct physical or telecommunications access to the key nodes of any computer system we wish to disrupt or disable. The second major shortcoming of our cyber programs is the inability to preclude detection when the programs are introduced into a computer system, thus allowing the operators of the computer system to initiate early counter measures once our program is identified and restore operations in a relatively short period of time."

As the officer was explaining this to Ali Hassan, he could see that the General understood the big picture but was having problems understanding the technical considerations.

"And what is this Bengali going to be able to do for us?" Ali Hassan asked.

"This young fellow is a brilliant researcher and experimenter with computer viruses. We have set him up in a safe house with a complete computer diagnostics lab and all the technical support he needs. The problems we have given him are to answer the questions, 'How can one disrupt and disable a mega-major computer system such as those found in the major Western industrialized countries? And secondly, how can this be done without early detection, thereby avoiding timely countermeasures?'"

"And will he not be suspicious of our ultimate intentions?"

"A certain amount of suspicion, of course, but we have represented to him that we are doing this purely to protect our own systems and for scientific research which is exactly what so many others around the world are doing today. And even if he suspects, he is greedy by nature and he is being well-paid."

"And will he be successful for us?"

"Oh, I think you can conclude that the worst he can do is to make suggestions on how we can improve our systems, and perhaps he can make a breakthrough. This is the best equipment he has ever had, the most support, and an unlimited budget. I am optimistic, sir."

"What about the security considerations and termination of his contract?"

"Well, that is somewhat sticky. We have hired him for six months—more money than he dreamed of in his lifetime. I'd suggest we postpone that decision until his work plays out more. In the meantime, he will be under strict control and when the time comes for the security consideration and contract termination, we'll bring that back to you for your decision."

"Yes, I am sure of that," Ali acknowledged, thinking, "one more nail in my coffin," but aloud saying, "Let there be no doubt, Colonel, I am expecting something I can go forward with and I am holding you responsible to make that happen. Do I make myself clear?"

"Perfectly clear, sir," the colonel replied, rising and hurrying out the door.

After the officer had departed, Ali took a sheet of paper from his desk drawer and began to think aloud what he would say, relieved that it was mostly good news. As he voiced his thoughts, he jotted down a few notes for his update with Saddam:

- *Coordination with W.M. continues. Targets passed. Phase two training begun.*
- *Special weapon acquisition finalized. Deposit made. Delivery date and place agreed upon.*
- *C and B weapons identified and available.*
- *Cyber weapon progressing. Recommendations expected soon.*

When Ali Hassan finished these notes, he folded the paper twice and placed it inside his coat pocket. He then realized that Captain Bassari was standing anxiously in front of his desk to remind him he was dangerously close to being late.

"Sir, I have already called the Security Detail and they are waiting outside. They said no blind fold today."

"Yes, yes, of course. I'll be back later," he said and hurried out the door. Once outside the building, he quickly got into the rear seat of his unmarked car, instructed the driver to follow the waiting security sedan, and soon both vehicles were crossing downtown Baghdad on the way to Saddam's location.

Ali Hassan tried to relax during the ride, but as always, was nervous about seeing Saddam. To calm his nerves, he reached into his pocket and pulled out the paper containing the briefing notes for Saddam. At precisely that moment, a taxi ran a red light, broadsiding Ali Hassan's sedan. The sedan rolled over twice, throwing Ali from the car.

CHAPTER 13

ANKARA

On a Monday morning, at the U.S. Embassy in Ankara, Turkey, the U.S. Naval Attaché Captain Ben Alvarez knocked on the open door of the Defense and Air Attaché Colonel Walt Lipmann. Lipmann's head was bowed, concentrating on a stack of messages he was reading. He looked up and said, "Come on in, Ben. What's up?" motioning for Alvarez to sit in the chair to the right of his desk.

"Just wanted to check in before I leave this morning on my trip to Sinop."

"I suppose you are going to go by car rather than use a perfectly good airplane?" quipped the DATT.

"Absolutely. No offense to your service, of course, but I enjoy seeing the Turkish countryside and people although I must admit it is a long trip."

"Are you are taking the family with you?"

"Not this time. Rhonda and the kids are heavily involved in summer activities."

"What do you hope to accomplish?"

"It's just a routine liaison trip. I'll visit the Turkish Navy Black Sea Unit, the military unit at Sinop and the province governor."

"That's right. You were stationed at Sinop when we had U.S. Forces there."

"Yep. It was a great tour in those days. Our unit was known as Diogenese Station."

"How long will you be gone?"

"About five days. A day up, a day back and three days on the ground."

"Well, pass my regards to the Governor. He's a great guy. And drive carefully."

An hour later, Captain Alvarez was on the outskirts of the Turkish capitol in a small DAS sedan headed north toward Sinop. The air conditioned Toyota was comfortable in the very hot, dry, and dusty Turkish summer, although the driver's space in the small car was somewhat cramped for the 6'2" former Naval Academy basketball player. The traffic was heavy on the two-lane highway now filled with a combination of heavily loaded trucks, private cars, motorcycles, motorbikes, and just about anything that had wheels. The private cars particularly jockeyed for position, taking any chance to gain even one more position in the long line of traffic. None of this bothered Ben Alvarez. He was resolved that the trip would take him the best part of eleven hours, allowing for stops for lunch and dinner so there was no point in being in a hurry. He would enjoy the trip.

Captain Alvarez had twenty-one years of service in the U.S. Navy. He was a ship driver with a Naval Intelligence sub-specialty and he'd previously served in Turkey for a year in 1989-90. As a Catholic, he had studied Latin early and when he went to language school as a Lieutenant, Turkish came easily for him. He thoroughly enjoyed his first tour in Turkey and when the opportunity came for service in the DAS, he jumped at the chance. Although the job wasn't going to lead to Flag rank, he and his wife enjoyed foreign service and the unusual opportunities with such assignment offered. He and his family had not been disappointed. Although the Turks tended to be closed-mouthed and secretive about their military activities, Ben Alvarez's linguistic skills and easy going personality made him welcome at Turkish naval facilities throughout the country. "He's a natural," his boss, Colonel Lipmann always said.

The day passed without major event as Alvarez drove through the mostly rural countryside with the elevation gradually increasing as he neared the northern portion of Turkey. The small hotel where he had made a reservation in

Sinop faithfully kept his room. Although it was after 9:00 p.m., the manager insisted he have a light meal of fish and vegetables with one of the local beers in the hotel's congenial dining room. Alvarez pleaded that it wasn't necessary because he had stopped for a snack on the road, but knew he could not turn down the hospitality. He acceded with good humor and feinted reluctance, a style the Turks loved and after taking his seat at a prepared table, was immediately joined by the manager and two of the hotels regulars for an hour of jovial conversation.

The next morning after a breakfast of local fruit, fresh yogurt, and the strongest of Turkish coffees, Alvarez set out in his car for the twenty minute drive up to the military installation atop Sinop's highest hill overlooking the Black Sea.

It was a clear day with a white chop on the dark waters and more than a mild wind blowing from the sea. When he pulled up to the gate of the old military post, the two Turkish sentries signaled him to stop and asked for some identification. When he replied in Turkish and told them "I am the American Naval Attaché here to see your commanding officer," they were surprised, quickly came to attention, and said they would have to call their Headquarters for further instructions. Then one of the sentries immediately turned and ran to the guard shack and picked up a phone. Alvarez smiled, having been through this type of routine many times before. Soon after the guard had completed his call, a Jeep drove down from the top of the hill containing a Turkish Army driver and officer. Ben saw that the officer was the Installation Commander Colonel Dregan whom Ben knew from an earlier visit to Sinop.

"Captain Alvarez. Welcome," the Colonel said getting out of his Jeep and walking over to Alvarez's car.

"Colonel Dregan. Good to see you again. Thanks for coming down to meet me," Alvarez replied getting out of his car and exchanging salutes with the Turkish Officer.

"Please park your car here at the gate and we will go in my vehicle."

Ben then moved the car, locked it, and climbed into the back of the Turkish Army Jeep.

"I brought the Jeep instead of my official sedan because I knew you would like a tour of the installation first thing. Right, Captain?" The Colonel spoke in English and Alvarez in Turkish, both out of respect for the other's language and to improve their own proficiency.

"Yes, sir. It is always great to return to Diogenese Station. I have very fond memories of the year I served here. Most impressive for Americans was the history of this area and realizing that the famous philosopher, Diogenese himself, actually walked this very ground more than 3,000 years ago looking for one honest man."

"Yes, yes. We are still looking for that man," remarked the Colonel and laughed heartily.

Most of the morning was spent driving around the old installation that had been one of the key Cold War monitoring locations where the Turks and their American Allies looked and listened across the Black Sea into Soviet territory. For years, American servicemen and women of all services and their Turkish counterparts sat side by side in one of the most forward and dangerous outposts keeping tabs on the Great Russian Bear. Captain Alvarez thought to himself that Sinop was now only a specter of the dynamic activity, excitement, and numbers of people that were once there. The huge operations building, the rows of barracks, the dining hall, the movie, the library, the headquarters building, the motor pool, and the many maintenance shops all seemed to be at about one-tenth utilization.

"Sad," he thought. "But times change and our technology has improved so much that it has made places like Sinop almost obsolete."

Alvarez's visit to Diogenese Station was concluded at Colonel Dregan's Headquarters after a briefing on the current

Turkish activities at Sinop and more Turkish coffee than the naval officer could drink.

"Captain, it's time for you to go," the colonel said, looking at his watch and smiling. "I promised our Navy you would not be late for lunch. They are... how you say it... a little pissed... that you, a navy officer, visits the Army first, but of course, I know it is because of my rank and the protocol, right?"

"Yes, sir. We military diplomats must always follow protocol and you, sir, are the senior Turkish officer in the area."

Colonel Dregan's driver returned Ben to his car and as Ben started the car and headed down the hill, he took one more look at the large building on the very top of the hill. It was the building that served as the Bachelor Officers Quarters for the officers assigned to Sinop during Ben's tour. Ben remembered his time there fondly and thought once more of the Officer's Club in the basement of the BOQ known as the DOOM Club, as in Diogenese Officers Open Mess. He had spent many nights there enjoying the camaraderie of his fellow officers that comes when Americans are serving their country in far away lands. "Many a good night," he remembered.

The Turkish Naval Base was not far away. As he drove down the narrow road leading back into town and further down the coast to the base, he went over the itinerary in his mind. He would first join the Senior Officer Present Ashore and his staff for a formal luncheon in the Commander's Mess at the base. Following that, he would spend the afternoon visiting the shore staff officers to discuss Turkish naval operations on the Black Sea and particularly, U.S. military assistance to Turkey which had declined dramatically in the last few years. He knew the Turks were hopeful that their support to NATO in the actions against Serbia would result in increased aid from the U.S. He expected to receive a number of pitches this afternoon for needed naval equipment. Tonight the officers would host a dinner for Ben at one of their favorite watering holes that would be fun, but would probably test his stamina for beer and raki. Then tomorrow, Ben would get his sea legs back by spending the day aboard one of the Turkish patrol boats on the Black Sea. Ben couldn't wait for that; it would be the best part of his visit.

The afternoon went pretty much as Ben expected except at the end of the day, when he went by the base commander's office to express his appreciation. The commander, Captain Outziz, was with a Turkish Customs Officer who worked closely with the Turkish Navy in Sinop. Outziz explained that the Customs Officer had just related a story to them that might be of interest to Captain Alvarez. The Customs Officer then told Alvarez the following:

"Since the end of the Cold War, the commerce between Turkey, Russia, and the Ukraine has markedly increased. The seabourne traffic across the Black Sea is now very heavy and keeps Turkish Customs and the Navy very busy. More Russian and Ukrainian tourists come to all our ports along the northern coast of Turkey. This has been good for trade and our country. And many of our ships carry cargo to and from many Russian and Ukrainian ports. One such small ship that is home-ported in Sinop has been particularly active in this regard. We watched this fellow very carefully and found he was breaking the rules. We then... how do you say... 'busted him.'" This last lost something in Turkish, but Ben nodded to indicate he understood. The Customs Officer continued:

"Because his infraction was relatively minor, we told him we would allow him to keep his license and Captain's papers if he agreed to keep us informed about other unusual activities taking place, particularly at the Russian ports. He agreed and has been quite helpful to us, particularly regarding smuggling activities. He recently told us a story that we are not sure what to do about and thought maybe you could help us."

"If we can, we will certainly try," Ben replied.

"Very well then, the Captain informed us that he had been hired by a shipping company in Odessa to deliver a cargo of caviar to a destination in Alexandria, Egypt. The company that was shipping the cargo was identified as the Black Sea Fisheries of Kiev. The shipping company advised our Captain that the cargo would be accompanied by three BSFK escorts who would load and unload the cargo and then require return passage to Odessa. When our Captain asked the tonnage of the cargo, the shipping company replied that they didn't know for sure; however, they had provided his hold capacity to the fish company in Kiev who responded that they would pay for the ship's full capacity roundtrip. When our Captain asked if there would be a return cargo, he was told by the shipping company that it was unknown."

"Did the Captain pick up the cargo?" Ben asked.

"Yes. He said that the pick up time for the cargo was designated as 11:00 p.m. in the evening in spite of his request that any loading be done during the daylight hours. According to the Captain, just before the designated time, a small truck of no more than one ton capacity showed up at the dock in Odessa. A man dressed in work clothes suitable for a sea voyage introduced himself in Russian as Mr. Sarnov and told the Captain that he and the two others with him were prepared to load the twenty-four ten kilo containers of caviar by hand. The Captain was surprised by the small size of the cargo and his offer to let his crew assist in placing the cargo inside the hold, was refused. Sarnov himself only supervised the other two, but the unloading from the truck marked on the outside panels in Cyrillic alphabet 'Black Sea Fisheries' and loading into the ship was completed in less than 30 minutes. The driver of the truck departed the dock immediately after the last container was removed. Mr. Sarnov then advised the Captain that he would like to get underway as soon as possible. Sarnov also told the Captain that one of the two other men accompanying him would remain in the hold with the cargo and be relieved periodically by the other man. The Captain advised Sarnov that the security wasn't necessary, that he could vouch for his crew, but Sarnov was adamant. Sarnov then departed for the cabin space the Captain had made available and remained there until the ship was close to Alexandria.

"The designated location in Alexandria was an anchorage furthest from the port. When the ship arrived four nights later, there was no other craft in the anchorage to meet it. Sarnov then advised the Captain to anchor and make a cell phone call. A small launch appeared shortly thereafter with three crewmen who looked Arab. Sarnov and his two helpers transferred the cargo, gave the Captain instructions to standby, and all six of them and the cargo left in the launch. It returned after about three hours and Sarnov directed the Captain to get underway. The Captain noted that the launch that returned Sarnov to the ship had its name on the stern covered with a hanging canvas, but as it pulled away, the wind lifted it slightly, revealing three Arabic characters."

The Customs Official then passed a copy of a small piece of paper with the three Arabic characters. "Our translators say that these three characters translate into English to the word, 'AMIR'."

The voyage back to Odessa passed without incident according to the Captain, with Sarnov and his two assistants staying in their cabins and having their meals there. In Odessa, the three men departed on foot immediately after docking. The Captain did not note anyone meeting them."

"What do you make of this, sir?" Lieutenant Commander Alvarez asked the customs official.

"According to the Captain, the cargo had already been cleared by the Ukrainian Customs. It was so indicated on the bill of lading that he picked up from the shipping company at the dock in Odessa. Caviar is certainly a valuable cargo but in that small a quantity? And with the security and the unusual circumstances of not wanting our ship captain to know who the cargo was delivered to? We suspect a major smuggling operation. Maybe gold, jewels, drugs, who knows?"

"Have you tried to identify the ship in Alexandria from the three Arabic characters, sir?" Alvarez asked.

"Yes, we asked the Egyptian Customs counterparts but they said they could not help us, given only the three characters and the not unusual appearance of the launch."

"So, how might the U.S. be of assistance, sir?"

"Well, we asked our headquarters in Ankara to assist but they didn't sound very hopeful. Very busy, of course. You know how it is in higher headquarters don't you Captain?" The Customs Official said somewhat sheepishly looking and smiling at the others in the room for support.

"Well, I'm not sure there is anything we can do. We might help you with the mystery launch's name, but as the Egyptians said, three characters and an ordinary small boat are not much to go on. Nevertheless, when I get back to Ankara, I'll see what we can do. It'll take some time, but I can promise you an answer, even if it's negative. All right, sir? The minute I find out anything I'll send it back to you through Captain Outziz," Alvarez concluded, gesturing toward his Turkish Navy hosts.

That night, while changing clothes for his dinner with his Turkish Navy friends, he made a few notes on the story the Turkish customs official had related. "The Turks think they are onto a smuggling operation. But could it be something more sinister?" Alvarez asked himself.

CHAPTER 14

WASHINGTON

June and the long hot summer were ensconced in the nation's capitol. And that's exactly what it was for the group of people who had dedicated their lives to protecting America's national security interests at home and abroad. Long hours, long days, and hot, sticky problems almost everywhere. The conflict continued in Serbia almost unabated. NATO bombing of Yugoslavia continued relentlessly without obvious effect on the Serb's resolve. The proponents of the bombing in the NATO nations daily recounted the massive damage to the country's infrastructure and the increasing pressure on its leader, Milosevic. Still, Milosevic refused to cave in. The U.N. War Crimes Tribunal indicted Milosevic and several of his henchmen for crimes in Kosovo. But many felt the Tribunal's timing only undermined efforts to reach a diplomatic solution. And NATO began marshalling upwards of 50,000 peace enforcement ground forces.

Congress released its report on Chinese nuclear espionage theft of America's nuclear secrets calling for blame to be placed on the Clinton administration, the National Security Adviser, the Secretary of Energy, the Attorney General and the Justice Department, the FBI, and a host of others. Two nuclear powers, India and Pakistan, resurrected their long standing Himalayan border disputes over Kashmir and began exchanging significant artillery fire, and rattling their nuclear sabers. In Jerusalem, Israeli police beat off Palestinian demonstrators in a violent confrontation following the election of a new Israeli Prime Minister. The FBI's web site was shut down by hackers in the United States and around the world. It was the first publicly acknowledged attack against the FBI from cyber space. It caused quite a stir. And the State Department, DAS, FBI, and CIA became increasingly concerned that a terrorist group would strike an American embassy somewhere in the world this summer. Yet, no firm indications were evident—just a feeling of anticipation.

On a Monday morning at 7:30, Bart Lowe was just crossing the 14th Street Bridge heading south on I-95 toward Washington Boulevard that would lead him to the DAS Headquarters building in Ballston. He normally left his quarters at Bolling Air Force Base no later than 7:00 a.m. because of the heavy traffic going into Washington. Once he reached the 14th Street Bridge however, the traffic was lighter and he would be at his desk by 7:45.

Bart felt tired this Monday morning—a new feeling for him. But "why not?" he thought. He had been back at the DAS job for more than three months now and the pace seemed to be greater each week. Not the pace he was setting like in the old days but a pace dictated by world events and the many masters that could pull the strings of the DAS and its "new" Director. He had worked seven days the past week; at the office, at the many high level meetings in town, and at the mandatory social events that were a must in order to keep tabs on foreign policy matters in Washington.

He had left the office yesterday at mid-afternoon. Not because he was caught up, but because he had fallen so far behind in his personal affairs and correspondence. He stayed with that until ten last night and then fell asleep while trying to read a John Grisham book. And he wasn't tired because his deputy or his people were not pulling their weight. Quite the contrary. The dedication of the people in the DAS was extraordinary; "even the civilians," he chuckled to himself as he drove along. He practically had to order Barbara Barnsworth not to come in to the DAS yesterday. She had been putting in twelve-hour days since Bart arrived back at the job.

He turned off Washington Boulevard into the DAS secure underground parking garage. Once he was recognized by the garage security guard, he parked and locked his car, went into the building, took his security badge out of his inside coat pocket, and placed it above his coat lapel and was waved through the electronic security gates by the entrance guards. Riding up to the 14th floor on the elevator, he took out his day's schedule that Joan had given to him on Friday night and reviewed the very full day, and especially the last item, an office call by an old friend, Ed Royster, who had been the Director of the Defense Intelligence Agency during Bart's last year at the DAS in 1991. "It'll be good to see Ed," he thought as the elevator doors opened at the 14th floor. Bart realized he wasn't feeling tired anymore as he headed down the hall for his office at a brisk pace.

The morning World-Wide Operations Update or WWOU as the DAS staff liked to call it, was limited, at Lowe's direction, to one hour in duration. This morning, Bart knew the Operations Staff was really constrained to get in all the developments taking place around the world. Based on a multitude of new requirements coming from national and theater consumers, along with the initiative coverage by attachés in response to events in their countries, DAS information reporting was at an all time high—up a full 25% over what was considered normal. In addition, General Lowe's recent requirement for New and/or Dangerous Contingency Area reporting had sensitized the U.S. military and other government agencies and had the effect of generating even more specific requests for information. One of the DAS staff officers quipped, "Information and Intelligence reporting is a lot like sex. Everyone wants some. And the more you get, the more you want." Bart believed it. He also spent an inordinate amount of time on the telephone either talking with the DATTs in troubled areas or responding to requests from J2s and CINCs for even more information.

When the update was over, Bart glanced down at his notebook and realized that he had taken a full page of notes on items for which he personally needed to take some action and he suspected that Barbara had made an even longer list.

When Bart and Barbara walked back to their respective offices together, Barbara added, "I see that Ed Royster is on your calendar today. What is that about, if I may ask?"

"You may, but I don't know. Joan scheduled it and according to her, Ed just called and said he wanted to stop by and see me. No particular subject mentioned."

"Have you seen him since you've been back?"

"Nope."

"He's one of my favorite people. He was at DIA when I worked there and he was very helpful to me with career advice. I haven't seen him either in some time and if you don't mind, I'd like to stick my head in the door and just say hello."

"Certainly. As soon as I find out what he wants, I'll give you a yell and you can join us. I'm sure he'll want to see you," Bart replied. "By the way, Barbara, do you know what Ed is doing now? Is he retired?"

"I don't think so. I believe that he went to work for one of the Washington area firms that provide military expertise and training to developing countries. I think it's known as MILTRAIN."

"Oh, yeah. I've heard them mentioned by the State Department. They evidently have a number of contracts with State. Okay then, I'll let you know when he's here."

"Thanks. Oh, Bart, I almost forgot. I meant to give you an update on the program for periodic briefings that we worked out for Senator Karson. We've done three now and Maureen says the Senator is very pleased. I must admit it was a good idea for you to suggest that Lieutenant General Eways at DIA take the lead for the substantive intelligence updates for the Senator with DIA analysts, with our guys who have served in the Mid-East countries going along to answer his 'What's it really like on the ground,' questions. And DIA each time has included our favorite analyst, Tony Roper, for the terrorist perspective, which is one of the main areas of interest to the Senator."

"Great, Barbara. And what's in it for us?" Bart asked.

"I've forwarded to Maureen our top-ten unfunded requirements and she is optimistic that at least some of them can be supported."

"I love a win-win situation. Take a pat on the back for that action, Barbara."

"Oh, no. It was your idea, Bart."

"Okay, we'll both take credit. Here's to us," he said, rising his right thumb in the air.

When Bart was seated at his desk, he looked first at the intimidating stack of actions labeled "hot," then paused, remembering how disappointed he was that in the more than three months that he had been back at the DAS, he had only been able to visit a relatively few attachés in Europe and the Balkans. "Can I re-prioritize?" he wondered. And almost before he could finish the thought, Joan entered and said, "Ready with your secure conference call to Mr. Kitchen at the FBI and Ms. Softly at CIA."

Bart must have stared blankly at Joan because she quickly picked up the card schedule from his desk and pointed to the 9:10 a.m. item. Jarred back to reality, he remembered. "Good morning, John. Good morning, René." Because of the time lapse since the last bin Laden terrorist attack against the U.S. Embassy in Nairobi, and the increasing tension anticipating the where and when of the next attack, Bart found himself talking with Kitchen and Softly three to four times a week. "Maybe this time," he thought, "there will be a breakthrough on his whereabouts and his next target." But after fifteen minutes of shared information and exchanges, it was once again clear that the United States was no nearer to solving the bin Laden problem.

The day went by quickly for Bart and before he knew it, it was 6:00 p.m., and Joan, still at her desk, announced on the intercom, "Sir, General Royster is here."

"Great. I'll be right out. And Joan, will you get us some iced tea?" Bart asked. He rose from behind his desk, and walked over to the office door to welcome Royster. Bart had not seen Ed since Bart's retirement in '91. Ed was Bart's senior, but a good friend and mentor, and he'd retired one year before Bart. He remembered Ed as a Hollywood casting, picture perfect, West Point graduate General. He was handsome, athletic, capable, respected, and liked by almost everyone who knew him. As Director of DIA, he had been Bart's and the DAS' strongest supporter.

As Bart greeted General Royster, he was not surprised to see that time had been kind to his friend. The sandy brown hair had thinned some and he had grayed at the temples. But his deep blue eyes set in a tanned face were as honest and penetrating as Bart remembered. His blue shirt and perfectly tailored blue suit would be admired in any of the power circles in Washington.

"Ed! It's great to see you," Bart said, sincerely glad to see such a respected soldier again. He grasped Royster's outstretched hand and placed his other hand on Ed's shoulder. "Please come in and make yourself comfortable."

After they were both seated, Royster on the couch and Bart in the nearby leather easy chair, Ed began by saying, "Bart, congratulations on your new, old job. I was out of town at the time of your swearing-in ceremony but I was delighted to learn that you were coming back to Washington. Did they have to drag you kicking and screaming?" This question asked mostly in jest.

"Thanks. I received your nice note and was sorry you couldn't make the swearing-in. And no, they didn't. You know me. I guess I have never been able to say 'no' to the call of a bugle. But Ed, frankly, since I've been back, I have begun to wonder if I made the right decision. The pace seems even faster than when we were together. I just hope that I can keep up with it and provide the leadership that our attachés need in these crazy times."

"There's no doubt in my mind Bart, that you're the right man for the job. And I've heard a number of others in this town say the same thing. Speaking of crazy times, that's kind of why I'm here today. By way of background, when I retired, I had an offer from a West Point classmate to join a firm he founded, MILTRAIN. Perhaps you know of it?"

"Yes. I know that it has an excellent reputation with the State Department."

"Well, we try. We do a lot of work for them as an extension of U.S. foreign policy. When I first joined the firm, they wanted me for my intelligence background so that I could advise them on the intelligence community's thinking on the strategic role of many of their clients. However, and this is a big however, they wanted never to be perceived as playing an intelligence role. They were concerned about credibility with their clients. So I have been squeaky clean with respect to any intelligence activities."

Bart acknowledged this from his old friend but was not sure where the conversation was going.

"However, again, a big however, something recently came to my attention that I can't sit on. I've been agonizing for the past few days on how to handle it. But, fortunately, it doesn't impact adversely on our customer so I decided to pass it you and let you decide what to do with it," a small smile appearing on Royster's face.

"Ed, it seems to me that we went down some similar paths in our earlier association. And if I recall correctly, those paths always meant something of a headache for me." Bart responded with his own smile.

"Well Bart, your job at that time was clearly with delicate matters, wasn't it?" Ed asked, breaking into an even bigger smile.

"Yeah, right. Particularly when my friends made it so!" Bart said and laughed.

"At any rate here's what I have," Ed said, opening a small leather note pad and removing a folded piece of paper. He carefully unfolded the paper and Bart could see that it was quite dirty and charred on one end. He passed it to Bart and said, "This paper contains four items, apparently handwritten in Arabic. One of our contacts that we have worked with for a number of years gave this to me and claims that he obtained it in Baghdad approximately two weeks ago while visiting there. According to him, he was crossing a street in downtown Baghdad and witnessed a terrible auto crash. A taxi ran a red light and ran into another car. The car that was hit rolled over several times and burst into flames. Our contact, along with other pedestrians, quickly ran to the scene to see if they could help. Several men were able to free the driver of the burning car, but his injuries looked very serious. Another man had been thrown from the car and was unconscious and looked as though he had several broken bones. Close to the burning car, our contact noticed this piece of paper. It was just starting to burn. Our contact assumed it had fallen from the car and thought it could be something of value, so he quickly stepped on it to stop the flame and then put it into his pocket. Ambulances and the Iraqi police arrived shortly thereafter and took the three injured people away. Since none of the three were conscious and he was reluctant to talk with the police, he just kept the paper. After the crowd thinned out, he took the paper out of his pocket and looked at it. Shocked at what he read, he was nervous about carrying it around, but decided to hide it in his sock. He was able to conceal it when he returned to his own country of Bahrain. When he arrived here last Friday for a scheduled meeting with State and us, he passed me the paper and his translation. And here's his English translation which one of my Arabists says is correct. The translation read:

- *Coordination with W.M. continues. Targets passed, Phase two training begun.*
- *Special weapon acquisition finalized. Deposit made. Delivery date and place agreed upon.*

- *C and B weapons identified and available.*
- *Cyber weapon progressing. Recommendations expected soon.*

"Holy shit!" Bart said, feeling a nausea in his stomach, and thinking "What could this mean?"

CHAPTER 15

ISLAMABAD—FLORIDA—NEW YORK

On a hot afternoon in July, on a busy street not more than a mile from the U.S. Embassy in Islamabad, Pakistan, a well known shop that specialized in fine wooden jewelry boxes of all shapes and sizes was busy, as usual, with a large number of western tourists. The shop had reopened its doors at 4:00, after the noon break, and more than twenty people were now browsing through the shop's many wares, being helped by the six men who handled the sales, wrapping and special orders. The craftsmen who actually built the inlaid teak boxes worked twelve hours a day in four large workshop rooms in the rear of the store. The shop was well known for its quality workmanship and was recommended by most hotels in Islamabad to their guests. What was not known, except by a few key officials in the Pakistani government, was that behind its excellent reputation, the shop was also the headquarters for bin Laden's al Qaeda organization in Pakistan.

In a suite of simple rooms behind the workshops, Wadih Mohammed sat alone going over in his mind the planning for the greatest undertaking by al Qaeda since its inception. Wadih had been with bin Laden in 1989 when he issued his own fatwa (*religious decree*) for the killing of U.S. military in Saudi Arabia and Somalia. He had assisted bin Laden in 1991 in moving from Peshawar to the Sudan when pressure from the United States made it impossible for the Pakistani government to continue its overt support. And again, when the Sudan became too risky, to Heimand Province in southern Afghanistan, and now, to the northern mountainous region of Afghanistan. Wadih Mohammed was the chief architect of bin Laden's terrorist organization with cells in more than twenty-five countries and its key operations planner.

He and bin Laden had been suspicious of the action proposed by Saddam Hussein, but to date, Saddam had fulfilled each promise made and, wonder of wonders, had delivered the nuclear weapon, a feat that the al Qaeda organization had been trying unsuccessfully for years to accomplish. And their own expert had inspected the devices in Egypt and assured its genuineness. It was now in safe al Qaeda hands on its way to the United States. "Allah be praised," Wadih thought with near orgasmic thoughts.

Both Wadih and bin Laden knew that the chemical or biological and cyber weapons, not nearly so difficult to make, and with the required expertise present in Iraq, would be forthcoming soon. Bin Laden had given Wadih the order to proceed with the full operational planning for *Retribution*.

Wadih Mohammed had returned last night after spending two days in Afghanistan, one day with bin Laden and one day with Abdul Khalid. Bin Laden had instructed Wadih to resist any urging from Ali Hassan and Saddam Hussein to hurry *Retribution*. Bin Laden said, "I suspect that Saddam's anxiousness to carry out the strike is based on concern for his own longevity. Saddam has many enemies and only Allah knows how much longer he can be the master of Iraq."

Bin Laden told Wadih that he had decided that a diversion somewhere else in the world would be required prior to executing *Retribution* in order to shift some of the security concerns that presently existed in the United States. When this was discussed, they both agreed that a strike that had already been planned for the fall would serve that purpose. Bin Laden directed Wadih to implement its execution.

The self-appointed Holy One was optimistic that Saddam and he could reach agreement on the final three targets and alternates. This, he said, was because of the good faith shown on Saddam's part in agreeing to the ten targets used for the ongoing phase two training. Nor did bin Laden believe that General Uday would play any significant role beyond that already played in the building of the first target list. Then too, bin Laden said, "Saddam will have no choice but to agree with our final judgment as the strikes will be carried out by our al Qaeda soldiers of Allah." As always, Wadih was inspired when he was with bin Laden.

In the day he spent with Abdul Khalid, he witnessed the target-specific training that Khalid had designed and the impressive results and motivation that Khalid's nine trainees exhibited. At least three of the nine were personally known to Wadih Mohammed and as he heard and watched each of them describe in detail and then demonstrate how they would successfully reconnoiter, access, defeat or bypass security systems and then attack mock targets with explosives, simulated chemical or biological agents and cyber weapons, he came away impressed that bin Laden's decision to select Khalid to carry out al Qaeda's most holy mission was Allah inspired.

After the training demonstrations, Wadih had taken a walk alone amid the then quiet, desolate, Afghanistan mountains and thought about his role and the role of the believers he had just seen in mock action and was inspired to do all that he could to make *Retribution* a blow the United States would never forget.

That night, after evening prayers, Abdul Khalid outlined for Wadih his thoughts on which targets would be the most accessible and what support would be required in the United States and elsewhere for his three teams to be successful in their attacks. Because Wadih Mohammed had always suspected that Khalid had somehow been at least partly responsible for to the failure of the Trade Center Bombing, Wadih questioned Khalid relentlessly, attempting to find fault in his approach and thinking, but could find none. He was impressed at how much forethought, reasoning, and operational expertise Khalid obviously applied. "The man must never sleep," he thought. So thorough, so detailed, so well laid out was Khalid's approach that by the time they had concluded their discussions, Wadih had made up his mind to provide Khalid everything he wanted, "Inshallah."

Now back in Islamabad, Wadih knew the things he must do. He rose from the cushion where he had been sitting and padded barefoot over to a small desk made of cedar sitting on a brilliantly colored Persian rug. He slipped into the small, but sturdy, handcrafted chair and removed paper and pen from the single drawer in the desk and began slowly writing some very important instructions to the heads of the al Qaeda cells at five locations: Cairo, London, New York, Washington, and Miami. When he finished writing the first set of instructions, he picked up a small bell from the desk and shook it three or four times creating a pleasant metal against porcelain sound. The assistant, who sat outside Wadih's door whenever Wadih was there, heard the summons and entered the room immediately.

"Chie, mayherbonnie, dood or cheeni, naheen." *(Tea please, no cream or sugar).*

The assistant bowed his head in acknowledgement, quickly left the room and was back in less than five minutes with a freshly brewed pot of tea, and a cup. He knew that whenever Wadih Mohammed was writing at his desk, he would consume large amounts of tea.

After Wadih had poured the first cup of tea and tasted it with satisfaction, he sat the cup down and reached into his pocket for a small key ring. He found the key he was looking for and used it to unlock a small safe that was located behind the desk. He reached inside and shifted a number of packets of foreign currencies until he found what he was looking for—a 6 x 4 inch pad containing about a hundred sheets of paper with row after row of letters. He removed the one time pad of encryption codes and began the laborious process of encoding the five different texts of instructions to the cells. He knew it would probably take him about four hours. And although he didn't look forward to it, he had done it many times before. When he finished, the encoded texts would be put onto the global Internet.

The next night at 11:00 p.m. in a comfortable, but not up-scale, housing development in Cape Canaveral, Florida, Samir al-Misri, a former Egyptian citizen, said good night to his wife and two sons and sat down at his computer located in a small room behind the garage. Sam, as his friends in the neighborhood liked to call him, enjoyed sitting at the computer and surfing the 'Net for 30 or 45 minutes before turning in.

Sam and his wife took advantage of the liberal immigration laws and emigrated to the United States ten years ago and were now both naturalized U.S. citizens. He owned and operated two shrimp boats that fished the waters of the Atlantic between Cape Canaveral and Key West. In addition to his regular wholesale accounts for the fresh shrimp and some fish, his wife helped him operate a small stand at the Canaveral docks. Business was good and as a result, life was good for Sam and his family and for the crew members that operated his shrimp trawlers. Several of his crew were recently arrived Arabs from several countries in the Mid East. Sam went out of his way to assist Arabs coming to the States and was always successful in getting them settled. It was easy for Sam. There was always work for people on the many shrimp boats operating out of Cape Canaveral. And Disney World in Orlando and other attractions there, were always looking for low wage people—the same for Miami and the rest of the tourist industry. Sam never had any trouble in getting people jobs in Florida. Sam was of the Islamic faith but kept a low profile, and when he worshipped publicly, it was at a mosque in Orlando.

Tonight, Sam, following his normal routine, pulled up an international chat room on the 'Net and was surprised to recognize a message for him. He promptly downloaded the message and logged off. Leaving the computer on, he got up from his seat and went to the garage. He took a short ladder off a hook on the wall and positioned it in front of several shelves he had put up on the inside of the garage wall. From the very top shelf, he pulled down a large coffee can. He took the lid off the can and reached inside and pulled out a long, narrow pad. Climbing back down the ladder, he retraced his steps back to his computer table and, using the pad, began to decode the message that had been sent to him from al Qaeda headquarters somewhere in the Middle East. When he finished, he learned that he was to receive three more individuals at the beginning of September and get them settled into suitable covers for some future task.

Sam had been the head of the al Qaeda terrorist organization for the southeastern United States for almost ten years. He had never taken an active part in an actual terrorist action; his role was too important for such a risk. Mostly, he received al Qaeda soldiers, pre-arranged safe houses, transportation, financing and covers. His family had no idea of his covert life and they would have been shocked if someone suggested that Sam was a terrorist. But Sam felt an intense inner pride in what he was doing for the cause and would, without hesitation, be willing to become a martyr if required for the Jihad.

After deleting the encrypted message from his computer files, returning the decoding pad to its hiding place in the garage, and shutting down the computer, Sam turned on the TV, but muted so it wouldn't wake the family.

He confirmed the earlier weather reports that he had seen and as he switched off the remote control, he thought to himself, "Another ninety-six degree July day. It should be a good day for the shrimp!"

The following day in New York, a vehicle that many motorists took to be a police sedan, was heading north on the

New York Freeway toward Brooklyn. The car, a 1998 Chevrolet, was painted blue and white, had a panel of emergency lights across its top and was marked "Metropolitan Security Service" on both sides of the car. The midday traffic pulled to the right of the freeway to permit the vehicle to pass. There were two uniformed individuals in the front of the car. The driver was a young probationary officer with less than one year's employment with the Metropolitan Security Service. The individual on the passenger side was a veteran of eight years of service with Metropolitan and wore the gold bars of a lieutenant. His name was Nasim Haddad. They were on their way to Fort Hamilton where Lieutenant Haddad would spend two hours with the Metropolitan Security Service Detachment that provided security for the historic old Army fort. Up until a few years ago, the Army had provided its own security with military police, but the cutbacks in military manpower had caused the Army at Fort Hamilton to contract out some of its routine duties like security. The security detachment there was one of ten Metropolitan Security Service contracts that Lieutenant Haddad supervised. Metropolitan had more than 200 security services contracts in and around New York City and an excellent reputation for its security expertise and the quality of the company's personnel. Lieutenant Haddad was originally from Gaza. When he first came to New York, he worked a number of jobs so that he could take college level courses at night. After two years of college, he applied for and received an appointment to the New York City Police Academy. After graduation, he spent three years as a New York patrolman. He had a perfect record as a patrolman and when he applied for a position with the Metropolitan Security Service, he was quickly hired as a security guard with better pay, benefits, and hours.

In the eight years Haddad had been with Metropolitan, he had advanced rapidly to corporal, sergeant, lieutenant, and in one month, he would be promoted to captain and take on even more responsibility for Metropolitan. Haddad liked his work and was well thought of by his subordinates and superiors. He was well paid and lived in a roomy bachelor apartment in Brooklyn. His apartment was near the Verrazano Bridge and he could see Governors Island from his bedroom window. He was quite proud of his stereo and computer systems and spent much of his leisure time listening to music and working with computer programs on his computer. He also used the Internet to continue to improve his expanding knowledge of computer security systems. Haddad used his email to stay in touch with his Islamic friends throughout the seven boroughs—and his friends were many. His advice on security matters was often sought and often given.

Haddad's trip to the United States from Gaza many years ago, was financed by the Islamic Resistance Movement (known as Hamas). He was told at the time that he would be called upon to repay that debt. Over the years, many Muslims had asked him for non-sensitive information, which he had gladly passed on, but no one from Hamas had asked him to do anything. Perhaps they had forgotten. He was aware, of course, of the large number of militant Arab groups in New York and because of his contacts at the FBI, had some idea of their activities. He wasn't sure how he would react if someone from Hamas showed up and asked him to do something that would endanger his job at Metropolitan or that could be considered support to terrorist activities. He'd thought about it many times but then shrugged it off thinking, "I might never have to face that problem. I'll just have to wait and see."

That July night, after he had walked the six short blocks to his apartment building from Fort Hamilton, he used his outside entrance key to get into the lobby, checked his mail box, and then walked over to the open elevator and pressed the number six on the panel. Coming out of the elevator, he walked to his right and passed three doors to apartment 604. A second small key was produced and he opened the door, removed his hat, unfastened his pistol belt, and hung the black leather belt, holster, pistol, and hat, on top of the wall clothes tree. He then went quickly into his bedroom, changed into shorts, tank top, and moccasins, and returned to the kitchen to retrieve a Pepsi Cola from the refrigerator. He opened the can, took one long pull on the cold, sweet liquid, and wandered into the room that housed his computer system. He logged on, pulled down his email, and began to browse through them. Most of the messages were routine, but one caught his eye. It said, "Urgently need your help," and had an email return address he did not recognize.

CHAPTER 16

WASHINGTON

It was a Saturday night during the last week in August. Bart Lowe was sitting at his desk in his quarters at Bolling Air Force Base, finishing up some personal notes thanking a variety of people for their assistance to him—his broker in Florida, his doctor at Walter Reed Medical Center, and the Air Force NCO in charge of the Base Automotive Hobby Shop who had given him some helpful advice on maintaining his revered, but temperamental, Jaguar. He was dressed in dark trousers, a fresh shirt and tie, having showered a short time earlier. Before sitting down at the desk, he had fixed himself a Manhattan on the rocks and put a CD on the player. When he finished the correspondence, he noticed it was 6:30. He wouldn't leave the house for another thirty minutes. He was going to the Kennedy Center to its annual presentation of Swan Lake. He planned to pick up his companion for the evening, Maria Salah, at 7:30 at her apartment at the Watergate and walk the short distance from there to the Kennedy Center.

Relaxing now to the pleasant voice of Tony Bennett, he eased back in his high back leather desk chair and took a pull on his Manhattan and thought about how quickly the summer had passed. When Ed Royster had dropped by the office, and passed the cryptic note to him that was allegedly found in Baghdad, his first thought was that maybe they were onto something really big. But when he had summoned Jim Poreman and Barbara Barnsworth, they didn't necessarily agree. Jim pointed out that there were several possibilities. One—that it was some project being worked on by any one of several Iraqi ministries for a military exercise. Two—that the note was written by a member of the group that opposed Saddam. And three, that some form of deception was intended. Barbara agreed and suggested that the source of the info, Ed Royster's client, be investigated to determine his reliability and that CIA and Tom Mellon and the Defense Human Intelligence Service be requested to see if their assets could learn something more about the people who were involved in the automobile accident in Baghdad.

Bart reluctantly accepted their assessment and recommendations but directed that the information also be shared with John Kitchen at the FBI. René Softly at CIA, and Brigadier General Great at CENTCOM. And he told them to make sure that General Eways and Tony Roper at DIA were aware of the report. The important thing, they all agreed, was to protect the source of the information, indicate to all concerned that the information came from a "usually reliable source," and be on the lookout for anything else that might relate to the subject.

The rest of the time had been spent on the continuing high interest areas of Serbia and Kosovo, India and Pakistan, China, and North Korea. Milosevic had finally agreed to a peace plan, a compromise between the NATO and Russian proposals and a cease-fire had been declared. The occupation of Kosovo by the NATO and Russian contingents began and the first refugees had returned to Kosovo. All of the European DAOs had been impacted, reporting continued at an all time high and the DAOs in the Balkans were operating around the clock. The operations people at DAS headquarters concerned with the Balkans were on twenty-four hour a day shifts. The Chinese had suspended their military to military agreement with the U.S., and communications between the Chinese and the U.S. Embassy and DAO were strained. The resentment against Americans in Beijing and other Chinese cities made life very uncomfortable for embassy personnel and their families.

Bart had attended a DATT Conference at the SOUTHCOM Headquarters in Miami and from there, flew back with the U.S. Defense Attaché to Colombia for a two-day visit. It was a good change of pace from the stifling and humid hot days in Washington but Bart felt uncomfortable being away from DAS Headquarters too long given the major crisis situations in Europe and China. He was shocked to learn that the illegal drug situation in Colombia was no better in 1999 than when he had left the DAS eight years ago.

Bart left the quarters at 7:00. He went through the kitchen into the garage and got into the Jag, S-model convertible, backed out of the driveway and was soon out the guarded front gate and on his way to Washington.

There was still about an hour of daylight left when he pulled into the underground parking garage of the Watergate. Maria had suggested that he park in one of the two garage spaces allocated to her apartment. The spacious apartment was leased by the Lebanese Embassy and Maria had only one private automobile, a Lexus. Bart parked and locked the green Jag and headed for the elevator to the lobby. Marie was waiting on one of the lobby sofas and spotted Bart immediately as the elevator door slid open. He walked across the small lobby and reached for Maria's hand as she was rising. She took his hand and drew him near and kissed him softly on both cheeks. With high heels, she seemed as tall as Bart and her dark eyes met his with clear intensity. She was dressed in a black, sleeveless, floor length sheath dress. Her long hair was piled high on her head and she looked as though she had just stepped out of a fashion show. "Striking," Bart thought to himself. He couldn't remember seeing or knowing a more attractive woman.

"I don't think I will need this," indicating the white shawl that could be wrapped around her shoulders, "but sometimes the Kennedy gets cold."

"Would you like for me to carry it?" Bart asked.

"No, thank you. It's no trouble. We had better get started if we want to be on time for the first curtain."

"Then let's go," Bart answered with a smile and offered Maria his arm. They went out the revolving front door and began walking toward the Kennedy Center.

Once inside the Kennedy Center Opera House, they proceeded to the balcony level and received two programs from the waiting attendant who led them down the stairs to the box Bart had reserved.

"I don't think anyone else will be joining you tonight, sir. The show will start in seven minutes," the attendant informed them as he pushed the other two chairs aside in the four seat box.

The advantage of the Opera House boxes was that the view included only the front center stage. Velvet drapes were on both sides of the box and blocked the seats so that no one from the neighboring boxes could look across and see inside. Bart and Maria took advantage of the semi-bright overhead light to read their programs. They both had seen Swan Lake several times over the years but the cast tonight was a new one for them both.

As the lights dimmed, Bart glanced out of the side of his eye at the beautiful woman sitting beside him. He thought again that her beauty was striking. She could pass for an American anywhere but there was a certain look about her olive colored skin and high cheek bones that gave her a Mediterranean look.

They had seen each other about a dozen times since first meeting at the Lebanese Embassy three months ago. She had followed up quickly with an invitation for him and Jim Poreman to return to the Embassy of Lebanon for an in-depth briefing on her duties in Washington. Following that, she had asked him to join her at the Chevy Chase Club for lunch so that they might get to know each other better. And after that, a third invitation had been forthcoming from another friendly Embassy for an evening affair where he found himself as Maria's dinner partner. Her good offices with the wife of the military diplomat who hosted the party led Bart to believe that Maria had arranged the whole thing. At that point, he became nervous that perhaps he was being targeted by Maria for other than friendly reasons.

There was no question that he enjoyed her company but, "My God," he thought, "she is from a foreign intelligence service." Before anything went further, he felt compelled to ask John Kitchen and René Softly what they thought. They both had laughed. John had said, "Bart, she has been helpful to us for all intents and purposes for years. When our intelligence exchange first started years ago, we were suspicious as we always are. But this is one of the rare ones that we have gotten more out of than what we have put in. And I don't know a single U.S. spook in town who doesn't trust her. Let me suggest that you make a memo for your own security people of her interest and if anything untoward should ever take place, and I don't believe it will, then you'll be covered."

René told him, "Bart, Maria is one of the best. I don't know what we would have done without her in our coverage of the Middle East. She has given us so much over the years, I don't think we can ever repay her or her country. Her interest in you is probably as a woman and because you are a bachelor. Hell, I know if I wasn't married, I'd be interested in you!" Although they were on the phone, Bart suspected that he probably reddened slightly at René's remark. "I have a suggestion for you, Bart. Why not ask Maria why she seems so interested in you. I'll bet you'll get an honest answer."

Bart liked René's suggestion and the very next afternoon, when he and Maria were both at an Armed Forces Day Ceremony at the French Embassy, Bart took Maria aside and put the question to her. "Why so much interest in me?"

She had replied, "I would have thought you could have figured that out. I have been in this town for five years and you are the first real bachelor I have met. Everyone near my age in this town, in our business, is married. I have met my share of 'geographic bachelors,' but that's not my way. When I first met you, and Jim Poreman had told me that you were not married, I liked you right away and I thought you liked my company. Just because we each do classified work for our countries doesn't mean we can't be friends. But if you are uncomfortable with that, then so be it." And with that, she smiled and walked away.

For three days, Bart stewed over what to do. He had had a defense security clearance for years. He knew the questions that investigators asked about foreign contacts. He also knew how to recognize improper questions by a foreign person. And he sure as hell wouldn't answer any questions that were inappropriate. He did like Maria's company. So Bart dictated a memorandum to the DAS Security Division informing them of the contact with Ms. Salah for official and non-official purposes. Then he called Maria, said he was sorry and hoped that she would join him for dinner the following weekend. Since that time, they had done a number of social things together and thoroughly enjoyed each other's company. And tonight at the ballet, was no exception.

Shortly after the opening scene, Maria reached for Bart's hand and held it tightly. It was a warm, comforting feeling. The only other time in his life that Bart had held the hand of someone not American was during his first visit to Russia in the 1980s and his Intourist guide, Tatyana, had wanted to share an emotional moment in the old theater in Leningrad.

Bart looked over at Maria and could see she was very much involved in the stirring music and artistic presentation as the white costumed dancers moved gracefully across the heavily draped stage. They had not been intimate yet. Not even kissed—except Maria's traditional Lebanese greetings. Not even exchanged a real hug, but Bart had been close to her, helping her put on her coat, opening doors, pushing elevator buttons, and tonight in this dimly lit, romantic setting in the Kennedy Center. A little later, Maria shifted in her chair to be closer to Bart, released his hand and moved her hand up under his arm and placed her other hand on his arm so that she was holding his arm very close and the proximity of her caused Bart to be extra aware of her nearness and warmth. He desired her very much at that moment. He turned his head, leaned toward her and softly kissed her cheek. She, in turn, turned toward him and stared deeply into his eyes conveying a warmth that transferred to the pit of his stomach.

After the Swan Lake troupe had taken its last bow in response to the standing ovation, Bart and Maria walked back to the Watergate, joined closely by her holding on tightly to his arm and him being very conscious of the warm, full bodied, exceptionally attractive woman at his side. When they exited the elevator on the 7th floor, and walked down the plushly carpeted hallway to her apartment door she said, "You will come in for a drink, won't you, Bart?"

"I thought you'd never ask," replied Bart, resorting to an old cliché he had used for years, throwing his arms out in mock surrender.

Once inside, Maria suggested that he take off his jacket and make himself comfortable. She then kicked off her shoes and said she would get the liqueurs. As he waited, he surveyed the tasteful furnishings in the oversized Watergate apartment suitable for diplomatic entertaining. As he stretched out in an especially comfortable easy chair, he thought to himself, "I wonder if I will make it home tonight!" He made sure his beeper was on.

While Bart Lowe and Maria Salah were watching Swan Lake from a box in the balcony of the Opera House, there was a man downstairs in an aisle seat in the orchestra section, who was a regular patron of the Kennedy Center and had held season tickets for more than ten years. He, like Bart and Maria, had seen Swan Lake several times but it was one of his favorites and he was thoroughly enjoying tonight's performance. When intermission came, he walked out to the refreshment stand, purchased a small bottle of Perrier water, and made his way through the crowd to a corner where he could look out the tall, front windows, across the Potomac River to the skyline of Northern Virginia. He looked to the southeast to see if he could see the Pentagon. He could not because of the darkness and the trees along the Virginia side of the river. Nevertheless, he knew just where it was because it had been in his thoughts since last March.

Shar Baker was a chief engineer for the Bell Atlantic Telephone Company of Virginia and Maryland. He had been an American citizen for seventeen years and had worked for Bell Atlantic for fifteen years. When he first came to America from Palestine, his name had been Sharif al-Bakr. He decided to change it to Shar Baker to have a better chance for decent employment. As a young man, Bakr was drawn to the precepts of Islamic fundamentalism and joined the Abu Nidal Organization (ANO) in Palestine. He was later recruited by the intelligence arm of the ANO to become a "sleeper agent" in the United States. Bakr's instructions were to make a life for himself, acquire legal status, and when he was settled and in place, to report back to the ANO for further instructions. He was given five years to establish his cover. In compliance with his instructions, Bakr settled in the Northern Virginia area close to Washington. He used the small amount of money given to him by the ANO to educate himself, establish a residence, and find employment. He married an American woman, fathered two children, and later divorced. He performed well for Bell Atlantic, was regularly promoted, and lived comfortably in a high rise apartment complex in Arlington, Virginia. Over the years, he acted primarily as a reporting agent responding to various tasks received from the ANO, and he successfully arranged accommodations and meetings for visitors. In earlier years, he was disappointed in not having a more active role but in the last few years, he had lost some of his earlier fervent feelings and enjoyed his very pleasant life in his adopted country.

At the end of 1997, the Defense Department had announced a renovation of the Pentagon that would be ongoing for ten years. He reported this item at that time, along with several other items to the ANO, via a code system hidden in innocent appearing letters sent to family members still living in Palestine. He was surprised in the interest shown by the ANO in the Pentagon item and their subsequent tasking for further information on this subject. There wasn't much additional information that he could find other than the public announcement that large segments of the Pentagon staff would be moved out of the Pentagon temporarily to permit renovation of their portion of the building. Then, last March, an interesting thing happened. Bell Atlantic received a request from the U.S. Defense Department for emergency assistance. In the construction work being done at the Pentagon two floors underground, one of the workers using a jack hammer had inadvertently broken through the floor and cut a number of power and fiber optic communications cables. This accident resulted in more than half of the Pentagon's communications being lost. Baker was assigned by Bell Atlantic to head up the emergency repair team that deployed to the Pentagon. The Pentagon communications people, the military, Bell Atlantic and Virginia Power Company, worked together to restore the communications and power. The problem turned out to be a complex one and the power and communications diagrams for the entire building, the third largest building in the world, were poured over for hours before the determination was made as to the best way to repair the ruptured fiber optic cables. After nearly twelve hours, a solution was found and the cable spliced, but only after the most serious disruption in Pentagon communications history.

When Baker returned to his Bell Atlantic office at 4 a.m., he left a note for his secretary saying that he would take the day off to get some sleep. When he returned to his apartment, he spent the next four hours at his desk reconstructing all that he could remember about the power and communications diagrams for the Pentagon. Surprising even to him was the simplicity and access to the key power stations and communications nodes in Northern Virginia that supported the Pentagon and across the Potomac River, the White House. Baker was not entirely sure what to do with what he had, and his sketches could not be clandestinely sent to Palestine. He decided to report what he had and ask for instructions. His communiqué was acknowledged within a week and he was told he would be provided further guidance. Then nothing came all summer. He concluded that what he had discovered must have already been known. Then, just yesterday, a message came with surprising instructions!

CHAPTER 17

RETRIBUTION UNLEASHED

It was Wednesday, the first of September in Baghdad, and the heat was still brutal, but some relief in the weather would be coming later in the month. Ali Hassan was sitting uncomfortably at his desk with his right leg propped up on the corner of the desk. The cast on that leg ran from his foot to his knee. His left arm also bore a cast from his wrist to his shoulder. The pain from the three broken ribs he had sustained in the automobile accident in June, in addition to the broken arm and leg, had eased, but he was still miserably uncomfortable. It was after 6:00 p.m. and he was probably the only one left in the building except for his aide, Captain Bassari, who he insisted remain until he departed. Since he had come back to his office after four weeks in the hospital, he had returned to his former angry self, treating his staff like servants because he, himself, felt so terrible. He hated the stupid imbecile of a taxi driver that caused the accident and felt frustrated that the idiot had been killed in the accident, denying Ali Hassan the pleasure of killing him. And he had little remorse over the death of his driver, also a fatal victim of the crash. "The stupid dog should have been able to avoid it," he thought. He could not remember a time in his life when he was so miserable and worried.

While he was in the hospital, Saddam himself was his first visitor, which created quite a stir. Saddam was not known for his caring or sympathy for the sick or wounded. Ali knew, of course, why Saddam was there. He wanted to determine if Ali could continue his important role in *Retribution* or if any compromise of security had taken place in the accident.

At the time Saddam visited him, Ali was still groggy from his injuries that were severe, but not life-threatening. Ali, although medicated, had enough presence of mind to assure Saddam that he would be able to continue his direction of *Retribution* from his hospital bed, by using his trusted assistants. He could see that Saddam had his doubts but Saddam told him that he would have his security people make special arrangements at the hospital for him to have a private suite with all the necessary secure communications he would require. Saddam directed that Ali's room be guarded twenty-four hours a day. Ali suspected that was more to make sure that Ali Hassan did not go anywhere than for his protection. The doctors quickly got the message that Ali was important to Saddam and Ali got the best of care. Even General Uday Hussein, Saddam's son, came to visit Ali on his third day in the hospital. He didn't say much and Ali guessed that Saddam had sent him around to see if Ali was going to live and be able to continue *Retribution.* He must have passed Uday's inspection because after that, Ali's own people then came to the hospital and set up a twenty-four hour watch so that Ali could work whenever he felt like it.

Ali's worst moment at the hospital, far greater than the pain from his injuries, was when Saddam had leaned over his bed and whispered in his ear, "Was anything lost or compromised in the accident that can pose a security threat to *Retribution?*"

"No, sir," Ali had whispered back to Saddam. "You know that I never carry sensitive papers in the car or on my person. It would be too dangerous." Ali had lied and prayed to Allah that nothing in his voice or facial expression would suggest he wasn't telling the truth. Saddam seemed satisfied and had not raised the question again.

As soon as his own people had set up at the hospital, Ali had them search the vehicles involved in the accident and the clothes worn by himself and his driver. Nothing out of the ordinary was found. Only Ali remembered the cryptic note that he had in his pocket at the time of the accident. He also remembered taking it out of his pocket just before the crash. "What could have happened to it?" he had wondered a hundred times. He knew the vehicle had burned and wanted to believe the small piece of paper had also burned. He also knew that he had been thrown from the car before it exploded, but did he take the paper with him? He could not remember anything after a sense of flying through the air. In his worst nightmares, he wondered if Saddam's security personnel in the lead vehicle had quickly returned to the accident, found the paper and turned it over to Saddam who was now just letting Ali play out his usefulness. And then, when the time came to accuse Ali of betrayal, Ali knew beyond a shadow of a doubt who would win that argument.

In spite of Ali Hassan's personal fears and discomfort, *Retribution*, like a storm cloud rising on the horizon, continued on schedule. Ali Hassan himself, while in the hospital, was able to complete the project to select a chemical or biological weapon for use in *Retribution*. He simplified the final selection by reducing the candidates to two: VX, a deadly chemical nerve agent and anthrax, a deadly biological spore. Iraq had long had expertise with both these deadly agents; however, the research and production capabilities had mostly been directed toward military weapons means of delivery. Ali Hassan directed his people to develop delivery means that could be accomplished by a few people in a terrorist type attack. He instructed them to consider and recommend options that would allow for a safe, protected delivery by a terrorist, and options that would, if necessary, infect the terrorist. He had his experts design options that would allow for relatively small amounts of the agent to be spread with maximum lethal results. He had them rank the degree of difficulty of getting the agents into the United States without detection. And finally, he had them figure which agents when used, could best be denied by Iraq.

The analysis conducted by Ali's team of experts was persuasive. Of VX, the nerve gas, and anthrax, the biological agent, anthrax was clearly the better choice. Both could be spread by a single terrorist using a truck or a small plane which could carry 200 or more pounds of either VX or anthrax under the right atmospheric conditions and expect to kill one-to-three million people in a city the size of Washington, DC. But in addition, the anthrax offered an even more destructive capacity in the long term that would be more difficult for medical authorities to deal with. It offered more possibilities for dispensing, and it was the easiest to conceal.

Ali had no difficulty convincing Saddam that anthrax was the weapon of choice for *Retribution.* Saddam had always trusted Ali's judgment on chemical and biological warfare. The next step was getting Wadih Mohammed's agreement on the choice of anthrax, sending some people to Afghanistan to a location of bin Laden's choice, and training the terrorists on the safe handling of the deadly spores. The last step was the coordination involved in passing the anthrax to Wadih Mohammed's people for safe transport to the United States. All this was accomplished before Ali left the hospital.

The cyber weapon, however, had remained a problem for Ali until just a week ago. The hoped-for weapon that the Bengali had been hired to develop had not materialized and Ali Hassan's experts began to think the Bengali wasn't capable of a breakthrough. This caused Ali to go through a terrible period making excuse after excuse to Saddam and Wadih Mohammed on reasons for the delay. Even bin Laden complained to Saddam that the training of the strike teams was near completion and could not be concluded without knowledge of the cyber weapon to be used.

During that time, Ali's sweating intensified, even in his air conditioned office, to the degree that he had to change clothes twice a day. To tolerate the arm and leg casts, he chose to wear traditional Arab garb. The shalwar qamese was easier to get on and off although he had to cut the left arm area to permit getting it over the cast.

He had tasked his experts that were working with the Bengali to resurrect some of their own proposals as alternatives, but when he heard them, he knew that they would not do the job against sophisticated American anti-virus systems and he also knew that Saddam would see through any ruse. Two weeks ago, he had seriously begun to mentally review his options. "I could continue to plead for more time hoping the Bengali will come through with the weapon we need. I am losing confidence in this approach. I can kill off my experts, blame them for the failure, and try to convince Saddam that I need more time. Saddam would probably see through that; he has used that approach a number of times himself. I can defect to the west and get out of this hellhole of a country forever. To do that I would need to have some excuse to get my family close to a border, probably Kuwait or Saudi, where I can make a break for it, but Saddam is probably having me watched now."

Nothing seemed feasible to Ali; he had feared the worst and thought his run as one of Saddam's longtime favorites was about to end.

Then last week, he could scarcely believe his ears late one night when one of the cyber people told him the breakthrough had taken place. At first he doubted that it was true because he had been putting terrible pressure on his people to make something happen and he feared that this might be their feeble attempt to placate him with something that would never stand up to Saddam and bin Laden. Fortunately, he was wrong. When his experts came the next day to brief him and show him the new cyber weapon, he quickly shared their belief that a breakthrough had been achieved. He could recall with pleasure the briefing he received from an Iraqi Army lieutenant colonel who was the Army's and government's foremost expert on computer technology, who told him that.

"The essence of the weapon, sir, is a virus. That in itself is nothing new, but this virus is new in its methodology and techniques of application and may be undetectable without knowledge of its origin. We propose calling it 'Desert Mist.'"

The officer had brought some charts along to illustrate and he now turned to those. The first one contained the names of five countries in alphabetical order:

- France
- Germany
- Great Britain
- Japan
- United States

"As you know, sir, our Bengali had done some impressive work in the virus field and we gave him these five western countries as case models for computer system penetration and disruption. He and we are familiar with their military, government, commercial and financial systems because of their proliferation throughout the rest of the world. We started with the most successful and recent attacks against their systems by professionals and amateurs. You may recall the 'Solar Sunrise' attack in February against the U.S. Defense Department and the more recent Melissa attack. The challenge for our weapon was not so much how to attack; rank amateurs and hackers are doing that daily from within those countries or from an international base or through several other countries. The challenge was to create a virus that could first penetrate the security firewalls or multiple lines of defense in a computer and then, and most importantly, render the penetration undetectable until such time as the system is degraded to an unusable level or completely destroyed. That's what we have accomplished in 'Desert Mist'!" the lieutenant colonel had said proudly. He then took Ali through the rest of the charts to explain how the virus worked.

"'Desert Mist' is a vicious virus. Once inserted into a system, it mutates and begins to change the names of the operating system files. It adds new names and bogus files and destroys other original existing files. It then mutates to any connected or supporting system and to any other system that contacts the infected system. It is difficult to detect because of its ability to change file names. If a user attempts to delete unrecognized files, the user may be deleting the existing files and thus aiding in file destruction. And it can hide from all known anti-virus software."

Ali Hassan had a number of questions relating to testing the virus to determine its reliability and all were answered to his satisfaction. And then he was told about its employment.

"This little disk," the Lieutenant Colonel had said, holding up a 3.25" floppy, "is most effective when entered directly into the system from a system node. It can, however, be hacked in from a nearby location."

It was clear to Ali Hassan at that time that the lieutenant colonel and all his colleagues were ecstatic at the development of so capable a computer virus. To Ali's mind, "Computer nerds are the same the world over!" and he really didn't comprehend the significance of the development. What he did understand was that he couldn't afford the security risk to *Retribution* by letting the Bengali leave Baghdad alive. His instructions to his people were, "Make sure you have picked his brain for everything useful and that you and your people can train others in the use of the virus. Then see to it that he has an accident—a fatal accident. Make a settlement with his family through our contact in Abu Dhabi and destroy any records of his participation in our efforts."

At that moment, he had felt like the old ruthless, get the job done at any cost, Ali Hassan.

Now, as he sat in pain in his office and remembered the other things he had accomplished once the cyber weapon was assured, he wasn't so sure of how he felt and what his status was with Saddam. He had informed Saddam of the development of the virus. Saddam was relieved and agreed that the rest of *Retribution* could move ahead. Saddam, like Ali, wasn't really sure how effective any computer virus could be, but he knew that the other two weapons could wreak havoc in the United States and was arranging to get on with it. Ali completed the arrangements with Wadih Mohammed to send the cyber weapon trainers to Afghanistan and then realized that after that, most of his work on *Retribution* was done. All that was left for him was to coordinate the timing of the strikes and the final target selections. Saddam could, of course, take care of those final items himself directly with bin Laden. Ali made a mental note to convince Saddam that the presence of Ali and his team would be required right up to the strikes being carried out, in the event anything went wrong and Ali's help was required. Ali thought of this as his best life insurance policy. He realized that if and when *Retribution* was successfully, or otherwise, accomplished, Ali Hassan would be the "smoking gun" that could link Saddam Hussein with *Retribution.* "Maybe," Ali thought, "I need to think again about defecting."

Abdul Khalid was standing at the window of his room at the "Goat Farm." It was almost six o'clock on Thursday evening, the 16th of September. He was looking at the purple hues on the mountain and could feel the cool evening breeze blowing as the sun slowly sank from view. The cooler weather had called for a change in clothes starting about two days ago, but "no matter," he thought, his charges were trained and would be departing soon. The last of the training at the "Goat Farm" had taken place last week when Ali Hassan's trainers had instructed each of the nine "soldiers of Allah" as bin Laden and Abdul Khalid liked to call them, on the use of the Desert Mist. Only three would be used in the cyber attack but Khalid had cross-trained each individual to do each other's job on the nuclear weapon, the biological agent, and finally, the cyber weapon. Then, if anything should happen to one, the next one could take his place. Cross training was a technique that Khalid had learned in the

Special Forces and was one that would now, to his mind, "serve the cause of Allah."

As he stood looking out the window, Khalid went over yet again, in his thinking, "What else needs to be done before my work is finished here?" Wadih Mohammed and several of his people spent the week at the "Goat Farm" going over the cover, identity, and travel plans for the nine trainees and Khalid. The nine would all be traveling separately by different routes. Three would be going to Florida, three to New York, and three to Washington, D.C. The travel would be phased so that no connection could be made between travelers. All would be met by what Wadih Mohammed called "reception stations" who would facilitate their covers in the United States and provide them the necessary support to carry out their own *Retribution*. One individual on each team of three had been chosen to be the strike team leader. They were all aware of the ten possible targets but none knew the three primary and three alternate targets. These would be decided on by Saddam and bin Laden and passed to Abdul Khalid before he departed Afghanistan to join the three teams in the United States. Khalid would wait until all nine team members were in place and their covers secure before he departed for the United States.

Extra care had been taken with Abdul Khalid's cover. He was the only one of the strike team that was wanted by the FBI for questioning in connection with the New York World Trade Center bombing. His appearance would be altered so that none of his former military associates or co-workers in New York would recognize him. Wadih Mohammed had also informed him that each of the weapons to be used in the strike would be delivered by separate courier and Khalid would only be advised of their location and how to obtain them when he was safely in the United States.

All of the team, including Khalid, would be in the United States by the 30th day of September. Once there, Khalid would be responsible for coordinating and conducting the reconnaissance of the specified targets and coordinating the final phase of training with each strike team and, when ready, would so inform Wadih Mohammed, who, in turn, would determine a "go date" from Saddam and Osama bin Laden. Bin Laden was coming in the morning to personally send off his soldiers on the holiest of missions.

That night Abdul Khalid could hardly sleep. He had great confidence in the true believers like himself that he had trained and now felt with every fiber in his body that his whole purpose for living was about to be realized. He was wide awake long before dawn, his usual wake up time, and rose with great anticipation of hearing the Holy One's charge to his deadly flock.

CHAPTER 18

LONDON

It was 7:45 on Thursday morning, the 30th of September. The night cleaning crew at the U.S. Embassy was just finishing up its work and would be gone by 8:00 a.m. There were twelve people on the night crew and six on the day crew. Nine men and three women. They wore blue coverall uniforms with U.S. Embassy written on the back in white letters. Most of the people were Indians or Pakistanis. A few were British citizens. And most had worked faithfully and were well-liked and trusted at the Embassy. This was particularly true of Thomas Mandi, the cleaning crew chief. Thomas, as everyone called him, was a Pakistani and he had worked on the cleaning crew at the Embassy for eight years. He had been Chief of the cleaning crew for five years.

Thomas came in at 4:00 a.m. most days and left at 1:00 in the afternoon. He believed that if his night crew did a thorough job of cleaning, there would be no complaints from anyone during the day and the smaller day crew could look after the routine job of maintaining waste cans, towels, and toilet paper in the bathrooms, and cleaning up spills. The cleaning crew were reasonably well paid, liked their jobs, and the U.S. Embassy always looked clean.

This morning, Thomas planned to leave shortly after eight o'clock, just making sure that all members of the day crew showed up. Thomas was beginning six weeks of leave today. He had made the request for leave three months ago. It was approved without any problem because it was the only leave he had asked for that year. Thomas went into the basement of the Embassy where his locker was located to change clothes. After he slipped out of his blue uniform and into a wool suit, white shirt, and red tie, he checked to see if he had his bankbook, plane ticket, and passport. With those items secure, he took a small travel case from his locker, re-locked his combination lock, and headed back upstairs. At the main entrance, he left his travel bag with the receptionist and reentered the Embassy proper, his security badge clipped to his lapel. The security guards and the Marine sentry waved him through and one asked, "Where are you off to so early this morning, Thomas? You are looking mighty spiffy today."

Thomas repeated what he had already told a number of other people, "I'm off on home leave."

"That's a good lad," was the frequent reply. Thomas was well-liked by the security guards. He knew them all and always chatted with them as they moved between the three security posts at the Embassy—especially the rear one where the loading dock was located. Everything had to be run through xray and metal detector machines but the guards often cut Thomas some slack when he was unloading cleaning materials in bulk, particularly paper towels and toilet paper.

Thomas took the elevator to the third floor. He then followed the corridor to the rear of the building and turned left. This corridor was a dead end except about halfway down on the right where a door led into the Embassy conference room. It was one of those areas known as a "secure area" meaning that Thomas and his cleaning crew could only enter when they were escorted by an Embassy Marine. Thomas and his crew had been in the conference room at 4:00 a.m. this morning. They had vacuumed the heavily carpeted floor and dusted the large conference table and the leather chairs surrounding it. They had also cleaned all of the pictures hanging on the wall. The cleaning crew always cleaned the conference room on Thursdays because that was the day the Ambassador held his weekly staff meeting.

Thomas walked past the door toward the end of the corridor and stopped at the cleaning cart that he had left there earlier that morning. He could see it was exactly as he had left it—nothing disturbed. It wasn't the first time that Thomas had left the cleaning cart at that location on Thursday or at other out-of-the-way places in the Embassy. It was never questioned. In fact, Thomas had been placing cleaning carts at various places in the Embassy for more than two years. The only time he had ever heard anything about it was if it was blocking the way, then someone would complain. This morning, Thomas checked the cleaning cart carefully to see that it still had a full complement of cleaning materials. You never could tell when someone would need something cleaned. He opened the side doors on the cart and found the packages of paper towels still fully stocked. He hesitated, then looked back down the hall to make sure no one was there and then reached in, found a small clock attached to a large package behind the cartons, and set the alarm for 9:15 a.m. That done, Thomas closed the doors, retraced his steps to the elevator and pushed the down button.

Within a couple of minutes, Thomas Mandi had collected his travel bag, exited the main entrance of the U.S. Embassy, gone to the nearest corner and hailed a taxi. Thomas would ordinarily have taken a bus, but, this day, of all days, he didn't want to risk being late for his plane to Peshawar.

That same morning, just a few moments earlier, Colonel Richard Beemer, United States Air Force, the Defense and Air Attaché to the United Kingdom, had locked the front door of his three-story townhouse that was just six blocks away from the Embassy. The near Grosvenor Square flat was the envy of the entire embassy staff. It had originally belonged to the U.S. Army Air Corps, later, the U.S. Air Force, and now, DAS, since the 1940s. It was an extremely valuable piece of property but because of its center of London location and the age of the old house, it was extraordinarily expensive to maintain. Each time the DAS had a new Director, the DAS staff recommended that the DAO London DATT house be sold and every time a new DATT was sent to London, he was enjoined to look at alternatives. Colonel Beemer was no exception. "I tried," he told himself, "I really did." But when he found out how incredibly valuable the place was for liaison purposes, not to mention the location, in one of the world's largest cities, he, like his predecessors, began a crusade to convince his DAS and embassy leadership that it made imminently good sense to retain the townhouse.

This rainy morning, Colonel Beemer was dressed in a suit made by an English tailor and carried, as do most English gentlemen, an umbrella. He could have passed for an English gentleman, particularly with the black Bowler hat, except for his haircut. That was still at a U.S. military acceptable standard. The walk from his house to the U.S. Embassy was just twelve minutes. He could, as he had this morning, leave his flat at 7:45 and be at his desk at 8:00.

As he walked along at a good military pace, smiling at fellow passersby, he thought to himself about how much he enjoyed his attaché job. That was true also for his wife, Jean. He had twenty-seven years of service had had the honor of commanding a wing, but fell just short of making Brigadier General. He had no idea that something so meaningful as his attaché role in London was possible after the two great years he had spent in command. When he finished his command at Offut Air Force Base, Nebraska, he was about ready to hang it up. But his Assignments Officer at Air Force Headquarters knew that he would make an outstanding diplomat and persuaded him, and Jean, too, that they should volunteer for the DATT/AIRA London job. They had talked it over. Both kids had been educated and were on their own now. "What the hell," they had thought, and they did it. They had been in London for a year now and had loved every minute of it. "What a city; what a place!" they said often.

London was one of the largest DAOs. Twenty-one people and a well balanced mix of officers, NCOs and civilians. Dick Beemer loved his team and he loved his work. He got along so well with his British colleagues that they regularly accused him of being an anglophile. He had to admit he liked their good-humored life style. "It hasn't been all play," he thought, "not by a long measure." The thing in

Kosovo alone had kept the DAO more than busy. It was clear from the beginning that the efforts of the U.S. and United Kingdom were going to be the chief ones that kept the alliance within NATO viable for the war against Serbia. The coordination between the U.S. Air Force and the Royal Air Force at the national level fell to DAO London, and that had proven to be a seven day a week job up until the bombing halt. In fact, DAS Headquarters had to provide two additional Assistant Air Attachés to them on temporary duty just to keep up with the daily requirements. And once peace was declared, the workload had shifted to many new items of coordination with Whitehall, the British Defense Department, on the U.S. and British roles in the Kosovo Peacekeeping Forces.

"Well, all in a day's work," thought Colonel Beemer as he reached the Embassy. As he went up the front stairs of the relatively new building, through the security checkpoint, and up the elevator to the third floor, he began to think about the day's schedule and the Ambassador's Country Team Meeting that would take place that morning at nine o'clock.

By 8:45, Beemer had reviewed the night's cables from Washington and Europe, taken three phone calls, placed two, and made some minor changes to the day's schedule. He had met briefly with the Army and Navy attachés, made a note to write an Information Report on a matter that he had been working on for some time with the FBI Legal Attaché and MI-5 stemming from a request from DAO Kiev, and had drank two cups of coffee. He thought about a third one but remembered he would be drinking coffee in the Country Team Meeting and decided "the kidneys can take only so much."

Dick Beemer departed at 8:50 for the short walk down the hall. The DAO and the Ambassador's Conference Room were both on the third floor. He would be early but that would give him a chance to do a little informal coordination with some of the other early arrivals. When he entered, he saw eight others already at the conference table. He said, "Good morning," and took his regular seat at about the mid-point of the table. There were twenty-five principal staff heads at the U.S Embassy in London counting the Deputy Chief of Mission or DCM. Seating would be twelve on one side of the table, twelve on the other, with the Ambassador on one end of the table and the DCM at the other.

Colonel Beemer hoped to talk with the FBI Legal Attaché who always sat next to him in the Country Team Meetings but unfortunately, he did not arrive until just before the Ambassador. "Bob, if you have a minute after the meeting, I have a question or two about the Kiev matter," Beemer requested.

"Sure, Dick," the Legal Attaché replied.

Just then the Ambassador was announced and everyone stood.

The Ambassador walked to his place at the head of the table and taking his seat said, "Good morning ladies and gentlemen. Please take your seats. Let's go around the room and see what folks have to report."

The Political-Military Counselor, known in Embassy parlance as the POL-MIL was the first to report. "If he is consistent with his track record," Dick Beemer thought to himself, "he'll take the longest."

It was 9:10 by the time when the POL-MIL finished his report on supposedly "must know" items for the Ambassador. Colonel Beemer noted, "Still five people to go before I give my two-minutes-max pitch," he was thinking. A minute for the Econ, a minute for the Commercial, a minute and a half for the Admin, and less than a minute for the Regional Security Officer. Then Colonel Beemer began, "I have three items today, Sir. First...."

Dick Beemer never finished his report. The explosion that went off at exactly 9:15 a.m. blew out every window in the front of the U.S. Embassy, instantly injuring scores of passersby on the street. Inside the Embassy, the blast obliterated the conference room and collapsed the fourth floor into the third. Of the twenty-six people in the conference room at the time of the explosion, only one would survive—

an assistant from the Economic Section who was seated in the projection room behind the conference room. For the Embassy Security personnel, their worst fears had been realized. The Embassy had been penetrated, a bomb internally detonated, and the safeguarding of American lives defeated. Angela Roxbury, the State Department's Assistant Regional Security Officer for the Embassy, sitting in her office on the first floor of the Embassy near the front entrance was thrown out of her chair by the blast, she instantly recognized the sound of a bomb explosion and anticipating its destruction screamed, "GOD HELP US!"

At 9:45 at London's Heathrow Airport, Pakistani Airlines Flight 442 with service to Lahore and Peshawar announced its first call for boarding. At almost the same time on the small television set in the corner of the waiting room, the British Broadcasting Corporation (BBC) interrupted its regularly scheduled program to announce, "An explosion has taken place at the U.S Embassy at Grosvenor Square in downtown London. Authorities now on the scene report that damage appears to be significant and emergency crews are expecting heavy casualties. The BBC will follow the situation and interrupt our regular programming as soon as further information is available."

Thomas Mandi was one of the passengers sitting in the nearby row of seats watching the "telly," as the Brits say. When the announcement ended, he picked up his cap, double-checked to make sure he had his boarding pass, a window seat, and his passport, and calmly headed toward the orderly boarding queue—one of the customs of British life he rather enjoyed. Once on board and in his seat, he accepted the offered cup of English tea—another British custom he liked. "And after all," he thought, "it might be a long while before I have any more English tea."

Thomas Mandi was pleased that the Pakistani Air Lines plane took off on schedule. Once the aircraft was airborne and the "fasten seat belt" sign was turned off, he removed his shoes, pressed the seat button to recline and thought he might catch some sleep. "After all," he thought, "I was up for most of the night." During that warm fuzzy time just before the mind and body fall into sleep, Thomas thought of his years in England. They had been good ones for him and he knew he would miss them. He had always liked the people at the U.S. Embassy and he knew that they liked him. He couldn't recall doing a better cleaning job than the one he did last night. "Just so," he thought.

Ten years ago, Thomas was one of the first Muslims in Peshawar to be recruited by bin Laden and the al Qaeda organization. When he was sent off to London years ago, he was never sure for what purpose, other than to serve Allah. He always followed his instructions and then a little over a year ago, it all became clear. Now as he returned to Peshawar, he did not know what would be ahead of him but he knew it would be in the service of Allah, and for that he was grateful. His last thought before dozing off was, "Praise be to Allah."

At 4:15 a.m. in the early morning of September 30th, Bart Lowe was awakened by the phone on the table next to his bed. "General Lowe, this is Barbara. I am sorry to wake you.

"A few moments ago, our Ops Center picked up an unconfirmed report from the Associated Press wire service of an explosion at the U.S. Embassy in London. Shortly after that, CNN reporting from London televised coverage of the scene and the massive damage. Emergency vehicles are in place, there is a fire still burning and it looks like chaos everywhere!"

"Jesus H. Christ! Do we know anything else? Have we been able to reach our people?" Bart shot back quickly and with obvious concern.

"Nothing else yet. There is no response from our people, but the damage to the DAO area of the embassy looks extensive and the Embassy COMMs seem to be out. State doesn't know anymore than we do."

"What the hell can we do, just wait?"

"The Ops Center will get what we can from CNN and they are now tuned to ABC, NBC, and CBS. They will all be covering it and we will just have to standby until we hear from our people in London or one of the other agencies in town. We're trying to contact the U.S Navy Europe headquarters on Grosvenor Square and I've got a call into the Brit Defense Attaché here in Washington."

"Okay. I'll get dressed and get into the Ops Center ASAP," Bart replied, a feeling of helplessness running through his body.

CHAPTER 19

AFTERSHOCK

By the following Monday, the fourth of October—one of the saddest in memory—most of the details of the bombing of the U.S. Embassy in London were known in Washington. The Ambassador and all his senior staff had been killed, including the Defense Attaché. In addition to Beemer, a Warrant Officer, two NCOs, and three civilians from the DAO were killed in the blast. Total deaths were estimated at seventy, including ten visitors to the Embassy. Total injured, some critically, was placed at 147. It was the worst single violent incident against Americans since the downing of the Pan Am Flight 103 in Lockerbie, Scotland, and the bombing of the Marine barracks in Beirut, Lebanon. Bin Laden had his diversion.

The horrific memories of the earlier U.S. Embassy terrorist bombings in Africa in 1998 were resurrected with the loss of life and destruction at U.S. Embassy London. Great Britain which prided itself in its anti-terrorist security measures was shocked and embarrassed. The United States was in mourning. The President had gone on national television to denounce the cowardly act of terrorism and vowed that the perpetrators would be found and brought to justice. The entire U.S. military was placed on higher alert status indefinitely and every U.S. Embassy throughout the world was directed to heighten security measures. No major federal agency in town was left untouched. They all had casualties. Black armbands and black ribbons were everywhere. The first word of the news quickly initiated the launching of assistance teams from all the affected government and military departments. The British opened their facilities and their hearts to the arriving teams offering every possible assistance. The FBI's bomb and forensic experts assisted by their military counterparts were on the scene in just hours working with their British hosts in looking for bombs and clues in the Embassy debris. The most gruesome task that fell to all on the scene was the finding and careful removal of bodies and body parts that were from those who had been closest to the detonating bomb blast. Then the slow, painful, identification process. This, of course, delayed the notification of the next of kin and hours and days went by while families awaited the already anticipated, dreaded news. It was a heartbreaking and anguished time for all involved.

Next came the return of the fallen heroes to Washington and their various homes throughout the nation. A national period of mourning was declared by the President with flags at half-staff throughout the country while more than a dozen separate memorials and interments took place. Five of the DAO London dead were buried in Arlington National Cemetery at services attended by the Secretary of Defense, Chairman of the Joint Chiefs, Chiefs of the Military Services, and the entire DAS Headquarters. Until then, Bart Lowe remembered the earlier time in the 1980s when he had stood at the gravesite of the assassinated U.S. Defense Attaché to Greece as the saddest day of his life. And now on this occasion, in the crisp October air, he listened to the mournful sounds of the bugler's taps. His heartache was even greater as he empathized with the military families' grief. Bart Lowe, in a way, felt responsible for their deaths. "I was after all," he thought, "their commander. The one who sent them away to a foreign place and thus, the one ultimately responsible for putting them in harm's way."

General Lowe's deep seated feelings of remorse were made even greater by a growing feeling of frustration, of helplessness, of not being able to personally do something about righting the wrong. As a soldier for most of his adult life, he understood that when an enemy strikes you on a battlefield, you must sustain your losses, but then you plan your counterattack and how you will ultimately defeat that enemy. In defeating the enemy, in striking back, your honor is restored and the wrong is righted. In his country's approach to terrorism, the wrongs never seemed to get completely righted. Chet Baldwin, the U.S. Navy officer killed in Greece by 17 November terrorists—his killers were never brought to justice. The bombers of the U.S. Air Force Khobar Facility in Saudi Arabia—not apprehended. The terrorists who bombed the embassies in Africa—most of the perpetrators still not caught, nor brought to justice. And the ones who were tracked down, the Libyans who bombed the Pan American Airlines Flight in Scotland—turned over after ten years? But what about their bosses? The ones who ordered the bombings? Still at large. Free to plan other terrorist acts. The same went for the Trade Center bombing in New York. Some of the perpetrators were indicted, even some of the higher up middlemen. But what about those leaders in foreign countries who were ordering these attacks against Americans? And now London. "How far do they have to go before we say enough is enough?! What will it take before we say this shit has got to cease? Does someone have to pop a nuke? Is that what will finally do it?!"

For the rest of October, these kinds of thoughts continued in Bart Lowe's head. His frustration seemed to grow and he became short tempered and impatient with his people. He had always been a man of action and now he found himself in a position of wanting desperately to take action, positive action, and yet, not knowing what that action should be. His diplomatic manner and persuasive skills that had served him so well seemed to have taken leave. His staff checked the morning operational updates—dreaded his obvious disappointment when they had no developments to report relating to the bombing of the Embassy in London. Even his personal staff and closest associates in Washington grew wary. Each Monday, they were hopeful that the weekend, even as short as it was, would somehow allow Lowe to get over the shock of the loss at DAO London and return to his normal, affable, self.

On Monday, the 20th of October, almost three weeks after the London Embassy bombing, Bart Lowe entered the DAS front office at a brisk pace. Without breaking stride or a "good morning," or any word of greeting to Colonel Ted Wenke or Joan, he directed, "Joan, get John Kitchen on the phone," and then entered his office and closed the door.

"Oh, my," said Joan, looking at Colonel Wenke, "looks like another one of those days."

When Joan took Bart's coffee in a few minutes later, without acknowledging the coffee he said, "Where's John Kitchen? What's the hold-up?"

"I am sorry, sir. Mr. Kitchen was tied up and his secretary said he would call back as soon as he was free."

"All right. Let me know the minute he calls," he replied without taking his eyes off the cables he was reading or saying "thank you" for the coffee. The minute Joan left the office, Bart buzzed Barbara Barnsworth on the intercom.

"Yes, sir."

"Barbara. Are there any new developments in London?"

"Only those that are contained in the Operations Summary that is already on your desk. Have you seen the Summary?" Barbara answered with a slight tone of irritation.

"Yes, yes. But I thought maybe you might have something else."

Barbara sighed thinking to herself, "Here we go again," and then said to Lowe, "Bart, we really must talk. May I come over?"

"Talk, talk? About what? Well, at any rate, not before I speak to Kitchen and Softly. I'll buzz you when I've finished." And the intercom connection was broken.

"Christ!" Barbara thought to herself.

Thirty minutes later, Joan's voice came on the intercom and said, "Mr. Kitchen is holding for you on the Stu-3, sir."

Bart grabbed the secure phone receiver and immediately said, "Let's have an update, John."

"Jesus Christ, Bart, who the hell do you think you are talking to? I'm your friend! I'm not one of your... Colonels. Did you forget that we just talked yesterday? And before that, at noon on Saturday? The FBI isn't a currents Operations Center. You have one of those of your own. Ask them for the latest developments or have them call my guys. I've got a whole freaking Bureau to run here—not just a single terrorist incident, no matter how bad it was!" Then a pause, then, "Oh, shit. I don't mean to take my wrath out on you, Bart, but you have got to cut me some slack. We are practically working around the clock here and I don't think I have been at home for more than a couple of hours for the last two weeks."

John's outburst, or perhaps because it demonstrated genuine anger and frustration—those exact emotions that Bart was feeling—got Bart's attention. The thought quickly raced though his mind, "My god, what am I doing? Transferring the grief and anger I am feeling to my friends, to my own people?" Then to John Kitchen, "John, John, my friend, I'm sorry. I can see now how much of a royal pain-in-the-ass I have been. I am not certain what came over me but I can assure you that it won't happen again. Your wake-up call has hopefully brought me back to my senses. Can you put it behind us Old Buddy?"

"Of course I can, Bart. Take it from one who has been there many times. It goes with the territory in this town. It's feedback that we are human."

"John, I sincerely regret being such a pest and promise I'll just let our folks do the talking for awhile. I know that they will do a good job."

"Fine, Bart. But as long as you're on the phone, let me share with you the summary I was just handed this morning. As you know, the Embassy, or what's left of it, remains shut down so that our guys can continue to sift through the rubble looking for clues. My experts now believe that the explosive used was the old plastique type."

"Really, wouldn't that take a large amount to do as much damage as it did?" Bart asked.

"Yes, quite a large amount. And the question is how could anyone get that much into the Embassy? They would have had to have had inside help or perhaps have taken small amounts in over a long period of time, hiding it somewhere in the Embassy."

"And do they know yet where it was located? Was it in the conference room?"

"We believe it was not inside the conference room because the east wall was blown inward. It was most likely in the hall adjacent to the conference room."

"How could that be, John? Was someone holding it?"

"No. We suspect that it was concealed in something, but whatever it was, it may have been completely destroyed. Our people will continue to sift through everything and may yet turn up something."

"Any suspects yet, John?"

"No, Bart. And no group has come forward yet to claim credit. But, and this is only for your ears, Bart, our best guess is that bin Laden is responsible. We believed for some time that he was going to strike again, and we and CIA believed that it was going to be here in the United States. We may now have to reassess our thinking. It could be that because of the Trade Center fiasco and our heightened awareness, bin Laden concentrated on only foreign targets figuring hitting us here would be too tough."

"I don't know, John, that's more in your bailiwick!"

"Well, we will be working it hard with René Softly and are going to try to figure out where we may be the most vulnerable."

"My bet will still be right here in the good old U.S. of A., John."

"Whatever, Bart, we have a lot of work ahead of us. I'll be in touch."

"Many thanks, John, and once again, I am sorry to have been such a pain-in-the-ass!"

When Bart broke his connection with John Kitchen, he immediately dialed the CIA's Counterterrorism Center and asked to speak to René Softly. When she came on the line, he said, "René, this is Bart. I have my hat in hand and ask that you accept my humble apology."

"Apology. For what, Bart?" she tentatively asked, not knowing what to expect.

"For being a complete asshole the last couple of weeks."

"Would you believe a complete 'flaming' asshole?" René responded.

"Flaming?"

"Yes. Flaming, a degree beyond normal assholes," René responded, now laughing. My god, Bart, you have been a bastard the last couple of weeks. I was beginning to think that you had fallen into that well-known Washington malady known as CIA bashing. When anything goes wrong, blame it on the CIA!"

"I can only say guilty as charged, René. And throw myself on the mercy of the court."

"Mercy granted, Bart, and welcome back to the real world."

"Can you stand one question this morning, René?"

"Since you turned on the old Bart Lowe charm again, how could I say no?"

"John thinks that the bombing in London is bin Laden's work. Do you agree?"

"Although there is no direct evidence to tie him to it, he would be our first choice."

"Does this take the pressure off the U.S. as a target for the time being?"

"Maybe yes, maybe no. Probably too soon to say, but it could suggest that he believes the foreign locations are easier pickings, and if London is any indication, maybe he is right. Bottom line, Bart, all your people abroad, and all our people abroad, better watch their six!"

After his call to René Softly, Bart walked over and opened the door to Barbara Barnsworth's office and, seeing that she was alone, walked in. Barbara, sitting behind her desk, looked up and mentally braced herself for Bart until she saw he had half a smile on his face.

"John Kitchen and René Softly tell me I have been a flaming asshole for the last few weeks. I suspect that is what you wanted to talk to me about."

Barbara let out a sigh of relief, smiled, and said, "It's going to be good to have the old Bart Lowe back again."

CHAPTER 20

HOMECOMING

It was a homecoming of sorts for Abdul Khalid. After he had his final instructions from Osama bin Laden, he had been smuggled into Saudi Arabia where he was given a cover that would allow him to enter the United States. His cover was that of a representative of East Wind, Ltd., a successful, Saudi, high tech firm that was looking for long term investment opportunities in Florida's fast growing space coast. The diversity of his firm's interests and his portfolio would permit him to travel to anywhere along the East Coast of the United States from Florida to New York. And, if necessary, it would facilitate his cover to Texas and California. And, of course, a visit to the nation's capitol to visit the numerous space lobby groups there would be appropriate.

Khalid departed Riyadh on 29 September and flew first class in keeping with his cover, to Atlanta, Georgia. He changed planes in Atlanta after only a two-hour layover and flew on to Miami. Before leaving Riyadh, Khalid's appearance was altered. His beard had been shaved. He sported only a thin mustache and a neatly trimmed goatee. His hairstyle was changed and dyed from its natural brown to a deep black color and he was outfitted with dark prescription eyeglasses and a new wardrobe consistent with the garb worn by successful Saudi businessmen. Wearing Armani suits was different for Khalid but he knew he would have no difficulty in adjusting to his new lifestyle.

He was given $1,000 U.S. dollars in cash, $8,000 more in American Express Traveler's Cheques, and the number of an account in the United States where he could draw up to $90,000 to cover any expenses he incurred.

There had been no difficulty in passing through the U.S. Customs in Atlanta. His Saudi passport was recognized immediately and he was welcomed to America by just about everyone he encountered. In Miami, just as he left the airport by limo bound for his hotel in downtown Miami, he realized he had not been back to the U.S. in six years; and it was good to be home again, or at least to a place he had once called home.

Once he was settled in his suite on the 16th floor in the Miami Hilton. He ordered half a dozen bottled Cokes from room service. The Coca Cola was one of the things he had missed most about the United States and he planned to get his fill of them while he was here. He had arrived in Atlanta in the afternoon at three o'clock, departed at five o'clock, and now it was almost eight. Given the time gained between Saudi Arabia and the U.S., he decided to turn in early so that he would be fresh for his meeting tomorrow and the important tasks that he was here to accomplish.

Khalid was a devout Muslim and before going to bed, he washed up, changed his clothes, spread his prayer rug onto the hotel room floor facing east, knelt on the rug, and said his evening prayers. After reciting the required traditional prayers, his most fervent plea was for Allah to be with him as he carried out *Retribution.*

The next morning, he rose at dawn and ordered a light breakfast of yogurt, fresh fruit, and tea. After he had finished eating, he moved a chair in front of the large window overlooking Miami's Biscayne Bay, sat down, folded his arms across his chest, bowed his head and began staring at the brilliant green waters. An observer would probably have thought that Abdul Khalid was meditating. Actually, he was going over in his mind all that he needed to know and do in the days and weeks ahead.

"First," he thought, "I need to remember the ten potential targets that bin Laden and Saddam agreed on—four nuclear, three biological, and three cyber."

"Those targets, three are in Washington, two are in New York, two in Florida, and one each in Virginia, Texas, and California." Much information from Iraq and the target holdings of al Qaeda had been available on the ten chosen targets and one other one in New Mexico, but recent events made access to that one too difficult.

In Yazdan, Khalid and his three teams of three individuals each had spent many hours in training on breaching and attacking each of the candidate targets. When Khalid was convinced that each target could be successfully attacked, he and the teams then brain-stormed those that could be best attacked, and made their own list of which of the ten targets should be the three primary and three alternate targets. When Khalid was confident that his rationale for the three best and the three second best targets was well thought out and achievable, he approached first Wadih Mohammed and then bin Laden with his recommendations. They both agreed. Bin Laden told Khalid that when the time came, he would urge Saddam to support the three targets that Khalid recommended. And in private, bin Laden told Khalid that even if Saddam did not agree, unless his reasons were compelling, bin Laden would likely give Khalid the go-ahead on the three recommended targets. "After all," bin Laden had said, "we are the field soldiers of Allah, and unlike the West, I will rely on the best judgment of my field commander. And Khalid, that is you."

Khalid's first order of business was to personally conduct a reconnaissance of each candidate target and then review with his teams the support apparatus and people that Wadih Mohammed had put in place. Together they would go over again all available information to validate, or, if necessary, modify their plans for attacking the targets. Khalid would have the month of October to accomplish this and at the same time, continue to age his cover and that of the individuals on the three teams.

Following the reevaluation of the targets and the selection analyses that he had done in Yazdan, Khalid would begin the final training phase of rehearsing in the actual target areas, the attacks to be carried out. At that time, the weapons to be used would be placed in the hands of the three teams. When Khalid was convinced the teams were strike-ready and present with their weapons, he would report that to Wadih Mohammed and stand by to receive the command to strike.

Khalid had committed every aspect of the operational planning for *Retribution* to memory. His only written material was the legitimate schedule of places he would visit and people he would contact in working his cover. But sufficient time and flexibility was built into his itinerary to allow for his *Retribution* work and the contacts from al Qaeda that would be supporting him. His schedule on the portions of the plan that applied to al Qaeda had already proceeded him and was in the hands of those who would be assisting him and his teams. "Now," he said aloud, "I am ready," rising from the chair and heading into the bathroom for a shave and shower and then to dress in his Armani suit. His first appointment was picking him up at 9:00 a.m.

Abdul Khalid was a man of exceptional energy and dedication and in his heart-of-hearts, he believed he was a man of destiny involved in a cause that he had taken on as a teenager with blind faith and allegiance. He would be hard pressed to explain in a rational way why he felt an obligation to carry out the orders he received from those higher up in the pecking order of his cause, but he believed he was willing to give his life for that cause. When those people or organizations engaged in terrorism recruited and obtained the services of an Abdul Khalid, they had acquired a formidable weapon. His resolve would now be tested.

October was also a particularly busy time for Bart Lowe and the person who had become his ardent romantic interest, Maria Salah. Bart worked his way out of his funk of grief and feelings of helplessness for those killed in the U.S. Embassy London bombing and plunged himself back into the DAS Headquarters' constantly changing agenda. An agenda that mirrored the international events or crisis that filled the daily newspapers of the world. If anything was happening in the political-military conduct of a nation, then Bart Lowe and the DAS had an attaché involved in observing and reporting. Bart once again became the lead by example—care for his people, no problem is too great if we do our best—leader that had earned him a well-deserved reputation in most circles in Washington in which he moved. The London aftermath, the expanding peacekeeping role for the United States in Kosovo, and the working toward a return to normalcy in relations with China, were still the major claimants of his time. Nevertheless, he made extra efforts not to neglect more than a hundred other countries that he and his attachés were responsible for watching.

Maria Salah, who had always been a busy person, was someone who led several lives. She was many things to many people. To her Ambassador and the other people in her Embassy, she was a wealth of knowledge about the USA and a walking reference library of the right contacts throughout the Washington government. She simply knew more about America than anyone else and she was very much in demand. Her own headquarters at the Lebanese Intelligence Service in Beirut, viewed her as simply their best resource in the most important country in the world. As a result, she could almost always call her own shots. No one would ever think of ordering her home. And from the American perspective, she was the darling of the friendly foreign intelligence services. When the answer to a question dealing with the Middle East seemed too difficult for a U.S. agency to handle, they usually turned to Maria Salah. And she hardly ever disappointed them. Many of the higher ups in the FBI, CIA, NSA, and DIA had, from time-to-time, doubted her, thinking she was just too good to be true. But she had come through for them so many times that after awhile, their doubts went away and they accepted her for what she said she was—a true ally of the United States. And in reality, that's what she was, a friend. That part had been easy for her. The United States could do, and had done, so much more for her country than she or Lebanon could repay, that the information they asked for was willingly given. Her phenomenal success was based on her true expertise. She knew the Middle East like the back of her hand. She knew the main players like she knew herself. She had grown up there, had survived the worst years, and had never forgotten an important event, political group, or leader. She was genuinely that good.

In the spying, espionage, and intelligence business, information is the chief currency. Information provided now to a needy person becomes a debt that can be reclaimed later. And Maria Salah had acquired a lifetime of IOUs that she was regularly calling in while at the same time, collecting new future ones, as she moved into the senior years of her career.

Maria Salah had first learned about America from her Catholic father, a professor at Beirut University. He believed in the western world, in America, and in those who advocated democracy and freedom. She followed his teachings and as a result, she was able to carry out her responsibilities for Lebanon and the United States with a clear conscience. There was only one flaw. She had some baggage that no one knew about. No one in the leadership of the Lebanese Intelligence Service, no one in her government, and certainly, no one at the Lebanese Embassy. And she was almost certain that no one in the U.S. Intelligence agencies knew. The problem was that many years ago when her country was torn apart in war and many people were just trying to survive, a group of people had helped her family and had saved Maria's life. Without their help, she and her family would have died and she was naturally very grateful. This group of people made it clear after she was no longer in danger, that at some time in the future, she would have the opportunity to repay them for their help. As those things go, it was several years later when she was asked for something in return. The request was so trivial and unimportant, and she just a junior officer in her intelligence service career, that she did not hesitate to comply. The requests for assistance continued over the years, but always were for such small non-sensitive matters that she couldn't say 'no' and after a time, she was lulled into thinking that the routine, nothing important, requests would be all she would ever receive. Then finally, too late, she realized that she had fallen into one of the oldest techniques of the spy business. She couldn't say 'no.' If she did, the information would be leaked to her bosses and she would appear to be a traitor—she knew that. It was only a matter of time before something very important was asked of her and she would be faced with a major decision that could bring her world, a world she cherished, to an abrupt end. Unfortunately, that request had arrived in Washington a short time ago and she was agonizing over how to deal with it. She had always prided herself in being in complete control of her life and now that control was in jeopardy.

Maria Salah also had another challenge to the control of her life. She was worried that she was falling in love with Bart Lowe.

Maria had started her relationship with Bart as one more close liaison arrangement that would benefit his agency, the DAS, and at the same time, be helpful to her in her job in Washington and to the Lebanese Intelligence Service. Her expectations going in were no more than good offices with a senior level official in an important U.S. agency who could be called upon when the need arose. But she quickly found out that she liked Bart Lowe. They had a lot in common. Although they were from different cultures and backgrounds, they were both over achievers, who had dedicated their lives to their professions and serving their countries, and both were workaholics. At the same time, they both liked to have a good time and appreciated participating in the many cultural and entertainment opportunities in Washington. And perhaps most importantly, Bart had rekindled strong romantic and physical urges in Maria that she hadn't felt in years. She had simply been too busy in a man's world. Bart was responsible for resurfacing a feminine feeling of warmth that Maria had forgotten she had.

By the last week in October, they had moved into a full romantic affair. In planning her schedule for the week, she carefully planned the times she would be available to be with Bart. She suspected that he did the same thing. They had been intimate a half dozen times and each time, Maria thought it was better than the last. And recently, she had found herself thinking with anticipation about their next romantic encounter. This was in sharp contrast to her cultural upbringing about the role of women in her own society. She had not yet thought about where all this was going but she knew for certain that she wanted her romantic involvement with Bart Lowe to continue.

Saturday nights were usually free nights for diplomats in Washington. Most of the official functions took place during the week or on Friday nights. Bart and Maria had eased into a pattern of getting together on Saturday nights even though they may have seen each other officially during the week. On this Saturday, the last Saturday in October, at 2:30 in the afternoon of what looked like a good day, Bart Lowe sat in his office playing paper catch-up for those things he didn't get to during the past week. It was quiet in the office, the others having left about noon, and Bart breathed a sigh of relief as he initialed the last paper he was going to review and threw it into his out box. He glanced at his watch, saw that he was running on time for his three o'clock racquetball game with John Kitchen at the Pentagon Athletic Club, and picked up the phone for one more call. He punched in a now familiar Washington, D.C. exchange number that was answered on the third ring by a husky voiced woman.

"Yes?" the woman's voice asked.

"Maria. Is that you?" Bart asked.

"Of course it is, Bart. Who else do you think would be foolish enough to be in the office on such a gorgeous Saturday afternoon—except you and me?"

"Naturally. But somebody has to do it. Right, Maria?"

"If you say so."

"Right. I'm just calling to confirm that we're still on for tonight."

"To be sure, moi General!" Maria replied. She was a master of six languages and liked to mix her light conversations with various foreign words and phrases.

"Six-thirty for cocktails and dinner at my place?"

"I wouldn't miss it for the world, Bart. I love Sergeant Child's cooking."

"And casual dress?"

"I'm not sure I have anything, as you Americans say 'casual' but I promise to look presentable."

"I'm sure of it. Whatever suits you, Maria. I'll be in a shirt and cords and maybe if it's as cool out there as it looks now, a sweater."

"Okay," Maria said lightly, smiling at how Bart always told her what the dress would be. She supposed it was his military background always wanting to be in the appropriate uniform.

"And the other…" Bart's question trailed off.

"Yes, to that, too, Bart," Maria replied, smiling even more now at Bart's awkward attempt at asking did she intend to spend the night and not wishing to reveal even a hint of such activity over the phone.

"Great," Bart said with almost little boy enthusiasm. "I'll see you then," and smiling, ended the call.

That night turned out to be one of the most romantic that either Bart or Maria could remember. It started with cocktails on Bart's rear deck facing the wrap around hedge, manicured lawn, and the last beautiful flowers of the season. The cool air caused them to sit close together on the green striped, canvas covered, deck swing. Bart had converted Maria to sharing his favorite cocktail drink—Manhattans over ice. She now enjoyed them as much as Bart but limited herself to one. The speakers on the deck played soft music from the small library in the house. They filled each other in on the highlights of their workweek and before they knew it, the cocktails were gone, and SFC Childs was summoning them for dinner.

He had prepared a chateaubriand surrounded with carrots, green asparagus, and roasted small potatoes. Maria called it a meal fit for a sultan. The food was complemented by a red Cabernet Sauvignon and the candlelight setting for two with string music now in the background made for a perfect, private and singularly tasty meal, unlike either of them could remember on the Embassy circuit.

"Is SFC Child's really this good," Bart thought to himself, "or is it the company?" He decided it was probably both.

SFC Child's, before departing for the night, served homemade Key Lime Pie, one of Bart's favorites, and something altogether new for Maria. Her obvious pleasure as she sampled it and the following compliment made SFC Childs' day.

"Sir, I have set the coffee pot and cups in the library along with some liqueurs. If you have nothing more for me, I'll say goodnight."

When General Lowe nodded and said, "Well done, Bill. I can't remember a better meal," SFC Childs turned to Maria and said, "It was good to see you again, Ms. Salah. I must tell you that whenever the General knows you are coming, he is in the best of humors."

"How nice to know, Sergeant Childs. Thank you," Maria replied and beamed at Bart.

After dinner, they moved into the library, drank their coffees, and topped the evening off with beakers of Kahlua over crushed ice. Listening to the soft strains of music from Bart's carefully selected CDs, they kicked off their shoes and danced to several romantic tunes they recognized. Holding Maria closely and swaying slowly to the music gave Bart a contentment and excitement he had not felt in some time. And if he was any judge of women, Maria felt the same way.

By eleven o'clock, they had drained their glasses, drank their last cup of coffee, and danced their last dance.

Holding Maria in his arms, Bart asked, "Are you ready for bed?"

"More than ready, Bart," Maria replied with a gleam in her eyes and a softness in her embrace that promised the pleasures that only a woman can bestow upon a man.

Later, as they lay naked side-by-side in Bart's king-size bed, neither was in a hurry to consummate their lovemaking. Rather, both were more concerned with prolonging their foreplay as they tenderly and sensually touched each other in the most intimate ways.

Although their relationship was still in its early stage, Bart felt that Maria was the best and most passionate lover of any woman he had ever made love to. And she, in turn, was confident that Bart had the most sensuous hands and touch of any lover she had ever had. Both were caring and considerate lovers doing all that they could to arouse, excite, and please, the other. After some time together, when they both sensed that they couldn't stand waiting any longer to take that final step to ecstasy, Maria gently, but firmly, pushed Bart from his side facing her onto his back. Then she slowly, but very deliberately passed one leg over him until she was tightly astride him and then she lowered her mouth to him and as her tongue sought his, she slowly, warmly, and wetly, lowered herself onto his manhood. As he received her and the indescribable warmth he was now feeling, he uttered, "Oh, my god."

CHAPTER 21

COUNTDOWN

Sitting at his desk at the DAS Headquarters on a Monday morning in late November, Bart Lowe had just finished reading *The Washington Post*. He found that the *Post* was a good barometer on what was going on around the world and usually provided good news coverage of most political-military events—the DAS' stock in trade. In this morning's paper, the major stories read almost like the Information and Intelligence Reports he read from his attachés. Except the paper rarely had to worry about questions like: Was the information complete, accurate, classified, or sensitive? Did the source of the information need protecting? Nevertheless, the *Post* sometimes offered insight into matters taking place in a foreign country that were of interest or potential interest to the Defense Department and the U.S. military, and Bart had used information from the *Post* on more than one occasion to task his attachés to find out more on the subject. "Today's paper," Bart thought, "smacks of a return to normalcy." The U.S. Embassy bombing investigation had moved to page four although all of the U.S. embassies abroad remained on heightened alert. The peacekeeping mission in Kosovo, the return of the ethnic Albanians, and the disarming of the Kosovo Liberation Army had all moved to routine reporting, as had the Indian-Pakistani conflict. China remained on the front burner, chiefly because Congress was still looking for a scapegoat to blame the Chinese espionage on, and most of the federal government had a plan for better counterintelligence protection of the Nation's secrets.

In the way of new developments, Iraq had returned to a more aggressive posture, regularly firing against the U.S. aircraft patrolling the "no fly" zones. That reminded Bart of something he had not checked on in a while and he made a note to do so. Beyond that, football was in full swing again and Bart was a die-hard fan of the Florida Gators, the Florida State Seminoles, the Miami Hurricanes and the Washington Redskins, and in that order. Monday's paper, with the college ranking polls, contained good news for all the Florida teams. The Redskins were a different matter. With no change in the coaching staff, Bart, like most critics, believed that the leadership necessary to turn the team around was not present and the outlook for the season was bleak.

"Joan, will you see if Mr. Mellon is in the building and if so, ask him to come up and see me," Bart asked his secretary over the intercom. "The subject is Iraq."

"Yes, sir."

In less than five minutes, Tom Mellon, the head of the Defense HUMINT Service, knocked on Bart's door, entered and said, "General Lowe, you wanted to see me?"

Bart, rising from his desk and walking over to greet Mellon with a handshake said, "Tom, good to see you. Thank you for coming up so quickly. Have you had coffee yet?"

"I have, but not enough to refuse some of Joan Weber's good 14th Floor coffee. Black, please."

"Fine, please have a seat, Tom." Bart walked over to the door, stuck his head out, and asked Joan to bring them coffee.

"Joan said the subject was Iraq?" Tom asked after Joan handed him a steaming cup of coffee.

"Yes, Tom. Did we or CIA ever learn anything more about that scrap of paper that Ed Royster turned over to us?"

"Funny that you should ask. We had a report that just came in over the weekend from a legal traveler in Africa. When you asked us to see if we could find out more about the automobile accident in Baghdad, I checked our sources and found we had a stay-behind contact there who is a doctor. He's been with us since we had to pull our DAO out of Iraq before the Desert Storm war. He hasn't given us much of value over the years but he is loyal and I thought it might be something he could find out about. The problem was contacting him. It's difficult. We have used legal travelers in the past but we didn't have anyone who could go right away. So we waited for the source in Africa to make one of his scheduled trips. And apparently, he was able to contact the doctor and the Doc had some information."

At that point, Tom Mellon reached in his inside coat pocket and took out a small notebook. He referred to it and then told Bart, "According to the Doc, on the date that Ed Royster's contact said the accident took place, a high-ranking officer was admitted to the hospital in critical condition as a result of an automobile accident. The Doc didn't know anything about the accident but the guy was someone very important because none other then Saddam Hussein visited him at the hospital and according to the Doc, Saddam had never been there before. Also, the Doc said that the VIP was at the hospital for about a month recuperating from his injuries and they gave him security guards around his room and he had many visitors at all hours of the day and night."

"Did the doctor know the man's name?" Bart asked.

"Oh, yeah," Tom replied referring once again to his notes. "The Doc says his name was Ali Hassan al-Majid but it wasn't a name he recognized. I didn't plan to tell you about this report until the analysts had a chance to look at the report and check out this guy's name."

"Okay, Tom, that's interesting. Please make sure that Tony Roper at DIA sees it right away and put it on the wire for the CIA and FBI counterterrorist people. Anything else coming your way on the London bombing?"

"No, sir, nothing definitive, but the word on the street is that it is probably a bin Laden job."

"Okay. Thanks, Tom. Please keep me posted."

When Bart returned to his desk, he looked through the stack of "hold" items until he found a copy of the scrap of paper given to him by Ed Royster.

- *Coordination with W.M. continues. Targets passed, Phase two training begun.*
- *Special weapon acquisition weapon finalized. Deposit made. Delivery date and place agreed upon.*
- *Chemical and biological weapons identified and available.*
- *Cyber weapon progressing. Recommendations expected soon.*

He looked at the four points and the English translation, but he still did not know what to make of it. He made another note to himself on his scratch pad to talk to Roper.

Later that same day, John Kitchen called Bart on the secure line.

"Bart, we have a development on the London bombing. I don't know if it will prove to be anything but right now, it's the only viable lead we have turned up. It seems there is a Pakistani who is employed by the Embassy named Thomas Mandi. In fact, he is head of the Embassy Cleaning Team. He is well liked and the embassy people were concerned that he was one of the people killed in the blast that the Brits or we have been unable to identify. Now someone remembers that he was scheduled to go on home leave to Pakistan for six weeks on the day of the bombing and one of the surviving Security Guards remembers him departing that morning. His leave time was up a week ago and no one has heard from him and according to the Brits, all of the records that would have shown a leave address were destroyed in the bombing. In London, where the guy lived, there was no additional information and the Brits say that there is no record of his departing the U.K. or his arrival in Pakistan. Of course, if he is involved, he could have used a phony passport to depart the U.K. and to enter Pakistan. Looking for male Pakistanis going from London to Pakistan on any given day will be like looking for the proverbial needle in a haystack with only lukewarm support from the

Pakistanis. They have never forgiven us for holding up their money and the jet aircraft we promised them a few years ago.

"Still, there is one other piece of evidence that suggests that he could be our guy. The forensics experts came up with eight caster wheels in the bomb wreckage that, based on the damage to them, suggest that they were at ground zero of the blast. The experts have postulated that the bomb was somehow rolled into position in close proximity to the conference room. Now when the lead about the cleaning guy comes along, our group finds out that the cleaners use a standard cleaning cart that rolls around on four sets of caster wheels. The problem is, no one seems to know exactly how many carts there were and if one's missing because a number of others were also destroyed. Bottom line is, our group believe, and the Brits agree, that a cleaning cart probably contained the bomb."

"John, I know exactly what you mean by the cleaning carts. Hell, we use them in this building and probably most of the buildings in the U.S. government. But how in the hell could you get enough explosives in the embassy to do that much damage?" Bart asked.

"If the cleaning guy is our bomber, perhaps he brought in the bomb material over a long period of time and stacked it somewhere in the embassy. At any rate, this looks like our best lead and we will be following it up."

"But is there a connection to bin Laden, John?"

"We are not sure, Bart, but remember that bin Laden started the al Qaeda movement from Pakistan more than a decade ago and many of his recruits for the Holy War were Pakistanis."

"And do they still have a safe haven there?"

"The Pakistanis say 'no' but we think 'yes'."

"Alright, John. Thanks for the update. Anything else we can do?"

"No, Bart, your people in London and here at home have been very helpful. We'll be in touch."

Bart made the third note of the day to himself to discuss with, and pass on some guidance regarding this latest development to the DATT in Islamabad.

During the month of October, Abdul Khalid had carried out his *Retribution* duties in several places in the United States. He had met with the three teams, who had all arrived safely in the USA and were in place at their locations. Working together they had verified their targets. He had personally met with those who would be giving him and his teams support, although they had no idea what the support was for or what it was intended to accomplish. He was pleased and came away with even greater admiration and respect for Wadih Mohammed and Osama bin Laden for the support bases they had organized in America over the last ten years. He had personally been aware of how extensive their organization was in New York but he had no idea of the al Qaeda capabilities in other areas. "Allah had, no doubt, smiled on bin Laden," he thought. And for the others involved in this Holy War undertaking, Khalid's leadership was inspiring. His confidence, competence, and enthusiasm made all things seem possible. His fellow conspirators were convinced that they were going to be successful in carrying out this most holy of holy missions, *Retribution.*

In November he had returned to each target area to oversee a "dry run" of the target strikes by each team against the primary and alternate targets. Some in bin Laden's movement would have argued that the rehearsals were too risky and if they failed, it would put the real operation at risk. However, Khalid believed in what he had learned in the U.S. Army—that training and practice make perfect. And the dry runs, short of detonating any weapons, did reveal several flaws that were corrected. Khalid was pleased with the results.

Now Khalid, having returned from New York, was back in Florida at the furnished condominium in Cape Canaveral that his cover company in Saudi Arabia leased for visiting executives to the nearby Kennedy Space Center. This location was close to his principal support base for *Retribution.* For the remaining days of November, Khalid would put into motion the movement of the weapons to the three teams' locations. The arming of the teams was the last phase of putting *Retribution* into its strike-ready posture. As was his habit when he was at the condominium, he rose early and went for a two-mile jog along the beach. He used this time to mentally go over the next steps he would take. Most importantly, he recounted, would be the movement of the "suitcase nuclear bombs," not one, but two, Allah be praised, from Florida to New York. They would be going by truck concealed in a load of fresh citrus fruit—oranges and grapefruits. They would arrive in northern Virginia and be joined together by the Washington strike team with the detonating devices that were already present in a cleverly disguised cache. The Washington team leader was a nuclear arms specialist and he would advise Khalid when the bombs and the detonating devices were assembled, armed and ready for strike. The bombs had arrived by an Egyptian ship destined for the Canaveral port during the summer and off-loaded onto a shrimp boat in the waters off the Florida coast.

The biological weapon had been hidden in a 2,000 pound shipment of dates that arrived in Miami from Morocco and was presently located in south Miami in a gourmet market that featured fruits and wines from the Middle East. It would remain there in cold storage until picked up by the Florida strike team the day before execution.

Already present in New York, the cyber weapon was in the form of six small computer disks. The disks were being held by an individual who was a known computer nerd who had hundreds of disks in his possession. He would turn the six disks over to the strike team when he received a prearranged phone call. This call would also take place the day before execution. Khalid anticipated that all would be ready by the first of December and he planned to send the ready-to-strike message to Wadih Mohammed on that day by a coded message over the Internet. In the meantime, Khalid's itinerary of work for the cover firm in Saudi Arabia was scheduled through the end of the year and regardless of the strike time, he would complete his cover work and then return to Saudi. He had, of course, allowed sufficient time and flexibility so that he could change the schedule and go wherever he felt he might be needed. As he finished up his run, he had worked up a good sweat, his mind was clear, and he was looking forward to swimming a few laps in the condominium's beachside pool before getting dressed and starting the day in his cover role.

Maria Salah's dilemma had increased in the last month. She now realized that she had fallen in love with Bart Lowe and she was beginning to receive vibes that he felt the same way. She had begun to have thoughts that earlier would never have entered her mind, like: "What would it be like to be married to a Bart Lowe? To live in a large house in suburban Virginia or Maryland? To give up the various power positions I have worked so hard to get and to hold." It had not been easy for her as a woman in her country or in the Arab world. And she was proud of all that she had achieved. If Bart asked her to marry him, and if she said 'yes,' she would have to forfeit her position with the Lebanese Intelligence Service. And what was really surprising to her, she was beginning to think she would be willing to risk it all to be Mrs. Bart Lowe and share the rest of her life with that kind and loving man. And although she was embarrassed to admit it, she found herself daydreaming about their lovemaking. And it sometimes made her angry. "Imagine me—Maria Salah— after all the danger and conflicts I have been through and survived in my career in professional espionage, feeling that way about a man—an American man at that!"

The other side of her dilemma was the increasing taskings she had had of late from the group to whom she believed herself to be indebted. Although she had made the decision to comply with the first detailed request for information about some things purely American that she had received during the summer, she wasn't sure from what level of the organization the tasking had originated. In answering the tasking, she pleaded that she would not be able to respond to future taskings due to her own very heavy workload. That plea, unfortunately, had quickly been rejected and a specific threat of compromise had been tendered. Also, there was no doubt that the threat had come from the very top. While there was no explanation as to how the information she had been asked to provide would be used, she had been in the intelligence business long enough to know that it related to some kind of targeting. The information requested related to a number of government facilities in the Washington area and at other locations in the United States. Maria suspected that the intention of seeking information about several facilities was to conceal the single location that was to be the target. She also knew that because of the bombing of the U.S. Embassy in London, the American authorities had shifted their concern from an internal threat to one abroad and thus, could be more vulnerable. Maria feared that the group that was now asking her to provide additional information, recognized that vulnerability in the United States, and was readying some kind of attack.

The problem, Maria worried, was that she could be viewed as part of the conspiracy for any attack or incident by either the perpetrators, or by the Americans if somehow they learned of her involvement. Not knowing what else to do, she had continued to provide the requested information although she had hedged by not reporting all of the information to which she had access pleading that what she was able to provide was all that she was able to obtain. She knew that the group would recognize that and probably get back at her in some way. Then she received a communication that really alarmed her. The group told her that her name had been given to "someone" who, in the event of an emergency, could contact her for help. The message was clear that the "someone" would be on an important mission for the group and if things went wrong, would expect her to provide a safe haven and assistance.

This, more than any previous request led Maria to believe that the group was definitely planning some action to take place in the United States. Her dilemma was growing.

CHAPTER 22

INDICATIONS AND WARNING

The U.S. government and military have, for years, spent billions of dollars on creating, maintaining, and improving the capability to detect the imminence of foreign hostilities in order to preclude surprise attacks against America such as the Japanese attack on Pearl Harbor in 1941. The use of superior technology to detect organized military activities, weapons, and threats anywhere in the world, together with dynamic collection, analysis, reporting, and rapid dissemination of threat information served the nation well throughout the Cold War years and into the 1990s.

The rise of terrorism in the 1990s and particularly those terrorists interested in inflicting mass death and destruction posed one of the deadliest and most difficult to detect threats ever faced by the United States. The traditional indications and warning signs that U.S. professionals were so used to seeing in dealing with sophisticated enemies and weaponry were not present when dealing with terrorists. The importance of human intelligence and human infiltration of terrorist groups by intelligence and law enforcement agencies and others became exponentially more important. Agencies such as the FBI and the CIA Counterterrorism Center relied heavily on these techniques to provide indications and early warning of terrorist attacks; at the same time estimating that both international and domestic attacks would increase and that terrorists' operational techniques and weapons would become more skilled. Their fears were realized when the embassy bombings in Africa and London came along.

The intelligence analysts and intelligence and security professionals in Washington were worried. They were worried beyond the warnings that the President and his national security people had given the nation last January. There were no new developments concerning the London perpetrators. Then, on the first of December, the State Department was forced to make the decision to temporarily close six U.S. embassies in Africa. The six had all reported being under surveillance by suspicious individuals. The six—Gambia, Togo, Madagascar, Liberia, Namibia, and Senegal—had, like the rest of the U.S. embassies around the world, been on heightened alert since the London bombing.

Officials in Washington were concerned that the U.S. Embassy bombing in London reflected a continuation in a number of worldwide attacks against the United States. They suspected that America, at home and abroad, would be more vulnerable and less security minded during the Christmas-New Year holidays. Security managers everywhere were doing everything possible to remind Americans of the danger of terrorist attacks. The warnings, however, largely fell on too-busy-with-other-things ears as Americans shifted into high shopping gear with only twenty-four days left until Christmas. In fact, on the second of December, a poll conducted in several cities in the U.S. revealed that, of ten problems that concerned Americans the most, completing their Christmas shopping ranked number one. Number two was paying for the Christmas holidays and three was concern for the impact of Y2K. Terrorist threats against America was ranked tenth. The poll was carried by the AP Wire Service and appeared on the front pages of most of the world's newspapers. It was read with interest by a disparate number of people.

In Iraq, the article was highlighted to Saddam Hussein in his morning briefing by Saddam's public affairs officer who was surprised when Saddam asked him to repeat the item. To himself, Saddam thought, "Of course. Why didn't I think of that?" The other senior Iraqi staff members who were present at Saddam's morning briefing remarked on Saddam's good humor afterward. "He smiled," they said, "throughout the entire briefing."

Ali Hassan later that same morning in his office in Baghdad noted the article as he was going through the translated major western wire service stories provided to him daily by the Iraqi Intelligence Ministry. "If they only knew," Ali thought. Just yesterday Ali had delivered the word to Saddam Hussein that he had received from Wadih Mohammed that the strike teams were in place in the United States and were prepared to strike on order. Saddam had only nodded and dismissed Ali without another word. Having worked with Saddam for so long, Ali took Saddam's nod to mean, "I'll let you know when I have decided."

Already that morning, Ali had saturated his handkerchief with perspiration. His sweating was caused by his continuing dilemma. He knew that if Saddam was going through with *Retribution*, and Ali believed Saddam was mad enough to do so, it would be soon. Saddam, he reasoned, would not want to wait too long for fear that the plan or the terrorists would be discovered and compromised. "Mother of Allah," he said aloud to himself and then thought, "the minute Saddam gives the word for the strikes to take place, my usefulness to him will be over and my days numbered. My only hope is for Saddam to hold onto me until after the attacks are carried out in case anything goes wrong. But that may only be a matter of hours, or at the most, days." Once again, Ali began going over in his mind what he considered to be his options. None of them seemed to be good ones.

The "What are America's Problems?" poll article was highlighted in Ambassador B.J. Ross' United States Information Agency read file in Kiev in the Ukraine. She, like most U.S. diplomats serving outside the country, had reacted to the embassy bombing in London and closures in Africa, and was nervous about her own embassy's security posture. The longer she sat at her desk late in the afternoon, the more concerned she became. Then suddenly, she picked up her secure telephone and punched in the DATT's number. Colonel Farrar answered on the second ring.

"DAO."

"Joe, is that you?"

"Yes. Who's this?" Farrar replied not recognizing the Ambassador's voice because of the security sound distortion.

"Joe, this is B.J. Ross. I take it nothing ever came of that report you forwarded in May?"

"Well, not exactly. The DATT in London, as well as the COS there and the FBI Legal Attaché picked it up for action at my request.

"And?"

"There was also a possible lead coming out of the DAO in Ankara, Turkey, that might have been related but the lead petered out in Egypt. Quite frankly, the action probably came to a halt when the embassy was bombed in London."

"Well, Joe, I want to resurrect it. You get a hold of Arlen Garrand and tell him I want to put a full court press on this thing. I am going to send a cable to your headquarters, CIA, and the FBI and see if we can get this thing moving again."

"Yes, ma'am. Roger that."

At Bolling Air Force Base in Washington, at DIA's Defense Analysis Center, analyst Tony Roper, who had just returned from a week long trip, settled into his small cubicle on the third floor for three to four hours of catch-up reading. He noted that there were two yellow phone messages marked 'urgent' in a stack of about twenty. The urgent ones were from his point-of-contact at CIA's Counterterrorism Center and the other from the J2 at CENTCOM, Brigadier General Great.

"Urgent?" he thought, "lots of people in this business think their questions are urgent." He decided he would wait until he had at least scanned his piles of reports and information before returning any calls. Then he would be in a better position to answer questions.

"But, first things first," he said aloud. He then removed his coat, rolled up his sleeves, picked up his coffee mug from his desk, and walked around the corner of his cubicle to the main corridor where the admin shop was located with the never-empty pot of coffee. When he had filled his extra large mug with the black, hot, almost syrupy liquid, he returned to his work area and settled into his plain but lumbar supported desk chair. He first read the past week's newspapers—*The Washington Post* and *The New York Times*. As he quickly scoured the front-page stories, he used his highlighter to mark something he might want to read again later. When he noticed the 'America's Problems' poll, he said aloud to himself, "So what else is new?" Tony finished the seven days' worth of newspapers in an hour, his self imposed limit.

After the papers, Tony went on to the all source Intelligence and Information Reports regarding terrorism that had been received by DIA the last week. Tony guessed that the reports would number about 200 judging from the size of the stack. The Admin people had sorted them alphabetically by country. The reports were from a wide variety of sources, including the DAS, CIA, FBI, NSA, the Military Intelligence Services, the State Department, and several friendly allied Intelligence Services. The volume of reporting had been high since the London bombing.

By the time Tony got to the J's, he had finished his coffee and was thinking about a second cup. Then he saw a HUMINT report from the Defense HUMINT Service that almost made him fall out of his chair. It was the report that Tom Mellon had briefed Bart Lowe on at the beginning of the week. What got his attention was the name appearing in the report, Ali Hassan al-Majid. Tom recognized the name of one of the really original bad guys in Iraq. Tony was confident if Ali was involved, that Iraq was up to something no good. "No wonder CIA and CENTCOM said their calls were urgent," he said to himself and immediately reached for his "hold" box and looked for the copy of that scrap of paper found in Baghdad.

In Dhaka, Bangladesh, it was Friday evening and Lieutenant Colonel Frank Windom and his wife Jan were having an after dinner coffee at their favorite Bengali hangout, the Compute-a-Cup. It was crowded but they managed to get a booth from a Bengali couple who were just leaving. Shortly after their coffees were served, the owner, Turan Dey, appeared and asked if he could join them.

"Of course, Turan. We haven't seen you in awhile. How have you been?" Frank asked, moving over in the booth to make room for Dey.

"Good, my friends. Busy, but that is good for business. How are things at the U.S. Embassy?"

"As you say, busy. Since the bombing in London, all of our people have been concerned over security." Colonel Windom told him.

"I am sure it must be a stressful time. But then your American holidays are coming up. Your Christmas. Your New Year's. That should bring better times."

"We certainly hope, Turan," Jan Windom replied.

"Speaking of the holidays," Dey continued, "did you see the article in *The New York Tribune* international edition this morning about what Americans see as their problems?" Turan Dey asked.

"Yes. We did," both Windom's answered, looking somewhat sheepish.

"I couldn't help notice that the American concern for terrorism was very low. I would think that after these earlier bombings of the U.S. embassies in Africa and the most recent one in London, the concern should be quite high. Is it because you Americans have great confidence in your internal security and believe that nothing could happen?"

Frank looked at Jan and smiled.

"We do, of course, have confidence in our abilities to detect and protect against attacks by those who would do us harm. But this is possibly something else that relates to the American psyche. If there is a clear and present danger or threat, Americans will react accordingly. Absent that clear and present danger, and it must be obvious, American tend to go about their business as usual and take a wait and see attitude," Frank explained. "I don't know if that answers your question very well, but it is probably the best I can do."

Jan nodded in agreement.

"We live and learn," Turan Dey acknowledged. "At any rate, when I read the article, and I'm not sure exactly why, I was curious to know what had happened to the young man I told you about in May or June. Do you remember?"

Frank nodded. Jan wasn't sure what Turan was talking about, but listened attentively.

"I rang up the number of his family here in Dhaka to see if he had returned to India. His mother told me a fascinating story. She said that he had told her that he had been hired for a special research project by a firm in Abu Dhabi. That he might be away for six months and that he probably would not be able to write. She did, however, receive a large check each month from the firm in Abu Dhabi to be deposited in her son's bank account. Then in October, she was notified by the firm in Abu Dhabi that her son had been killed in a freak oil-gas explosion related to his research. Due to the intensity of the blast, there were no remains. Fortunately, the Abu Dhabi firm told her, that they carried substantial insurance policies on all their contract employees because of the hazardous nature of the work. The insurance paid his mother the equivalent of $100,000 U.S. dollars. The mother was saddened to lose her son; he was one of six children, but his insurance policy would look after the family's welfare and for that, she was grateful," Turan Dey concluded.

"Whew. That's quite a story, Turan. What do you make of it?" Colonel Windom asked.

"Maybe it's just as his mother said, but I don't like it. Remember the part my friend Aziz told me about the mention of Baghdad. I don't trust those people."

"I hear you, Turan. I hear you," Windom replied.

A week passed.

It was 4:00 a.m. on Saturday morning, the 11th of December, at Bolling Air Force Base. Bart Lowe was sleeping soundly after a late night of embassy receptions. He thought he was dreaming about a buzzing sound. Then the sound woke him and he realized that the sound was coming from his STU-3 secure phone located on the desk in his small work-study adjacent to his bedroom. Once awake, he could see clearly and he then got out of bed and padded barefoot through the adjoining door to the desk and the ringing phone. He switched on the desk lamp, found a pencil and paper, and lifted the ringing receiver.

"Lowe here."

"How the hell are you, Soldier? Hope I didn't get you out of the sack too early."

Although the voice was scrambled by the security device, Bart recognized the caller by the choice of words.

"Is this the famous onward and upward Ambassador?"

"None other, Soldier."

"This old soldier's okay. How's everything in Kiev?"

"You received my cable last week to you and others?"

"Yes, indeed. And we do share your concern. I think you got everybody in town's attention."

"Well, wait until you read the latest. We have just put it on the wire and it's a joint message from me, your guy and the COS. The bottom line is that your guy's source has good reason to believe that a nuclear weapon was sold to someone and departed here sometime ago. The Russians working here with the Ukrainians that are in contact with the COS won't confirm it, but their denials are weak. We are going to try to put pressure on the guys in Moscow to own up. I know it's the weekend there and I wanted to make sure our cable doesn't get lost in the shuffle. This thing has me really worried, Bart, and you know I do not do that very easily."

"I'll vouch for that, B.J., and I'll run your cable down as soon as I get into work."

"Good old Bart. Still doing the Saturday Drill?"

"Have to, just to keep up with the young guys."

"I'm not buying that, Bart. You have always been the pacesetter. And on the diplomatic grapevine, I hear that you have a Lebanese beauty on your arm at all the best places in town."

"Yes, that's true, but only because my first choice had to go off to conquer the world."

"Believe me, Bart, there are days when I truly regret that decision."

"I hear you, B.J. But your country needs you and you still have mountains to climb."

"That's me, the climber."

CHAPTER 23

THE TWELFTH HOUR

Another week had passed. It was now one o'clock on the 20th of December. It was the first day of the official holiday period whereby all departments of the U.S. government and military begin a liberal leave policy allowing civilian workers and service members to take leave and spend time with their families. It meant that the U.S. government and the military would be at reduced strength for the next fourteen days.

Bart Lowe, Barbara Barnsworth, and Tom Mellon were in an official sedan heading west from DAS Headquarters toward Langley and CIA Headquarters. It was a beautiful but cold, clear, winter afternoon. The night before had brought Washington its first snow of the year and the trees that lined the George Washington Parkway were stately with their white coats. An Intelligence Community meeting had been called for 1:30 at the request of Bart and the Director of DIA, Lieutenant General Pat Eways, to be held at the Counterterrorist Center and chaired by René Softly.

As the sedan turned off the parkway and moved slowly along the winding road that led to the sprawling complex of buildings that was the CIA, set well back into the forest alongside the Potomac River, Bart was struck by the beauty of the CIA grounds. The natural beauty and serenity seemed to him to be in sharp contrast to the purpose of the meeting that he was about to attend. When the sedan reached the security gate, it was halted by the armed guards. General Lowe, Ms. Barnsworth, and Mr. Mellon's identification cards and Defense Security passes were verified and their names checked against the posted list of those attending the meeting. When they were cleared for entry, the sedan proceeded to the main entrance of the building that housed the CIA Headquarters and dropped its passengers. They entered the building and, after repeating the security checks at the visitors' registration desk, were met by an escort to take them to the Counterterrorist Center. At the Center, they were taken to a large conference room and offered coffee and refreshments prior to taking their seats. The time was now 1:27, and the other attendees were already present and seated around the large table. Bart shook hands with a number of people and said hello to others.

The principals of the meeting were seated at the table and their back-ups—for Bart, that was Barbara and Tom—were given chairs along the conference room walls. Bart and Lieutenant General Eways were in the first two chairs at the front of the table closest to a briefing lectern and a screen for visuals. At the other end of the table, seated at the head, was René Softly, the Chairperson for the meeting. The others present were Major General Don Odom, the Deputy National Security Advisor and former head of the DAS; Tom Glynn, Deputy Director of the National Security Agency; CIA's Deputy Director and Deputy Director of Operations; John Kitchen from the FBI; Ambassador Warren Forthwright, the Assistant Secretary of State for Intelligence and Research (INR); Robert Softly, a retired Army General Officer and now Assistant Secretary of Defense for C^3I (and René Softly's husband); Bernie Meurrens the Deputy Director of the Department of Energy (DOE); Senator "Kit" Karson from the SSCI; Lieutenant General Ben Holland, the J3, JCS; the J2s from EUCOM and CENTCOM; Major General Len Fisher; and Brigadier General Keith Great; and the Deputy Commandant of the Coast Guard, Admiral Will Sayers; and the Deputy Director of the U.S. Customs, Beth Rollins.

At exactly 1:30, René Softly called the meeting to order.

"I thank you all for being here today and responding so quickly to our call. I know that is not easy, given your own demanding duties, particularly during this holiday period. Today we are going to discuss a case code named DISCOVERY."

This brought some laughter around the table.

"I know, I know," René responded. "There is no intention here. The name just came out of the random selection of code names. And as you will see, for those of you who are not already familiar with elements of the case, the subject is a serious one."

René Softly had everyone's attention again.

"Also, as I think you all know, General Pat Eways and General Bart Lowe requested this meeting. Mr. Tony Roper, DIA's National Intelligence Officer for Terrorism will now give us an overview of DISCOVERY."

Tony Roper, dressed in a dark blue suit, white shirt, red tie, and black wing-tips, moved to the podium. He pressed a button on the podium to indicate to his assistant in the room behind the visuals screen that he was ready for his first graphic which was a simple one containing only one word— DISCOVERY.

"What we are calling DISCOVERY today, first surfaced to our attention last May in two reports written by the Defense Attaché and CIA's Chief of Station in Kiev. Both reports are contained in the folder in front of you for those of you who have not see them. The essence of those reports suggests that up to five of the forty-eight missing nuclear suitcase bombs in the former Soviet Union are, or were, located in the Ukraine and that a buyer with Arab connections made an offer to buy one or more of the bombs. The buyers in this report were allegedly based in London; an attorney and an oil company conglomerate representative. Leads were passed to the DATT and COS in London for follow-up and MI-5's cooperation was requested by our people, the Ukrainian and the Russian Intelligence Service. The bottom line of those efforts by MI-5 was that both suspects had traveled to Kiev but both were able to substantiate legitimate business reasons for their trips. They believe both individuals have been involved in several illegal arms transactions, but MI-5 has not been able to prove an actionable case. Then, when the embassy was bombed in London, the priority of interest was lost with the death of the DATT, COS, and Legal Attaché and the shift in urgency by MI-5 to the embassy bombing.

"We then had movement again two weeks ago at the request of Ambassador Ross in Kiev and INR here in town." Roper said, nodding at Ambassador Forthwright.

"Just last week we had a flurry of activity again based on a joint report from the embassy in Kiev. That report is also in your folders. This report provides information about a former Russian military officer who was also mentioned in the earlier report. His opulence as a member of a Russian crime syndicate increased dramatically this past summer. In addition, he tried to recruit a member of the Russian Nuclear Control Organization in the Ukraine. The Ukrainian authorities arrested the former officer on the charge of espionage, and they suspect that he has been involved in illegal arms sales, but they have no proof, and he has been released on bail. The State Department, Defense Attachés, and the CIA in Moscow have all pressed their Russian counterparts there to come clean on any information they may have involving any unaccounted for suitcase nuclear bombs in the Ukraine. They have all maintained that they know nothing, but their denials are weak, and thus, we believe, suspect. If the Russian end is a dead-end and it probably is, we have explored other possibilities that we believe relate to this matter."

At this point, Roper paused briefly to pour himself a glass of water from a small thermos sitting on a shelf in the lectern. He then signaled for another graphic—a map of Russia and the Middle East—to be displayed.

"In July, the DAO in Ankara, Turkey, reported that a Turkish sea captain had delivered an unusually small cargo from the port of Odessa, on the Black Sea," Roper said, pointing to the location on the graphic map, "to an anchorage off of Alexandria, Egypt. The cargo originated in Kiev and reportedly consisted of several large containers of caviar and was accompanied by three armed Russians. The cargo was offloaded onto a small launch with Arab crewmen. The Turkish sea captain said the launch had Arabic script on it that spelled 'Amir.'

"DAO, Ankara, queried DAO, Cairo, in an attempt to identify the 'Amir,' but the Egyptian port authority had no launch by that name registered. A query to DAO, Kiev, by DAO, Ankara, to locate 'The Black Sea Fishing Company' that had been listed on the Bill of Lading, also met with negative results. However, a second request to DAO, Cairo, and the Chief of Station there, two weeks ago with some urgency added by CIA and DAS Headquarters caused the Egyptian Maritime Ministry to locate a ship, the 'Sheik,' that had previously been named the 'Amir.' The ship is a 165 foot, privately owned, luxury cruiser currently registered in Saudi Arabia. The U.S. Coast Guard determined that the 'Sheik' was in the Alexandria anchorage in June and sailed from there to New York with enroute port stops in the Azores, Miami, Cape Canaveral, Charleston, and Baltimore. It left New York Harbor in October for its return voyage to its home port of Jiddah, Saudi Arabia," Roper said, pointing to the ship's routing on the graphic map.

"Requests for information made to the Saudi government concerning the 'Sheik's' cargo and business in the United States have thus far provided no additional information. CIA is exploring other sources, and the State Department has requested a priority response from the Saudi Embassy here.

"In a possibly related event, a mid-eastern businessman from a friendly country traveling in Iraq witnessed an automobile accident in June in Baghdad and recovered a small piece of paper from the wreck that contained four cryptic handwritten notes in Arabic. This graphic shows the English translation of those notes," Roper said as the next graphic came up on the screen.

"Copies of the note were passed to CIA, DIA, FBI, NSA, and the analysts at CENTCOM." At this point Roper picked up a pointer and used it to explain the words on the graphic.

"While there were some worrisome terms on the paper such as 'Special weapon acquisition, chemical or biological weapon, and cyber weapon,' there was no other frame of reference to tie this to, and none of us came up with anything solid. Then, just two weeks ago, a Defense HUMINT source living in Baghdad identified the sole survivor of the accident as Ali Hassan al-Majid. If that information is correct, it means that one of Saddam Hussein's most ruthless lieutenants is involved in whatever the notes relate to.

"I know that General Great remembers Ali Hassan from Desert Storm. He has headed up their chemical and biological efforts for years. He was responsible for the use of chemicals in the Iraq-Iran War and for the chemical attacks in Kurdistan.

"Some of our analysts believe that this note refers only to resumed activities in the weapons of mass destruction area now that Iraq no longer has to fear the United Nations Inspectors. However, with the help of some of my colleagues here at the Counterterrorism Center, we took these initials." Roper then pointed to the 'W.M.' on the graphic and ran it against other known personalities in Iraq and in the major terrorist organizations. "One hit we came up with is this man." A graphic now appeared on the screen containing the name, 'Wadih Mohammed,' and several aliases and some personalia.

"If the W.M. should stand for this individual, Wadih Mohammed," Roper continued, "he's a Pakistani who has been with Osama bin Laden since the beginning and we suspect that he is bin Laden's operational planner. Unfortunately, we have never been able to come up with a picture of this person and do not know his present whereabouts.

"Tony, was this the only 'W.M.' hit you came up with when you checked the databases?" Tom Glynn, the Deputy Director, NSA asked.

"No, sir. We came up with a total of eighteen names with these initials. Seven in Iraq and eleven spread across the known terrorist organizations. This one seemed the most logical one to be mentioned by a high level Iraqi official such as Ali Hassan."

"Were there any hits at the Iraqi weapons or munitions ministries?" Glynn pressed.

"Yes, sir. There were two Lieutenant Colonels."

"And couldn't they logically be in contact with Ali Hassan?"

"Yes, sir," Roper admitted.

There were some looks around the table. Not wanting to get bogged down at this point, René Softly said, "Let's move on."

Tony Roper once again used his pointer and returned to the graphic with the notes from the Baghdad auto accident.

"Please note the reference here to a cyber weapon. We know the Iraqis have, for a number of years, been involved in cyber research but with no breakthroughs. Quite frankly, our computer experts tell us, they have never had the quality of talent to compete in this area. Again, in two possibly related reports coming out of Bangladesh in June and earlier this month, the DAO, Dhaka, obtained information from a usually reliable source that a young Bengali living in New Delhi and well-known in both countries for his cutting edge research in computer viruses was hired by a firm in Abu Dhabi in the United Arab Emirates for a special research project. Before leaving New Delhi, the young man intimated that his work was going to take place in Baghdad. Our source in Dhaka learned this month that the young man had not returned to India and allegedly died in an explosion.

"We asked the DAO and COS in Abu Dhabi to obtain information about the young man and the firm who supposedly hired him. The firm refused to provide any information. COS Abu Dhabi has suspected for some time that the firm in question is acting as a front for several illegal activities, but the authorities in the Arab Emirates say the firm is legitimate.

"And that concludes my briefing on DISCOVERY."

Before the group could bombard Tony Roper with questions, René Softly quickly interjected, "Thanks, Tony. Pat, do you want to take it from here?" She nodded to Lieutenant General Eways.

"Yes. Thank you, René. As you are aware, we have asked each of you and your people to assist us in obtaining additional information about DISCOVERY. The assistance has been good, and we appreciate it. The bottom line now, folks, is that we may have only a bunch of reports that appear to relate to each other, but in reality, do not. On the other hand, it is possible that we have discovered, pun intended, a plot on the part of Iraq or Osama bin Laden, or in the worst possible case, both, to strike an unprecedented, deadly blow, or blows, against the United States.

"General Lowe and myself, and General Great from CENTCOM, and of course, Mr. Roper, believe strongly that it is the latter, and we are asking the Counterterrorist Center to declare a country-wide full-scale security alert to guard against such a possibility."

A number of sighs and deep breaths could be heard around the table.

"Keith, would you like to add anything?" René asked General Great.

"Yes. Thank you, René. We don't know for sure that this thing, if there is such a thing, is directed against the continental United States as compared to U.S. interests abroad. CENTCOM does, however, feel strongly that Saddam Hussein is up to something. It's been too quiet for too long. This is uncharacteristic for Saddam. We have to believe he is planning something. His response to us for the last year has been too measured. And we have always believed that his use of weapons of mass destruction has been just around the corner. But this whole thing could be directed against Israel, for example. If so, he would be in a better position to claim some form of provocation."

"Thanks, Keith. Now let's open the floor to questions, comments, and discussion," René Softly announced.

The ensuing discussion lasted a little over an hour and was, at times, quite heated. It was a dilemma no one relished, particularly at this time of year. It also became obvious that no clear consensus was going to be achieved. When she was satisfied that everyone had had his or her say, René Softly exercised the role of the Chair.

"Well I think that about covers most pertinent discussion. Unless someone feels strongly that we have missed anything, I will try and summarize the salient points."

Bart was tempted to make one more attempt at convincing the table of the possible gravity of the situation but on reflection, was satisfied that Tony Roper and Pat Eways had done a good job at that and Bart didn't want to beat a dead horse.

"Very well. Department of Energy opines that if a nuclear suitcase bomb is already in the United States, detection will be difficult. Detection would be somewhat easier after the device is assembled. However, DOE is willing to conduct random radiation detection tests in Miami, Charleston, Baltimore, Cape Canaveral, and New York. DOE and Coast Guard do not believe access to the ship, 'Sheik' would necessarily reveal any past presence of nuclear weapons, but State Department will request access from the Saudi government. Coast Guard will conduct further investigations of the 'Sheik's' port calls in the U.S.

"U.S. Customs and the Immigration and Naturalization Service, in coordination with FBI and CIA and State's Passport Control Office will review all foreign entries into the United States for the last six months, searching for any possible connections to Middle Eastern or Iraqi terrorist groups.

"NSA, FBI, and CIA have not noted any communications that could be related to DISCOVERY but will increase their efforts, particularly on the Internet, now thought to be the international terrorist communications of choice.

"Defense and the JCS do not believe that DISCOVERY is compelling enough to further change the alert status of U.S. Military Forces in the continental United States or abroad but will continue to reinforce the importance of the already heightened security alert status. State Department, CENTCOM, and EUCOM concur.

"General Odom believes that the National Security Council and the President would view a nationwide alert as not politically feasible, particularly at this time of the year given the tenuousness of the DISCOVERY case. Further compelling information could change that view.

"Do we all agree with that summary?" René asked. And seeing nods of agreement around the table, proceeded, "Then my ruling on behalf of the Counterterrorist Center is that the DIA and DAS request for a nationwide terrorist alert is not approved. Reconsideration will, of course, be given if additional information becomes known." René looked for and received nods of agreement from her CIA colleagues.

Senator Kit Karson had the last word. "I'm not sure I like it, but I don't know what else can be done at this time."

After the meeting adjourned, when Bart Lowe, Barbara Barnsworth, and Tom Mellon were riding along the George Washington Parkway on their way back to DAS Headquarters, Bart turned to the other two and said, "Have you ever had that feeling that some great disaster is about to take place and you are helpless to do anything about it?"

They both nodded their heads but had nothing to add.

CHAPTER 24

CHRISTMAS

At the same time that Bart Lowe was experiencing feelings of impending disaster in Washington, Ali Hassan was having similar feelings in Baghdad, but for altogether different reasons. His were personal.

Earlier that day, he had been summoned by Saddam and given Saddam's approval of the three targets recommended by Osama bin Laden and a strike timeframe to be passed to bin Laden via Wadih Mohammed. Ali had at first been surprised at the timing for the strike but then recognized Saddam's intention. "Brilliant," he had thought.

Saddam directed that bin Laden must acknowledge and confirm the targets and timing within twenty-four hours. Ali had immediately passed the message to Wadih Mohammed and surprisingly, had received bin Laden's agreement in less than four hours. The answer came with a cryptic message saying that the "go" had already been passed to the strike teams and now the strikes could not, or would not, be recalled for any reason.

When Ali had passed bin Laden's answer to Saddam that afternoon, Saddam smiled broadly and said, "Allah be praised!"

"Shall I pass the word to your son, Uday Hussein?" Ali Hassan asked.

"No," Saddam had replied, "say nothing to anyone and continue your work with the ministries and your people as if nothing has changed."

When Saddam had summoned Ali that morning, Ali did not know what to expect. He worried that it could be the end of Ali Hassan. He had grown increasingly alarmed as the time had passed since hearing, on the first of December, that

228

the teams were in place and ready to strike. He thought that Saddam had somehow cut him out and was communicating directly with Wadih Mohammed and bin Laden. Then, he was relieved initially this morning when Saddam verified that the original plan was still in being. Now, however, he realized that since everything had been set in motion and all that was left was to await the results of the strikes, Ali Hassan's usefulness was probably at an end, other than being Saddam's scapegoat if Iraq's role in *Retribution* should be discovered.

"What to do?" he thought as he tossed and turned in his bed.

By morning, and after a sleepless night, he had decided.

Later, sitting at his desk, Ali saw that it was 11:45. He reached for his intercom and pressed his aide's button.

"Yes, sir," Captain Bassari answered.

"Come in here."

The Captain quickly left her desk and entered Ali's office. When she was beside his desk, she said again, "Yes, sir?"

"How would you like to go to lunch today with me to the Majestic Hotel? I sometimes take lunch there and the food is good."

The Captain was stunned. Ali Hassan was not known for his generosity or even his civility, especially with subordinates. A short, awkward silence ensued and finally Captain Bassari replied, "That would be very nice, sir."

"Good. We'll leave in ten minutes. Tell the driver to have the car ready." Ali had noticed that morning that Captain Bassari was dressed in western attire and thought she would provide good cover for what he was about to do.

The dining room in the Majestic Hotel in downtown Baghdad was pleasant and the service and menu catered to foreign visitors to Iraq. Captain Bassari was even more surprised at the kind, almost engaging way that Ali Hassan talked to her during their lunch. It was a first for her. She didn't know, of course, that he was trying to give the impression—if anyone was watching—that he was romantically interested in his attractive companion and that was their purpose for being at the Majestic. She did not know that he had something altogether different in mind.

After they had finished their meal and coffee was served, Ali said, "My dear, while you are finishing your coffee, I am going into the lobby to the tailor's. I buy my shirts here and it is time I bought some more. I'll be right back."

Ali had never bought a shirt at the Majestic, but he was about to take the biggest risk of his life. He had known for some time that the tailor, a Jordanian, was suspected of being a spy for the British. In fact, he was under surveillance by Iraqi Intelligence, but they had not caught him doing anything illegal. When Ali entered the shop, he was relieved to find it empty of people other than the tailor—a short, well dressed man about fifty years old—Ali approached him directly.

"I understand you make shirts."

"Yes, sir. Any size, any color," the tailor replied. "Here are the sample colors and materials," handing Ali a sample board.

Ali looked at the samples briefly, returned them to the tailor, then took a business card out of his pocket, turned it over, wrote something on the back of the card in English, and passed it to the tailor saying, "Good. I'll take three of the white linen shirts. I have written the size on the back of my card. Can you make those for me in three days?"

The tailor looked first at the back of the card and saw that Ali had written, *I am seeking British asylum. I have important information.* He then turned the card over and read the Arabic that said *Ali Hassan al-Majid, General, Iraqi Army.*

The tailor's heart started pounding. He fought not to show any emotion. "Is this a crude attempt at entrapment?" he wondered.

Then, looking up at Ali, he saw something in Ali's eyes that made him believe that the request was genuine. The tailor said, "I think I can make your shirts, but three days may be difficult. I am very busy, but I think in four days for sure. Shall I deliver them?"

"No, that won't be necessary," Ali said, breathing a sigh of relief and wiping sweat from his brow. I'll have my assistant pick them up. Her name is Captain Bassari."

"Good. I'll include a bill in the package I give her," the tailor said.

Then Ali returned to the dining room and Captain Bassari.

"I have ordered some shirts. I will want you to pick them up later this week," Ali told his aide.

"Yes, sir," Captain Bassari replied, "I'll be glad to do that," wondering if she had misjudged the General.

Ironically, on the evening of Monday, the 20th of December at almost the same time, Bart Lowe in Washington, and Abdul Khalid in Florida, received enlightening telephone calls. The time was 11:10 p.m. and both men were watching the late news on CNN.

Bart's caller was the DAS Operations Center Duty Officer reporting that a DAS C-12 Aircraft, overdue at its destination in Africa and presumed lost, was, in fact, safe. According to the Duty Officer, the aircraft had developed engine trouble and made an emergency landing at an undeveloped strip and had been simply out of communication.

"Thank God for that! And thank you, Major Jimmons. Anything new in terrorist activities?" Bart asked, his concern continuing over the possible threat.

"No, sir."

"Then, Merry Christmas to you and your family."

"Thank you, sir," Major Jimmons responded to his boss, happy that he had good news for the 'Old Man.'

Khalid's call reached him at his condominium and came from his contact in Cape Canaveral, Sam Misri. Sam used Khalid's Saudi cover name and told him that he had some free space on his fishing boat the next day if he was interested. This was a prearranged signal to indicate that a message had been received for Khalid over the Internet and would be available for him at Sam's Cape Canaveral seafood stall.

"Thanks for the call, Sam. I would really like to go out, but unfortunately, I have a full day tomorrow. Maybe another time. And Merry Christmas to you and your family." A nice cover technique the Muslim thought to himself.

That night, Abdul Khalid, like Ali Hassan, was restless and didn't sleep much. His insomnia, however, was caused by adrenaline and the anticipation that the message to strike had finally been received.

The next morning, Khalid was not disappointed. Sam gave him the message he had printed out for him in a small envelope tucked inside the newspaper he used to wrap the pound of fresh shrimp that Khalid purchased at the fish stand. He could barely contain himself, but waited dutifully until he was back inside the condominium. After he had closed and locked the front door, he went into the kitchen, unwrapped and trashed the newspaper, removed and washed the shrimp, put them into a bowl, covered it, and placed it in the refrigerator. He then picked up the sealed envelope, opened it, and read the three sentences on the sheet of paper. Satisfied he understood the message, he reached for and struck a match from the box on his stove and burned the message, washing the ashes away in the sink. The message would not have meant anything to anyone else, even Sam, but he wanted to be careful. It was based on a prearranged code between Khalid, Mohammed, and himself.

He had to admit that he had been concerned, not hearing sooner, but when he saw the time selected, he immediately understood the logic and believed it would enhance the strike teams' element of surprise. He then went about planning exactly how he would use the available time until the strikes took place. He was relieved he would not be rushed. After it was clear in his mind those things he had to do and oversee for the strike teams, he set in motion the prearranged notification of the strike teams. He went into his bedroom, opened his briefcase, and took out the cover schedule for the rest of his visit in the United States. He sat down at the small desk in the room and figured out the changes that would be necessary. When he was finished, he picked up the phone and called Delta Airlines. After a lengthy wait, and considerable holiday music, he finally was connected to a weary, but determined to be helpful, reservations woman. "I need to make some changes to existing travel plans--" he began.

"During the Holiday Season?" she interrupted.

"Yes."

"I am sorry, sir, but all of our flights are booked and that will be very difficult, maybe impossible," trying to discourage any timid travelers.

"We need to try. I am a first class passenger and money will not be a problem. I know the rules of the advance purchase and we won't worry about those things," a determined Khalid told her.

"Well, sir, that will be a help."

Although it took him almost forty-five minutes, Khalid was able to make all the changes he required.

The rest of the official Christmas week passed without incident for Bart Lowe and the DAS. The mornings were spent trying to get as much work done as possible because the afternoons were taken up by the perennial office Christmas parties that take place throughout the U.S. government in Washington. Every major agency in town had a Christmas party for its employees and their families and friends. In addition, the major Western embassies all had holiday celebrations that week. By the time the DAS held its own internal Christmas celebration on Thursday afternoon, the 23rd of December, Bart counted nineteen other parties or celebrations that he had attended—it was an opportunity for agency heads like General Lowe to show their employees that they valued their support and friendship. It meant a lot to them.

His secretary, Joan Weber, who knew better than anyone the demands of his schedule, kidded him on Thursday morning saying, "General, I am guessing that by this time you have had just about all the goodwill and holiday cheer that one person can stand."

He smiled at her and suspected that she was right, but replied, "No, not at all. It's all great fun and I treasure seeing people enjoying themselves at this time of year. As you know, Joan, I am an only child and my immediate family is all gone. However, the holiday season always turns up the calls, cards, greetings, and remembrances of so many friends that I have had the pleasure of knowing over the years. So it is a special time of the year for me and I don't mind the pace. Besides that, by next Monday it will be all over... so there is light at the end of the tunnel."

Joan, recognizing the serious personal, but good-humored side of her boss, ventured further. "Oh, yes, sir, I agree. And I bet that this Christmas and holidays will be even more meaningful to you because you have someone special to share it with...?" her voice trailed off into a question.

"Do you mean Maria Salah?"

"Yes, sir, I can't help but notice from your schedule the time you are spending with her."

Bart laughed, and threw his hands up in mock surrender. "You've got me Joan. I have to plead 'no contest.' And yes, you are right. She is a wonderful person. She has added a dimension to my life that has been missing for some time and I am happy for it. In fact, she is coming to the Christmas party here this afternoon and I want you to meet her."

Maria also joined Bart on Christmas Eve and she spent the Christmas weekend with him. On Christmas Eve they attended the candlelight service at the Bolling Air Force Base Chapel, made eggnog afterward and listened to Christmas music until the wee hours. When Bart came into Maria's life, she began following more Western customs—Christmas gifts a notable highlight. On Christmas morning, the traditional opening of presents from under a magnificent Christmas tree, found and decorated by Sergeant First Class Childs, seemed like a contest between two spoiled adults trying to outdo the other. The 'contest' was declared a draw. Bart took Maria through the steps of preparing the traditional turkey and dressing dinner and even convinced her to have a cold turkey sandwich and a glass of cold milk at midnight—although she confessed to him that she preferred goat's milk.

Sunday was a reflective day whereby both Bart and Maria were thankful for all that they had, including each other, and discussed the serious subjects of "peace on earth and goodwill toward men" and the prospects of that ever being a reality in their lifetimes. Neither was too optimistic given their backgrounds and the current conflicts around the world. Without revealing any classified information or sensitive methods, Bart shared with Maria his continuing concern over the terrorist threat to Americans around the world, and to his mind, now within the United States. Maria had received no further requests for information from the group she feared, but the thought of something happening and those that made it happen coming to her for help or safe haven was ever present on her mind. She was tempted, when Bart raised the subject of a threat, to tell him all, but could not muster the courage and settled for the solace she found in being in his arms.

Bart received no calls from the DAS Operations Center over the Christmas weekend. "Maybe," he thought, "I'm overly concerned about the threat."

Ali Hassan had never given much thought to the real meaning of Christmas. However, Christmas Day 1999 was going to be a special day for him. On Thursday, when Captain Bassari returned from the Majestic Hotel and handed him the wrapped package from the tailor, he said to her, "Close the door and no calls. I'm going to try these on." He then quickly tore the paper away and opened the cardboard box containing three hand sewn linen shirts. Under the shirts was a sealed plain envelope containing two pages. The first was the bill for the shirts on the tailor's letterhead. The second was a plain piece of stationery containing the following typewritten note:

```
Regarding a ride for your friend
to Jordan. If your friend can leave
right away I am driving to Amman
Saturday night. If he is not in a
hurry or perhaps would like to take
his family with him we could make
other arrangements later. I plan to
leave promptly at 8:00 p.m. Your
friend could meet me at my car,
lic. no. 9174, parked in the
concessionaire reserved parking
space, no. 13.
```

As soon as Ali had finished reading the note, he copied the license number and parking space number on another piece of paper, he then took a cigarette lighter from his desk drawer and burned the note in an ashtray. He rose and started pacing the floor. Although his casts had been off for some time, he still had a slight limp and his arms ached. He grabbed the box of shirts and unfolded one to try on. After he removed his shalwar qamese, he was only wearing his undershirt. He realized he was struggling and suddenly just wadded-up the new shirt and threw it on the floor.

"Do I have the guts to pull it off?" he wondered. "What if I have been followed by Saddam's men? And now they're just waiting for me to leave with the Brit spy. And what if the Jordanian isn't a Brit spy and he has turned me in? They will be waiting for me when I go to the tailor's car." These and a thousand other thoughts had gone through Ali's mind the next two days.

He wanted to take his family with him but he knew there wasn't time. By Saturday morning he had convinced himself that it was the only thing left that could save his life. He made sure that he was very visible to all his people all day Saturday and let them think he was not feeling well and planned to stay in his quarters to rest all day Sunday, December 25th. When he left his building on Saturday night at 7:00, he told Captain Bassari and his personal aide at his quarters that he was going straight to bed and should not be disturbed before Monday morning. They were glad to have the unexpected time off.

He changed his clothes, put on a dark suit and hat, and slipped out of a private entrance at the rear of his quarters. It was 7:45 and he knew that he could walk unnoticed through the suburban neighborhood to the Majestic Hotel in ten to twelve minutes. His calculations were good. He arrived at the Majestic at three minutes to the hour, went around the rear of the hotel, saw no movement in the large parking lot, and located parking space number thirteen. A blue sedan with license number 9174 was parked there. He hesitated in the shadow of the building momentarily and then saw a man he recognized as the Jordanian tailor walking toward the car. They both reached the car at the same time. The tailor unlocked his side, reached across the seat, and unlocked the passenger side door for Ali, who immediately climbed into the car.

The tailor said nothing to Ali for about forty-five minutes until they had cleared the outlying suburbs of Baghdad. Then he said, "There is a Jordanian passport in the glove compartment along with a wallet, several pieces of identification, and a small amount of currency. As soon as we get into the countryside, I suggest you crawl into the back seat of the car and change into the clothes I laid out for you on the seat. There are also some shoes, size ten. I hope that's large enough."

Ali nodded affirmatively.

After Ali had changed and had thrown his clothes into a waste dump area by the road, the tailor explained their journey.

"We are going to take Highway No. 4-West all the way to the Jordan border crossing at Trebil. That's about 500 kilometers and it will be a long haul. But I have done it many times and we should be able to make it shortly after daylight. You should have no problem with your Jordanian documents leaving Iraq. Once in Jordan, the Jordanian authorities are cooperating with the British and you'll be turned over to them. It should all go smoothly."

Ali had a number of questions for the tailor—most of which he could not answer. The night air was cool, there was very little traffic on the road and Ali started to feel some of the great tension of the last week start to leave his body. The night passed quickly and with no signs of anyone following them, Ali thought to himself, "Can it be this easy?"

He wouldn't have had that thought if he had known that at that very moment there was an Iraqi Republican Guard helicopter with an infrared tracking device just above and behind, but well out of sound range of the speeding car. Its job was to fly the special surveillance team observing Ali Hassan at the express direction of none other than Saddam Hussein.

If, for any reason, Ali or the Jordanian tailor had decided to turn around and head back to Baghdad, it would probably have saved his life, at least for a time.

As the first light broke, the tailor announced, "We have made good time. I make it we are no more than ten kilometers from the border."

The start of a smile appeared on Ali's swarthy, and now beard shadowed face. But just then, Ali spotted something on the road just on the horizon.

"Is that the border?" he asked.

"Not hardly. We are not that close."

As the light improved and the distance closed, it became apparent that what they were seeing was a roadblock. When the Republican Guard Surveillance Team determined that the vehicle was clearly headed for the Jordanian border with its important passenger, they had radioed Baghdad for instructions. The order had gone out for a roadblock and to take the subject of the surveillance into custody.

Ali had another 'what to do' decision to make—this one even more critical than the earlier ones.

He turned to the tailor. "What if we leave the road before we get to the roadblock and make a run for the border. Can we out run them?"

The tailor, now realizing that, what a few moments ago appeared to be a major coup, had turned completely to shit, made an instant decision and turned off the road to the southeast and pushed the accelerator to the floor.

"The terrain is rough, but mostly flat. Maybe we can make it. Or maybe a Jordanian border patrol will see us and give us a hand," he said, his own adrenaline flowing at full speed.

What they hadn't counted on was the helicopter. When the car left the road, the helicopter quickly closed the distance, flying now at a low altitude directly above them. Its megaphone was turned on and the car was ordered to stop.

The tailor looked at Ali who shook his head and gave a sign with his hand to press on.

The pilot of the helicopter asked permission from the Surveillance Team Chief to fire.

"What will we fire?" The Team Chief asked.

"A heat seeking missile."

"Will that stop it?"

"To be certain. One will destroy it. Two will obliterate it."

"Just a moment." Because of the seniority of the officer in the car, the Team Chief felt duty bound to get permission from Baghdad. When the Chief of Saddam's Security was informed, he felt it was important enough to interrupt Saddam's breakfast.

Three minutes later, the Team Chief told the pilot, "Fire both missiles." The pilot was right about the results.

In Baghdad, when Saddam Hussein finished breakfast, he had his aide get his son, Uday, on the phone.

"Uday?"

"Yes, Papa."

"I have a mission for you. Prepare a military funeral with honors. A brave soldier, and my close friend, Ali Hassan al-Majid has just died in a tragic training accident. The country will mourn him.

CHAPTER 25

RETRIBUTION

The last week of the year at DAS Headquarters was a catch-up one for those who were working. About half of the headquarters' staff was on leave, and the communications from around the world was at twenty percent of its normal level. Bart Lowe increased his newspaper reading time to a full hour—a luxury he could rarely afford. The papers had begun the countdown to the millenium and the hype on what could happen at Y2K. Barring any unforeseen events and with Christmas behind them, Bart anticipated that the media would have the whole country thoroughly whipped up by midnight on Saturday. It was probably, he thought, going to be a frenzied New Year's Eve. He and Maria planned to have a quiet dinner at her apartment at the Watergate.

That afternoon, Bart received a call on his Stu-3 from René Softly.

"Bart, glad I caught you in. There was an interesting development over the Christmas weekend. Our new Chief of Station in London was informed by MI-6 that they were expecting a high-level Iraqi defector coming out through Jordan. He was being escorted by one of their agents and was supposed to be at the Trebil, Jordan, border crossing point Christmas morning. Neither person showed up, and all attempts to contact their agent have failed. Now, are you ready for this? The defector was supposed to be Ali Hassan."

"You're kidding!" Bart replied in disbelief.

"No. I'm not. Of course, we don't know how accurate this information is. It could be some kind of ruse from the Iraqis or misinformation from their agent."

"Will we find out anymore, René?"

"Who knows? It could be just a delay, or the guy could have gotten cold feet, or the Iraqis could have caught them. At any rate, I'll pass this along to Pat Eways, Tony Roper, and the FBI. NSA is checking for any related Iraqi Comms."

"Thanks, and if you don't mind, Keith Great at CENTCOM will be interested."

"Of course, Bart, and if anything else develops we will keep you in the loop."

"Thanks, René, and here's hoping you and Bob have a great New Year."

"Right you are, Bart, and don't let the Y2K bug get you."

On the morning of 31 December, Abdul Khalid was up at the first light in Cape Canaveral. He was going to have a very full day. He would be going to Orlando this morning, then flying to New York, later to Washington, and then returning to Florida at 10:00 on one of the last flights out of D.C. The past week had been spent in the final preparations for *Retribution*, and everything had gone according to plan.

The biological weapon team had moved the anthrax from Miami to the Cape on Wednesday. The two hundred pounds of anthrax was in liquid form ready to be dispensed automatically from two mist dispensers concealed in two large picnic style ice chests aboard one of Sam Misri's fishing boats. The primary target for the biological agent was Walt Disney World and the other entertainment locations in Orlando, Florida. The secondary target was the John F. Kennedy Space Center at Cape Canaveral Air Base. Khalid and the biological weapon strike team had devised a plan to strike the primary target and achieve some damage to the alternate target.

The team leader was a medical technician thoroughly experienced in the handling of deadly chemicals and biological agents. His two teammates were both pilots. Since coming to Florida in September, one of the pilots, documented as a licensed instructor pilot, had been checked out at a local Orlando airfield and had regularly rented a small Cessna single-engine aircraft twice a month on Fridays. The two-hour rental was for the purpose of providing flying lessons to two students—his teammates.

On Friday, the thirty-first of December at 8:00 a.m., the team departed in two cars from the fishing docks in Cape Canaveral where Sam kept his boats. The Team Leader was in one; the two pilots in the other. The anthrax was in the trunk of the Team Leader's car. The drive to the first airfield, located east of Orlando, where the pilots would pick up the rental aircraft, took forty-five minutes. Meanwhile, the Team Leader drove onto a second, smaller and less used, airfield located on the west side of Orlando, arriving there at 9:10. The instructor pilot checked in at the small flight operations office, was recognized and greeted warmly by the airfield personnel, obtained the keys to the rental, gave them his two-hour flight plan, and was joined by his student for the pre-flight checks. They were airborne by 9:30. The flight to the second airfield for the purposes of a practice landing by the student and the pickup of a second student had already been coordinated and took just twenty minutes.

They landed at the second airfield and taxied to the ramp where the Team Leader had parked his car. The ramp was at the end of the field and they were able to load the two ice chests in the aircraft unobserved. The aircraft was quickly airborne and checked in again with the air control center located at the Orlando International Airport. They were given clearance for their flight. The altitude assigned for the flight was five thousand feet. The pilot flew west and kept them well beyond the five-mile restricted area radius of the international airport. When they reached the unrestricted area west, they turned and headed north. This flight pattern took them parallel to Disney World and the four other entertainment centers. As the aircraft came alongside of the Disney World complex, the pilot turned off the transponder that allowed the air control center to track the location of the aircraft. With the heavy air traffic in the area, he knew it was not likely that the small aircraft would be missed immediately. By that time, the anthrax would be dispensed.

When the transponder was turned off, the small aircraft descended to one thousand feet.

At a designated point on the flight chart that they were using, the pilot signaled to the Team Leader. The door of the aircraft was then opened and the Team Leader, after putting on protective gloves, slid the first ice chest into place, removed the mist dispenser, and began dispensing the deadly anthrax. They had previously calculated that the prevailing winds were from the southeast, and today was no exception. The mist would be carried by those winds from their present altitude across the open acres of Disney World and the other entertainment complexes. The mist was too fine to be felt by the unsuspecting crowds of people, men, women, and children, estimated to be close to five hundred thousand, visiting Disney World attractions on the New Year's Eve day.

The strike team and Abdul Khalid had all been inoculated against the anthrax spores. Nevertheless, the aircraft doors would be wiped clean with sterile antibiological rags placed for clean up in the ice chests and the members of the team would all shower and wash thoroughly after the mission.

The effects of the anthrax would not be noticed until approximately two weeks later when the people who had visited Disney World returned to their own homes throughout the United States. Then people would begin to fall seriously ill with flu-like symptoms and a mortality rate of eighty percent, or higher, would take place.

The small Cessna continued along its assigned vector but at one thousand feet, until one hundred and seventy five pounds of anthrax had been dispensed. At that point, the aircraft returned to 5,000 feet altitude, switched the transponder on, and flew on until it reached its northern-most vector and received permission from the air control center to fly east. The flight continued until the blue of the Atlantic Ocean was in sight and the aircraft reached the restricted area of the Kennedy Space Center. Permission was received to turn south, placing the aircraft now parallel of the Space Center's main administrative area where most of the Space Center work took place, clear of the restricted area where the Visitors' Center was located, and where the majority of people worked. The Team Leader repeated the earlier procedure and the twenty-five remaining pounds of anthrax were dispensed as soon as the transponder had been turned off and 1,000 feet altitude reached. The southeasterly winds continued and the deadly mist once again found its mark. Then, regaining its altitude, the aircraft continued south until its vector was reached. The flight and descent into the second airfield was completed on schedule and the Team Leader and the ice chests and dispensers unloaded. The aircraft quickly turned around, taxied to the take-off runway, received permission for take-off, and was enroute to its home airfield.

The Team Leader, after watching the take-off of the Cessna, got into his vehicle and drove out of the airfield for his return trip to Cape Canaveral. As he exited the airfield entrance, there was a car beside the road with a lone, male occupant behind the wheel looking at a map. As the Team Leader's vehicle passed the other car, he raised his left hand and gave a thumbs-up. Abdul Khalid nodded and looked at his watch. The time was 10:45. Pleased, he thought to himself, "I have plenty of time to make my twelve o'clock flight to New York."

Neither Khalid, nor the strike team, gave much thought to the future effects of the anthrax, but thought of their work that day as the successful completion of an important mission. Nor did they foresee the indirect consequences of the anthrax attack on the population of the surrounding areas. Some of the mist would drift into Orlando and into the communities surrounding Cape Kennedy. The State of Florida and many towns and cities in the United States would find themselves completely unprepared to cope with the subsequent panic and attempted exodus that would occur.

When Abdul Khalid settled back into his first class seat on Delta's Flight 602 non-stop to the JFK Airport in New York, he sipped his second Florida orange juice with relish. His time spent in Cape Canaveral had increased his appreciation of the fresh citrus fruit. The oranges in the Middle East could not compare in flavor with the larger and much sweeter ones grown in Florida. Even better, he thought, than the ones he had tried when he made his trip to California.

The Delta jet took off into the southeasterly winds, banked to the west and the pilot came on the intercom and announced, "For our visitors, you may want one last look at Disney World. We are just coming up on it now and it will be visible from the right side of the aircraft."

Khalid joined the other passengers in looking at the great arrays of fantasy rides and fairyland-like buildings. "If they only knew," he thought.

When the stewardess came around after takeoff, and took lunch orders, she was surprised that the handsome, probably foreign, man in seat 2C, refused a drink—not even champagne with his orange juice. Most of her first class passengers wanted all they could have of the complimentary booze.

By the time the lunch service was over, Khalid was already thinking ahead to the events that would take place in New York City later in the day. He had to be careful, of course, in returning to the city where he had lived and worked. The danger was of someone recognizing him. However, he had confidence in his disguise and Saudi Arabian businessman cover. This was his fourth trip to New York since October and he felt confident that this one would be as successful as the earlier ones.

His plane arrived on schedule at 2:20 p.m. and, without baggage, he was able to get to his reserved limo for the trip into the city and arrive in plenty of time for his 3:30 cover appointment at the New York Stock Exchange (NYSE). The "market" would be closing at 4:00. The strike team who had "The Stock Market" as its primary cyber target estimated that because of the many New Year's Eve celebrations, the market and the building would quickly empty. All indications that Khalid could see and that his anxious-to-finish-up-on-time cover contact expressed to him, said, "A mass exodus like you have never seen will take place just as soon as that bell goes off at four o'clock."

Khalid became a part of that exodus and went directly across Broad Street to a popular coffee shop. He was able to get a table by the window with a view of the market entrance. He ordered a pot of tea and waited for the next step in the cyber attack against the world's largest equities market with an estimated capitalization of twelve trillion dollars.

Sitting with his teacup in hand, he thought back to the time in Yazdan, Afghanistan, when he and the strike teams were training for and planning their operations. The thinking, at first, was that the NASDAQ, the world's first completely electronic stock market, a fully automated stock market, transcending the trading from the floor found in the NYSE, should be the primary target. Appealing also was the NASDAQ's location in Trumbull, Connecticut, as a place that access might be more easily achieved. But then the al Qaeda support organization provided an asset that made access to the NYSE the obvious choice and the primary target. The asset was Captain Nasim Haddad of the Metropolitan Security Services. Information was developed that Metropolitan had the computer security contract for the NYSE. Knowing that Haddad was an employee of Metropolitan, he was tasked to provide information on the security of the NYSE. At first he was reluctant, but when he found out that most everything he had been asked to provide was public knowledge, he agreed. When Haddad was promoted to Captain and placed in charge of the Computer Security Unit, it was a gift from Allah. The more information Haddad provided, the more deeply he was involved, and when he was told in no uncertain terms that his own life depended on his cooperation, he caved in and fully cooperated. It was said that when he first met the Cyber Strike Team Leader and learned that no loss of life was intended in their operation, he was greatly relieved.

At 4:15, Khalid saw a Metropolitan Security Services van stop right on schedule in front of the market and discharge six uniformed security officers. Five of the individuals were carrying small diagnostic equipment cases and the sixth was a supervisor, Captain Nasim Haddad, that Khalid recognized from a photo he had been shown. The van was scheduled to pick up the officers at five thirty. As part of the NYSE's preparations for Y2K, the Computer Security Team had been running diagnostic tests after the close of the market every weekday for the past six months.

Metropolitan's computer security support was actually provided to the NYSE's data processing subsidiary, the Securities Industry Automation Corporation (SIAC), which acted in the building as project coordinator for NYSE's system changes and associated testing and conversions. SIAC, because of the Y2K concern, had been involved in industry-wide testing of NYSE's automation equipment and was confident that when the double-zeros rolled over on January 2000, all systems would be A-OK. The tests for the thirty-first of December that Metropolitan would run for SIAC would be short test runs on the systems and programs dealing with stock order processing, data sorting, money calculation, and changing "99" to "00." Three series of tests would be run: one with the system date set at 31 December, one with the system date set at 1 January, and one with the system date set at 3 January, the first day the market would be open in the year 2000.

As part of SIAC and Metropolitan's efforts to support NYSE Member Firm's 2000 Order Processing testing requirements, on Friday of each week, any firm with a test system and test communications line could run a test with the system date set for January 3rd, 2000.

In working with Haddad, the Cyber Strike Team had developed a dummy test line. And one of the strike team members, a computer expert documented as a former law enforcement officer, was hired as a part-time employee for Metropolitan to fill in when regular employees were either sick or required time off. There was no problem in finding someone who wanted time off and substituting the strike team member on the 31st of December.

That strike team member, at 5:20, finished his last member firm's Year 2000 (Y2K) test and then pulled up the "dummy" firm line where his two teammates were waiting to enter the 'Desert Mist' virus. Five minutes later, the strike team member at the NYSE restored the system's firewalls and security barriers and prepared to leave. Over the next sixty-plus hours, the 'Desert Mist' would run rampant through eight hundred million files. The chaos that it would cause would be incalculable.

At exactly five-thirty, the Metropolitan Security Service van pulled up in front of the NYSE and picked up the six uniformed security officers.

Abdul Khalid, watching from the coffee shop, paid his bill, wished the waiter a Happy New Year, and left in search of a pay phone to confirm what he believed had already happened.

Abdul Khalid's limo pick-up at 5:45 got him back to JFK in time to make his 6:40 Delta Flight to Washington's Ronald Reagan National Airport. The first class section was full and the man in the seat next to Khalid was overly friendly and anxious to talk. Once the plane was airborne, Khalid pleaded a long day, and reclining his seat to the maximum, he feigned sleep. Khalid knew that this next and final phase of *Retribution* was the most complex and difficult of the three strikes and he wanted to be sure that he had overlooked nothing.

The terrorist organizations of the world, particularly the Middle East ones, sometimes share information and assets when the purpose is against a common enemy. And Wadih Mohammed was a master at obtaining information and assistance for bin Laden's al Qaeda organization. This was particularly true when Wadih became aware of an Abu Nidal asset with exceptional knowledge of the Washington area power and communications network to include the Pentagon. When the information from their asset was shared by Abu Nidal with al Qaeda, it made the choice of the Pentagon the obvious candidate as primary target for the Nuclear Strike Team. Moreover, Shar Baker, a chief engineer for Bell Atlantic, became the ideal technical adviser for Abdul Khalid and the strike team.

Al Qaeda already had an asset in the Pentagon, a Sudanese man—a green carded alien—Jeri Barobbi, who had held a job there for the past three years. He had begun in the Pentagon Cafeteria as a food server, but because of his excellent work ethic and recommendations by his supervisors, he had moved to a better job in the Pentagon Book Store located on the Pentagon Mall. Barobbi was a key part of the nuclear weapon strike. He had provided a way to get the weapon inside the Pentagon.

The suitcase nuclear bomb—and Khalid and his strike team had two of them that the Iraqis had bought from the Russian Crime Group—consisted of five components that, when assembled, would barely fit into the largest of suitcases. The first component was a projectile of HEU (highly enriched uranium); the second was a hollow receptacle (cylinder) of HEU, closed on one end; the third, a tube-like structure with tungsten at one end and, fourth, a propellant to fire the projectile into the receptacle forming a supercritical mass and thus, a nuclear explosion. The fifth and final component was a detonating device and timer. Each of the components of the nuclear weapon, the strike team had learned, fit nicely into five standard 19" x 13" x 6" bookcase cartons like those used by the Pentagon Book Store.

At three o'clock that afternoon, Jeri Barobbi had gone to his personal vehicle in Lane 25 of the Pentagon's south parking lots. Lane 25 was used exclusively by the concessionaires who worked on the Pentagon Mall and their employees. Barobbi's five-year-old Toyota hatchback had proven useful for short run book carton pick-ups. Most of the books coming to the Pentagon Book Store were delivered in bulk either by the U.S. Postal Service, Federal Express, or United Parcel Service. The books were normally picked up by Barobbi at one of several outside loading docks after they had already been run through x-ray machines and received security clearance. But frequently, a best seller, would sell out quickly and Barobbi would be dispatched to another bookstore in the area that was overstocked to pick up books, so that Pentagon customers wouldn't be disappointed. When he did this, he had two ways of getting the books through the Pentagon Security system. If it was a small number of books, say just a box or two, he could put them on a small carrier with wheels that he kept in the car and just take them in the south parking entrance to the building and roll them through the metal detector and right down the mall to the Pentagon Book Store. If it was a larger load, he took the boxes in his car to the Church Street X-ray Station that was two blocks from the Pentagon, had his car x-rayed, and was given red security check stick-ons for each box. Then with his Pentagon Building Pass, he could drive into one of the internal roads that run under the Pentagon and deposit his cargo at one of the internal loading docks close to the Mall. And then, drop off his cargo, park his car again at Lane 25, and return later and pick up his cargo with a dolly from the bookstore. And that is what he had done this afternoon with one exception. Instead of going directly from the Church Street X-ray Station to the internal Pentagon road, he returned to Lane 25 long enough to switch five book cartons and red security stickers with five identical cartons from the trunk of two strike team members who were parked there.

The two strike team experts, waited in their car thirty minutes more, until 4:30 p.m. At that time, both dressed in winter-weight business suits, walked into the Pentagon Mall area through the Security Check Point flashing their counterfeit—but exact replicas—Pentagon Building Passes. Then they strolled around the mall looking in the store windows and observing the large numbers of military and civilians leaving the building for the holiday eve. At 4:50, they walked up to the Pentagon Book Store and received a nod from Barobbi indicating that the other employees had all departed. They entered the store and browsed briefly until five o'clock when the other customers departed. Barobbi closed the steel curtain gate on the front of the bookstore and then showed them into the storeroom in the rear where he had placed the book cartons. They immediately removed their coats and began assembling the first nuclear weapon to ever be inside the fifty-six year old building.

In a remarkable coincidence, the two terrorist weapons experts on the nuclear weapon strike team, finished their work, told Barobbi—tongue-in-cheek—not to work too late, and left the Pentagon at almost exactly the same moment as the Metropolitan Security Team was coming out of the NYSE. They still had work to do.

When the two men had departed the Pentagon Book Store, Barobbi at first resumed his regular end of the day work. Then suddenly, it dawned on him. There was no point in doing anything else because tomorrow, there wouldn't be anymore Pentagon Book Store—anymore Pentagon.

Oddly enough, when Barobbi went out the mall entrance door for the last time, it wasn't himself that he felt sorry for, it was the beautiful, tall and stately, middle-aged woman who owned the bookstore and who had been his friend for the last year. She wouldn't have a bookstore to come to work to anymore.

*   *   *

Khalid's flight from New York was almost fifteen minutes late getting into Ronald Reagan Airport. He disembarked quickly and walked rapidly through the baggage claim area and then took the elevator up to the second level and walked across the bridge to the Metrorail line that ran parallel to the main terminal. He purchased a three-dollar ticket from the vending machine that would be sufficient for a round trip return to the airport. Then he checked the large posted schedule on the wall for the Blue Line that ran to Rosslyn. He saw that the Blue Line ran every ten minutes and the next metro train would be at eight o'clock. It was then 7:55. The Metrorail arrived right on time and as he boarded, a man dressed in dark trousers, sport coat and tie, and wearing a black raincoat, followed closely behind him and sat in a vacant double seat with Khalid. The man was the Strike Team Leader and had been waiting for Khalid since seven-thirty.

After the Metrorail was underway, the man struck up a casual conversation about the holidays and the fear of Y2K. Their words were lost in the sounds of the speeding train and the noises of the other passengers. Their meeting would seem normal to any casual observer. The man managed to tell Khalid that all had gone well at the Pentagon and in just a short time, as he would see, the other preparations would be in place.

The ride from Ronald Reagan Airport to Rosslyn took just ten minutes. When they arrived, they separated, as they would have if they had not known each other. They both took the stairs up a half level to the walkway across two sets of tracks and down to the platform for the eastbound Orange and Blue Lines to Washington and Ronald Reagan Airport. Taking up different positions, they awaited the next Orange Line Metro that was scheduled to arrive at eight-twenty. The platform was very crowded with people heading into Washington for various millenium celebrations or just to be on the streets of the Nation's Capitol with others when the bells sounding the New Year rang. At 8:23, the Orange Line arrived already full, but most of the people tried to squeeze into the Metrorail cars anyway. From the last car, Khalid watched a man of medium height, dressed in the blue trousers, blue jacket, and matching blue shirt of the Metro employees, come off the car, pushing on rollers, a very large suitcase, much like the many seen in any U.S. airport. Without hesitating, he went directly to a door in the platform wall, produced a key, unlocked the door, and quickly placed the suitcase inside the small room, closed the door, and quickly departed the platform heading up the main stairs toward the Rosslyn exit. Khalid and the Strike Team Leader had stood in the back of the rushing crowd to get on the car, and like many others, gave the appearance that they would wait for the next Metrorail car, hoping it would not be as crowded.

The door in which the man had placed the suitcase was a small broom closet used by Metrorail clean-up crews for their brooms, mops, and cleaning supplies. However, the last clean up had been performed at eight o'clock that night and nothing more would be done until the 4:00 a.m. crew arrived. The man, however, had left a handwritten note that said, "This is the property of Robert Walter. Do not move. I will be back to pick it up on 1 January 2000. Thanks. Robert Walter."

Neither Khalid nor the Team Leader noticed anyone paying attention to the man placing the suitcase in the small room. The man, of course, was not a Metrorail employee, but a strike team member posing as one.

It had been a simple matter to buy the uniform, take an impression of the door lock, and have a key made, and observe the door to determine when and how often it was used. The suitcase nuclear bomb, like its companion in the Pentagon, was set to go off at 12:01–just a minute past midnight. The 1 KT bomb in the subway closet, two stories below ground, was directly under a Virginia power station that was the main power grid for the White House and most of the government buildings in Washington. If the Iraqi targeteers that did the estimates of the effects of two 1 KT nuclear bombs within a half a mile of each other, going off simultaneously were correct, then in addition to destroying the Pentagon, and a large portion of downtown Rosslyn, as well as taking down at least the west end of the three major bridges running from Northern Virginia into Washington, the results would leave the President, and the key U.S. government departments in the dark, without connection to their worldwide communications and isolated from Northern Virginia.

All of this was going through Khalid's mind as he saw the Team Leader nod to him ever so slightly signifying that all aspects of *Retribution* were in place and he was taking his leave as planned. Khalid watched him disappear up the long, steep escalator stairs. He looked at his watch. It was 8:29. He was supposed to catch the eight-thirty Blue Line Metro back to the airport. It would be along in just a minute or two. He would then be back at the airport by 8:45, relax, have a cold drink, and catch the ten o'clock flight back to Orlando. The Metrorail pulled up, only two minutes late, and Khalid started to get on the half empty car. Then, something caused him to hesitate, wait, and then decide to catch a later Metro. "I've got plenty of time," he thought. Maybe it was the element of danger–being so close to what was going to happen in just a little over two hours. For whatever reason, Abdul Khalid decided he would go up the stairs and outside on the streets for just a few moments to get a little fresh air and be back in plenty of time to get back to Ronald Reagan.

It was a mistake. It was the biggest mistake that Abdul Khalid would ever make. When he reached the last exit of the Rosslyn Metro Station, he turned right, went to the corner, and headed down the hill toward the Potomac River. He calculated that he could walk to the road that ran by the river, have one last look at the skyline that in just a few hours would be changed forever. Khalid was full of himself. He was almost bursting to think what he had achieved against the most powerful country in the world. Back in Yazdan, he was sure that he was willing to give his life for bin Laden and Allah's cause, but something had happened to Khalid the month he had been back in the United States. Maybe it was a taste of the good life his cover had given him. Maybe it was the brilliance of the plan that he had worked so hard to design and achieve. At any rate, Khalid had decided almost a month ago that he, of all people, should not be martyred. He should be the living legend, the terrorist who pulled off the single most successful and yes, destructive attacks in history. "By tomorrow," he thought, "I will have done even more than Carlos the Jackal, perhaps the most famous of terrorists. I shall live to enjoy that well earned reputation." The idea of the Jihad, the holy war, that motivated bin Laden and most of his followers now seemed less important to Khalid.

These lofty thoughts made the adrenaline flow through Khalid's body and raised his body temperature to the point that he felt flushed and hot, even though the night's temperature was in the low forties. When he reached the river road, he turned around, took his green London Fog raincoat off, loosened his tie, undid the top button of his shirt, and headed back up the hill toward the Metro Station. As he was passing the Orleans House Restaurant and Bar, a very popular watering hole anytime and a bedlam on New Year's Eve, a rambunctious group of a dozen or more visiting college fraternity men from West Virginia, who had already had too much to drink, and had been asked to leave the bar, came staggering down the steps, pissed off and looking for mischief. They fell in step behind Khalid who was still in a state of euphoria. One particularly obnoxious and intoxicated young man saw Khalid's raincoat draped loosely on his shoulders and decided to have what he thought would be some fun. He said loudly, "Nice raincoat. Thank you very much," and yanked the raincoat off of Khalid's shoulders.

Because he had been deep in thought, Khalid took a reflex action that he had learned in the Special Forces. He whirled around quickly and with an open hand, thrust the butt of his palm in an upward blow against his assailant's nose. He could hear the breaking cartilage and what seemed like a quart of fresh blood sprayed on him and down the shirt front of the young drunk. Khalid almost regained his senses and ran, but before he could, two of the drunk's larger friends grabbed Khalid's arms and two more started punching him. He used his feet against his attackers, but there were simply too many of them, so he relaxed thinking that he would take the beating and then get on with his plan. However, to complicate matters, several soldiers from nearby Fort Myer, walking on the other side of the street saw the attack on the pedestrian and went over to help. A full-scale melee occurred. The last thing that Khalid remembered was being hit on the head with a full bottle of whiskey, the bottle breaking, and the liquor soaking him to the skin.

When Khalid recovered, he was in an Arlington County, Virginia paddy wagon, heading toward the Arlington County Jail. When they were unloaded at the jail with several other men, nothing that he could say would convince the booking police officials that he was merely a victim. He reeked of alcohol and the young tough with the broken nose had told the police that Khalid had started the whole thing.

By the time he was booked, it was nine-thirty. When he inquired about bail, he was told that the instructions to the police were to hold all drunks arrested on New Year's Eve until eight o'clock the following morning. Khalid's plea to the Desk Sergeant that he was an important Saudi Arabian businessman who could not miss his ten o'clock flight fell on deaf ears. The Sergeant opined that even if the prisoner used his one call on the Saudi Embassy, he would only get an answering service. He did agree that if Khalid knew how to reach someone in an official position who could come to the station, vouch for him, and sign a release, that they would consider letting him go.

Khalid was near panic. The strike team would, by now, be on their way out of the area and Shar Baker had departed yesterday for Richmond. His only hope now was the emergency, safe haven contact and numbers he had been given–if only he could remember them. The Police Sergeant gave him a pencil and paper and Khalid wrote down the three numbers, a daytime one, an after hours one, and a cell phone. The name he had been given was Maria Salah. The Sergeant told him that, normally, they allowed only one call, but since it was New Year's Eve, he could try the three. Khalid knew that it would be no use to call the official number, so he dialed the after hours number and got a message machine and left a plea for help. He then dialed the cell phone and his heart dropped when an answering message came on the line. But at the end of the message, a female voice said, "If this is an emergency that cannot wait until morning, press nine-nine." Khalid pressed nine-nine and waited for what seemed like forever.

At the Watergate, it was 9:45 when Maria heard her emergency buzzer go off on her cell phone.

"Who could that possibly be?" she wondered. She and Bart had had cocktails with the Ambassador from Honduras and his wife who lived across the hall from Maria. Then she had fixed Bart a Middle Eastern lamb dish for dinner that he raved about. She believed him–it was one of her specialties. They ate late and were just taking their coffees into the front room to watch the New Year's Eve countdowns on television when Maria's cell phone rang.

She explained her system to Bart.

"Can't you just let it go?" he asked.

"Would you let yours go?" she asked in return and knowing the answer said, "I'll just be a minute," and left the room.

"Hello."

"This is Lawrence," Khalid said. He explained his situation to Maria and ended with, "You must believe me; this is a matter of life and death–mine and yours."

"Mine? I don't understand that. Are you threatening me?"

"No, that is not my intent nor my meaning. It is all I can say now. I was told you would help me if I needed it and you must believe me, I need your help desperately. You must come soon–every minute counts."

Before returning to the front room, Maria put on a pair of heels, and a winter jacket over her eveningwear pants suit. She grabbed a scarf and her purse. She checked to see if car keys, her official diplomatic identification, and her official checkbook were in the purse. They were.

"What the hell?" Bart said, surprised when he saw she was dressed to go out.

"Bart, I am sorry but I must go out for awhile. You must understand it is business. I won't be long, an hour at the most," she told him and started out the door.

"Not so fast," he said, grabbing her arm. I'm not so sure I'm letting you go out by yourself on New Year's Eve, unless you tell me where you are going."

"Well, alright," she gave in. "I am going to the Arlington County jail."

"One of your relatives in jail?" Bart made an awkward attempt at humor, but realized it failed when he saw the worried look on Maria's face.

"Okay. I'll wait here," Bart said, "but take your cell phone and call me if you need help."

"I need to hurry," she said, closing the door and becoming preoccupied with what the call could mean. She was certain that whatever it was, it would be a problem for her relationship with Bart Lowe. "More lies," she thought, as she entered the elevator and pushed the button for the garage.

Only eleven minutes lapsed from the time Maria left Watergate until she drove up in front of the Arlington County Jail.

She hurried from the car. Maria had been to this jail on more than one occasion in the past trying to obtain the release of some important Lebanese citizen who had run afoul of the local authorities, so she knew just where to go.

The Desk Sergeant who had talked with Khalid was willing to let him go after seeing Maria's diplomatic identification, but when he asked her if she could vouch for the individual, Maria, almost said 'yes,' but instead said, "I'd like to talk to him first."

"Okay, ma'am, I'll have the jailer take you back," he said, motioning for one of the uniformed officers standing by.

When Maria went into the cell block area, it was bedlam. It looked as though thirty to forty people were in the central lock-up in various stages of drunk and disorderliness. Khalid was standing close to the bars waiting for her.

"You'll have to talk to him here, ma'am, until I get the go ahead to release him," the jailer said, walking away a short distance so that she could have some privacy with the prisoner.

Khalid had thought deeply over what he would have to say to Maria Salah to gain his release. He had assumed that she was a part of the al Qaeda organization, and as others had been, would be at his beck and call. In his phone conversation with her, he could sense her reluctance and he was prepared to tell her whatever was necessary to gain her cooperation.

The split second that the guard was out of hearing range, Khalid said, "Have you made the arrangements for my release? I also need a car to leave town immediately."

"I don't intend to do that until you tell me what this is all about. My instructions were that someone with the code name you used might require my assistance, but if that became necessary, your mission would be explained so that I, not you, could determine the best way to help. You could be an imposter for all I know. This could be an FBI sting." The latter part was not true, but the risk was too great for Maria unless she knew more.

"Woman!" Khalid hissed in Arabic, revealing a deep seated prejudice for the opposite sex, but quickly realizing the futility of that approach, whispered rapidly in Arabic, that in less than two hours, two nuclear bombs were scheduled to go off at the Pentagon and in the Rosslyn Metro Station just a few blocks away. He concluded with, "And if you wish to save your worthless ass, woman, you had better get me out of here NOW!" Finished, Khalid could see the look of disbelief on the woman's face and thought to himself, "Now we will get some movement out of this cow–now that she knows that she is in the presence of greatness!

Khalid could not have been more wrong. What he had mistaken for surprise in Maria's eyes had been shock and disbelief. "Bin Laden has gone too far this time," she thought, shuddered, and told Khalid, "I'll be right back."

Khalid, believing her, went to get his coat so he would be ready. "We can't afford to lose another moment," he thought.

Instead, Maria, escorted back to the Desk Sergeant's desk said, "I think he's a phony. Better hold him Sergeant," and went running out the door.

Meanwhile, back at the Watergate, Bart had switched off the television and turned the radio on and was listening to soft music. He glanced at his watch and saw that it was 10:05. "She's been gone twenty minutes," he thought. "I wonder how long Maria will be."

In Arlington, Maria came running out of the jail entrance like someone was chasing her and looked madly for her car. She found it, opened the door, climbed in, started the engine, and sped out of the parking lot heading back toward Washington. As soon as she could, she punched in her phone number and heard Bart answer, "Hello?"

Out of breath she said, "Bart, you are not going to believe this! But there are two nuclear bombs here, ready to go off at midnight! What are we going to do?"

Bart's first reaction was of disbelief thinking that Maria was part of some New Year's ill-conceived joke.

"You have got to be kidding me, Maria. Is this some Y2K joke?" he asked. Yet he was concerned over the alarm that he heard in Maria's voice.

"Bart, BART! Listen to me, I am NOT kidding you!" Maria screamed, and started pounding her fist on the dashboard of her now speeding car.

"Whoa, Maria," Bart said, trying to calm her and realizing that she was indeed serious. "Where are you and are you driving? If so, you need to slow down and get a grip on yourself!"

Maria temporarily regained some of her composure and said, "You will think I'm crazy, but let me tell you what I have." She was still driving like she was possessed.

He agreed and listened as she relayed, in an excited, high pitched voice, what had taken place inside the jail. "Maria, do you believe this man?"

"Yes, I do, Bart. I have known these goddamned idiots all my life and with every fiber in my body, I believe him."

"Okay. The main thing for you to do is to calm down and get back here as quickly as possible." Bart said in a commanding voice. "Then we'll figure out what to do. Just be careful."

"Alright," Maria replied, trying unsuccessfully to hold back tears and concentrate on her driving. "I should be there in five minutes." The cell line went silent and Bart moved over to the window to watch for Maria's car, thinking, "Nuclear bombs. Dear God, can it really be?"

Standing at the windows of Maria's apartment, Bart looked again at his watch and saw that it was 10:15. He was anxiously watching Virginia Avenue for any sign of Maria's Lexus. He knew that if she were coming from Arlington, she would take Wilson Boulevard to the Roosevelt Bridge, cross into the District, and take Virginia Avenue to the Watergate.

The route that Bart suspected Maria would take was exactly the one she chose. But she was having a hard time concentrating on her driving. She was near hysterical as the thought of a nuclear bomb going off in Washington flashed through her mind. Also, she knew that the life she had been so fond of with Bart Lowe was over. Her connection to bin Laden and his people could never be satisfactorily explained. Bart would never be able to trust her. Everything was ruined!

As she exited the Roosevelt Bridge, her front fender scraped the guardrail wall, and she saw that she was going sixty-five miles an hour. She didn't care. She knew she had to hurry—there was so little time. But Bart would know what to do. As her Lexus came onto Virginia Avenue, it didn't appear to Maria that there were many cars on the street, so she stepped down on the accelerator even more.

"I must get to Bart. He will know what to do," she thought. "If only I can stop crying," she said aloud, wiping her eyes with her sleeve.

Bart could see up Virginia Avenue for quite a few blocks and he noticed a set of headlights moving down the Avenue at a high speed. "My God! I hope that's not Maria!"

The Watergate sits at the intersection of Virginia Avenue and New Hampshire. What neither Bart nor Maria could see that night was a large United Postal Service (UPS) truck heading west on New Hampshire toward Virginia Avenue. Its driver, a young man age 27, was one of UPS' best employees. Always willing to work overtime. In fact, that night, he had been working for sixteen hours—a double shift. And he and his wife had a new baby and sleep around his house had been in short supply. He was dragging and starting to nod off. "I probably should stop for a Coke or coffee," he thought—he had delivered his next to last package on New Hampshire, "but, I've only got one more delivery to go on Virginia Avenue and I can go home to celebrate New Years' Eve with the wife." He negotiated the turn from New Hampshire onto Virginia Avenue and began to look for the address on his clipboard.

Maria had been unable to control her sobbing and felt herself becoming even more distraught. She didn't realize it, but she had gone into shock. She knew somehow that if she could get home and be with Bart that everything would be better and that became her objective over everything else. Her car was going too fast she sensed and she knew she should slow down soon. "Is that the red canopy of the Watergate ahead?" she wondered. And now there were very bright lights ahead coming toward her.

The driver of the UPS truck was having a problem locating the address slip for his final delivery on his clipboard and he couldn't stop yawning. Then he noticed that a delivery receipt had slipped to the truck floor near his right foot. "That's probably the missing one," he thought. He knew he should pull over and get it but he thought he could probably reach for it with his right hand and steer with the left. He looked down, stretched, stretched a little more, and then he had it. But when he looked up, he was horrified to see that his truck had drifted across the center lane and an oncoming car was about to hit him head on. He had delivered his last package for UPS!

Maria had begun to reduce her speed and she was sure that it was the red Watergate canopy ahead but she could not understand why the bright lights of the oncoming traffic seemed to be getting closer and coming directly toward her. "Perhaps," she thought, "it's because of the tears in my eyes." She hit the UPS truck head on without ever touching her brakes.

Bart Lowe could not believe his eyes as he watched from the apartment window, the collision of the two vehicles less than two blocks up Virginia Avenue. His heart leapt into his mouth and he muttered, "Please, God. Don't let it be." He wanted to believe with all his heart that the car that struck the UPS vehicle couldn't possibly be Maria's. But instantly, he knew that he had to find out for sure.

He broke into a run out of the apartment and down the stairs, worried that the elevator would take too long. He was almost out of breath from his fast dissent when he reached the ground floor, but yelled to the concierge to call 911 as he raced through the lobby. The concierge replied that they had already done so. As Bart went outside, he noticed that several people had heard the collision and were moving toward the accident.

When he was within fifty feet of the mangled vehicles, he could recognize Maria's Lexus. Both the car and truck had emptied their gas tanks and people were shouting about the danger of fire and explosions. As he arrived on the scene, he saw a body lying in the street. It was a man and people were going toward him. When Bart got to the Lexus, it appeared that the force of the crash had driven the engine back into the cockpit of the car and the metal looked as though it had crushed itself around the passenger. He could see Maria but she was pinned tightly within the car. Her body was covered with blood. Bart could not tell if she was conscious. He tried to move the driver's side door, but it was impossible. He ran around the car frantically looking for any opening, but found none and felt helpless knowing that Maria was probably near death and there wasn't anything he could do about it.

The police and emergency fire and ambulance people arrived immediately thereafter and began their accident scene work. They forced Bart to move away from the car until the threat of fire had been neutralized. They accomplished that quickly and when he told them that Maria was a loved one, they let him stand close to the car while they tried to free her. It looked impossible. The emergency ambulance doctor was able to reach inside the car through a hole that the firemen had cut and determine how badly Maria was injured. After only a few minutes, he spoke with Bart.

"It looks as though the impact drove the steering column into her chest and stomach causing massive internal injuries and severe bleeding. I have begun blood transfusions and given her an injection that may allow her to regain consciousness, but only briefly. She has little chance of surviving and I'm afraid that she may be dead before we can free her. You may want to sit there," he pointed to the opening in the car side where he had reached Maria, "in the event she wakes up."

Bart was stunned, but quickly moved to the car and, getting down on his knees, reached into the car and found one of Maria's hands. It felt cold but, wet with warm blood. Miraculously, there was not a mark on Maria's face and she looked peaceful except for her red, still tear-filled eyes. Bart moved as close to her as he could through the small opening.

In just a split second, Maria's eyes opened and she looked at him," Bart," she whispered, "I knew if I could get back to you, everything would be alright." Her voice was so low he squeezed in even closer to hear her. She smiled the faintest of smiles.

"That's right, Maria, everything is going to be alright. You don't need to worry about a thing. He hated to ask, but knew that he must, "Is there anything else you need to tell me?"

"Tell you?" she whispered.

"Yes. About the bombs?"

"No. I told you everything. But you said you would take care of it, right?"

"Yes, I did. And I will."

She hesitated and he was worried that he was losing her but then she said, "There is one other thing that I want to tell you and that is that... that... I..." she couldn't finish.

Bart, knowing what she was trying to say, said, "I know, Maria. And I love you, too," his voice cracking and tears welling up in his eyes.

And then she was gone.

The doctor moved to Bart's side and quickly confirmed Maria's death. Bart provided him the necessary identification information and, with tears still in his eyes and heavy heart, started walking back toward the Watergate. Then, time like a waterfall, hit him. "My God," he said aloud, "it's quarter to eleven, Maria's dead, there may be two nuclear bombs in Washington that are going off at midnight and I'm going to take care of it. Christ! I hope I know how," and he broke into a run.

CHAPTER 26

PUCKER FACTOR

On a dead run, Bart returned to the Watergate, went into the building, took a waiting elevator, retrieved his car keys and cell phone from Maria's apartment, ran down the stairs again—this time to the garage—jumped in his car, started it and screeched out of the garage heading toward DAS headquarters. Once underway, he took his cell phone out of his coat pocket and punched in the DAS Operations Center number.

A sleepy sounding voice answered the phone. "DAS Operations Center, Petty Officer Wilmot speaking. Can I help you?"

"Son, this is General Lowe. Get me the Duty Officer and make it quick!"

"Yes, sir!" And then five seconds later, "Lieutenant Colonel Roberts, sir."

"Roberts, this is General Lowe. I have a mission for you and it may be the most important mission of your life so listen carefully! I am on my way to the headquarters and should be there in five minutes. You start calling on the secure phone in this order, the FBI Operations Center for Mr. Kitchen, and the National Military Command Center for the Secretary of Defense, and the Chairman of the Joint Chiefs of Staff. Tell them I must speak only to those individuals, that my precedence is 'Flash Override,' that this is a national emergency involving a nuclear weapon, and that this is not, repeat NOT, a drill! Got it?!"

"Yes, sir!" the duty officer said, "I'm on it already," thinking to himself that either it was some kind of emergency planning drill or that the 'Old Man' had blown his cork.

Nine minutes later, when Bart Lowe came running through the doors of the DAS Operations Center with what looked like blood on his hands and down the front of his shirt and smelling like gasoline, the duty officer was convinced that General Lowe had taken leave of his senses, but he held up a phone receiver and said, "Mr. Kitchen is standing by."

Bart grabbed the phone from the duty officer's hand and said, "John?"

"Yes, Bart, what do you have? Bureau headquarters will record this so you won't have to repeat it."

"Roger. I understand."

Bart then relayed exactly what he had been told by Maria. When he had finished, John asked, "Is Maria available for us to talk to?"

"Maria is dead," Bart answered.

"Dead?! Maria? What the hell?"

"She was killed in an automobile crash on her way back to the Watergate. I'll explain later," Bart said, his voice cracking.

"Right," John replied, his own voice incredulous at what he had just heard. "Bart, we can't afford to take any chance with this kind of thing. We'll immediately send Arabic speaking agents from the Counterterrorist Task Force to the Arlington Jail to interrogate this 'Lawrence' to see if we can get further information. At the same time, dispatch the FBI Response Team to the two locations and notify the Department of Energy to get their response team moving. The Bureau's Ops Center will notify Justice and the White House Situation Room. I need you to continue to inform the defense and military people and be prepared to answer their questions. And believe me, they will have a few. Bart, if this crazy scheme is real, we only have sixty-one minutes. I'll be in touch again as soon as I get into Bureau headquarters. That is, if we are all still here!"

As Bart began his phone notifications of the Chairman of the Joint Chiefs, the Secretary of Defense, and the Director of the Defense Intelligence Agency through the patch lines at the National Military Command Center (NMCC) and the National Military Intelligence Command Center (NMICC), he grabbed paper and pencil and scribbled instructions to the Duty Officer to initiate the DAS' own emergency recall system of key personnel for those who lived within fifteen minutes of DAS headquarters. He knew that would include Barbara Barnsworth and Jim Poreman, the Middle East Division Chief. He then modified his note to instruct Poreman to go directly to the Arlington County Jail and call for further instructions when he arrived. He then added a note for the Operations Center to contact DIA's Tony Roper, whom Bart re-called, lived in nearby Shirlington, with the same instructions as Colonel Poreman.

An alert crew at the FBI Operations Center, when they were told by the DAS duty officer that General Lowe was calling about a nuclear weapon, set their communications to speaker phone and opened their lines to the others in Washington who respond to national crises: Department of Energy's Nuclear Emergency Search Team (NEST), and the Federal Emergency Management Agency (FEMA). As soon as the suspected locations were mentioned, NEST and the FBI dispatched response teams to the Pentagon and Rosslyn Metrorail Station and initiated coordination with their military and local bomb squad counterparts.

The White House Situation Room notified the National Security Advisor who, fortunately, was at the same private New Years Eve party as the President. Before he could notify the President, the FEMA Director was on the secure phone that the Secret Service had provided the National Security Advisor.

"Sandy, we need to evacuate the President and other government officials to Camp David."

"Jesus Christ, Jim. I haven't even told the Boss, yet. But, I know he isn't going to like it." The National Security Advisor said, looking at his watch and seeing that it was eleven-ten, "This whole thing could be some kind of a hoax."

"Yeah, Sandy. But what if it isn't and we all get blown to smithereens knowing we could have done something about it?"

The heavy-set National Security Advisor began to feel that his shirt and tie were choking him, and his stomach felt as if it was about to lose its contents. He realized now what some of his military colleagues meant when they used the term "pucker factor."

"All right, Jim. I'll tell him. Does the Secret Service agree?"

"You bet they do. And Sandy, I need the Boss' approval to implement the emergency evacuation procedures for Washington and the Northern Virginia areas."

Oh, my God, Jim. It's New Year's Eve. It will be utter chaos."

"I know, Sandy, but again, consider the alternatives. On the positive side, there will never be a better time to test our plan."

"Yeah, Jim. I hear you. Stay on the line. I'll tell the President."

The National Security Advisor signaled to the President's Chief of Staff to join him, and the two men moved across the room toward a group of six people standing around the President of the United States.

"Chief, I have some very bad news for the President, and there isn't time to say it twice."

"Oh? Why wasn't I informed?" the turf sensitive Chief of Staff who was the President's political closure guy asked.

"Believe me, Chief," a now heavily perspiring National Security Advisor said, "this is bigger than both of us."

When the President saw the serious look on the faces of his two principle assistants, he excused himself from the group and joined them in a quiet corner of the room.

The President was all smiles and enjoying himself. He was at his best when working a friendly crowd.

"What's the problem, Sandy? You look as though you just lost your best friend. I'm sure whatever it is, it can't be that bad," the President said, ever the optimist.

The National Security Advisor summarized for the President the information he had been given by the White House Situation Room and the Government security response that was already underway. The President, maintaining his good natured smile, said, "You're shitting me, right? This is some kind of Y2K prank?" Then, recognizing that the National Security Advisor was unusually serious asked, "Who the hell is this guy Bart Lowe?"

"Sir, Lieutenant General Bart Lowe is the Director of the Defense Attaché Service. He works for the Secretary of Defense and the Chairman JCS. I think you met him at one of the Foreign Receptions."

"Yeah, but where did he get this information? Isn't that the job of the FBI or CIA? And where is this coming from?"

"Ordinarily, yes. The intelligence community has been worried that something else beyond the bombing in London was coming but they haven't had anything definitive. Based on information that U.S. military attachés developed, Lowe believes that Iraq or bin Laden has been planning an operation. But his information was sketchy. Evidently Lowe got this bomb information from a reliable, friendly intelligence service source and the FBI believes it is probably true."

"Probably true? Jesus Christ, Sandy! Can't we do better than that?"

The National Security Advisor regained his backbone and now, with determination in his voice, said, "Not in the time we have left, Mr. President. I have FEMA on the line," holding up the Secure Phone, "and Jim recommends we implement the National Emergency Evacuation Plan. The Secret Service concurs and I agree. If you approve, I'll alert Camp David."

The President looked at his Chief of Staff, who rarely failed to comment on anything. He started to say something, changed his mind, and nodded his head affirmatively.

The President looked at both men. "Okay, but we are going to look like fools if this turns out to be some kind of ruse. Tell FEMA that I wouldn't mention nuclear bombs and to minimize any details as to why a national emergency has been declared until such time we can work a media briefing from Camp David. I'll expect a situation update every ten minutes after I arrive at Camp David. And Chief, alert the spin guys. We'll need to get our heads together on how to come down on all of this later." The President then left the room with his Secret Service escort. The time was 11:16.

At that same time, Barbara Barnsworth was hurrying into the DAS Operations Center and four FBI agents from the Counterterrorist Task Force pulled up in the front of the Arlington County Jail in two cars with sirens wailing. The agents hit the ground running. Prior to their arrival, FBI headquarters had contacted the Arlington County Police with a request to immediately place the Saudi man they were holding into isolated custody, fingerprint him, and consider him extremely dangerous and to provide the FBI an area that could be used by them for an intensive interrogation of the suspect.

Arlington County sent four policemen to the lock-up to secure the prisoner.

Abdul Khalid appeared calm in his outward demeanor but was seething inside as he paced back and forth in the large cell. He couldn't understand what was taking the woman so long. She had been gone almost an hour and time was fleeting. "Only forty-five minutes left," he thought, growing more uneasy with his situation. When the four policemen appeared and motioned for him to come forward to the cell entrance, he mistook their intention and said, "It's about time I was released. What is the problem?"

"Problem? There is no problem, buddy," the largest of the four policemen said. "You aren't going anywhere." And with that, they handcuffed Khalid and led him out of the lock-up cell and to another location in the building that was used to interview or interrogate suspects. When they arrived at the interrogation room, two other policemen were waiting to fingerprint him. Khalid protested saying, "Where is the woman who is obtaining my release? I want to see her immediately!"

The second policeman replied, "Don't worry, you're going to have some visitors real soon." And completed the fingerprinting.

Khalid knew now that his problem was even worse than he had imagined. "What has that woman told them?" he wondered. "She is some help!" And there were only forty minutes left.

Two of the FBI agents entered the interrogation room, identified themselves and one, speaking in Arabic, said, "We have been told that you have information about bombs located at the Pentagon and the Rosslyn Metro Station. What can you tell us?"

Khalid looked at the Agent and replied, "I am a Saudi business man visiting the United States on official business. As you can see, I speak fluent English and I don't know anything about bombs. A diplomat is working on obtaining my release."

Khalid was not sure how long it would take to check his fingerprints, and he planned to stay with his cover story as long as possible hoping that the woman would show up and get him out. Any hope that he had was destroyed three minutes later when the other FBI agents came into the room, and one whispered something into the ear of the lead Agent who then turned to Khalid and said, "You can drop the pretense now Sergeant Jabr. We know that you have been wanted for questioning by the FBI for several years in connection with the New York Trade Center bombing." The miracle of electronic fingerprint checking had revealed Khalid's true identity.

When Barbara Barnsworth walked into the Operations Center, Bart Lowe was pacing behind the secure communications console, still working the phones, and trying to respond to multiple calls from senior defense and military officials. She was shocked at his appearance. His coat was off, his tie loosened, and the front of his shirt was heavily stained. His hair was mussed and he was visibly agitated. Her first thought was "the boss has lost it and that's why I've been called in here on New Year's Eve." Then, she couldn't believe her ears when the Duty Officer filled her in on the situation himself having a hard time imagining, much less believing, what was going down.

"And," the Duty Officer concluded, "someone named Maria is already dead. I'm not sure of the connection."

"Maria Salah?" Barbara asked.

"I'm sorry, ma'am. I don't know."

Then, the professional that she was, Barbara started jotting down notes of actions to be accomplished to compare them with actions Bart had already taken. A moment later, Bart finished the call he was on and saw that Ms. Barnsworth was there. With a sigh of relief he said, "Barbara. Thank God you're here. Did Lieutenant Colonel Roberts fill you in?"

"Yes, Bart. Has DISCOVERY become a reality? What do you need me to do?"

"I'm not sure I believe what is happening. It may be DISCOVERY. At any event, we need to do anything and everything we can do to assist the FBI and others in the time that is left before midnight. First, double-check me on the things I've done. Then, tell me what else can be done."

Barbara ran through her list of notes and Bart nodded yes or no.

"Okay, then the only two things that you haven't done is notify René Softly, and the Counterterrorist Center, and Senator Karson."

"My God, yes, the CIA and the Counterterrorist Center, but do we really need to notify Karson?"

"However this thing turns out, he will continue to play a major role in counterterrorism, and he'll be grateful to be included."

"You're right, of course," Bart replied.

"I'll take care of that and the CIA. What did you have in mind for Jim Poreman and Tony Roper?"

Just then the Duty Officer interrupted and said, "Colonel Poreman on the line for you, General."

Bart picked up the phone and answered, "Jim?"

"Yes, sir. I'm here at the Arlington County Jail. I see that the Bureau guys from the Counterterrorist Task Force are here also. I suspect that's why you sent me here, Boss. Am I right?"

"Right as rain, Jim. Now listen carefully. This is an open line so what you don't get from me, try to get from the FBI guys.

"No problem, General. I know them well."

"The drill is two big bombs. One at the Pentagon and one at the Rosslyn Metro Station set for midnight."

"Tonight?" Poreman interrupted, looking at his watch and seeing that the time was 11:25.

"That's affirmative. The police and FBI are holding an Arab man who should know the exact locations of the bombs. He may be our DISCOVERY guy. And he contacted Maria Salah earlier tonight."

"Oh my God," Poreman said now realizing the full impact of what was going on. "Weapons of mass destruction," he thought to himself and felt a "pucker."

"Your mission is to offer assistance to the Bureau guys and figure out a way to get this guy to come clean ASAP. Tony Roper, I'm told, is on his way to give you back up. The DISCOVERY information may give you some leverage. I'm contacting John Kitchen to make sure the FBI accepts our offer of assistance!"

"That won't be a problem, I'm sure. I know these guys well and they're the best," Poreman assured Lowe.

Barbara's question about Poreman and Roper was answered by his phone conversation and she moved to the bank of secure phones to notify CIA and Senator Karson.

The two NEST and FBI Response Teams received notification of possible nuclear bombs at the Pentagon and Rosslyn Metro Station at 11:01 and were on site at 11:20. They were told that the bombs were set to go off at a minute past midnight and the teams were accelerating their normal procedures. At the Pentagon, they were met by the Pentagon security force who, with their own bomb squad augmented by military specialists from nearby Fort Myer, had begun the evacuation of the building of all people except those in the underground bomb secure areas. A Command Post had been established there and a systematic search scheme of the unsecured areas of the building was being readied. Given the size of the Pentagon, seventeen and one-half miles of corridors spread over 583 acres of land; a search without a clue as to the exact location would be monumental under any circumstances and nearly impossible in the time available. Nevertheless, Pentagon contingency planning had addressed the possibility of a bomb in the areas that were thought to be the most susceptible to an enemy or terrorist hiding a bomb. Those areas were prioritized from one to a hundred and these were the areas selected for the NEST and FBI teams to begin their deadly search. The nuclear detection devices and the bomb dogs were quickly moved into the building and the searches begun at 11:30.

Prior to arriving at the Rosslyn Metro Station, the FBI had contacted the Washington Metropolitan Area Transit Authority and Arlington County bomb squad and directed the closure of the station as soon as possible, but not later than 11:20. Despite the Transit Authority protests due to heavy New Year's Eve crowds, the Rosslyn Station and its tracks leading from Virginia and from the Nation's Capitol, were closed at 11:14 and the stations emptied by 11:25. Large crowds gathered outside the metro station and poured over into the streets, confused as to what was happening. The

NEST and FBI teams, with their nuclear detection devices and bomb dogs, started their searches on the street level on the assumption that that level would be the easiest one to conceal a bomb. There were three levels at the Rosslyn Station and the possibility that the bomb had been placed alongside of the four separate sets of tracks leading to Virginia and Washington. While the search area was not nearly as large as the Pentagon, it was a difficult one and the bomb professionals were very concerned over the time limitations.

Following the President's approval at 11:16 p.m. of a National Emergency in the Washington area, in accordance with its longstanding plans, FEMA contacted the D.C. government and the state emergency authorities in the adjoining states of Virginia and Maryland. They announced that, based on multiple bomb threats, FEMA was executing a National Emergency Evacuation Plan for parts of Washington, D.C. and Northern Virginia. The District of Columbia and the affected states were directed to implement their supporting roles on a 'no prior notice' basis and not later than 11:30 p.m. eastern standard time.

The first public announcements were made over pre-empted national and local television and radio stations at 11:25. Maps of the areas to be evacuated were shown and the evacuation routes were announced. By 11:30, sirens of federal and local police, fire, and other emergency officials were beginning to be heard throughout Washington and the areas of Northern Virginia adjacent to the bridges leading across the Potomac to Washington. Roadblocks were being formed and uniformed officers with flashlights appeared everywhere directing traffic and trying to move a stunned New Year's Eve crowd. The chaos had begun.

By 11:35, Khalid had given up all hope that somehow his contact, Maria Salah, would obtain his release. He could only conclude that she was responsible for his detention by the FBI. If the information had come from his own team, then the FBI wouldn't be so concerned about the exact locations of the bombs. It was also apparent to him that his interrogators were very concerned about the time left before detonation. They consistently watched the clock in the interrogation room. They tried to conceal their nervousness from him, but he could see it in their eyes. They were thinking he suspected, "In twenty-five minutes, we could all be dead." And it was true. The police station where he was being held was only a few short blocks away from the Metro Station.

In his mind, Khalid was going over his choices. "If I say nothing, the bombs will go off as scheduled and I will be a martyr to all who oppose the United States and thinks of it as the Great Satan. If I tell them about the bombs, I will probably spend the rest of my life in prison, and that's not a future I want to look forward to." He had pretty much made up his mind that he would stonewall them.

The lead FBI Agent from the Counterterrorist Task Force knew Colonel Jim Poreman well and respected his linguistic abilities and his Middle East expertise. At 11:36, he was talking with Poreman and Tony Roper. "Jim, we have made zero progress with this guy. He is a tough apple. We thought that the knowledge that we know who he is and his suspected affiliation with bin Laden, plus the threat that he will lose his own life if we continue to sit here, would break him. But, he hasn't budged an inch. If anything, he appears to be resolved like he accepts the whole thing. Any ideas?"

"Tony and I were just thinking that if you took Tony in and Tony revealed to him just how much we learned and know about his operation and how hopeless his situation is, that might give you some leverage."

"Okay, it's worth a try. Let's go Tony." The DIA Counterterrorist Analyst followed the FBI Agent into the interrogation room and sat down with Khalid.

At 11:40, the National Security Advisor called the President at Camp David from the bomb shelter beneath the Old Executive Building where the White House Situation Room had set up operations.

"What's the latest, Sandy?" an unusually solemn voice of the President asked.

"The NEST teams have found nothing yet. FEMA reports that the two-mile radius areas around the Pentagon and Rosslyn have been cordoned off and all entry cut off. The evacuations are proceeding well, but FEMA estimates that several thousand people will probably still be in the area at midnight."

"What's the problem, Sandy? Isn't FEMA getting out the word?"

"Oh yes, sir. The announcements are being made continually over the television and radio networks, loudspeakers have been set up in key locations, and vans are roaming the neighborhoods. The reality is that some people just won't get the word in time or will ignore it and think it is some kind of Y2K stunt the government is staging."

"Also, Mr. President, the Department of Energy advises that if the bombs have not been located and disabled by 11:57, the searches will have to stop in order to safeguard the lives of the search teams."

"I understand. Anything new from the FBI in questioning the suspect?"

"No, sir. I'm afraid not."

"Sandy, any suggestions for feed to the media? The Press Secretary is engaged in a media frenzy."

"Again, no, sir. They will have to wait just like the rest of us."

"Understand, Sandy. Over and out," a helpless feeling President said, his concern over being the first president to suffer a nuclear blast against the United States increasing by the minute.

At 11:41, Bart Lowe learned from the FBI that the NEST teams had, as yet, found nothing and that their search time would be limited to 11:57, the last possible minute for the teams to relocate to a safe bomb haven.

Just then, Barbara Barnsworth reminded him that it was time for the DAS Operations to shift to the bomb shelter in the basement beneath their headquarters building. Once they were there, they both took seats in the small office set up for the Director.

"Bart, there wasn't time to say anything before, but I know how much Maria's death must have hurt you. I am so sorry."

"Thanks, Barbara, but the most haunting thing about all of this is that this man telephoned Maria for help. I can't help but believe that she was somehow involved and because of my relationship with her, I might have some complicity in all of this," Bart confessed to Barbara in a tired voice.

"Bart, that is the worst kind of bullshit! Maybe Maria was somehow involved, although I have a hard time believing that, but you are one of the straightest arrows I have ever known, and I know that you could never aid or abet, knowingly or unknowingly, anything such as this. And let's not forget that you were the single voice in the U.S. intelligence community who warned and believed that something like this could happen."

"I appreciate your confidence, Barbara, but I guess the only thing left to us now is to wait and see," an unhappy and bone-tired Director of Defense Attachés replied.

At 11:45, at the Arlington County Jail, the lead FBI Agent and Tony Roper came out of the interrogation room and huddled with Jim Poreman.

"Nothing doing, Jim," the FBI Agent said, "Roper's DISCOVERY information seemed to surprise him, especially the part about the possible collusion of Iraq and bin Laden, but he's still tight as a clam refusing to say anything."

Poreman looked at Roper and Roper shrugged his shoulders. "Look, there is one other possibility," Poreman told the FBI Agent. "Can I take a shot at appealing to this guy's ego?"

"I'm not sure I know what you mean, but we are out of ideas and almost out of time. My instructions are that if we don't get anything out of him by 11:50, we need to move him to a federal holding cell at Fort Belvoir so that we don't lose him if the bombs do go off. He is our only link. You have five minutes, Jim."

Before Poreman went into the interrogation room, during the one moment or so that Khalid was alone, he again mentally reviewed his situation. He had been genuinely surprised that the American authorities seemed to know about Iraq's involvement with bin Laden and their knowledge of the cyber and biological operations. Was it possible that they knew even more and that one of his team members had defected and told all? Was it possible that they already knew the bomb's location and were just trying to get him to cooperate? And if so, where would that leave him? A life in prison? Not a martyr? Not recognized as the most successful terrorist in history? He wasn't sure anymore.

Just at the moment Khalid was rethinking his dilemma, Jim Poreman came in. Khalid recognized him as a military man. Without losing any time, Poreman quickly told Khalid who he was and about his experience in many Middle Eastern countries and his respect for people of Islamic faith.

Khalid was impressed with the man's sincerity.

"Look, I'm sure you're faced with a great dilemma— whether or not to let the bomb-thing take place or at the twelfth hour, stop it from happening. If you let it happen, the FBI is going to move you so that you won't be killed and martyred. In fact, they are getting ready to move you now and will do so as soon as I have finished talking to you. And if as much as one person dies as a result of the bombing, you will be prosecuted, found guilty, and executed. You will be hated by both sides. The ones who put you up to this for getting caught and endangering their safety and remembered in America as a hated terrorist.

"If, on the other hand, you give this thing up, save the lives that are at risk, you will be rewarded for your assistance and although you will be subject to penalties under the law for what you have already done, your success of being able to pull this operation off, the first of its kind in the United States, will instantly make you a world famous person. The

United States will do almost anything to gain your full cooperation. And you will be of tremendous assistance to them in learning how to guard against such a thing happening again. People will write books about you. Hollywood will want to make a movie about you.

"So, it's up to you, Sergeant Jabr, do you want to be remembered as the man who was the pawn of a cause that most of the civilized world detests, or the man who saved the United States from its worst terrorist act?"

Just then, the door opened and the FBI Agent said, "Jim, time's up."

Khalid, seeing that the clock in the room showed 11:50 said, "The bombs are located in the Pentagon Book Store and in the third level platform cleaning closet of the Rosslyn metro station."

CHAPTER 27

AFTERMATH

Front page headlines of *The Washington Post*, January 1, 2000:

Bombs at Pentagon and Rosslyn Metro Station Disrupt New Year's Eve

WASHINGTON, DC—A national emergency was declared last night at 11:15 p.m. for the District of Columbia and parts of Northern Virginia... According to a White House spokesman, the threatened areas were evacuated and the powerful bombs were disabled just minutes before detonation by federal explosives experts... Y2K terrorist actions suspected...

Other Y2K related stories on page A9.

The previous night, when Khalid had revealed the bombs' locations, the FBI had flashed that information to the two search teams. The Counterterrorist Task Force Agents then complied with their instructions to move Khalid to a safe location. They asked Colonel Poreman and Tony Roper to accompany them and to continue to participate in the interrogation of the terrorist suspect.

The bomb at the Pentagon was disabled at 11:58 and the bomb at the Rosslyn Metro Station at 11:59. The President was informed at 12:01 of the new millenium, by the

National Security Advisor, that the bombs were, indeed, nuclear ones. He recommended that the Evacuation Plan remain in effect until 7:00 a.m. the following morning so that the bombs could be thoroughly examined by the NEST teams and removed safely from their locations. When this was accomplished, the curfew would be lifted. The FBI also wanted additional time to continue their interrogation in the event that there were other bombs in the Capitol area. The President approved.

On the thirty-five minute trip in the FBI sedan from the Arlington County Jail to the federal holding area at Fort Belvoir, Virginia, Abdul Khalid was able to collect his thoughts and come up with a plan. When he arrived and was unshackled and placed in a detention cell, he was officially arrested, Mirandized, and told he was being held on a Justice Department warrant.

In the short time Abdul Khalid was in FBI custody, they had determined from his airline ticket and Delta Airlines that his trip on Friday, 31 December, began in Orlando, Florida, then to New York, and from New York to Washington. He was scheduled to return to Orlando that same night. They intended to use that information as the basis for further interrogation to find out what he had done at each location. However, at 1:00 a.m. when they began, Khalid told them: "I have additional information of vital interest to the United States. I will not, however, reveal a single word unless I receive an assurance from the highest level of the U.S. Government that, in exchange for my information, I will be free from prosecution and my personal future freedom will be guaranteed."

The FBI interrogators laughed at Khalid and said, "Nice try. But forget it. Don't you know that the U.S. Government's position has always been that we don't bargain with terrorists?"

Khalid was not rattled. His interrogators tried all the approaches they knew for the next two hours, but could make no headway with Khalid.

The lead Agent then compared notes with Poreman and Roper. Tony Roper said, "My guess is that there is far more to this operation than just what we stumbled on tonight."

"Like what," the FBI Agent asked, "more bombs?"

"Maybe," Roper said. "But maybe something else equally as bad as the bombs. What we suspected in our DISCOVERY operation also involved chemical, biological, or cyber agents."

"Jesus Christ!" the FBI Agent said. "Do you think something like that could be around here, too?"

"I don't know, but from what you say, he seems pretty sure that he has something we would really want to know." Tony Roper offered, and then asked, "What do you think, Jim?"

"It seems clear that something has caused him to believe he can stonewall us without fear," Poreman replied.

"Well, I need to go back to the Bureau for further instruction."

By 4:00 a.m., the FBI interrogator's questions had been addressed at FBI Headquarters and by the Justice Department. The official answer to Khalid's question was "no."

In the interim period, Colonel Poreman updated Bart Lowe and told him, "It's my gut feeling that this guy really has something big that he is hoping to bargain with and if we don't reach some accommodation, I fear we will regret it."

"I have been on the horn with John Kitchen and he says that Justice is hard over and believes the guy is just looking for a plea. Maybe if you can convince him he has to offer us some specifics, then maybe Justice and the FBI will support his request." Bart suggested to Poreman.

"Okay, Boss, we'll give it another try."

At 4:30, after comparing notes on an approach with the FBI agents and Roper, Poreman went into the cell alone with Khalid. Poreman was sure he looked dead tired, but Khalid looked to Poreman as though he had his second wind.

"Sergeant Jabr, it looks as though this thing is going to end in a stalemate. The Justice Department figures they already have all they need on you and that you are just trying to improve your position. If you don't come up with something else, they are not going to offer anything. Now you have to ask yourself, where does that leave you? If there is something else bad out there that we don't know about and it happens, then you are going to take the blame for it. If, on the other hand, you give us enough to convince the Justice Department that it's worth trading for, then you have given yourself a fighting chance. Do you follow?"

Khalid followed. He had thought that out and knew he still had several hours to play with before the damage the anthrax would do could not be stopped. He had been told that the incubation period was 24 to 48 hours. "Still," he thought, "What the Colonel says makes good sense. 'I'll think about it,'" he told Poreman.

At 5:30 a.m., Khalid motioned for his interrogators to return. When they were present he told them, "Please tell your superiors that I am aware of a second offensive strike against the United States that will result in thousands of casualties if not prevented. It is not too late, but time will run out quickly. However, before I will reveal this information, I want to see U.S. agreement to my earlier demands in writing and I want an attorney who will represent me to review the document to make sure that the U.S. cannot go back on its word to me once I have given you the information."

Khalid could see the surprise, even shock, on the face of his interrogators at the mention of "thousands of casualties." In spite of all that had gone wrong for Khalid since leaving the metro station last night, he was beginning to feel again that he was in control and that he had the necessary leverage to make the most powerful country in the world meet his demands. At that moment, he remembered a slang expression from his military service days and thought, "I've got them by the short hairs."

His FBI interrogators were indeed alarmed at Khalid's mention of thousands of casualties and immediately reported the new demands to the Bureau.

Khalid's new revelation quickly resulted in a conversation between John Kitchen, his boss, the FBI Director and his boss, the Attorney General.

"Can't we lean on this bastard and persuade him to tell us what we need to know?" the Attorney General asked.

The FBI Director turned to Deputy Director John Kitchen, "John, is there anything else we can do to persuade him to cooperate?"

I don't think so. The interrogators are our best and they don't believe he will break. We can continue to try but they have been with him about six hours now and say he is tougher than ever.

"But look, why don't we counter with, we'll do it provided that he tells us everything; who planned and financed the operations, all the details, etc., and then act as our material witness against the others. If he buys it, and if Bart Lowe and the DIA guys are right, we'll have the smoking gun against bin Laden and Iraq."

"I like it," the Attorney General said. "Our people will do the paperwork and we'll get an attorney for him off of the Defense Attorneys list."

"Try to select a former federal prosecutor that will understand where we are coming from," requested the FBI Director.

"Good idea. I'll brief the National Security Advisor and ask him to get the President's approval. We should be ready in a couple of hours," the Attorney General told them and reached for her secure phone.

The agreement promising immunity from prosecution and protection under the Federal Witness Protection Program for Abdul Khalid (under his true name) and signed by the Attorney General of the United States was not ready until 8:30. The President did not approve until the White House Council had reviewed the document. Two Assistant Attorneys

General, along with a court appointed defense attorney for Khalid presented the document to Khalid, and after discussing it privately with his appointed attorney, Khalid signed the agreement.

The FBI interrogators were augmented by additional members of the Counterterrorist Task Force and officers from the CIA Counterterrorist Center, and DIA to participate in the debriefing of Khalid following the signing of the Justice Department's agreement.

At 9:15 on New Year's day, Khalid revealed the details of the anthrax spraying in Florida and the cyber attack in New York. The several Americans—including Poreman and Roper—could not believe their ears as Khalid calmly described the operations directed against Disney World, Kennedy Space Center, and the New York Stock Exchange. They had all been aware of the threat of biological attack against the United States for years, but did not believe it would ever really happen. It had happened!

The same reaction of revulsion was felt by every person up the National Security chain to include the President. The President had returned to the White House from Camp David after the bombs were cleared at the Pentagon and Rosslyn. He had scheduled an emergency meeting of the National Security Council for 1:00 to discuss the nuclear attack and had retired for a short nap at 8:45. He had the feeling that he was dreaming when his aide woke him to tell him that the National Security Advisor was on the secure phone again. "What the hell is it now, Sandy? Can't it wait until the one o'clock meeting?"

"I'm afraid not, Mr. President," and then he revealed the unthinkable to the Commander-in-Chief. The President's first reaction was one of complete disbelief and silence. He was silent so long that his Security Advisor thought they had been cut off and said, "Mr. President, are you still there?"

Then finally, "Yes, Sandy, I'm still here," the President replied, sounding exhausted. "Is there any chance that this information is false?"

"I suppose so, but given the severity of the nuclear bombs and the details this terrorist gave the FBI, it's probably true. We won't know for sure until a sample of the surrounding soil is taken."

"Can we do that right away?"

"We need to think that over very carefully, Mr. President. There will be massive panic in Florida and perhaps in the whole country when this is announced or if it leaks."

"My God! Yes. What do you recommend?"

"I suggest we stay with the National Security Council meeting to discuss it, but move the time ahead to noon. That will give me time to get FEMA and the Health Department to come up with a reaction plan and we will be able to discuss it with the principals at the meeting."

"Let's go with that, Sandy. And button this up until we can decide what's best. And we have just given that scumbag immunity? Can we shoot him?" the President directed. He got out of bed, and headed for the shower saying, "Happy fucking New Year!"

The catastrophic possibilities of what had taken place in Florida and the question of what to do about it so overshadowed the stock market attack that it was temporarily put on a back burner until a coherent plan for Florida could be agreed upon by the President and the National Security Council. The Desert Mist virus—now in its fifteenth hour—continued on its file destruction way.

By 1:30 on New Year's Day, most of America was watching the annual college football games on television. People had taken note of the mysterious bombs found in the Nation's Capitol on New Year's Eve, but the television and print news was scanty and they were content to hear the inevitable follow-ups. The National Security Council was briefed on the anthrax attack and was stunned to learn that close to 500,000 people had been at the Disney and other entertainment complexes in Orlando, Florida the previous day. FEMA recommended a plan to immediately notify and immunize all those exposed as soon as a sample of the anthrax could be obtained and the appropriate antibiotic inoculations prepared. The plan, a massive one involving FEMA, Health Department, the U.S. Military, and the Florida National Guard, was agreed upon by the National Security Council and approved by the President.

At 1:45 on New Year's Day, the President called the Governor of Florida on a secure phone.

"Jeb? This is Bill Clinton."

"Yes, Mr. President. To what do we owe this honor?" the Governor responded, surprised that the President was calling him.

"Jeb, I wish it were just to wish you and the State of Florida Happy New Year, but unfortunately, I have some unthinkable information to pass to you."

"Unthinkable?" the Governor replied, the smile on his face quickly turning to a frown.

The President related to the Governor the now apparent connection between the bombs in Washington the previous night and the terrorist's description of anthrax seeded in Florida.

"Surely Mr. President, that cannot be true."

"Unfortunately Jeb, we now know that it is true."

"True... How?" an aghast Governor asked, feeling a shortness of breath.

"When we first learned of this earlier today and not wanting to alarm anyone unnecessarily, we dispatched a medical team from the FBI office in Orlando to obtain a soil sample to check for the presence of anthrax. They reported anthrax at Disney World and the Space Center at Cape Canaveral and believe they will find it at the other amusement parks in that area."

"When was this, Mr. President, and why wasn't I informed?" a rattled State Executive asked, already wondering how he was going to handle such a disaster.

"Jeb, it wouldn't have been prudent to alarm you without thinking out what we could do about it **if** it was there. And we have done that now. I have just come from a National

Security Council meeting and FEMA has proposed a comprehensive plan to deal with the problem."

"And what is that plan?"

"Sitting beside me is the Director of FEMA who will brief you on the plan and with your concurrence, will have his people begin coordination with your emergency management people. The bottom line is that we must inoculate all those who have been exposed and that could be upwards of five hundred thousand people."

"My God. But will it be in time?"

"The answer to that is, yes, we hope. Our medical experts tell us that anthrax exposure can probably be defeated if inoculation occurs as soon as possible after contact."

The President obtained the Governor of Florida's agreement to the Plan and for the decision to hold back the necessary public announcements and news releases until the FEMA Health Task Force, being readied at Andrews Air Force Base in Maryland, was in place in Orlando and the Florida authorities were prepared to orchestrate "Operation Vaccination." The target time agreed upon for the beginning of "Vaccination" was 6:00 p.m. and would be initiated by an announcement to the Nation, first by the President, followed by the Governor of the State of Florida.

Because of the threat to human life in Florida, the President did not address the cyber problem at the New York Stock Exchange until four o'clock. At that time, he met with the National Security Advisor along with the Director of the National Security Agency (NSA) and a group of experts from NSA whose job it was to look after the security of the U.S. Government's vast communications network. It was their opinion that if a destructive virus had been introduced into the market's system almost twenty-four hours earlier, then the result would likely be more than fifty percent of its files destroyed or irreparably damaged. NSA had organized an assistance team that could be immediately deployed if the Stock Exchange leadership, when informed, requested assistance.

The Governor of New York, who was hosting a New Year's Eve Day reception in Albany, was contacted by the President at 5:00 p.m. and informed of the suspected cyber attack against the New York Stock Exchange. He was advised that the Chairman of the Board of the NYSE had also been contacted, informed of the Government's information about the suspected attack, and offered the assistance of an NSA team to investigate, conduct a damage assessment, and recommend remedial action. The offer of NSA assistance was accepted and agreement reached that no public announcement of the attack would be made until such time as any impact on the United States and the world markets could be made in coordination with the Secretary of the Treasury. The Governor was asked to support the no public announcement policy until the extent of damage was determined and the government continued its investigation of the perpetrators. The NSA team departed Fort Meade, Maryland, for New York at 6:00 p.m., almost to the moment that the President of the United States announced to the country that, "A senseless act of terrorism has taken place in Orlando, Florida, putting thousands of Americans at risk from a deadly biological agent. Fortunately, the attack was discovered shortly after it took place and the Federal Emergency Management Agency, in coordination with the State of Florida, will be providing vaccinations to all the people who have been exposed."

The President asked the American public to listen carefully to the public service announcements that would be made every thirty minutes on nationwide television and radio for the next three days in all fifty states to learn who was affected, and concluded with "the perpetrator or perpetrators are not known at this time, but the FBI is conducting an around-the-clock investigation."

The panic that seized the American public was greatest in Florida, but in truth, was felt throughout the country. Terrorism took on a new meaning for almost every American and the news coverage was constant. Unknown to the public was the somber, close hold, estimate given to the President by the Health Department that said, with Herculean effort, FEMA would be able to reach and vaccinate upwards of 98% of the people exposed, but some would unintentionally slip through, not be vaccinated, ultimately get sick with flu-like symptoms and die. And the risk of the illness being spread could not be ruled out. This would be America's first real experience with anthrax and the actual outcome was unpredictable.

By 7:00 a.m. Sunday, January the 2nd, the NSA team in New York, working with the people who operated the Market computer systems concluded that the damage to the Market files was even more extensive than estimated. The systems' managers' knew that the files could be reconstructed because all the files were in other locations in part, but they believed the reconstruction effort would take at least two weeks and possibly up to thirty days. The Treasury Department experts opined that the United States and the affected international markets could not sustain such a downtime without dire economic results. The Secretary of the Treasury advised the President that alternatives would have to be devised between Government and U.S. corporate industry and probably the other major economic powers of the world.

After his revelations about the anthrax and cyber attacks on the morning of January 1st, Khalid was permitted a few hours sleep while preparations for an extensive debriefing and interrogation were put into place. That afternoon, he was moved into an FBI Safe House in Northern Virginia used exclusively for lengthy interrogations. Colonel Poreman and Tony Roper were included as part of the debriefing team. As the interrogation proceeded, Khalid refused to name, or to provide information, on those individuals whom he had trained and who had actually carried out the attack. In his mind, he knew that he would eventually have to do so, but he felt a sense of loyalty to the strike team and he wanted to buy enough time for them to get away from the United States. Instead, he began relating to his interrogators. The *Retribution* meeting that had taken place almost a year ago in Iraq, and how Osama bin Laden had taken on responsibility for carrying out the attack with the support of Saddam and a handful of people in Iraq.

As he provided the information, it was summarized by the FBI and passed to the National Security Advisor and other key officials whom the President had designated.

By 8:00 p.m. January the 2nd, the "Smoking Gun" that Khalid had promised, was evident to the President and his closest advisors. At 9:30, he called a mini-National Security meeting, that included the Vice President, National Security Advisor, Secretary of State, Secretary of Defense, Chairman of the Joint Chiefs, Directors of the CIA and FBI, and the Director of the Defense Intelligence Agency.

By midnight, the President had directed the Secretary of Defense and the Chairman of the Joint Chiefs of Staff to implement existing contingency plans to seize and/or neutralize Osama bin Laden wherever he might be and to begin planning for the military take down of Saddam Hussein and those elements of the Iraqi government that were known to be involved in *Retribution*, or involved in the support of terrorism.

On their return to the Pentagon, the Secretary of Defense and the Chairman of the Joint Chiefs conducted a secure conference call with the Commander-in-Chief of Central Command and the Special Operations Command with directions to execute their long-standing plans for the capture and/or neutralization of Osama bin Laden. They also received their first alert for Iraqi operations.

At 6:00 a.m. on January 3rd, the President sat down at the White House to breakfast with the leaders of the Congress to brief them on the events of the last three days, inform them of his actions already underway against Osama bin Laden and to ask their support for a "war powers" vote against Iraq.

At 9:00 a.m., the President addressed the Nation to inform the American public of the senseless Pearl Harbor-like attack against the United States, and that the United States, in the days and weeks ahead, would be moving against the terrorist perpetrators.

"Terrorism. Those who support it and those who carry it out have finally crossed an unacceptable line with this Great Nation. It is our intention to stamp it out," the President concluded.

Monday, the third of January, was the scheduled New Year's holiday. Technically, the U.S. government was closed down. However, the terrorist events leading up to the President's address to the nation that morning, ensured that all those involved in the work of national security and the aftermath of the anthrax and cyber attacks were working around the clock. The Y2K concerns that the nation carried into the last days of December 1999 paled in comparison to what New Year's Eve actually wrought, or nearly wrought. Y2K was all, but forgotten.

Bart Lowe sat in his office in Ballston, Virginia, late that afternoon talking on a secure conference call with John Kitchen and René Softly. They were discussing how lucky the United States was to have discovered the *Retribution* plot conceived by Saddam and bin Laden and carried out by a relatively few, but well-trained terrorists. This, in spite of the U.S. having the best intelligence and counterintelligence capabilities in the world.

"It's alarming to realize how vulnerable we are to hostile attacks in so many different places," René said to Bart and John.

"I don't think any of our FBI people are too surprised," John answered. "We have been beating the vulnerability drum for a long time with only limited results. Maybe this will be the wake up call America needs."

"Let's hope so," René added with heavy fatigue in her voice. "Anyway, Bart, we all now know that you and the guys at DIA were right on the mark about DISCOVERY. My hat's off to you and your attachés."

"Amen to that," John said.

"It was a team effort, René, and you're right, we were lucky," Bart replied. "And what would I do without you and John?"

"Do you think, Bart," René continued, "the mainstream military action that the President has directed will be the solution to the terrorist problem?"

"I'd like to think that it could be, and I certainly believe we have reached a point in time where a line in the sand must be drawn. When we take the war to the terrorists, it will require new capabilities, doctrine, tactics, and equipment. American lives will be lost, and we must have the balls to carry it through to the finish. I also know that to be successful, in a greatly expanded counter-terrorist mission, our military cannot continue to endure the downsizing, budget cutting, and continuous new mission deployments they have suffered in the last six years. We will need to do better by them." René and John agreed and concluded the call.

Late that night, Bart Lowe climbed slowly into his car for the twenty-five minute drive to his quarters at Bolling Air Force Base. He was dead tired and deeply saddened by the loss of Maria and the terrorist actions that had brought about her death. He also knew that the military attachés around the world, the Defense Attaché Service, the U.S. military, and the most powerful nation in the world—his country—would have no shortage of important and difficult missions and would need his leadership, dedication, and hard work. When he was needed, he would be there.